STONE
HEART

Luanne Rice

STONE HEART

Bantam Books

STONE HEART
A Bantam Book

PUBLISHING HISTORY
Viking hardcover edition published 1990
Ballantine mass market edition / January 1992
Bantam trade paperback edition / April 2005

Published by Bantam Dell
A Division of Random House, Inc.
New York, New York

This is a work of fiction. Names, characters, places, and incidents either are the product of the author's imagination or are used fictitiously. Any resemblance to actual persons, living or dead, events, or locales is entirely coincidental.

Grateful acknowledgment is made for permission to reprint an excerpt from "Easter, 1916" from *The Poems of W. B. Yeats: A New Edition* edited by Richard J. Finneran. Copyright 1924 by Macmillan Publishing Company, renewed 1952 by Bertha Georgie Yeats. Reprinted with permission of Macmillan Publishing Company.

Book design by Virginia Norey

Bantam Books and the rooster colophon are registered trademarks of Random House, Inc.

ISBN 0-7394-5226-6

Printed in the United States of America

For Susan Robertson

PREFACE
to the 2005 edition

Like all of my novels, *Stone Heart* is a love story at the heart of a family. What that means to me now is, in some ways, quite different from what it meant to me back when I wrote this book. I can see, rereading this novel for the first time since I wrote it fifteen years ago, that I was just beginning to question the idea that the things I loved would last forever. It was unthinkable to me that they wouldn't. . . .

I wrote *Stone Heart* during a period of tumult in my life. My mother was very sick, and I was in the process of leaving a marriage. I moved from Paris to New York City and then home to shoreline Connecticut—so I could be near my mother. The house I rented faced west across a bay toward three small granite islands and a distant point of land. My mother lived on that peninsula.

One morning, having my coffee, I stared across the water. Unfocused, half asleep, just-about-to-start-writing gazing into space . . . and I saw a tiny red light, flashing in the distance. Grabbing the binoculars, I realized that I was seeing an ambulance at the bottom of my mother's hill. I jumped into my car and rushed over. Later, when I asked her why she hadn't called me to say she needed to go to the hospital, she said, "Oh, honey, I didn't want to disturb you."

It didn't matter that I'd moved home to be close to her—to help her. As much as we love each other, our family has always had some issues with asking for help. In that way, I suspect we're not alone. It's hard to let the love in. To open up, reach out, pick up the phone, open the door, call your daughter from just across the bay. As much as we say we want closeness, there's a deeply ingrained instinct to push each other away.

Stone Heart came about through needing to understand that paradox. I wanted to write about a woman who returns home after many years away, who finds that everything has changed. She loves her family as much as ever, but she has to find new ways to understand them—and herself.

The title is taken from the poem "Easter, 1916," by William Butler Yeats:

> *Too long a sacrifice*
> *Can make a stone of the heart.*
> *O when may it suffice?*
> *That is Heaven's part, our part*
> *To murmur name upon name,*
> *As a mother names her child*
> *When sleep at last has come*
> *On limbs that had run wild.*

The poem is enormous, politically and personally resonant, many lines longer than those I've quoted here. Yeats commemorates the Easter Uprising in Dublin, the plight of Ireland, the emotional and experiential turmoil of revolution. He writes of passion, terrible sacrifice, vain hopes. Our family is Irish—one ancestor died fighting in that siege. Others eventually emigrated to America to escape hunger.

But I've come to understand, as I've gotten older, that there are many hungers, many ways sacrifice can harden a person's heart. There is such pain in love, in loss, in trying to help a person who won't be helped, in being rejected by someone you think you would die for. More than anything, that is what my writing has been, and is still, about.

Oddly enough, the family in *Stone Heart* is old Yankee, as far from Irish Catholic as you can get. I set the novel on my beloved

Connecticut shoreline, but I wanted to write about people just different enough from me that I could have some distance and perspective.

One thing I've learned since writing this book is that when it comes to the heart, there are no differences at all. People are moved by the same things. Sisters want to help each other; mothers think they know best; nieces are amazing. I borrowed some local legends that thrill me still: the real-life Bride Brook becomes, in these pages, Bell (as in "Wedding Bell") Stream . . . and lovers still cross the swollen banks to get to the wedding, if not the church, on time. On marine charts, the three small barren islands are called something else; in this novel, they are the Haunted Isles. The town here is called Hatuquitit; readers of other books of mine will know it as Silver Bay. Visitors to shoreline Connecticut will know it as Niantic.

> *Too long a sacrifice*
> *Can make a stone of the heart.*

Those lines have proven almost truer than I can bear. This novel was, and is, my attempt to soften hearts, including my own. What else matters, other than love? Fifteen years after writing this book, I can tell you: nothing.

STONE
HEART

PART ONE

THE HAUNTED ISLES

1

MARIA DARK FLEW NORTH, FROM ONE AMERICA
to the other, with a bag of treasures between her feet. The man
beside her spoke Spanish into a cassette recorder. He seemed
hardly to notice the lightning at their wings. The plane lurched,
then continued to glide; orange strobes reflected on the clouds
that surrounded them. A flight attendant cruised the aisle,
checking seatbelts.

"What time will we land?" Maria asked her.

"We're in a holding pattern over Philadelphia," the woman
said. "This storm is turning to snow in New York."

"You mean we might land here?" Maria asked.

"We might."

Lightning split the sky, and for one instant Maria wished to be
on the ground anywhere: Philadelphia, Miami, Machu Picchu.
Then she thought of Sophie and Nell, waiting at JFK, ready to
drive her home to Hatuquitit; almost absently Maria reached into
her bag for a talisman to guide the plane safely north. Her hand
closed around the gold goddess she planned to give Sophie. She
felt like the mysterious stranger going home, bringing storms
with her.

"Pretty," said the man beside her, admiring the small statue.
"Is it Incan?"

"No, she's Chavín," Maria said. During their excavation at
Chavín de Huántar, she and Aldo had found several statues like
her, and Maria, thinking of a present for Sophie, had commissioned a local goldsmith to copy one.

"That belongs in the national museum," the man said reproachfully.

"She's a replica. A present for my sister," Maria said. Aldo had taught her that foreign archaeologists were always suspected of trying to remove antiquities.

"That's too good for a present," the man said. He flinched at a crack of thunder, then resumed recording.

Maria figured he thought she'd robbed a grave. She'd have to tell Sophie about it; it would add to Sophie's pleasure in the goddess. Sophie would want details: the fact that the man wore thick glasses and had hairy nostrils, the fact that he began every other recorded sentence with "And furthermore." From his litany, Maria pegged him as a low-level lawyer for the local government.

Sophie and Nell would be at the airport by now. Just before leaving the mountain, Maria had called Sophie; the connection had been terrible, full of static, but Maria thought Sophie had said she and Nell would come alone. Like the old days, Maria thought. Before Maria married Aldo, before Sophie married Gordon and had Simon and Flo, before Nell married Peter and became their sister-in-law and Andy's mother instead of just their best friend.

The plane had been veering right, circling for forty minutes, but suddenly Maria sensed it change course. Heading for home, she thought she could smell north. She opened the hand clutching the statue for one quick look. The goddess was fine and slender, nearly as beautiful as Sophie.

For one moment Maria wondered whether Hallie would meet her at the airport. Of course she would not. Sophie had a ringleader's knack for setting a scene, assembling a party. Sophie would know that their mother had no place at this homecoming. Hallie wouldn't think it seemly to stage a big welcome for a daughter who had left her husband to his glamorous dig, to Chavín mysteries, to the thin mountain air, who had left him to all those things forever—and for what?

To return to a place where she hadn't lived for seventeen years, where her mother's house sat on a hill overlooking meadows bordered by Bell Stream on the east and the Hatuquitit Correctional Institute for Women on the west. To return to a town settled by Puritans who had called the Native Americans "fiends of hell."

To find work in a place where archaeologists taught at colleges or lectured at local Native American museums instead of making discoveries destined for display in the Smithsonian or the British Museum. Hallie would never understand why her only child to escape the ordinary would want to return to it.

Or so Maria thought as the plane from Peru rode the storm's front edge northeast and became the last flight to land before JFK closed down.

Sophie and Nell stood amid the crowd, whistling and waving so that Maria would see them. Sophie's whistle, incredibly piercing, was unmistakable and took Maria straight back to when the three of them would roam the Hatuquitit hills pretending to be Indian scouts. Now their thick New England clothes—red and blue down jackets, corduroy pants, Nell's sailcloth purse—looked startlingly bright in the fluorescent light.

"Anyone escaped lately?" Maria called across the crowd. To children growing up next to a women's prison, that question had been as natural to them as "How are you?" or "Do you like the weather?"

"Not this week," Sophie called back.

Suddenly the three of them were holding each other in a tight circle. Maria had to drop her bags to hug them properly. Then Sophie and Nell dropped theirs—their six legs formed a cage around the bags, protecting them from the thieves they imagined swarming around the arrivals area.

"Are you okay? Did you have a good flight?" Nell asked.

"It was bumpy," Maria said.

"But are you okay?" Sophie asked, her question meaning something different from Nell's. Maria took a second before looking straight at Sophie. Sophie, like all the Darks, had black hair, fair, unfreckled skin, and blue eyes that hid nothing. Right now they were full of grief for Maria's marriage. Their depth of sadness distracted Maria from her first shocking thought: that Sophie had gained a dangerous amount of weight.

"I wanted to leave," Maria said. "It was my idea."

Sophie nodded as if she knew better. Maria, three years older, had felt like Sophie's mother when they were children. But somewhere in mid-adolescence the roles had shifted and Sophie had taken charge.

"Let's get on the road," Nell said. "We want to beat the storm. . . ."

"How is everyone?" Maria asked on the way to the car. They shouldered into the driving snow. Her bags had been evenly divided among the three of them; she carried the heaviest two herself—a big metal one full of photographic equipment and a canvas one full of presents. The icy February wind stung her face and reminded her of nights on the mountain, at the dig site near Chavín de Huántar.

"Peter wanted to come," Nell said. "I made him stay at home with Andy. They're having dinner with your mother tonight. Someone has to keep her at bay—otherwise she'd freeze her ass off waiting for you at the end of the driveway."

"The driveway of her mind," Maria said, and Sophie snorted. Their mother would wait in the driveway for no one; she had perfected utter devotion to her family without ever showing any overt signs of affection. Somehow, Nell refused to see this.

"Here we are," Nell said, stopping at a red Jeep four rows into the short-term parking lot.

"Aren't you forgetting something?" Sophie asked Maria while Nell checked all her pockets for the car keys. Ice crystals frosted Sophie's black lashes. She smiled expectantly.

"What?" Maria asked.

"To ask about Gordon and the children. They're fine."

"That's great. I'm sure they are," Maria said. She wondered why Sophie wanted to make her feel guilty for not asking, but

Sophie continued to smile. If her face was plump, it was as radiant as ever.

"I'm just so proud," Sophie said. "I'm an idiot on the subject. Gordon's planning to put a gazebo near the brook. He knows I've always wanted one. . . ."

"A gazebo? Everyone has those now," Nell said, letting Sophie into the front and Maria into the back. She revved the engine.

"Gordon's will be different. He's designing it himself," Sophie said, giving Nell an oddly triumphant look.

Nell pulled up to the parking lot attendant and handed him the ticket. She rummaged through her bag. "Oh, no!" she said.

"What is it?" Maria asked, leaning forward.

"My money," Nell said. "Where did I put it?" She stared into her wallet, riffled through papers in her bag.

"That airport is full of pickpockets," Sophie said, grabbing her own bag to check for anything missing. "I'll bet it happened when we put everything down to hug Maria."

Maria smiled; she had lived away long enough to have lost the New Englander's provincial view of New York as a den of crime.

"No, a pickpocket would have taken the whole wallet," Nell said. "I'm sure I left home with money . . . didn't I pay the tolls? Did I drop it?"

"Here's five," Sophie said when horns behind them started to blow.

Maria felt exhausted and wished she were home. But where was that? Her mother's house in Hatuquitit or Aldo's tent in the Andes? An image of night in Peru filled her mind: the mountain air so clear and cold no scents came through it. She saw herself wrapped in her sleeping bag listening to Aldo in the next tent with his students and assistants. She would fall asleep to his voice lecturing and waken to it whispering *"Buona notte."* She heard herself sigh.

"What's wrong?" Sophie asked.

Maria opened her eyes, shrugged. She heard the click of a seatbelt buckle and saw Sophie hoist herself over the front seat into the back. "You need a traveling companion," Sophie said, settling next to her. She slid her arm around Maria's shoulders. "Take a nap. We'll be home in a jiffy."

With her head on Sophie's shoulder, Maria thought her sister felt ample, just like a mother. The extra weight gave her a lush roundness about the cheeks, breasts, hips.

"Do you want to tell me about it?" Sophie whispered in a voice too low for Nell to hear. "Did he find another woman?"

"No," Maria said. "We just stopped loving each other." That was the truth, but who could believe anything so bizarre? She had been brought up in a town choked with Puritanical roots, where decent people divorced only after suffering heartbreak, betrayal, flagrant infidelity. She and Aldo had been student and teacher, then lovers, then husband and wife, now friends. Maria believed that everything would be easier if they were not, if she could hate him. The discoveries of treasures and civilizations had made their days wild and exciting. But at night in the tent she would fall asleep alone while Aldo shared his rapture with his students.

"I can't imagine it," Sophie said. "I'm sorry. I could never stop loving Gordon."

"Then you're doing something right, you two," Maria said.

"We all thought you were so happy," Sophie said.

"I know," Maria said. She had heard that so many times already from professors and archaeologists and students on the dig: Maria Dark and Aldo Giordano, the husband-and-wife team known for their meticulous excavations, their investigative approach. One critic had called them archaeological detectives, saying that they uncovered lives—the people of the culture, not only the artifacts. Their faces and stories had been in *Geo, National Geographic, Smithsonian.*

"The good part is, you're coming home," Sophie said.

"Home" to Sophie had always been Hatuquitit. She had commuted to college in New Haven, married a man from the next village, persuaded him to cross the town line and build a house on Bell Stream.

"How's Mom?" Maria asked.

"You know Mom," Sophie said in a voice inviting Maria to complain about their mother. Maria recalled Sophie once telling her that she could not remember her mother ever hugging her, not once, all through her childhood.

Nell sped them east on the New England Thruway. They flashed through blocks of orange light thrown by the highway lamps. Snow fell steadily. Maria shivered slightly and Sophie tightened her grip. Plows heading in the opposite direction sprayed snow into the air. Nell switched on the radio, found a jazz station. Maria felt the rhythm lulling her, felt herself nodding.

She must have slept. The sound of paper rustling wakened her. Her head rested against the Jeep's door; her neck ached in the thin stream of cold air blowing through a crack. Maria opened her eyes. Sophie was bent forward, rummaging gently through Maria's bag of presents. Maria watched, and from Sophie's measured movements Maria knew she was trying not to disturb her. Suddenly she stopped, as if she had found what she was looking for. She withdrew her hand and there, closed in it, was the small Chavín goddess. Her eyes wide open, Maria watched Sophie slip the gold statue into her pocket. Then, just as Sophie was turning toward her, Maria closed her eyes again and pretended to sleep.

2

WIDE-AWAKE IN HER BED THE NEXT MORNING,
Maria heard a pebble strike the house. The sun was just up. She
nearly tripped over her long flannel nightgown getting to the
window that overlooked the long snowy meadow leading to Bell
Stream. Golden marsh grass spiked through the snow; the rising
sun turned it pink. Maria peered into the driveway where Nell
stood waving. Maria waved back. She threw on her old plaid robe
and hurried downstairs.

"It's freezing out there," Nell said, stamping snow off her
boots. "Is Hallie up?"

"Not yet," Maria said.

"And she was sleeping when you got home last night?"

"Yes," Maria said. "I sort of thought she'd wait up."

"Well, she'll be up soon," Nell said, filling a kettle with water,
measuring coffee into a filter, just as though it were her house.

Maria turned up the thermostat. Nell wanted to ignore the
fact that Hallie had gone to bed and Maria might be hurt. But
Sophie had understood. Last night, walking into the empty
kitchen, Sophie had given Maria a knowing shrug and a kiss good
night. But by then Maria had seen Sophie steal the goddess and
felt too bewildered to accept her comfort.

"What brings you here so early?" Maria asked. Sitting at the
old oak table, she traced the familiar grain with her thumb. This
had been her "place" since childhood, and at various times she
had seen in the oak grain a witch, her father's nose, mountains,
sailboats, a Pequot sachem.

"This is hard to say," Nell began, frowning. "I know how close you are . . ."

"It's about Sophie, isn't it?" Maria said with an ache in the pit of her stomach.

Nell nodded. "Something's happening to her. Most of the time she seems the same, but not quite."

"Did you hear her last night, when I'd forgotten to ask about Gordon and the kids?" Maria asked.

"I know," Nell said. "She took it as some sort of insult. She gets very defensive about him. She always imagines you're slighting him—when it's actually the last thing on your mind."

The coffee was beginning to smell good, and Maria craved a cup. She wanted to tell Nell about the goddess, but she hesitated. Nell's theory sounded crazy: Sophie imagining people slighting Gordon? As much as Maria loved Nell, she knew that Nell tended to exaggerate and romanticize the Dark family. "What does Peter think?" Maria asked.

"He doesn't see it," Nell said. "Neither does Hallie. They think I'm being paranoid and unfair."

Maria set two thick white mugs on the table. She poured the coffee, not bothering to offer milk or sugar: since high school she, Sophie, and Nell had drunk their coffee black, thinking it sophisticated and, as a bonus, calorie-free.

"They've noticed that she's gained weight, haven't they?" Maria asked.

"Hallie says that happens to all young mothers," Nell said.

"It didn't happen to Hallie," Maria said, picturing her mother as slim and beautiful as Sophie had been the last time Maria saw her.

"Remember that money I lost last night? Sophie stole it," Nell said bluntly.

Maria paused, stung. "How do you know?" she asked finally.

"Because every time she leaves my house, something is missing. Because I know I had ninety-seven dollars when I left Hatuquitit yesterday and I know it wasn't taken by pickpockets."

"How do you know Sophie took it?" Maria asked, afraid to hear the answer.

"The only time I let my bag out of my sight was when the gate at the parking lot jammed and I left the car to find a guard."

"I believe you," Maria said.

"You do?" Nell asked, sounding surprised.

"Last night I saw her take something out of my bag." The memory of it was so vivid: the hiss of snowplows, a lone trumpet on the radio, Sophie's glossy blue-black hair, her lowered head, the tension in her shoulders as she searched Maria's bag. "Something stupid—a little goddess. I'd planned to give it to her anyway."

"But valuable, right?" Nell asked. "She always seems to take things worth money. Your mother's silver gravy ladle is missing."

Hallie's gravy ladle made Maria think of family Thanksgivings and Christmases, the only times it was used. There was no way Sophie would steal it. Instantly the thought of Sophie as a thief was impossible. There had to be some explanation. Maria tried to block what she had seen last night; if she hadn't herself twice checked the bag for the gold figure, she could almost have believed she had dreamed the scene.

"I'm glad you're back," Nell said awkwardly. The terrible things they had said about Sophie hung in the air. Sweeping them away for now, Nell cleared her throat. "Do you have plans yet? Peter said you might teach . . ."

"I'm not sure," Maria said. "I've always wanted to dig around here." Her interest in archaeology had been born in Hatuquitit. She had found arrowheads in the meadow. The local tribes, the Pequots and the Hatuquitits, had been warriors, and Maria had imagined Indian wars fought in her own yard. At school they had learned legends of the Haunted Isles, three offshore islands said to be haunted by the spirits of Native Americans who had lived and traded there.

Nell nodded eagerly. "I always assumed you would. I remember Aldo at Christmas that year, saying all the important finds had already been made around here."

"Until the next one, anyway," Maria said. She wondered whether her family knew what an archaeological snob Aldo was, how boring he would find the relics of Eastern Woodland Indians.

Upstairs her mother began to stir. They heard her bedsprings creak, the toilet flush, the soft scrape of her slippers on the wood floor.

"I'd better go," Nell said, rising. "Peter has an early meeting, so I have to give Andy breakfast."

"I'm glad you told me everything," Maria said, hugging Nell.

"You can't possibly be," Nell said. "I know how you love Sophie."

"You love her just as much."

"I'm going to scoot," Nell said, glancing nervously at the door. "Hallie's not very happy with me. Peter told me she thinks I'm stirring up trouble."

"Don't worry about her," Maria said, kissing Nell good-bye.

Maria sat down, found herself staring across the table at Sophie's place. Her parents had sat at the heads, with Maria on one side and Sophie and Peter on the other. It had been that way forever; she could remember when Peter, the youngest, had occupied his place in a high chair.

"My old Maria," said Hallie Dark, standing in the kitchen doorway. She stood tall, her posture regal as ever. Maria felt shocked to see that her hair, once as black as her children's, had gone very gray.

"Mom!" Maria said. They gave each other a back-slapping hug, then stood apart.

"Who was here?" Hallie asked, instantly spying Nell's mug.

"Nell," Maria said. "She was up early and felt like dropping by."

"This is *very* early," Hallie said, her expression suspicious. But she decided to say nothing; she poured herself coffee instead. She took her place at the table and stared out the picture window. Gulls flying from the marsh to the Sound swooped and cried. A yellow Lab hunted along the stream. Maria followed her mother's gaze and tried to imagine what she was thinking. Hallie's mornings always included many minutes of gazing out the window. Peter said it was a form of Zen. Sophie believed she was thinking of all the paths her life might have taken if she hadn't had children. Maria tried not to feel impatient with Hallie for doing it even now, their first morning together in over a year.

"I'm happy to be back," Maria said finally. "It was great seeing Sophie and Nell."

"Sophie has been excited for days!" Hallie said, suddenly enthusiastic, as if someone had thrown a switch. "She's such a good girl."

"I thought she seemed a little...nervous last night," Maria said.

"You've been talking to Nell, haven't you?" Hallie asked, exhaling with exasperation. "I love Nell dearly, but she's making things very difficult. She's full of theories about Sophie's mental health—can you imagine?"

In a way that felt familiar, Maria found herself wondering about the discrepancy between what Hallie said about Sophie and the way she acted. Of the three children, Sophie most clearly resembled Hallie: the surprising vibrance in their clear, blue eyes, their perfect oval faces, their straight, fine hair. Perhaps because of the similarities, Sophie was Hallie's favorite, and Hallie watched Sophie with special—if detached—interest, as if she were watching herself in some distant mirror. Hallie had been the only child of doting parents, and from what Maria could gather, her childhood had been full of praise and gala events: prizes in school, horse shows, cotillions and regattas. Hallie cherished her own childhood; nothing made her so happy as the chance to begin a story with the words "When I was a tiny child..."

"Tell me about Aldo," Hallie said. "Is he well?"

The abrupt switch in subject startled Maria. "He's fine. He's in Peru."

"Sometimes I wonder how you'll manage here in cold, gray New England," Hallie said. "After all that glamorous jet-setting. If you dig around here you're going to find clamshells and dusty old Indian bones instead of gold treasures."

"I love New England," Maria said. "I dreamed about it the whole time I was away." It was true: She had lived alongside the Nile, the Amazon, the Loire, the Yangtze, but many nights she had dreamed, asleep and awake, of Bell Stream. Of sugar maples, stone walls, the brightness of a sky reflecting Long Island Sound. She had dreamt of starting an excavation somewhere in the town where her archaeological interest had been born.

"You won't find a man like Aldo again," Hallie said. "Not around here. I thought he was good for you. He brought you . . . I don't know, *out* of yourself. I think Aldo made you shine."

"Thanks, Mom," Maria said sarcastically, feeling her face redden. In her mother's early scheme of things, Maria had been the introvert, Sophie the extrovert. Hallie wouldn't have been surprised if Sophie had married an Italian archaeologist and traveled the world with him, digging as they went, but she had hardly been able to hide her amazement when Maria had done it.

"Please don't be so touchy," Hallie said. "I'm just showing a little concern."

"Fine," Maria said quietly. Amazing how her mother still had that power over her. After twelve months of wrestling with the idea of leaving Aldo, of realizing that Aldo's qualities of charm and confidence were half the time pure manipulation and imperiousness, it took her mother only fifteen seconds to make her doubt herself.

And then it happened: just as it had so often during their lives, Maria would be wishing mightily for Sophie to appear, to witness whatever outrageous thing Hallie was saying or doing, and Sophie would walk in.

"Good morning!" the Littlefields yelled. Maria jumped up and ran to the door. She hugged Simon and Flo, then Gordon and Sophie. "Did anyone escape last night?" Sophie asked, grinning at Maria.

"No one but the axe-murderess," Maria said.

"I don't think that's funny," Hallie said. "You girls didn't have to spend last night alone in this big house right next door to the prison. This would be the first place an escapee would go."

"Alone?" Maria asked. "What am I?" She noticed how much easier it was to joke with Sophie, to ignore the fact that her mother always felt alone, even when one or more of her children was in the room.

"We're having doughnuts," Flo said.

"Really? I love doughnuts," Maria said, tugging Flo onto her lap, wondering if she was getting too old for that.

"Honey-dip and crullers," Simon said.

"I'll make some more coffee," Sophie said. Maria asked the children about school, and they told her their teachers had hung pictures of her and Aldo taken from *National Geographic* on the bulletin boards. Maria's gaze kept sliding to Sophie and Gordon, huddled over the coffeemaker. Gordon was tall; he seemed to surround Sophie with his movements. He touched her elbow, whispered something in her ear, reached around her to brush coffee grounds off the counter. Maria had never seen a man seem so loving and protective: Sophie is *twinkling,* she thought, disgusted by the jealousy she felt.

"Did you bring us things?" Flo whispered.

"Yes," Maria whispered back. "Run up to my room and get that big yellow bag. Be careful—it's heavy." Flo and Simon took off, and Maria's heart started to race at the thought of giving out the presents when Sophie already had the goddess.

Finally the coffee was poured and everyone but Gordon was seated. "Pull up a chair, Gordon," Maria said.

He leaned against the counter, grinning sheepishly. The expression was boyish, very attractive on a big forty-two-year-old. "Oh, you're in his seat, Maria," Sophie said quickly.

"His seat? But . . ." Maria felt momentarily confused. She had always considered this spot hers. But of course she had lived away from home for many years. Gordon had obviously taken her place at the table. She shifted to the left, took Flo onto her lap. "Do you mind sharing, sweet pea?" she asked, trying to sound offhand, to hide how upset she felt. But wasn't it ridiculous for a grown woman to feel territorial about her childhood place at the table?

"I like it better," Flo said as Gordon sat beside them, squeezing Maria's hand by way of thanks.

Maria leaned down to reach into her bag, and when she

emerged with packages, the little gold goddess stood at her place.

"Where did she come from?" Maria asked.

"I borrowed her last night," Sophie said. "You were asleep and I didn't want to wake you up, but she was glinting in that bag of yours and I couldn't resist. She's so lovely to hold! I had her in my hand, running my thumb over her body, and I felt so soothed I forgot to put her back."

Maria tried to match Sophie's explanation with what she had seen in the car, and she felt tremendously disturbed to discover that it didn't fit. "She's yours," Maria said.

"I adore her," Sophie said, reaching across the table for the goddess. She held it lovingly in her right hand, just as she said she had done last night. Maria passed out the other presents: jet beads for Hallie, a bright wool sweater for Gordon, suede slippers lined with alpaca fur for Simon, a gold bracelet for Flo. Everyone exclaimed over the gifts' textures and brilliant colors; they passed the things around. Maria tried to sound happy, telling about the mountain villages where she had found each present, but all she could think of was Sophie stealing the goddess and for some reason deciding to give it back.

3

MARIA WENT OUT TO THE BARN AND USED HALLIE'S
Volvo to jump-start her father's old Mustang. She hated driving
it. It rattled and quivered on the road; holes the size of half-
dollars had rusted away. Hallie kept it for sentimental reasons, in
memory of her husband. Maria barely remembered him. Malcolm Dark had been a big, jovial man thirty years older than Hallie, with whom he was said by one and all to have been besotted.
He doted on her as if she were his beloved child, while maintain-
ing a distant but fond formality with his real children. When she
was eleven Maria had indulged a fantasy that he was really her
grandfather, that her real (young, handsome) father would return one day to claim her.

By then Malcolm Dark had started needing the care an elderly
person requires, and Hallie had spent all her time with him. She'd
march around the house with the tip of her tongue showing between her clenched teeth. Sophie had called Hallie's expression
"that face." They hated it because it proved how unhappy their
mother felt. Maria would ask Hallie to take them to the beach or
down to the stream, but she could never leave Malcolm. She's like
a prisoner, Maria had thought angrily: she's just like the ladies in
jail. Sophie was kinder. She would follow Hallie around the
house, listening to stories of horse shows Hallie had won, of piano
recitals she'd given, of boys who were now successful doctors and
businessmen with whom she had danced at Yale. "You could have
married them, right, Mom?" Sophie would ask. "Some of them
asked," Hallie would say, by then smiling.

The next year Malcolm died in his sleep, transforming Hallie into a young widow with three children. Then she had the chance to realize how much she had really loved him, and she was struck with profound grief, closing her off to her children for the next few years. Sophie had hated to leave her alone. Sometimes she would fake a sore throat in order to stay home from school with Hallie. Maria would be dressing for school, trying to ignore Sophie lying in bed.

"Get up, you're not sick," Maria would say.

"Yes I am, and you could be too," Sophie would say hopefully.

Maria would imagine the fun all three of them could have if she stayed home. But she never did. She had a nearly perfect attendance record and felt ashamed of Sophie, who had forty-five absences one year. She also felt jealous. She hated to think of Sophie and Hallie spending the whole day alone together. Hallie didn't deserve it. Before Malcolm died, she'd been too busy even for PTA meetings or to attend Sophie's spring concerts. It made Maria furious to think of Hallie and Sophie drinking tea with honey—for Sophie's sore throat—at home all day while Hallie encouraged Sophie to daydream about a singing career that would make her famous. Sophie did have a beautiful voice, but the one who wanted to be famous was Hallie, not Sophie. If Hallie really cared about Sophie's singing, why didn't she ever go to Sophie's recitals?

The road into town had hardly changed since Maria's childhood. Every landmark brought back memories. Even the weather, warm and hazy for February, made her think of the springlike late winter days that had most tempted her to skip school with Sophie. She drove along Cove Road, past the prison, the marshes, the stately Victorian houses at the head of Summer Street. The boatyard was full of boats out of water, covered for the winter with sheets of royal blue plastic. Driving by, she imagined getting a small sailboat for the warm weather.

Maria parked between the laundromat and the Pequot Savings Bank. She sat there a minute, watching people walk past. She recognized one high school classmate whose name she could not remember. Also Miss Rogers from the bookstore, and Mr. Brown the butcher. After living so long in foreign countries, delving into ancient civilizations, it felt peculiar, as exhilarating as an adventure, to be parked in her hometown. She climbed out of the car, hesitating an instant before locking it.

Window-shopping seemed novel and delicious. She gazed at gold-foil coins and chocolate lobsters in the candy store; real silk long underwear on a mannequin in Josie's; copper elbows at Hatuquitit Plumbing; roses, daffodils, irises, and Mylar balloons in Sea Garden Flowers; Kastmasters and hip boots at James's Bait and Tackle. In Peru she had shopped at farms along dirt roads, in villages without electricity. Maria, who had been raised in this small town, had forgotten its pleasures. But remembering them filled her with guilt.

Guilt was her payment for the relief she felt at being without Aldo. Aldo had never understood her feelings for Hatuquitit. "Your pilgrimage," he had indulgently called her yearly visits. Aldo came from a Roman banking family, and he felt most comfortable with things happening on a grand scale: the Earliest pre-Chavín burial site, the Most Valuable pharaoh's treasure, the Largest spread in *Smithsonian,* the Most Devoted wife. Maria had always thought he was brilliant, and she still did. But she'd stopped respecting him. He valued fame above everything. She'd begun to feel like any other archaeologist in his orbit instead of his wife. During her last several months on the mountain, they hadn't made love once. It wasn't only Maria who hadn't wanted to; Aldo had always found reasons for staying late at the excavation or lecturing in the next tent.

Maria found herself staring at color photos of houses in the window of Shoreline Realty. On an impulse, she walked in.

"May I help you?" the realtor asked. She looked about Maria's age, but Maria didn't recognize her. Beside this dainty person with her blond pageboy, blue cashmere sweater, and gray skirt, Maria in her black jeans and black leather jacket felt like a thuggy witch.

"I'd like to rent a house," Maria said.

"What are your requirements?" the realtor asked. "How many are there in your household?"

"Just me," Maria said, liking the sound of it. She knew she would be welcome to stay with Hallie, but she wanted her own place. Her own bed, her own kitchen, her own floor: three things not available in the many tents she had occupied.

"What is your price range?"

"Um, medium," Maria said vaguely, trying to convert her idea of a reasonable amount of pesos into U.S. dollars.

"Why don't you look through the listings?" the realtor asked, showing Maria to a desk. "That way you can see what's available. I'll show you any property you think you might like to see."

"Thank you," Maria said. She smiled at the realtor, who seemed to hover, waiting to say something.

"I saw you on *Nova*," the realtor said, blushing. "Wait till I tell Steve you're moving back home. Do you remember my husband? Steve Grunwald?"

"Sure I do!" Maria said. She had gone to school with him; in fourth grade she had stolen his Sugar Daddy and refused to give it back until he gave her his sweater and let her throw it up into a tree. "How is he?"

"He's fine. He's a lawyer now—his office is in the same building as your brother Peter's. Our kids play with Sophie's."

"That's great," Maria said, thinking how nice it felt to be back in a small town.

"I'm Nancy Grunwald," she said, shaking Maria's hand and handing Maria a thick notebook full of listings.

"What brings you back home?" Nancy asked after a minute.

"I'm separated from my husband," Maria said. "And I didn't want to stay in Peru."

"You don't have kids?" Nancy asked.

"No," Maria said. Nancy's simple question made her uncomfortable. She glanced at Nancy and thought of her kids playing with Sophie's. Children seemed to bind this town together. She wondered how hard it would be to fit in without them. For twelve years her attention had been focused on the ground: on dirt and the things it contained. She wondered whether, if she had had a different sort of career, like real estate, she would have found a way to make time for raising children. But she knew the answer: not with Aldo.

"That must make it easier, not having children," Nancy said. "I know it must be awful, separating. But I think it would be worse with kids."

"I think so," Maria said.

"You know," Nancy said, as Maria idly flipped the pages, "I have a place you might like. It's definitely not for everyone. It's a little rustic."

"How rustic?" Maria asked. "Does it have heat?"

"Yes, and indoor plumbing, don't worry," Nancy said, smiling. "It's not primitive or anything. It's a bit isolated and not exactly a showplace. It's right on the water. A really beautiful location."

"On the water?"

"Yes, out at Squaw's Landing. It's unlisted—word of mouth only. The owner really loves it. She'd live there herself, but she's working in Montreal. It's been in her family for three generations."

"It has a view?" Maria asked.

"Of the Haunted Isles," Nancy said. "Wait till you see."

She tried the caretaker's number, but his wife said he wouldn't be free to let them in until four o'clock. "Can you kill some time?" Nancy asked.

"Sure," Maria said. Waving good-bye, she headed for the library. A cool salty breeze blew across the railroad tracks from the bay. She thought about calling Sophie or Nell, to ask them to drive to town and see the house with her, but someone was using the only pay phone.

The Hatuquitit Library was a stone house on Summer Street with white shutters and a wide front porch. Inside stood the librarian's desk, racks of periodicals, a sitting area with vinyl armchairs and long pine tables, and stacks of books. It seemed smaller than Maria remembered. She walked straight back to her favorite section: Local Lore.

The shelves were full of picture books and yellowing periodicals with titles like *Pequot Tales, A Visit to Devil's Chimney, Hatuquitit: Our Tricentennial.* Maria thumbed through *Pequot Tales.* Inside the front cover was a map of Hatuquitit, with *X*'s marking the sites of Indian burial grounds. Two were located on Squaw's Landing.

Maria turned past the section called "Colonial Trickery" to "Love Stories." She read about an English trader in the 1600s who convinced the Pequots to sell him their largest graveyard by promising to move the bones to some other sacred earth. He fell in love with a squaw, already married to a Pequot. "Her Indian husband, upon discovering her deception, shot her through the heart with an arrow," Maria read. "But that only deepened his grief. He decided to follow her spirit to the Land of the Dead. At nightfall she came out of her grave and walked across the bay to the Haunted Isles. Her husband had to paddle his canoe very fast to keep up with her. 'Do not follow me,' she begged.

" 'I cannot let you go,' her husband called. But she only walked faster, until she disappeared from his sight into the woods on the largest island.

"A sea hawk heard the man weeping. 'Young man,' he said. 'If you do as I say, you can be reunited with your beloved. Follow the shore path to the rock cliffs. When the sun begins to rise, climb them, and you will find your wife there. She will be alive, and you may take her home in your canoe. But do not touch her or allow another human to touch her for four days! If you do, she will die again, and you will never again see her.'

"And so the young man obeyed the hawk. He climbed the granite cliff just as the red sun emerged from the waves, and there sat his wife, a spirit no longer. He longed to touch her, but he remembered what the hawk had said. She smiled and said, 'Your love for me is true, even though I have loved another. I know because you have followed me here.'

"The brave paddled his wife across the bay, and he hid her from the other Pequots for three nights. But on the morning of the fourth day, the English trader who had also loved the squaw passed by. Upon seeing her, he rushed, overjoyed, to embrace her. And even as he kissed her, she shimmered and became transparent and disappeared forever. When the brave discovered what had happened, he killed the Englishman with his tomahawk. And so the Englishman could not keep his promise of moving the Indian burial ground, and for that reason, many of the houses in Hatuquitit are built on sacred earth."

Maria had heard part of that story before, about homeowners discovering Native American bones in their basements or while bulldozing for a swimming pool. But she had never heard the Pequot legend.

Now she reached for a small book she had read a hundred times before, *The Story of Bell Stream*. The book had a faded red cover with black letters and seemed much closer to falling apart now than it had twenty-five years ago, when Maria had first read it. Loose pages protruded. Inside the front cover were rows and rows of dates, going back only until 1982, made by the librarian's stamp. Maria felt positive that every child in Hatuquitit had read the book at least once. Maria began to read it again.

It told the story of a couple who were to be married. The year was 1679, the place Hatuquitit. She lived east of the stream and he lived west. On the night before their wedding, a storm broke. It rained till dawn. She dressed in her wedding clothes, constantly asking her mother whether her betrothed and the minister had arrived, but they had not. Hours passed. Word came that the stream had swollen into a torrent, that it could not be crossed. "Then we'll have the ceremony when the storm passes," her mother said. But the minister had come from Massachusetts, where he would have to return that same night. If the wedding did not take place that day, it would be delayed for at least a month. So the brave bride-to-be hopped into a donkey cart and drove to the brook. Across its seething surface she spied her true love. She waved wildly, and he called to her. The minister opened his Bible. And there, standing on opposite sides of the water, shouting to be heard above the howling wind, the couple recited their wedding vows. The church bell was heard all through the town, and continued to ring until the storm stopped and the bride and groom could be reunited. So from that day on, the stream was called Bell Stream.

How lucky Maria and Sophie had felt that Bell Stream ran alongside their yard! As children they were always reenacting the ceremony, trying to determine the exact places where the bride, groom, and minister had stood. Peter could not have cared less. One summer Sophie had placed stones they'd picked up on Town Beach to commemorate the most likely spots. Maria was thinking about that, so it took some time for Sophie's voice to enter her consciousness. But there it was, real and clear. Sophie stood in the next aisle, speaking softly.

"This time I mean it," she said. "I've already called the matron. I want you to stay right here and think about what you did while I go home to pack your things."

"Please, Mommy . . . ," sobbed Flo. "Don't make me go there."

"I have no choice. It's where bad girls go. You know that. I'm going to go home and pack all your things into a garbage bag and throw it away so Daddy and I won't have to think about you anymore. Don't you know how you embarrassed Daddy? You don't even care about him."

"I do! I *love* Daddy!" Flo said hotly.

Maria felt frozen with horror. She wanted to fly into the next aisle, but she couldn't move.

"You stay right here," Sophie said gently. "You think long and hard about your mistake, and when I come back I'll take you to the prison."

"Please don't leave me," Flo said. Sophie didn't answer. Maria heard her heels click away, and then there was only the sound of Flo weeping quietly.

Instantly Maria went to her. "Flo?" she said.

Flo was six. She wore braids. Except for a little potbelly she was skinny. She was crouched down, her mouth buried in her Minnie Mouse knapsack. "Flo?" Maria said again, bending down to touch her head.

"Is Mommy here?" Flo asked.

"No," Maria said. She picked Flo off the floor and hugged her. The little girl felt limp; she didn't hug back.

"Mommy is sending me to prison," Flo said.

"No, she's not," Maria said. "Sometimes mothers say things they don't mean when they're mad."

"Mommy is very, very mad," Flo said.

"Do you know why?" Maria asked, beginning to sway, wanting to rock Flo who still gulped with sobs.

"Because I cried at the dentist," Flo said.

Maria said nothing, only rocked back and forth. Her arms began to ache, so carefully she lowered Flo to the floor, then sank down and pulled her onto her lap. "When you feel better, in a minute," Maria said, "I'll take you home. You can come to Gram's with me."

"I have to stay here," Flo said. "It's the rule."

"What rule?"

"Mommy leaves me here because it's safe and a good place to think things over."

"She leaves you here a lot?"

"Not a lot," Flo said. "Sometimes."

"For a long time?" Maria asked.

"Until it gets dark," Flo said.

"Listen," Maria said, taking Flo's hand and pulling her to her feet. "I'm your mother's big sister, and I say it's okay for you to come with me. I'll tell the librarian, so she can tell your mother when she comes back."

Flo accompanied her wordlessly. Maria stopped at the desk; the librarian gave her a dirty look.

"I'm this child's aunt," Maria said. "When her mother comes back would you mind—"

"This is not a day-care center," the librarian said. "This has happened once too often. I'd like you to tell your sister the next time she leaves her child here I'll call the police."

"Not the police!" Flo said, pressing against Maria's leg and starting to cry again.

"Come on, Flo," Maria said, leading her out of the library.

* * *

They ate ice cream cones. Maria postponed her appointment to see the house on Squaw's Landing. She and Flo sat in the Mustang's front seat, watching the laundromat. "People wash their clothes there," Flo said.

"I know," Maria said. Her mind brimmed with questions, but she didn't know how to ask them without upsetting Flo again. She tried to think of ways to ask the unaskable, found herself concentrating on things that were beside the point. How could the librarian have let her simply walk off with Flo? What if she were a kidnapper lying about being Flo's aunt? Then she would hear Sophie's calm voice again, telling Flo she was going to prison, and Maria would feel helpless and her mind would empty.

"Do you think it's funny, eating ice cream after going to the dentist?" Maria asked slowly.

"Yes," Flo said. She licked her orange sherbet carefully, not letting it drip down the cone.

"Do you like your dentist?"

"He's nice. But it's scary to go. To the doctor, too."

"I used to feel that way," Maria said. She still did, but you weren't supposed to say that to a child. She wanted Flo to tell what had made her cry, why her crying had made Sophie so angry. "Flo, what's your dentist's name?"

"Dr. Kaufman. He comes to our house for dinner sometimes, and then he doesn't scare me. He isn't rotten."

"You mean Dr. Kaufman is a friend of your parents?"

"Yes. He's Daddy's *good* friend," Flo said, starting to sound anxious. "Will you take me home soon?"

"Sure I will," Maria said, starting the car. "To your house or to Gram's?"

"My house."

Sophie had created a perfect country cottage full of rustic antiques, durable furniture covered with chintz and plaids, with family photos and nineteenth-century landscapes on the walls, and a yellow kitchen with an open hearth and a braided rug on the red-tiled floor. Maria, holding Flo's hand, walked through the unlocked front door. They passed Simon watching TV in the den. Sophie stood at the kitchen sink cracking ice into a big glass bowl.

"Look who I found at the library," Maria said. Sophie turned and her face collapsed. She wore a red apron that strained across her bosom. A child, probably Flo, had stitched the outline of a blue heart on it. She opened her arms and Flo ran into them. "Thank heavens you're okay," Sophie said.

"Aunt Maria made me come with her," Flo exclaimed.

"God, Maria!" Sophie said, wiping tears off her cheeks. "I went back for her and she was gone."

"Didn't the librarian say I took her?"

"Yes, but you weren't here when I got home and Mom didn't know where you were. Maybe you meant well, but don't you *ever* take her again without asking me. If you had any idea of what I've been thinking . . ."

Maria herself felt sick with the worry she must have caused Sophie. She watched Sophie and Flo wrapped in each other's arms, petting and soothing each other. "I'm fine, Mommy," Flo whispered. "Everything will be fine."

"I'm so glad you're home, honey," Sophie whispered back, brushing stray strands of straw-colored hair off Flo's forehead.

"Can I talk to you?" Maria asked after a moment.

"Talk away," Sophie said.

"I mean alone." Maria smiled at Flo, trying to reassure her. The child stood ramrod-stiff, her eyes full of panic.

"Sure. Go find Simon, honey. Okay?" Sophie said.

"Okay, Mommy," Flo said in a thin voice. She ran out.

Maria took a deep breath. She knew that if she touched her chest she would feel her heart pounding. "I heard you at the library," she said. "I was standing in the next aisle."

"You heard what?" Sophie asked, whacking a towelful of ice with a hammer.

"I heard you tell Flo you're going to send her to prison."

Sophie grimaced and shook her head bitterly. "Talk to me

when you have kids," she said. "Every mother in Hatuquitit threatens that. No one means it." She ripped open a bag of chocolate chips and began eating them.

"Flo believed it. She was crying her heart out, Sophie. Didn't the librarian tell you about it?"

"She gave me a lecture about not leaving Flo alone there anymore. I mean, sometimes I leave the kids while I run to the market or the post office, but never for very long—everyone does! Don't you remember spending hours there without Mom?" Sophie asked, popping chip after chip into her mouth.

"Yes," Maria said, but she knew they had been much older than six. "Will you tell me one thing? Why did you get so mad at Flo?"

"She purposely dropped a jar of mustard pickles at the market. She's doing that a lot lately."

"I thought it was because she cried at the dentist."

"She told you that?" Sophie asked, looking straight at Maria.

Maria hesitated. She wanted to protect Flo, but she had to know what Sophie would say. "Yes, she did," Maria said.

"I really overreacted," Sophie said, her voice shaking. "Paul Kaufman is a good friend of ours—he and Gordon play golf together. He absolutely adores our kids, and I could see it really hurt him when Flo began to cry. He thinks he's such a *gentle* dentist. Flo isn't really scared of him—she cried because her friends tell her she should be afraid of the dentist."

"God, *I'm* scared of the dentist," Maria said, feeling slightly reassured.

"Well, after the witch doctors you're probably used to . . ." Sophie tried to smile.

"Sophie," Maria said, keeping her voice calm. "I'm worried about you. I love you."

"I love you, too," Sophie said, but her knuckles were white on the hammer handle.

"What's the ice for?" she asked.

"Caviar," Sophie said. "We're having it tonight. Petrossian beluga—Gordon's favorite."

"What's the occasion?" Maria asked.

"Absolutely no occasion," Sophie said. "That's how we do things in this house—it's why we're so happy. One reason, at least."

Listening to Sophie's warm voice in Sophie's cozy kitchen, Maria could almost believe she had dreamed the scene in the library stacks. Then she thought of the gold statue and the coziness bled away.

"Caviar on a Tuesday night," Maria said dully, wanting but not daring to delve deeper. "Pretty fancy."

"Are you saying Gordon's not worth it?" Sophie asked with a slight edge to her voice.

"Not at all," Maria said. "He absolutely is." Then, because it suddenly struck her as bizarre that Sophie would be cracking ice for caviar while her daughter was missing, Maria knew she had to leave fast. So she said good-bye.

4

"YOU'D BETTER BE VERY SURE BEFORE YOU START accusing someone of neglect," Peter Dark said solemnly. He wore his wavy black hair very short. He'd grown a mustache—neatly clipped, in keeping with his small-town-lawyer image—since last winter. His wire-rimmed glasses reflected the candlelight, and he fiddled with his utensils, using the bowl of his overturned spoon as a fulcrum and his knife as a seesaw.

"I'm not accusing anyone!" Maria said. "I'm speaking in confidence to my brother and my best friend."

"Just as long as you realize it's one of the most serious charges you can make. If Sophie hears you say it, she'll turn against you in a second."

"Or let the air out of your tires," Nell said. Maria sensed Nell's impatience with the way Peter thought like a lawyer first and reacted like a brother second.

Nell's frothy red curls looked really lovely against her black velvet blouse. Maria felt touched that Nell had invited her for dinner the instant she heard about what had happened with Sophie. "*If* something's going on," Nell continued, "we can't worry about Sophie's reaction. We have to think of Simon and Flo."

"Am I nuts?" Maria asked. "Or is it normal?"

"Which part?" Peter asked, spearing a piece of codfish. "Parents can get pretty bent out of shape. Everyone has their own way of disciplining kids."

"Would you tell Andy you're sending him to prison?"

"No," Peter said.

"You know, my mother once told me I'd go to the jail if I wasn't good," Nell said. "I think it's irresistible for mothers of daughters living in this town—I mean, you're at the end of your rope, and there's a women's prison two miles down the road . . ."

"It's the *way* Sophie said it," Maria said.

"She doesn't hit them," Peter said. "If she did, there would be evidence: bruises or something."

"Maybe this is worse than hitting," Maria said. She couldn't get their voices out of her mind: Sophie's gentle tone, Flo pleading with real terror and desperation. No matter what Sophie's explanation, no matter how badly Peter wanted to see the best in her, Maria knew that no six-year-old should experience either of those things.

"What about the stealing?" Nell asked. "And the things she eats?"

"Who cares what she eats?" Peter asked, beginning to sound impatient.

"She serves incredible things to Gordon every night," Nell said. "Tenderloin, lobster, foie gras—I'm not kidding. Every night! But I see her car in the McDonald's drive-through every time I go by. Haven't you noticed how fat she's getting?"

"Tonight she's serving caviar," Maria said.

"I don't know how she affords it," Nell said. "Unless that's why she steals. Gordon can't make that much in the hardware business."

"Let's quit dissecting the Littlefields, okay?" Peter said. "Come on, Maria. Tell us about the excavation. Did you find my nose ornament there? I'm thinking of wearing it to court tomorrow."

Maria gazed at him. She held herself back from answering right away because once she did the subject would change and the tension diffuse. Maria could think only of saving Sophie. But from what? "You really should," she said after a moment. "In the Chavín culture they were worn only by priests or political officers. A nose ornament is a sign of power."

"And you found it on your dig?" he asked.

"No—you can't take real artifacts out of the country. It's a copy of one we found near Chupas." The mournful face of Señora Hacha filled Maria's mind, and she laughed out loud.

"What?" Nell asked.

"Oh, I was just remembering the woman who owned the land where we wanted to dig. She farmed coca, and right in the middle of her land was a burial mound. In Peru all ruins belong to the government, so strictly speaking, you don't need the landowner's permission to dig. But Aldo . . ."

"Aldo would naturally ask," Nell said. She, like the rest of the Darks, considered Aldo's European courtliness slightly comical.

"He told her we'd pay for any crops destroyed in the dig," Maria said, "but Señora Hacha wouldn't hear of it. 'Those plants are my family,' she kept saying. 'I've raised them from sprouts.' She meant it!" Maria said. Telling the story, she relaxed. Memories of the mountains, the Chavín temples cut in stone, sentimental Señora Hacha, Aldo, all made her feel at home. In Hatuquitit, where everything familiar seemed changed, Maria felt like a stranger.

Nell started to clear the plates and Peter went to check on their sleeping son. Maria remembered that it was right after the dig at Señora Hacha's that she had begun to think of leaving. Crouched at the site, uncovering a tiny skull—perhaps that of a mouse—with her stiff brush, Maria had suddenly been aware of Aldo standing above her. "Why do you bother with that?" he asked impatiently.

Shading her eyes, Maria stared at him. "You sound like you're lecturing a student," she said.

"You're *digging* like a student. Concentrate on the tomb."

Maria pretended to ignore him. She uncovered the entire skeleton of a field mouse, then recorded it bone by bone. She knew that as finds went, this one was unremarkable. But she believed that everything found in an excavation should be recorded. Aldo would leave it to others or overlook it entirely. But it wasn't their professional difference that had bothered Maria: it was the way Aldo had spoken to her.

He hadn't always used such a tone. She remembered the first

time they'd dug together in Peru. Aldo had dug there many times before, but it was Maria's first. He had introduced her to it with pride, wanting her to love life in the high Andes, digging for what would almost certainly turn out to be gold artifacts. One night he told her he was taking her to a mountain ruin where a witch would call forth spirits to make their excavation a success.

"She can't come, *señor,*" said Pedro, Aldo's Peruvian assistant. "Women cannot be present at the witch's ceremony."

"Maria is an archaeologist. She's coming," Aldo said, closing the subject, as if he thought Pedro made no sense at all.

The archaeological team, all men except for Maria, trekked to the ruin one cold black night. The witch regarded Maria in stony silence, refusing to do any magic until Aldo demanded it. Finally the witch prepared fifty-two offerings to as many spirits. Each offering was the same: three perfect coca leaves powdered with dry llama fat, silver dust, and wild thyme. Kerosene lanterns sputtered in the wind and cast long shadows on the stone walls. "Mountain spirit, we beseech you for safety and luck," the witch murmured in Spanish fifty-two times, holding aloft each offering, then pitching it into the fire. Flames shot toward the dark sky. Maria huddled against Aldo, terrified because it seemed possible the spirits were about to descend.

"Scared, *bella?*" Aldo asked. "If you had a grandmother in Sicily you wouldn't think this was so crazy."

"This is supposed to protect our dig?" Maria asked.

Aldo smoothed her hair, put his warm mouth against her ear. "It's so when Pedro's cow dries up or Juan's hens stop laying, they can't blame it on the dig being hexed like they did last time."

Sitting in Peter's living room, Maria pictured Aldo's face: his classic Roman nose, the smile that was quick after he'd warmed to you, his sensual green eyes that filled with tears more readily than those of any man Maria had ever known.

"Too bad Hallie couldn't come tonight," Nell said. "She had tickets to Yale Rep. She was going with a friend."

"She has a date," Peter said, grinning. "None of us has met him yet."

"I'm glad for her," Maria said, trying to make the cultural leap from magic to her mother's social life.

"You know, maybe we're all wrong about Sophie," Nell said lightly.

Maria didn't answer. She was remembering the passion in Señora Hacha's voice, the feeling of Aldo's arm around her shoulder as the witch burned her offerings. She realized that Nell wanted to end the evening on a pleasant note, but she couldn't smile. Her breath came as fast as it had when she and Aldo had lived two miles high, and she sat at her brother's table thinking about the power of magic and the power of love.

5

AT TWO THE NEXT AFTERNOON, NANCY GRUNWALD picked Maria up at Hallie's house. Maria was just climbing into Nancy's red station wagon when Hallie came out the front door, wrapped in a yellow wool cape.

"Maria, I just wanted to remind you I'll be out when you get home," Hallie said. "Hello, Nancy."

"Hello, Mrs. Dark."

"Okay, Mom. Thanks for reminding me," Maria said. Since they had just discussed Hallie's invitation to a cocktail party in Slocum, Maria figured Hallie really wanted to speak to Nancy.

"Now, where's this place you're showing Maria?" Hallie asked.

"Squaw's Landing," Nancy said. "You know it, don't you, Maria? It's a colony of summer cottages, mainly, out on that headland—"

"I know it," Maria said.

"That's a lonely place to live in the winter," Hallie said. "It's easy to feel depressed when you're miles from anyone, with nothing but water to stare at."

Hallie had a talent for seeming terribly concerned about her children's well-being, while making them doubt their own judgment. But her comment about Squaw's Landing only made Maria think of storms blowing off the sea while she sat reading alone by the fire.

"It sounds wonderful to me," Maria said.

"I'm sure you know what you want," Hallie said.

As they drove away, Nancy watched Hallie in the rearview mirror. "I can't think of anyone else in Hatuquitit who could get away with wearing a yellow cape," Nancy said. "Your mother reminds me of a movie star."

People had said that before; Maria knew how pleased Hallie would feel to hear it. It was the effect Hallie had wanted since her kids were small, walking into the market with a cape swishing around her ankles and dark glasses pushed up on her head while all the other mothers wore kilts or blue jeans.

"Does your family live in town?" Maria asked.

"No, I'm from Chicago. I met Steve at a wedding," Nancy said. "But we usually go out for Christmas or Easter."

"The yearly visits," Maria said. "I used to make those here. Nearly every year, anyway."

Leaving town, they passed through the Lovecraft Wildlife Refuge. Cattails lined the marsh's banks; platforms on sturdy poles held last summer's osprey nests.

"Are there many osprey here?" Maria asked, remembering one clear November night outside Cuzco when she and Aldo had watched a golden eagle hunting in the moonlight.

"Yes, they're coming back. Salmon too. They're beginning to spawn in the river for the first time in fifty years."

Maria gazed across the amber marsh toward the sea. Most of the snow had melted. The three small uninhabited Haunted Isles dotted the horizon. Past them, it was a straight shot to Portugal. Nancy turned right into a long driveway lined with birch and scrub pines. A tiny gray shingled cottage nestled at the end. Behind it, even through its windows, Maria could see the sea. Snowdrops filled the yard.

"I'll take it," she said.

Nancy laughed. "Everyone loves the view, but there are some problems. It's not well insulated. Last winter the tenant complained his oil bill was very high. The house takes an awful pounding in storms. Let's see . . ."

"I don't care," Maria said, stepping out. "I want to live here." She smelled pine needles and the sea. Stone walls from the last century bordered the property. Granite boulders from the last ice age protruded through the earth. Someone had planted daffodils at the base of one large rock; Maria walked to it, noticing how the bulbs followed the rock's contours. It made her think of Peru. A Chavín might have thought this rock was one of her ancestors turned to stone.

Nancy joined her. "It's beautiful, isn't it?" she asked.

"It is," Maria said.

"I think this would be a good place to get over . . . your separation, I mean." Nancy spoke awkwardly, as if she wasn't sure Maria wanted to talk about it. "Peter told Steve you're eager to get back to work and all, but I know how it must be."

"Thanks," Maria said. She'd been feeling up and down, more confused than she had felt in Peru. When she thought of Aldo's superior attitude, the way he had loved her only when he thought he could mold her, the way he had lost interest after she'd acquired a style of her own, she felt glad she'd left. But when she remembered the intense pleasure they'd shared together, seeing that golden eagle soar, she missed him very much.

"I think Peter's worried about you," Nancy said.

"That's funny," Maria said. She couldn't imagine Peter talking about her at work. For one thing, it bordered on gossip, which he hated. "That doesn't sound like Peter. It must be fatherhood."

"It does change them," Nancy said. "Steve was a workaholic till Melissa was born. Now he can't wait to get home."

Maria smiled, thinking about her brother being a father now.

"Shall we go inside?" Nancy asked. "Now, if I can just figure out which key . . ." She removed from her bag an enormous ring so loaded with keys that they formed a sunburst. The second key she tried worked.

Inside, the house was simple. One large room with three picture windows gave onto a wooden deck and the sea just beyond. Standing at the window, Maria felt she was at the helm of a ship. The Haunted Isles lay half a mile offshore. Maria thought of the Pequot brave rowing away from her yard in search of his spirit wife.

"It's so bright in here," Nancy said.

"I love it," Maria said, noting the rattan sofa and chairs, the sea chests, the bookshelves built niftily under the staircase. She walked upstairs and found two bedrooms, two bathrooms. As she entered the second bedroom—a barnlike room running the width of the house, with a vaulted ceiling, silvery, unpainted wainscoting, a double bed, and a vast tattered Oriental rug—she felt a blast of cold air. Maria had never seen such a romantic place.

"This room isn't insulated," Nancy said. "One of the drawbacks." She spoke with the confidence of a realtor who already knew she'd done her job.

It felt as cold as Maria's tent on the mountain. "I could use a down quilt," she said.

"An electric blanket, maybe," Nancy said.

"Yoohoo!" came Sophie's voice from the front door. She ran up the stairs and came in breathless. "I've driven all over Squaw's Landing looking for Nancy's red car, and . . . wow!" she said, looking around. "What a room! It's a *bedchamber,* and a goddamned cold one, at that."

"Hello, Sophie," Nancy said, sounding suddenly more formal.

"Hi," Sophie said. She hugged Maria. "Take it. This is one great house."

"I'll take it," Maria said, grinning at Nancy.

Nancy drove away, leaving Maria to explore the house and pace the property. Alone with Sophie, Maria didn't know what to say.

"This is a beautiful place," Sophie said. "Does it cost a fortune?"

"No. Nancy told me it's hard for owners to rent their houses out here during the winter. The prices go up in June, unless it's a year's lease, like this one."

They walked through the upstairs in silence. After a minute, Sophie added, "I was just wondering how you're going to pay for it. Without a job, and without Aldo."

"Aldo never supported me," Maria said sharply. She still felt angry at Sophie after yesterday; she wanted to hurt Sophie, remind her that while Maria was independent, Sophie had to depend on Gordon. "Besides, I still have a job. I'll raise grant money and work for myself. I've saved enough from other grants to last me a year."

"You're lucky," Sophie said, as if Maria's pointed comment had missed its mark.

They wandered into the living room. "Remember rowing out to the Haunted Isles?" Sophie asked, looking out the window.

"And swimming," Maria said. The summer Maria was thirteen, she and her friends from Hatuquitit had amassed a flotilla of dinghies and packed them with beach blankets, food, and flashlights. Maria told Hallie she was spending the night with Nell, Nell told her mother she was spending the night with Maria, Sophie said she was staying with Diana Selden, Peter said he was staying with Bill Walker. They had rowed and swum out to the islands, planning to spend the night. They'd stayed long enough to roast hot dogs and watch the moon rise before being spooked by hoot owls, crickets, and Indian ghosts. As they rowed swiftly home in the moon's bright path, every wave seemed full of sharks, and the air full of menacing spirits.

"I wonder if anyone has ever dug out there," Maria said.

"Kids are still finding arrowheads," Sophie said. "Simon found one." She paused, then continued. "I stopped by Mom's, looking for you, and she said you'd come out here with Nancy. Do you mind that I found you?"

Who could believe that she did mind? Maria felt tense; what could she say? "Why did you come looking for me?" she asked finally.

Sophie stared out the window. A raft of fishing mergansers dived in unison. "I have to talk to you," she said in a very low voice.

Maria turned toward her slowly. Sophie's shoulders were shaking, her head was bowed. "What?" Maria asked, feeling alarmed. "Is it about the library?"

"I'm not acting like myself," Sophie said. "I know you all think something is wrong, and something is." She exhaled, trying to get up her nerve. Maria grabbed her hand and squeezed it to encourage her.

"I had a miscarriage," Sophie said. "It happened two months ago. We hadn't planned it, but I got pregnant. It seemed like the most wonderful thing. She would have been born in May."

"Oh, Sophie," Maria said, hugging her close.

"I've got two beautiful children," Sophie said, now crying. "We hadn't *planned* it or anything, but I was so happy to be having another. I just can't get over it. I keep remembering my other pregnancies; I know all the stages . . ."

"Why didn't you tell Mom or Nell about it?"

Sophie shrugged. "Gordon and I were so happy—we wanted to keep it our secret for a while. And then when I lost the baby, I just couldn't talk about it. I'm not dealing with it well at all. . . ." She grabbed her hand from Maria's and covered her eyes.

Maria felt like crying herself, but she couldn't stop thinking of Flo. "Sophie," she said, "now that you know how terrible it is to lose a child, aren't you even more grateful for the ones you have?"

"You're talking about Flo, aren't you?"

"Yes," Maria said. "I just don't understand how you could have been so mean to her—I heard what you said."

"I hate myself," Sophie said. "I've got two great kids, but all I want to do is sleep."

"You have to lean on us," Maria said firmly. "Me and Nell. I'll babysit, do whatever you need. And I think you should talk to us about it."

"I have Gordon," Sophie said, rubbing her eyes. "He's been so wonderful. When I started miscarrying . . . he carried me to the bed. He called the doctor, but it was too late. You know, a miscarriage is exactly like having the baby. You have contractions, then you feel like you're levitating. And then the baby . . . comes out. Gordon was with me when Simon and Flo were born, and he was with me for this child. God, he cried when it happened. . . ."

"I'm so sorry," Maria said, pierced by Sophie's sorrow.

"I can't talk about it anymore," Sophie said. "Can we take a walk outside?"

"Sure," Maria said.

But at the front door, Sophie turned to her. "We would have named her Maria," she said. Then she walked ahead of her sister into the sunshine.

6

THE FIRST NIGHT MARIA SLEPT IN HER NEW HOUSE,
she dreamed of the Haunted Isles. Tall pines grew close to the
water's edge and waves lapped the granite. High cirrus clouds
blew across the sun. Maria, Nell, and Peter dug holes on Sand
Beach. Sophie wasn't there. In Maria's dream, she felt the coarse
sand scraping her fingers. She dug like a child, not an archaeologist. In one hole she found a clam, in the next she found blue sea
glass, in the third she found Sophie's gold goddess.

She wakened to moonlight as bright as day. It filled the cold
barn room. Lying under her quilt, Maria could see her breath.
She didn't want to close her eyes again because she was afraid of
seeing Sophie's face imprinted on the gold statue.

Instead she imagined starting an excavation—this area would
be a great place to do it, either in town or on one of the islands.
Everyone who had ever planted a garden in Hatuquitit had found
signs of the Pequots—arrowheads, mainly, but hatchets and
stone bowls as well.

Aldo would take the mayor out for dinner and win permission
to dig on the town green—thus ensuring publicity as well as political cooperation. He would contact anthropology department
heads at Yale and the University of Connecticut and arrange to
deliver some visiting-archaeologist lectures. He'd get university
and foundation money, and whether he found anything or not
he'd be financially ahead of the game.

On the Haunted Isles, she decided: that would be the place
to start. She saw herself digging, not getting permission from

anyone. She had always dreamed of excavating around here. She wanted to dig for the love of it. She was tired of jockeying for grant money, of competition. In Peru, all the young archaeologists had wanted Aldo's praise. So had Maria, many years ago, when she first met him at Cambridge. She'd been there on a Fulbright, her last year of graduate school. Aldo was a visiting professor. Although he wasn't much older than his students, he seemed more experienced and sophisticated than anyone Maria knew. She fell in love with him that semester. His voice—so Italian, so melodic—came back to her, delivering its lecture on "the art of troweling." Maria blocked it out.

Aldo would dig through soil like a locomotive steaming into the station. He aimed straight at the bottom layer. His approach would be single-minded, designed to illuminate only the earliest civilization.

Maria would regard all layers equally: the 1970 penny dropped by a Hatuquitit schoolchild, the clamshells discarded by volunteer firemen at a clambake forty years ago, and at the bottom of everything, pottery and flint left behind by the Pequots. She knew Aldo would dismiss her method: he always had. She remembered the time he had directed an excavation of the castle mound at Hastings to prove it had been the one built by William I, depicted in the Bayeux Tapestry. In his furor to discover a near-Conquest pottery sequence, he had dug a long trench across the castle's inner bailey. Maria remembered how the trench ruined parts of the bailey's stone and timber, destroying evidence that might have shed light on the castle's construction, but Aldo didn't care. He found the pottery sequence along with coins of William I, and the dig was documented in *National Geographic*.

Maria lay awake, watching the moon set. She couldn't stop thinking of Aldo, but she was glad to be without him. They had never been "right" for each other. She couldn't imagine him kissing the back of her neck the way Gordon had kissed Sophie's while she made coffee. Maria thought of Gordon taking care of Sophie while she miscarried their child and her eyes filled with tears. For her lost niece, but also because the time had never been right for her and Aldo to have a child.

That was Maria's fault as much as Aldo's. All through their marriage they had talked about having children—Maria had longed to. She had always imagined getting pregnant one day between grants in the hazy future: after the dig at Hastings, after their visit to Cairo, after the excavation of Chavín de Huántar. But Aldo kept attracting grant money. They would pitch their tents at a new dig site, and Maria's dreams of having a baby would remain only dreams.

She lay there thinking of the baby Sophie would have named Maria. She and Sophie had always been closer than any two sisters Maria knew, and this was proof of it. Since returning to Hatuquitit, since the stolen goddess and the scene with Flo, Maria had felt disconnected from Sophie, but hearing about her lost baby restored Maria's feelings of closeness.

Now she was awake for good. Climbing out of bed, Maria raced through the cold room to the heated hallway. She dressed in the clothes she had worn yesterday, and in the kitchen she discovered that she had forgotten to buy coffee. Driving into town, she wondered whether any stores would be open. The sun glinted through the treetops; it was just past six.

The IGA and Caldwell's were closed. Maria didn't feel like driving to the next big town, across the state line in Westerly, so she decided to have a coffee at Kathy's Luncheonette. It surprised her to see so many people up this early, mainly men sitting alone at the checkered-clothed tables. Like worshippers, all faced the same direction: the window overlooking Summer Street. Maria ordered a black coffee and corn muffin from Kathy. While she waited at the counter, she noticed that only two men wore suits. The others wore heavy sweaters or uniforms, and Maria figured they were fishermen and workmen. Gordon walked in.

"Good morning!" Maria said. She slid her arm around his neck and stood on her toes to kiss his cheek; she thought he hesitated a moment before bending toward her.

"You're up early," he remarked.

"So are you. Do you really open the hardware store at this hour?" Maria asked. She wanted to tell him she knew about the baby, to console him, but the place was packed. She paid for her order and waited beside Gordon. Glancing around the room, she spied a prime table by the window.

"Carpenters and painters usually start at eight, so I open at seven. My usual," he said to Kathy. Then, turning to Maria, he smiled. "Sophie says you have a terrific house."

"I love it," Maria said. "It sits right on the water, out on Squaw's Landing. You'll have to come see it. When the weather warms up, we can all swim . . ."

Gordon's smile seemed a bit frozen, as if he had something on his mind. Maria imagined him preoccupied with thoughts of Sophie. She gazed down at his strong hand resting on the countertop and had the urge to pat it. When Kathy brought him coffee and a blueberry Danish, he asked her to wrap it up.

"To go?" Kathy asked, sounding surprised.

"Please," he said.

"You won't join me?" Maria asked, disappointed because she would have liked the company. It had seemed lucky, running into her brother-in-law when she had least expected it; she hadn't had many conversations alone with him before, and she liked the thought of all these people seeing her sit with the handsome, well-known owner of Littlefield Hardware.

"I have a delivery coming in," he said. "But thanks for asking."

"Another day," Maria said. She would have kissed him, but he was already walking away.

When Maria had entered Kathy's, the only sound had been seagulls crying overhead. Leaving, Maria heard cars and a few trucks passing: people on their way to work. She was enjoying the freedom of not yet having a routine, hadn't yet started to miss the rhythm of going to work. She strolled down Summer Street, turning left on the gravel path that led to the boatyard.

Maria loved this boatyard. Her father had brought her here as a child. The docks and finger piers were empty. Sailboats, fishing boats, and cabin cruisers hauled ashore for the winter rested on weathered wooden cradles. All topsides were covered with bright blue plastic tarpaulins. Gravel crunched under her boots as she walked around, looking up at the boat bottoms. She stopped beside a sloop called *Galatea*. It looked about twenty-five feet long; its blue bottom paint had once been vivid, but a season underwater had left it chalky. She imagined setting out for the Haunted Isles in a boat like this one: sailing into the wind, her hand on the tiller. Lying in bed she had made up her mind to dig out there; for that she would need a boat.

"Is that Maria Dark?" a voice called.

Maria turned, startled.

A man walked toward her, craning his neck to see if he was right. He wore a dark green parka and khaki pants, and he walked very fast.

"Duncan?" Maria said. She recognized him from her high school class: Duncan Murdoch. BOLD AND INTREPID BOATWORKS was stitched in red over his right pocket, and the name DUNCAN over the left. He grinned at her. They had been friends in school. They started to shake hands, but switched in midstream and, trying for a kiss, cracked foreheads.

"Ouch," Duncan said, rubbing his head, then touching Maria's in a way that felt to her like he was smoothing out her eyebrows. "Is that some tribal custom you picked up in South America?"

"Usually I just bow at the waist and break into song," Maria said. "Do you work here?"

"I manage the place," Duncan said.

"That's great." Maria remembered that Duncan had loved boats and hated school. By the time their homeroom teacher would notice Duncan was absent again, he would be halfway to Orient Point in his Boston Whaler. "You've stayed in Hatuquitit all this time?"

"Yeah," Duncan said. "While you and Guido were roaming the globe, I've been right here. You may not believe it, but Hatuquitit is the capital of the universe."

"You sound just like my sister Sophie," Maria said. "She's never left here. Neither has Peter and neither has Nell. And his name is Aldo."

"Aldo," Duncan said. "My wife's a friend of Sophie's. My son plays with Flossie."

"Flossie?" Maria asked.

"That's right—they call her Flo, don't they?" Duncan shook his head. "Too hard a name for a little girl. Sounds like part of a diesel engine. Let them call her Flo when she's forty and the CEO of some petroleum company."

"I love 'Flo,'" Maria said, bristling. Flo was named for the city of Florence, where Flo was conceived, and Maria loved both the name and the nickname. But Duncan misunderstood what she meant.

"I love her too," he said. "She's one of the sweetest kids Jamey brings home."

"Thank you," Maria said, proud as if Flo were her own child.

"Uh, Duncan?" An extremely tall bearded man hung back, not wanting to interrupt them. He wore a parka just like Duncan's, with BOLD AND INTREPID BOATWORKS over the right pocket and JIM over the left.

"Jim Markham, meet Maria Dark. Maria's famous," Duncan said.

"Shut up," Maria said, blushing. She and Jim shook hands, then Jim asked Duncan about fixing the keel on a boat that had run aground off Moonsilver Point last October. Everyone was starting to go to work now, and Duncan waved every few seconds when someone would beep their horn. The wind was picking up; the weather felt more like winter than it had since she had been back. "I think I'm in the market for a boat," she said.

"What kind? Sailing, fishing?"

"Nothing big," Maria said. "I want to get out to the Haunted Isles. I'm planning to dig out there."

"Far out," Duncan said. He seemed unable to stop smiling. "You'll want something with shallow draft. There's not much water out there. Something you can drag up on the beach, though it depends which island you're talking about. Little Shell?"

"I don't know their names," Maria said. "I thought of starting on the biggest one—the one with that little hill."

"That's Lookout," Duncan said.

"Remember Miss Laird telling us about a Pequot trading post out there? How they traded fish for quartz and flint quarried upriver?"

"Yeah, Miss Laird. It was the only class I could stand. So, you're staying in town for a while?"

"Through the summer, maybe," Maria said.

"You've got time to think about a boat," Duncan said. "It's too early to put one in yet. There's still ice in the river, and it brings logs and stuff into the Sound—you'd be liable to crash into an oak tree. Unless, of course, you want a tub like that. She'll ride over anything." He pointed past the boatyard office at the head of a dock where a scuffed, broad-beamed workboat was tied. Painted red with a blue boot top, it was called *Alicia*. Tools were spread across the engine box, and lobster pots were stacked three high on deck.

"Is it yours?" Maria asked.

"Yep," Duncan said. "We use it to set moorings in the summer, but with things so slow between October and March, I do a little lobstering."

"Must be cold," Maria said, thinking she should leave. Over Duncan's shoulder she caught sight of Jim coming toward them again. "So . . . Duncan. I'll think about the boat and get back to you."

"Good to see you, Maria," he said. "Is it strange being back?"

She thought about it for a minute, till she realized she didn't know the answer. It seemed to vary from moment to moment. Right then, she felt as though she had never left. She shrugged, smiled at him, and walked out of the boatyard.

7

"DON'T YOU REMEMBER WHAT A WILD CRUSH YOU had on him?" Nell asked. She, her son Andy, Maria, and Sophie sat at Sophie's kitchen table waiting for Hallie, Gordon, and Peter to arrive.

"I thought he was such a maverick," Maria said. She could see him now, Duncan, driving his Whaler past Hatuquitit High, fins of white water rearing in his wake while Maria and all the other good students watched him from their lab stations in chemistry class.

"Duncan Murdoch was always suspended," Sophie said. "I can't believe he's turned into such an upstanding citizen."

"Remember the time I got suspended for wearing a turtle-neck?" Maria asked.

"Can you believe we went to the only public school in the world with a dress code stricter than Catholic schools?" Nell asked. She held Andy, thirteen months old, on her lap. He had his mother's red hair, and its redness seemed to increase in direct proportion to his age and its volume. He babbled with apparent good humor, but only his mother could understand him.

"What's that, sweetie? Are you singing your song?" Nell asked.

Andy hit a high note, then looked around for approval.

"What's that, 'Itsy Bitsy Spider'?" Sophie asked, tickling his feet.

Andy giggled, then yelled, *"Dronkwout!"*

"That means 'down the water spout'!" Nell said, laughing with delight.

"What a big boy," Maria said, reaching out for him. Nell handed Andy to Maria; he instantly grabbed for her big hoop earrings.

The coq au vin—a community effort with chicken sautéed by Sophie, carrots peeled by Nell, and Côtes du Rhône added by Maria—smelled delicious. Sophie had tossed a salad of Boston lettuce and endive. For a head start on the cocktail hour, they each had a glass of white wine.

Flo came in with Simon and they stood in front of Maria, examining her big necklace of beads and shell fragments: a gift from Carmen Puño, her assistant at Chavín de Huántar. "Those look like the shells at the beach," Flo said.

"They're similar," Maria said. "If you pick some up, we can drill holes in them and make you a necklace."

"Gram has pop-beads that break apart and then go together again," Flo said.

"Yes, and it's very important to know the difference between Gram's pop-beads and her pearls," Sophie said, giving Maria a significant look.

Flo's chin quivered and her eyes squeezed tightly shut. "Don't tell about the pearls," she said.

"We know it was an accident, sweetie," Sophie said, pulling Flo onto her lap. She stroked her hair, tucking some loose strands into the braid. Simon—tall for a ten-year-old—leaned against her leg, his arm around her neck. Maria watched them, Sophie and her children, and thought how solid they were. The kids seemed to press into their mother, and she welcomed them. It made Maria wonder what kind of mother she would be: more like Hallie or Sophie? Hallie had never seemed comfortable giving hugs and kisses to her children, yet Maria could see that affection came naturally to Sophie.

Before Maria heard anything, Flo looked sharp and said breathlessly: "Daddy!" She and Simon ran to the kitchen door.

"Sixth sense," Nell said.

"Yes, when it comes to their daddy," Sophie said, beaming. "They see his headlights or hear his tires on the road or something.

Here he is!" She joined Flo and Simon at the door, and they all kissed Gordon.

Maria sipped her wine. She knew Nell was trying to meet her gaze, but Maria wouldn't play. Yes, it seemed overly sweet, the way the Littlefields banded together, and she knew Nell's theory about Sophie's—could you call it blind loyalty?—to Gordon. But what was so bad about that? Nell didn't know about Sophie's miscarriage, and Maria considered that a crucial bit of information when it came to analyzing Sophie's recent behavior. She let herself smile blandly at Nell without reacting to Nell's raised eyebrows, her wry smile.

"All my little chickens," Gordon said, his arms around Sophie and the kids. "Did you miss Daddy today?" It startled Maria that Sophie would be the one to answer. "Yes," she mumbled into Gordon's shoulder.

Then Gordon raised his gaze to look over Sophie's head at Maria and Nell. The initial lack of expression in his hazel eyes made Maria feel like a voyeur—he seemed unaware of anything but his arms around his family. But then a slow smile came to his face. He eased away from Sophie and approached the kitchen table. "Hello, ladies," he said.

"Hi, Gordon," they said at once. Andy banged a spoon on Nell's knee.

"How about a glass of wine, honey?" Sophie asked, coming forward with the bottle. "We're having some."

"Wine would be great. This has been one long day," Gordon said.

"Did you get that delivery?" Maria asked.

"Delivery? What delivery?" Sophie said, filling Gordon's glass.

The question made Gordon blush. Or perhaps he had taken too big a sip of wine. Maria waited for him to answer Sophie, but he didn't. Sophie stood over the table, seeming to expand as she waited for an answer. Her eyes darted from Maria to Gordon.

"What delivery?" Sophie asked again.

"A big order from Crosby Tools," Gordon said finally.

"What do you know about that?" Sophie asked Maria.

Sophie sounded menacing, but Maria wanted to treat it like a joke. She touched her throat and widened her eyes, the way someone caught in the act would fake innocence. But Sophie wouldn't budge. She towered over Maria. Her hands on her ample hips, she made Maria think of a prison matron. "I ran into Gordon at Kathy's this morning, and he told me," she said.

"Oh," Sophie said, not moving.

Could she be jealous? Maria wondered. It seemed more likely that Sophie would want Gordon to *think* she was jealous, that she would imagine it flattering to him. Maria remembered one time in Paris when she had pretended to feel threatened by a beautiful archaeologist from the Sorbonne. The wonders it had done for Aldo's already adequate ego! But Gordon was her brother-in-law, and Sophie had to know Maria wasn't interested in stealing him. Maria saw a theatricality in Sophie's posture, like a drama school student acting out "jealous wife." Maria found it unbecoming, unworthy of her sister, and turned her attention to Andy. Sophie's mood swings, the ebb and flow of her affection—miscarriage or not—were beginning to irritate her.

Hallie arrived on Peter's arm. "Here I am!" Hallie cried. She wore the black mink Malcolm had given her his last Christmas. It looked sadly squashed and tufted, and when Hallie swept past, Maria smelled mothballs.

"You look wonderful," Nell said, standing to kiss her.

"Thank you, dear. I took it out the other night, to wear to the theater," she said, pronouncing it "thee-ah-tah." "And I figured, why put it back?"

Everyone, even Sophie, smiled and exchanged wicked glances; they knew Hallie was referring to her date at Yale Rep.

"Care to tell us about him?" Maria asked.

"It's Mr. Porter," Hallie said, her spine stiffening. She touched her hair, which she wore in a French twist. "You know Mr. Porter— he used to work at the bank."

"Do you call him Mister?" Sophie asked.

"I call him Julian," Hallie said sternly. "But we're just friends. His wife died three years ago, and he's still mourning. But totally.

I think he considers me a sympathetic ear. We spend hours talking about Malcolm and Elizabeth. We're two old wrecks."

"Novel seduction technique," Sophie whispered to Maria, so Maria knew Sophie's jealous fit—or whatever it had been—had passed.

"I remember him from the bank," Nell said. "He always looks so dashing—am I thinking of the right man? He wears beautiful suits, and he always has a silk handkerchief tucked in the pocket."

"Yes, that's him," Hallie said, her smile giving her away.

"So, Gordo—how's business?" Peter asked, the family gossip obviously making him nervous. He liked discussions about baseball, law, or world events—things on a higher and less personal plane. Maria fought the urge to mess up his hair.

"You know, just when you stock your shelves with that hunter green everyone was using to paint their trim last summer, *House and Garden* or some damned magazine decides shutters and window trim have to be gray-blue. Do you know how many requests I've had for gray-blue this week? The mixing has to be precise, with the proper blue base—and we ran out."

"Naturally no one wants to wait for you to reorder," Sophie said.

"Of course not," Gordon said. "They go straight to Magnano's in Westerly. Last Saturday I saw three of my customers go in there. I'm talking about good customers—ones with charge accounts. There's no such thing as loyalty anymore."

"Your father would just die if he knew the Clarkes traded at Magnano's," Sophie said.

"I feel like keeping them right the hell out of my store," Gordon said.

"What did you do? Stake the place out?" Peter said, helping himself to a handful of mixed nuts. Maria laughed. Hardware espionage: Gordon slouched in the station wagon's front seat, a hat pulled low over his eyes, watching his customers enter Magnano's empty-handed and emerge with little brown bags full of wood screws and toggle bolts.

"Well, you have to keep track of the competition," Gordon said, and since he was serious, no one knew quite what to say.

"Maria, will you make your salad dressing?" Sophie asked, stepping toward the long kitchen counter.

"The one with all the secret ingredients?" Simon asked.

"Sure," Maria said. Simon had his father's chestnut brown hair and lanky build. When he hit adolescence, he would have to unfold himself out of chairs the way Gordon did. He preceded Maria to the counter; he gathered the opaque green glass mixing bowl, a whisk, tarragon vinegar, and extra-virgin olive oil in an obelisk-shaped bottle.

"What a helpful boy you are," Sophie said, standing back to watch him. From her distant tone, Maria could tell she didn't expect a reply.

Maria kept her back to the others, deliberately furtive, so Simon would think she was letting only him in on her secret. She assembled the other ingredients: powdered mustard, mustard seeds, a pinch of thyme from Sophie's window-box herb garden, a splash of heavy cream. She mixed them vigorously with the oil and vinegar. Her family's voices rose behind her, and she felt contented in a way that reminded her of holidays. Sophie opened the oven door to poke a long-handled fork into the chicken; a blast of warm air hit Maria's knees.

"It's about ready," Sophie said. "Stand back, Simon: this is hot stuff." With quilted mitts—one shaped like a lobster and the other like a shark—she removed the orange enameled casserole dish. She placed it on a cork mat. Leaning forward to smell the coq au vin, Maria felt Sophie grab the back of her neck.

"Shark bite," Sophie said, clamping the potholder's jaws to Maria's neck. Then she kissed Maria's cheek.

"I'm setting the table, Mommy," Flo said.

"The dining room table, right, Flo?" Sophie said.

"Daddy shouldn't eat salt because it makes his face red," Simon said, as if in confidence, to Maria.

"I guess we all should eat less salt," said Maria, who loved pickles, salted nuts, and pretzels. She figured it wouldn't do to let her niece and nephew know about her fondness for junk food. There had been so little of it in Peru. She and Aldo had lived on potatoes, custard apples, eggfruit, and strange cuts of meat fried in lard.

Nell came forward, Andy resting on her hip. "What can I do?" she asked. Since the party was just family, everyone but Peter, who had come from his law office, and Hallie, who always wore dresses, wore jeans and sweaters.

"Take a load off," Sophie said, pushing her into a kitchen chair. "When Flo and Simon were that age, I used every excuse possible to stay seated. *Prone,* if possible."

"Thanks," Nell said. "The kid gains a pound every time I pick him up—I'm convinced."

Gordon came to the counter, slung his arm around Sophie, and dipped a spoon into the casserole for a taste of sauce.

"Mommy, how many forks do we need tonight?" Flo called from the dining room.

"Just a second," Sophie called back. "I'd better help her," she said to Gordon. Standing on her toes, she kissed his chin. Maria couldn't miss the glow in her eyes or the way they darted to Maria to see whether Maria had seen.

"Imagine a six-year-old knowing about more than one fork at the same meal," Maria said. "When I was that age, I always thought it was wrong that the knife went inside the spoon—I thought the knife should go *outside,* for protection."

Gordon chuckled, taking another taste of coq au vin. Maria glanced around the kitchen. Peter and Hallie were discussing the Brecht play Hallie had seen, and Nell was trying to get Andy to count her buttons. Maria leaned toward Gordon and spoke in a voice too low for anyone but him to hear.

"I was so sorry to hear about the baby," she said.

"What baby?" he asked.

"Yours—the one Sophie miscarried," Maria said.

Gordon lowered the spoon into the pot and, looking Maria straight in the eyes with as cold a stare as she had ever seen, said, "I have no idea what you're talking about."

*   *   *

The evening, off to such a festive start, felt like a nightmare to Maria. Slogging through the usual—food, conversation, the rooms of Sophie's house—everything seemed to happen in slow motion. Maria listened to Peter and Hallie debate the qualifications of Ben Twining, the new probate judge. She watched Simon stab a pearl onion with his fork and send it flying across the table. Sophie and Nell served the meal, poured the wine, went to the kitchen for more bread and soft butter. Maria ate dinner and spoke very little. Like the dreamer of a nightmare, she wasn't tricked by the familiar. She knew everything would give way, end badly.

How could you lie to me? Maria thought, watching Sophie. Sophie ate with real enjoyment, cutting the chicken into small pieces, chewing each bite with a little smile on her lips, wiping her mouth with her plaid cloth napkin. Now and then she would bend over Flo, helping her cut her food, urging her to eat another carrot. With her pretty plumpness, her patient attention to Flo and Simon, Sophie seemed the picture of motherhood. So how could she make up that story about her third child, the one she would have named Maria, dying in her womb?

Gordon seemed undisturbed by what Maria had asked him. He, Simon, and Peter talked about building a tree house.

"Don't you like the chicken?" Sophie asked. After a few seconds, Maria realized the question was aimed at her.

"It's great," Maria said. She knew her voice sounded normal, but Sophie's antennae were up.

"You're probably used to chickens straight off the farm," Sophie said. "Gordon and I were thinking of getting some hens."

"Do yourselves a favor and don't even *think* of it!" Hallie said. "Don't you remember when you kids were little and we bought hens and that horrible rooster?"

Maria remembered the rooster crowing all night long. She and Sophie had been in charge of egg-gathering that spring; she had loved reaching under the red-brown hens, into the warm straw, and pulling one or two speckled brown eggs out of each nest. But she had hated eating them: many had double yolks, darker than those of store-bought eggs, and some even contained perfect chick embryos with beaks and feathers.

"They messed up the whole yard," Hallie said, "and I couldn't stand the way they ate gravel." She shuddered, remembering.

"That's just natural," Sophie said firmly. "Gordon and I think chickens would be good for the children. They need to see a little more real life than they get on TV and at school."

"What's so great about chicken-doo all over the yard?" Hallie said. "Buy them a dog."

After dinner Sophie ushered everyone into the living room and fiddled with the radio until she found Warlock Devlin playing a lonely sax solo. "Make yourselves comfortable while Gordon and I make coffee," she said.

Nell rested her head on Peter's shoulder. They, like Hallie and Maria, focused on Flo and Simon reading *Babar* to Andy.

"I wish Aldo were here," Hallie said.

"Mom . . . ," Maria said. She didn't want to start talking about Aldo.

"I'm sorry," Hallie said. "But he's so lively, so interesting. He added so much pizzazz to our family, always telling stories about working in Peru and Egypt and everywhere."

"I've worked in those places," Maria said quietly.

"If you had stayed down there, digging with him, who knows where your career was heading," Hallie said.

All her life Hallie had been obsessed by missed opportunities: things that might have made her or her children famous, happier, more successful. Perhaps she imagined that without Aldo, Maria would give up working, spend her days shopping at the mall or watching game shows on television.

"Maria will do fine on her own," Peter said.

Maria smiled at him, grateful.

"Maybe it's Aldo we should worry about," Nell said. Andy had come to play with her shoelaces, and he was trying out the word

Aldo. "Aldo, Aldo, Aldo," he said over and over, pleased by its sound.

"Why should we worry about him?" Maria asked. She glanced at the door, wondering why it was taking Sophie and Gordon so long.

"You guys have worked together for years," Nell said. "Maybe with you gone he'll lose his place. Weren't you sort of a team?"

"We were," Maria said. Together they would design the excavation, then Aldo would concentrate on making the big arrangements. He spent a lot of time on the phone and in offices. It frustrated him, being too busy to dig, to have his hands in the dirt every day. Fieldwork was his first love. But he had a talent for administration—no one could replace him—so Maria had taken over the actual site. "I'm sure his assistant will fill in for me," Maria said. But Nell was right: no one, even Aldo, knew the dig at Chavín de Huántar better than Maria.

"Just don't forget who gave you your start," Hallie warned Maria.

She meant Aldo, of course, conveniently forgetting that Maria had nearly finished Cambridge, had excavated an abbey in Nottingham and a village in Greece by the time she'd met him. Maria kept her gaze on Simon and Flo, who were trying to lure Andy away from Nell's feet with a box of checkers.

"Where's that coffee?" Hallie asked.

"I'll go see!" Simon said, leaping to his feet, running out of the room. Flo flew after him.

But Gordon intercepted them. He entered the living room with one hand on the shoulder of each child, a wry smile on his face. "My Sophie has a headache," he said. "I'm awfully sorry, but she asked if you'd mind a rain check on the coffee."

"Is it a *bad* headache?" Hallie asked, frowning.

"Well, she thinks it's a migraine," Gordon said.

"Oh, dear," Hallie said. "It must have been all that red wine in the chicken. Or did she eat some chocolate earlier?"

"I'm sure she'll be okay," Gordon said, patting Hallie's shoulder.

*   *   *

Maria was driving too fast. She felt nervous, thinking of Sophie and Gordon, and it made her press harder on the gas. They were probably having a fight, and Maria couldn't help thinking it was her fault. She had mentioned the miscarriage to Gordon strictly because she wanted to feel closer to him. She had always felt that he wanted to keep her at arm's length, and she thought that by showing sympathy she might make him like her more. Now she understood that Sophie had lied in order to explain her bad acts: stealing and hurting Flo. And now that Maria knew there had been no miscarriage, Sophie had no excuse for how she had treated Flo at the library.

Halfway home to Squaw's Landing, she knew she had to speak to Sophie. She stopped at the Shell station to use the pay phone. The Littlefields' line was busy. She drove straight back toward their house. What she would say to Sophie she didn't know; she knew only that she had to kiss her sister good night and let her know that she loved her no matter what.

The Littlefield house sat on four acres at the end of a long, hedge-lined driveway. Maria pulled into the yard. There, in darkness undiminished by any light, were Simon and Flo running in circles. At first Maria thought they were whooping with joy, in sheer abandon, for the fun of it, but then she realized they were crying in terror. She tore across the yard to them, held their arms until they stopped moving. The night was cold, but they weren't wearing coats.

"Simon, Flo," she said, hugging them. They struggled to get away, but she wouldn't let them. "Tell me what happened."

"We can't tell, we're not allowed!" Simon shrieked. He yanked himself free.

"Flo?" Maria asked, gathering the child into a bundle. Flo could only weep, so Maria picked her up and walked toward the house.

Was this dark place so recently the scene of a family dinner? No lights were lit. Maria could almost hear the voices of her family—they had said good-bye less than forty minutes before.

But these voices were real, coming from Sophie and Gordon's bedroom. Their tone was not unpleasant; they weren't arguing.

"Please put me down," Flo whispered urgently. "Don't take me in there."

"Were they having a fight?" Maria whispered. "Is that why you're so upset?" She didn't want to barge in on some romantic scene of Sophie and Gordon making up. On the other hand, she felt real terror. She sensed it, like the time she and Aldo, while excavating a pre-Chavín burial mound, had smelled blood, then come upon a grave robber with his throat slit.

"Go to your room," Maria commanded Flo. "I'll come say good night after I see your Mom and Dad."

"Don't go in there," Flo begged.

Maria felt too scared to reassure Flo; she hurried down the corridor toward Sophie's room. Light seeped around the door, open just a crack. Gordon spoke in a monotone that reminded Maria of the way Sophie had sounded in the library.

"It's sad to think of the children without a mother," he was saying. "Going to your funeral will be sad for them. So will scattering your ashes across the yard. We'll save some for Bell Stream. You do want to be cremated, don't you? Isn't that what you said?"

In response, Sophie croaked. The sound was guttural, full of horror and sorrow. Maria thought she had never heard a worse sound; tears came to her eyes and ran down her cheeks, and she pictured Sophie with her throat cut. Maria ran into the living room and grabbed the wrought-iron fireplace poker. Then she charged back. She peered through a crack in the door's warped panel, preparing herself to see something dreadful.

There was Sophie, in a thin pink nightgown, sitting upright in a chair directly opposite Gordon, who leaned casually against their bureau. Her face was white and lumpy, as if she had been crying for a long time.

"Do you want cremation, Sophie?" Gordon asked. "You'd better tell me now, so I'll know."

Sophie only shook her head and croaked again. She raised her hand feebly to her neck, then let it drop.

Maria walked into the bedroom. At the sight of her, Sophie's eyes widened with fear, then looked away in shame. The room smelled like perfume and urine. Gordon flashed Maria his boyish smile. "Uh, caught in the act," he said stupidly.

"Let her go," Maria said, her voice steady, her hand gripping the poker.

"Let her go?" Gordon asked, still smiling. "She's not tied up, she's free to move. She likes this."

"Sophie?" Maria said, feeling sick to her stomach. Color was flooding into Sophie's round cheeks; she began to smile a little.

"Sophie, you can come with me," Maria said, walking toward her. She hesitated when she saw a thin rope tied tightly around Sophie's neck, but she walked on. "Come on—stand up."

"I'm fine," Sophie said hoarsely, barely getting the words out. "Leave us."

"You heard her," Gordon said, now glowering. "Unless you want to stay and watch."

"Stand up and let me see you're okay," Maria said. She wouldn't leave until she saw for herself. She was going to force Sophie to get to her feet, to admit that she was letting Gordon do this to her. Maria realized that in forcing Sophie to prove that she was a willing participant, Maria was demeaning her as well.

Sophie eased herself out of the chair, a defiant look in her eyes. "There," she said. As she stood, her nightgown slipped off one shoulder, revealing a ring of bruises and a trickle of blood coming from where the rope cut into her neck.

"Good-bye," Maria said, walking out of the room. Gordon or Sophie slammed the door behind her. She headed straight for Flo's bedroom, where Flo lay at one end of the bed and Simon sat at the other.

"Is Mommy okay?" Simon asked.

Maria had no idea of how to answer. "She'll be okay," Maria said, hedging.

"Don't leave now," Flo said. "All right?"

Maria stood by the door, feeling like an intruder. "Why does Daddy hurt her?" Simon asked.

"That's Daddy's way of loving," Flo said.

Hearing Flo snapped Maria out of her indecisiveness. "That's not love," she said, unable to hold the words back. Then, "Come on, you two—pack your jammies. You're sleeping at my house tonight."

8

THE CHILDREN FELL ASLEEP IN THE CAR; MARIA had to waken them when they reached Squaw's Landing. She carried Flo into the house while Simon walked silently beside them. The big moon rode high in the sky, throwing a silver path on the black sea. Maria shifted Flo onto her right hip and unlocked the door. She bolted and latched it behind her.

Moonlight flooded the empty house. Maria turned on all the lights to make it less spooky. She had planned to make hot chocolate and cinnamon toast, but the children kept yawning and rubbing their eyes. Although they had never been to her house, they were too tired to explore. Maria tucked them into bed in the spare room and kissed them good night.

Alone downstairs, when she had a moment to consider what she had done, she panicked. "I've kidnapped Simon and Flo," she said out loud. She glanced out the window, half-expecting to see flashing red lights and an armed SWAT squad. There were only dark trees bending in the wind. She considered calling Sophie, to tell her the children were safe. Instead, she called Peter and Nell and asked them to hurry over.

"I would have done exactly what you did," Nell said, hugging Maria as soon as they arrived. Peter was upstairs, settling Andy into the Portacrib. Maria felt disheveled, as if she'd been roughed up in a high wind. Leaning against Nell, who smelled like she'd been sleeping, Maria felt herself trembling.

"The kids were so upset," Maria said. "I don't know how much they heard or saw . . ."

Peter came down the stairs looking comfortable in his wide-wale tan corduroys and navy blue chamois shirt. His eyes, like Nell's, looked sleepy. "They haven't called yet?" he asked. "To see if you have the children?"

"No," Maria said. Was it possible Sophie hadn't noticed their absence yet? The thought of what she had seen, of what might keep Sophie from noticing that her children were gone, filled Maria with panic. "We have to help Sophie," she said. "I think you and I should go back there now, Peter."

"Hold on," Peter said. "Sophie said she was fine. You said you believed she really wanted you to leave."

"Yes, but I've had a chance to think about it. He had a cord tied around her neck."

"God, if the children saw that . . . ," Nell said, wincing.

"What *did* they see?" Peter asked. "You said they were scream-ing in the yard when you got there? God, Maria. This is going to affect them for years, maybe their whole lives. I hope Sophie and Gordon know that."

Maria felt like screaming. "We have to do something," she said. "Right now. We have to save Sophie."

Nell and Peter stared at her helplessly.

"You weren't there," Maria said, wishing she could make them see what she had seen. "I know she wanted me to leave, but I'm scared. I'm really scared for her, Peter."

Peter stared into her eyes. She could see him starting to believe her. When the three of them were children, Maria and Sophie had loved to tease Peter. At various times they had told him he was adopted, that the entire family spoke a different language when he wasn't there, that Sophie wasn't really his sister but a princess Malcolm and Hallie had purchased to be Peter's wife when he grew up. But they had also relied on him to be their brother—the man of the family after Malcolm's death. Since he'd turned fif-teen, Peter had taken care of all Hallie's finances. He had walked both his sisters down the aisle at their weddings. He always did his best to take care of them.

"Let's go," Peter said.

"I'm not sure you should," Nell said. "You can't go charging in if Sophie doesn't want you. I'm so worried about Simon and Flo. Did they see? Were they really that upset?"

"They were," Maria said, thinking of Sophie. She couldn't get Sophie's defiant expression out of her mind. That was the worst part: Sophie tortured and humiliated by Gordon, daring Maria to realize that Sophie herself permitted it.

"What made you go back there after dinner?" Nell asked.

"Sophie told me she'd had a miscarriage," Maria said. "But when I told Gordon how sorry I was, he said he didn't know anything about it." And so he punished Sophie for her lie, Maria thought, imagining the chain of events. "I felt so bad—when Sophie didn't come down for coffee, I figured it was because she and Gordon were fighting over what I'd said to Gordon. I couldn't let it go—I was nearly home, and I had a really bad feeling. I tried to call her, but I couldn't get through . . . the phone was off the hook."

"She did have a miscarriage," Nell said, frowning. "She asked me not to tell anyone."

"Not even me?" Peter asked, looking hurt. He frowned, touching his mustache.

"She made me promise." Nell held both his hands and smiled into his eyes. "I'm sorry."

Peter said nothing, but his eyes showed how betrayed he felt.

"I'm going back to Sophie's," Maria said, rising. "Anything could be happening to her. I shouldn't have left in the first place."

"I think we should go, but let's call first," Peter said.

"Let's call the police," Nell said.

An arc of light swept across the ceiling; they looked outside in time to see headlights being shut off. Sophie and Gordon were coming up the walk. Maria, Nell, and Peter stood silently at the window. Maria imagined the three of them erecting an invisible barricade. But the sight of Sophie, wrapped in a thick down coat, a silk scarf wound around her neck, made Maria want to fly out the door and hold her.

"We've come for Simon and Flo," Gordon said calmly, with extreme dignity, when Maria let him in.

"Let's sit down a minute, Gordo," Peter said, clapping Gordon's shoulder. Sophie, her eyes cast downward, stood just inside the door.

"It's late and we're tired," Gordon said. "They're upstairs?"

"Yes," Maria said, hating the sight of him. She stared at Sophie, willing her to look up, but Sophie would not.

"Go up and get them," Gordon said to Sophie. She started toward the stairs, moving slowly, automatically. Peter blocked her way. He put his arms around her, and for the three seconds she let him hug her, there was no mistaking that they were brother and sister: their height, their dark hair, their affection. But then she tore free and gazed up in hatred.

"I want my kids," she said shrilly.

"Sophie," Maria said, moving toward her. But Sophie's fury stopped her short.

"Maria says they were very upset." Peter spoke in a clear, measured way: more like a lawyer now than a brother. "They were running around outside without coats on."

Hysterical, Maria thought, remembering them running crazed, without direction.

"You take every upset child away from its parents?" Gordon asked. "Doesn't Andy ever cry? Are you two perfect?"

"Gordon," Nell said soothingly. "We just want to talk. We all love you."

"Let me see your neck," Maria said to Sophie, taking a step toward her.

Sophie stared blankly. Gordon put his arm around her. His posture seemed more protective than proprietary, and she leaned into him as if she needed him more than anything in the world. He propped her up. "Do you think I'd hurt my kids?" Sophie asked. "I love them."

"I know you do," Maria said. For the first time, Sophie looked straight into her eyes. Her gaze seemed full of love and pain. Then, breaking free of Gordon, she walked up the stairs past Peter. Gordon followed her. They returned an instant later, each carrying a sleeping child. Maria, Peter, and Nell stood together. No one said anything; they could only watch, helpless, as the Littlefields walked out of the house toward their car.

9

THE NEXT MORNING MARIA, STILL IN HER FLANNEL
robe and alpaca-lined slippers, sat in front of the big picture
window. A pile of library books leaned against her chair. *Pequot
Tales* lay open on her lap, but she was staring west, toward the
Haunted Isles. The sun, rising behind the peninsula on which her
house sat, turned the sea deep blue and the islands' granite shores
golden.

She was thinking of Sophie, but not of what had happened the
night before. What she remembered made her smile. Maria
turned the memory over and over in her mind.

One summer during college, Maria and Sophie had shipped
out of Westerly on an oceanographic school ship. Fifteen students and a crew of seven had headed for Georges Bank aboard
the *Narragansett,* a hundred-foot diesel-powered steel staysail
schooner equipped as a research vessel, with a laboratory, bottom and water-column sampling equipment, and hydrophones
for tracking the migratory and mating practices of humpback
whales. They left port on deck, with the wind in their faces.
Sophie had tucked her hair under a Red Sox cap, and she had a
full-body tan from having spent the spring semester sunbathing
nude on the roof of her dorm. Maria hadn't been out in the sun
yet that year, and her face was starting to burn.

An hour later, as the ship passed the sea buoys, Maria felt
seasick.

"You okay?" Sophie asked, and Maria shook her head. The

ship's bow pitched up and down. Although the July day was cloudless, the gentle harbor waves were now ten-foot swells.

"Watch the horizon, you won't get sick," said a male voice. It had a slight Cranston accent and belonged to a freckle-faced college student. He had curly reddish blond hair, blue eyes fringed with pale lashes, and he was staring straight at Sophie.

"It's better to get it over with," Sophie said. "You know what I mean, don't you, Maria? Just do it."

Maria threw up over the rail; she felt the world spinning and knew she had to lie down. She stumbled toward her bunk, hearing Jack Frazier introduce himself to Sophie.

Maria and several other students spent the next twenty-four hours feeling deathly, violently ill. Lying in her bunk, trying to fight the nausea, Maria could hear other people moaning in their bunks. Late in the day, Sophie brought her some saltines. Maria felt miserable, irrationally irritated at Sophie for not being seasick herself. Sophie tried to act concerned, like a good nurse, but her eyes sparkled too much. Sophie was glowing.

"He's a great guy," Sophie said, leaning her elbows on Maria's bunk. "We climbed to the crow's nest last night and told each other everything."

"The crow's nest? How did you get up there?" Maria asked. Maybe if she pretended to be interested she would become interested and her stomach would stop churning. The only time she'd been on deck, she'd gotten the dim impression that the crow's nest sat about seventy-five feet up the main mast.

"Climbed the rigging. I dared him to do it. You've got to feel better, so you can climb up with us."

"It'll be the first thing I do," Maria said weakly.

"Look, you've got to snap out of this seasickness and get up on deck. We saw our first whale."

"Shit, I missed it," Maria said. She flushed with disappointment, but from that moment on she started feeling better. She made it onto deck in time for the sunset.

"Hi, Maria," Jack said. He had his arm around Sophie. He was wearing her baseball cap.

"Hi," Maria said. "Where are we? Have you seen lots of whales?"

"We're heading toward Georges Bank—we'll be there tomorrow," Jack said.

"The whale was incredible," Sophie said. "A humpback with her calf. They were so close to the boat. Wasn't it amazing, Jack?"

"Sure was," he said.

Maria could see what had happened during the day she'd been seasick. Sophie and Jack had fallen in love. They stood side by side, touching each other very lightly, as if to make their points, during the conversation. The ship's scientist, a thin, serious graduate student, walked over and asked them about their interest in oceanography. Jack said he wanted to become a marine biologist. Sophie and Maria told him they had signed on because they loved the sea.

The schooner's enormous sails filled the air over their heads. When the scientist asked if they would like to visit the lab and listen to recordings of humpback whales, only Maria said yes. Sophie and Jack walked toward the stern to watch the ship's frothy wake, beginning to glitter with bioluminescent plankton as the sea and sky darkened.

Jack was the love of Sophie's life. They were engaged by the following Christmas. They cooked exotic food on hotplates in their dorm rooms on weekends. They made love in hiding places in public. They had fun together. Jack proudly attended Sophie's music department chorales until she confessed to him she didn't want to sing anymore and he told her to stop if it didn't make her happy. He seemed to love Sophie without reservation, completely and unequivocally.

Their engagement lasted throughout their last three years of college and Jack's first of graduate school. It withstood the pressures of family: Jack's Catholic parents were not, at first, wild about his marrying an Episcopalian who had not set foot inside any church in many years. And the first time Jack met Hallie he and Sophie drank too much beer, and Hallie never forgave him for it. Yet their love never dimmed, or never seemed to, right up until the day Jack called Sophie and told her that he was break-ing their engagement, that he was in love with someone else.

Sophie's heart was broken. Sitting in her living room at Squaw's Landing, Maria remembered Sophie's agony. Maria nursed Sophie through the first few weeks. She would hold Sophie in her arms while Sophie sobbed, and shivered, and talked about Jack. Sophie had had no idea that he would leave. She kept covering the same ground, wondering aloud who the woman was, where Jack could have met her, how he could love someone more than he loved Sophie. "He's a bastard," Maria had said, wanting to kill the man who had hurt her sister.

"Don't say that," Sophie said. She would never criticize Jack. She had never met a man like him, a man who shared her inter-ests, who loved her for who she was. Sophie had told Maria she was so used to disappointing people—like Hallie, Maria knew—she feared she would never find another man who would love her the way Jack had.

Maria knew all about trying to please her mother, her teach-ers, her professors, boyfriends, and she had suffered for Sophie. Now, years later, it stung to know that Sophie had been right. It flashed through her mind that Aldo had never loved Maria with-out qualification either, but her thoughts stuck on Sophie. Sophie and the man she married three years after Jack abandoned her: Gordon.

Maria remembered that she had been in England when Sophie wrote the letter about Gordon. It was full of adjectives: "ador-able," "handsome," "successful," "athletic," "intense." Sophie wrote that Gordon's parents lived five miles away in the same house in which he had grown up, that Gordon owned Littlefield Hardware, that Sophie and he had met one night at a yacht club dance and fallen in love within days. Maria remembered feeling amused by Sophie's giddy descriptions of Gordon's physical at-tributes: his thick brown hair, his broad shoulders, his chest which was just hairy enough, his incredible lovemaking. Sophie had found it so touching that a man with Gordon's education—a Princeton degree—would take over his father's hardware business just because the family had always presumed that he would. Sophie did not compare Gordon to Jack in that letter. She didn't mention Jack at all.

Maria and Aldo hadn't been able to fly home for the wedding. They were in the midst of their excavation at Hastings; they had sent an outrageous Georgian tea service instead. Aldo had balked at the price. He would have caused a full-blown Italian scene in the tiny antique store if Maria hadn't explained—calmly, without tears—that she had only one sister, that if Aldo's work was going to keep them from Sophie's wedding, they were going to send her an absolutely fantastic wedding present instead.

Maria had always held it against Aldo, that his dig and the BBC camera crews had kept her from her rightful position as Sophie's maid of honor. Sophie had been terribly hurt; Maria felt sure that Gordon had never forgiven her.

Gordon's distance had always felt strange to Maria, considering how welcoming she felt toward him for entering Sophie's life and loving her. Maria credited Gordon with helping Sophie get over Jack. Maria had even convinced herself, as Sophie must have, that Gordon loved Sophie as well as Jack did—even better, considering that he married her.

By ten o'clock Maria was still in her robe. She had called Sophie five times and gotten no reply. She could not reach Nell. Maria couldn't seem to get dressed, to plan her day. Nothing, beyond talking to Sophie or, for a different reason, Nell—seemed to make sense. The telephone rang. She pounced, hoping for Sophie.

"Feel like taking a boat ride?" the voice asked.

"Is that Duncan Murdoch?" Maria asked.

"Yep. Arnie Pratt wants to sell his Damson boat. It's at a dock over your way."

Maria thought about it. She could hang around her house re-living last night, or she could test-drive a boat. Sunlight bounced off the sea's calm surface. "I'd like to see it," she said carefully. "Should I meet you at his dock?"

"Why don't I pick you up at your place?" Duncan asked. "I'll come by in an hour."

"Okay," Maria said. But an hour later she realized that she didn't know if he was coming by car or boat. She stood in the side yard, where she could see her driveway and the bay.

Exploring her jacket pockets while she waited, she found her trowel and brush. She had last used them in Peru, near a natural shrine where she and Aldo had uncovered three intact offering containers in the form of llamas. The Chavíns would fill them with a mixture of llama fat and blood, then place them in a pasture to ensure the fertility of the land. Crocuses blooming by her doorstep reminded her that March was a week off. In Peru in March the Chavíns would sacrifice black llamas to make the skies darken and the rain start to fall on the fields.

A motor droned, drawing closer. Maria walked toward the water. Duncan stood at the wheel of a long, ungainly green boat; it had no cabin and appeared, even at that distance, to have spent a tough winter. Pulling broadside to the stone jetty, Duncan held the wooden boat steady as Maria climbed in.

"Let her rip," Duncan said, relinquishing the controls.

Maria stood at the wheel searching for the gears and the throttle. The noisy engine sputtered and smelled like gas. She would have liked Duncan to drive away from shore and hand her the wheel when they were safe, in the middle of the empty sea, but pride made her back the boat out and steer west.

The engine's roar made conversation impossible. The boat's flat bottom made the calm water feel like the waves of a hurricane. Although the boat had very little freeboard, its prow rose mightily, blocking Maria's view.

"How much does he want for this boat?" Maria shouted.

"I can't hear you," Duncan shouted back.

"I can't see where I'm going!" Maria yelled, spitting a wisp of hair out of her mouth.

"I can't hear you!" Duncan shouted louder.

Slapping across the sea felt therapeutic to Maria. She gripped the wheel; by turning her head slightly to the left, upwind of the exhaust, she smelled salt air. It smelled like the sea and low tide—a fine combination of fresh and rotten. Although she hadn't driven a boat in years, the skill came right back. Duncan rode in the bow, the wind whipping his sandy hair. He pointed right, and she steered right. Then he pointed left. She figured he was taking her through shoal water; she pulled back the throttle. She knew they were headed toward the Haunted Isles.

Traveling slowly now, the boat leveled out. Maria steered into the passage between two islands and beached the boat on the one Duncan had called Lookout.

"I think this is the boat for you," Duncan said. "She drives well, I caulked her myself last month, and with her flat bottom you can bring her right up on the beach. You'll have to—there aren't any docks out here."

"Only problem: her nose goes up when I go over six miles an hour, and I can't see where I'm going."

"That's a deal breaker," Duncan said sadly, and Maria laughed.

"We'll fiddle with ballast," Duncan said. "Arnie keeps his gas cans and lobster pots in the stern. He's a lot taller than you are."

He shielded his eyes, looking up and down the beach.

"This is fun," Maria said. "Am I taking you away from your work?"

"Hell, I love any chance to take a boat ride," Duncan said. "That's why I'm in this business."

Maria surveyed the area. She imagined Pequots hauling their canoes onto the beach, unloading chunks of quartz, slabs of flint. Above the high-water mark, below a stand of pines, she spied the spot where sand changed to clay.

"Looking for a place to dig?" Duncan asked.

"Yes," Maria said.

"I've got some time," he said. "Would you like to take a walk around?"

"No, thanks," she said. She wanted to ask him about Sophie; he had said his wife and Sophie were friends, that their children played together. But what could she hope to learn? That everyone in Hatuquitit suspected Gordon was a wife-beater? That people were saying Sophie was mean to Flo?

"You know my sister, don't you?" Maria asked. "Sophie Littlefield?"

"Sure I do. She's a friend of Alicia's."

"Do you see her often?" Maria felt clumsy, like a private eye poking around someone else's business, with everyone seeing through her disguise.

"Not really. Sometimes I'd be there when Sophie came to pick up Flossie."

Flossie. That soft nickname for the niece she loved made Maria's lip tremble. She lowered her head, so Duncan wouldn't see. "She's a good little girl," Maria said after a few seconds.

"She is," Duncan said. From his solemn tone and the way he waited for what Maria would say next, she knew he'd seen her expression.

"Coming home to people you've known your whole life," Maria began, "you expect everything to be the same. The other day you asked me if it's strange being back, and I guess it is."

"Are you talking about Sophie?"

"You know, since I left home, Sophie's gotten married and had kids. She, Nell, and I were so close growing up. I'm an idiot to think that could last forever. I'm the one who took off—then, when I come back, I expect things to be just as they were when I left." Now Maria was talking more to herself than to Duncan.

"Well, this town doesn't change much."

The town hadn't changed at all, Maria thought. She gazed across the water at Squaw's Landing, the Lovecraft Wildlife Refuge, and the white spires of Hatuquitit. The morning sun struck the window of the prison's guard tower, and Maria knew Hallie's house was just two hundred yards west of it. Nell and Peter lived in town. Maria picked out the steeple atop the Congregational Church, closest to their house. The Littlefields lived in the pine barrens near Bell Stream, west of Hallie's, but Maria didn't look in that direction. Her hand closed around the trowel in her pocket, and she felt the urge to start digging.

"I want to buy this boat," Maria said. It was the only thing that had made her feel good in days.

"She's solid. Once we fix the bow, I know you'll be happy with her," Duncan said.

Maria nodded, but she felt anxiety growing again.

"You're still thinking about your sister?" Duncan asked after a minute.

"Yes," Maria said.

"You know, she's married to a real horse's ass."

"Gordon?" From habit, Maria bristled to hear someone criticize a member of her family.

"We're in the chamber of commerce together, and he's always got a chip on his shoulder—thinks people are against him."

"That must be hard on Sophie," Maria said, falling silent again.

Duncan walked toward the stern. There seemed a wordless agreement that he would drive home. The sun was in his eyes; he peered at Maria, his hazel eyes crinkled. Maria noticed that his hand on the wheel was tan and rough. She stood close enough to hear him over the engine.

"She needs a tune-up," he yelled. "We'll flatten out her bow for you, and she'd better be hauled. She needs to be sanded and painted. You can do that yourself, or we can do it at the yard. Of course, it will cost you extra."

He smiled, and her stomach flipped. Their eyes locked for just a few seconds, before she blinked and looked away.

"Do whatever it takes," Maria shouted into the wind as they slapped eastward, over the little waves, into the sun that was all she could see over the prow.

Duncan said something in a voice too low to hear. The wind took the words away.

"What?" she asked, leaning closer. He put his mouth to her ear. His breath was warm on her skin, and it made her blush.

"I said, a girl who loves boats," he repeated, his arm touching hers. "Wow."

"Wow," Maria said, concurring, as they flew across the waves.

10

MARIA SPENT A MORNING BACK IN THE LIBRARY'S Local Lore section, reading everything she could about Native Americans in Hatuquitit. She found an interview, in the *Hatuquitit Inquirer,* with Mathilda Brown, a direct descendant of Uncas, the Mohegan sachem. "Read the legends, if you want to learn about the Pequot," she said. "The man who married the moon, the man who used flute magic to make the women of another tribe fall in love with him, the brave who murdered his wife and her English lover and then followed her to the land of the dead—all of these stories are true."

Maria had heard the same thing about Peruvian legends: that even the most bizarre tales contained a morsel of truth. And she thought it interesting that the Pequots, like the Chavíns, had a myth about a man who married the moon. Maria checked her watch: it was two-thirty. She had told Nell she'd meet her at the village green. When she carried her books to the checkout desk, she came face-to-face with the librarian who had complained about Sophie leaving Flo. Maria's stomach tightened, but the librarian didn't seem to recognize her.

Walking toward the green, she noticed that Summer Street was crowded. Young women, their children in school, were doing their errands. Some of them clustered in shop doorways, talking a while before going inside. Passing the boatyard, Maria spied Duncan directing a truck loaded with pilings toward the docks. She watched for a minute, remembering their boat ride, wishing he would turn around and see her. But then she walked along.

Nell sat on a bench, rocking Andy in his stroller. His tiny hands gripped a bottle of apple juice. When Maria approached, he lowered his bottle to give her a terrific grin. Trying to wave, he dropped the bottle. His expression instantly turned so vaudeville-tragic, Maria had to hide a smile. But Nell retrieved the bottle, wiped the nipple with her glove, and handed it back to him before he had time to cry. His brow furrowed, he resumed drinking furiously.

"Good save," Maria said, sitting beside Nell on the bench, surveying the green. Several old men wearing dark topcoats sat in the sun. They made Maria think of Puritanical town elders.

"Have you talked to Sophie?" Nell asked.

"No. Every time I try to call, she hangs up on me. Have you?"

Nell shook her head.

"Did you have any idea this was going on?" Maria asked.

"No. I had a feeling she was stealing, and I noticed she'd seemed awfully protective of Gordon. But aside from that, nothing seemed wrong."

"I never thought I'd see her under some guy's thumb," Maria said, thinking of Sophie in high school and college. She'd always had boys begging her to go out with them. Her relationship with Jack had seemed so perfect; Maria had felt jealous of it. The way Sophie could convince him to put on a jacket while she wore a silk dress, high heels, and perfume and go out dancing all night, or the way they could just as easily take his kayak on a camping trip in Maine. But then Maria remembered how it ended and knew Sophie had felt her luck had abandoned her forever.

"When she first married Gordon," Nell said, then stopped. "God, she'd kill me for telling you . . ."

"Well, you'd better," Maria said.

"She'd send herself roses to make him jealous."

"You're kidding."

"No, I swear. Once a week, with a blank card. I knew she was getting roses from some secret admirer—the whole family did. Then one day I was driving home from Watch Hill, and I saw her car in front of a flower shop in Westerly. There she was, paying cash. She made me promise not to tell."

"Why would she send herself roses?" Maria asked.

"I could never figure it out. I mean, Gordon seemed to *worship* her from the very beginning. She certainly didn't have to make him jealous."

"Maybe he didn't worship her," Maria said. "Maybe he only pretended to in front of other people."

"Haven't you ever seen the way he looks at her?" Nell asked.

"Yes," Maria said, blocking an image of that night, the cord tied around Sophie's neck.

"Do you think he's brainwashed her?" Maria asked.

Nell frowned. "That's too bizarre," she said.

"More bizarre than everything else?" As she spoke, Maria began to see brainwashing as the only possible explanation. How would he have done it? She pictured Gordon dangling a pocket watch in front of Sophie's eyes, saying "You are getting sleepy . . ."

"I'm sure it's not that," Nell said. "Sophie's more in control than you think. Have you ever noticed that framed photograph in their dining room?"

Maria concentrated, came up with an image of a Halloween party. "People in costumes?" she said.

Nell nodded. "It was a Mardi Gras party a long time ago. Peter and I went. The couple in the middle—the ones dressed up like Rosie and Charlie in *The African Queen*? That's Sophie and Jack Frazier."

"Sophie keeps a picture of Jack in the dining room? Does Gordon know?"

Nell shook her head. "Definitely not. He thinks it's a picture she picked up at a flea market. One night they had a dinner party and Gordon was going on about what great taste Sophie has, how she decorated the whole house without any help. He was talking about the pictures on the wall, including that one, how she buys them all at some shop in Blackwood, and I was getting more and more nervous. I mean, they're not even wearing masks or anything. Sophie's head's turned away, but you can tell it's her."

"She didn't correct him?"

"No. She just sat there, looking serene. The way she always does when he praises her."

Maria could see it, Sophie fixing liquid eyes on Gordon, ready to flood straight into him across the table.

"And she never acknowledged to me that she'd lied to Gordon, that the picture had been taken at Mae Morgan's Mardi Gras party. Maybe she forgot I'd been there," Nell went on.

It pleased Maria to think of Sophie allowing herself some defiance—even just by displaying a photo taken with a former beau. It symbolized holding out: she was keeping something back from Gordon, hanging it proudly on the dining room wall. The thought gave Maria hope.

Andy dropped his bottle again. Leaning forward, Maria could see he'd fallen asleep. In spite of his having Nell's red hair, he reminded Maria of Peter when he was small.

"Has anyone told Hallie?" Nell asked. "About Sophie?"

"I haven't, if that's what you mean," Maria said, suddenly feeling tense.

"We haven't either," Nell said. "I think someone should, because I think Sophie really needs help."

"What makes you think Hallie wants any part of that?" Maria asked.

Nell looked up sharply, alarmed by Maria's bitter tone. "Because she's Sophie's mother," Nell said.

Maria had always found it easier to let her feelings about Hallie drift than to put them into words. "Hallie doesn't want to be a mother," Maria said. "Here's what Hallie wanted: she wanted cute kids so she could look like a cute mother. And now we're grown up, and she only wants to know what we can do for her."

"Maria . . . ," Nell said warningly. Nell came from a troubled family herself; her parents drank, and she had transferred her love for them to the Darks even before she married Peter.

"Well, tell me this: when's the last time she baby-sat for Andy?"

"A long time ago," Nell said.

"How long?"

"When he was first born, I think. About a year ago." At Maria's satisfied expression, Nell waved her hand. "But she's not that sort of grandmother. She made it clear right from the start that she didn't like baby-sitting."

"Well, she's not that sort of mother, either," Maria said, remembering how Hallie would stare into space, or listen to Maria Callas records; about the best she, Sophie, or Peter could hope for from Hallie was a long reminiscence about her own childhood.

"Maria, it sounds like you're blaming your mother for Sophie's troubles."

"Oh, I'm not," Maria said. "I'm just saying that we shouldn't expect much help from her now."

"It couldn't have been easy for her, taking care of your father. He was so old and sick when you guys were little. And Hallie wasn't very old herself."

"That's true," Maria agreed.

"You know, Peter's always been sort of jealous about the way your mother feels about Sophie."

"Sophie's her favorite," Maria said. That had been the family myth, but saying them out loud, the words lacked the ring of truth. Didn't "the favorite" usually get extra love? Instead of loving Sophie more than the others, Hallie had set her on the road to success. First came the piano lessons, then the singing lessons. "Make me proud," Hallie would say whenever Sophie practiced the piano or rehearsed for a concert. Yet Hallie rarely attended her concerts. It was as if she couldn't bear to see her second daughter occupy center stage. Maria remembered one time, in high school, when Sophie was singing two solos in the spring concert. "Break a leg, darling," Hallie had said, kissing Sophie as she left the house.

"You're not coming?" Sophie asked. She already knew that

Hallie wouldn't. But she had to ask again, as if to give Hallie one last chance.

"I've got a tickle in my throat," Hallie said. "I'm afraid I'll have a coughing spell and have to leave in the middle." Maria hadn't heard Hallie cough all spring, but she said nothing. She could tell how disappointed Sophie was, and she didn't want to make it worse.

"Come on, Sophie," Maria said. "You've got a curtain."

"Mom is one weird stage mother," Sophie said in the car. "It's like she'll die if I don't do this, and then she doesn't even come to hear me. Let's stop at the store, okay?"

"Why?" Maria asked.

"For cigarettes," Sophie said. "I want to make my voice all raspy and sexy."

"Really?" Peter asked. He was so gullible when it came to whatever his sisters told him.

"She's kidding," Maria said.

"I am not," Sophie said. "I want to ruin my throat. I mean it. Come on . . ."

Maria didn't even answer her, but kept driving. And Sophie didn't press it.

An hour later, sitting with Peter in the school auditorium, Maria watched Sophie take the stage. Hallie had bought her a new white dress with lace at the throat and cuffs—she looked to Maria like a bride, to Peter like an angel.

Sophie stood alone in the spotlight. She seemed to scan the darkness for a moment. Maria wondered whether she was look-ing for Hallie; or perhaps her eyes were adjusting to the bright light. Then, in clear, pure tones, Sophie sang "Somewhere" from *West Side Story*. By the song's end, tears were running down Maria's cheeks. Sitting beside Nell on the village green, Maria thought of Sophie singing that song and felt like crying again.

"Sophie's in trouble," Maria said bleakly. "I don't know what to do."

"We have to start somewhere," Nell said. "I think we should

tell your mother. She was the only person I told about Sophie's miscarriage. Can you believe that? I betrayed Sophie's confidence by telling something that wasn't true anyway."

"How did Hallie take it?" Maria asked.

"She was offended that Sophie hadn't told her herself. But I made her promise she wouldn't tell Sophie she knew."

"You shouldn't have said anything if Sophie asked you not to," Maria said, suddenly wanting to see her mother. Hearing about Hallie's selfish reaction brought back all Maria's old protective feelings for Sophie. It was just like Hallie to use Sophie's misfortune as an occasion to feel slighted. "Okay," she said. "Let's go see my mother."

"When I was a tiny child," Hallie said, "my father said I would run through the flower beds and get positively woozy from the smell of all those dahlias." She stood at the kitchen sink arranging daffodils and irises in a cut-glass vase. Mr. Porter had sent them. She loved flowers with long stems, and Maria could see she disapproved of the discrepancy in length between the elegant irises and the relatively stubby daffodils. But she couldn't bring herself to trim the irises' stems.

"You must have been so cute," Nell said, with just the right touch of irony. Maria knew that Nell loved Hallie. As children, Maria, Sophie, and Peter hadn't known about Nell's parents. The Drapers were always sober during the day, and Maria and Sophie had been jealous of Nell for having a mother who knitted sweaters, baked cakes, and taught them how to condition their hair with beer and mayonnaise; she could imagine Nell being jealous of them for Hallie and her movie-star looks, the romance of her widowhood, her big house on Bell Stream, the detachment from all things domestic that made her seem more like a contemporary than a mother.

"My father said I was hardly taller than the flowers myself, and he'd stand back watching my little black head bobbing through the garden." Hallie paused, cleared her throat, and gave

Maria a pointed look. "I hear you've been taking boat rides, Maria," Hallie said.

"Just one," Maria said, taken aback. Hallie's tone was extremely disapproving.

"Remember: this is a small town, and you're the dangerous divorcée. You don't want everyone talking."

"About Duncan Murdoch taking me for a boat ride? Who told you?"

"Ginger Talisker was out birdwatching in Lovecraft, and she saw you climb into his boat and zoom away. He's married, you know."

"I know he's married," Maria said, feeling defensive.

"That marriage is shaky," Nell said. "Alicia once told Sophie they were getting a divorce."

"Oh," Maria said, feeling an unwanted shiver. She wondered why Duncan hadn't told her himself.

"I'll say it again," Hallie said. "This is a small town, and people love that sort of thing. You can bet Ginger's told five or six people by now, and before long they'll have you in bed with him. It would give plenty of people satisfaction to spoil your reputation and tear down the Darks. You know what I mean."

"Don't worry," Maria said. "After I buy a boat from him, I'll never darken Duncan Murdoch's door again."

"Good," Hallie said. "He's not your type anyway."

"We want to talk to you about Sophie," Maria said sharply. By "your type" she knew her mother meant Aldo or someone like him: suave, famous, accomplished, someone who would convey distinction on the Darks. Not a local homebody like Nell or a local hardware store owner like Gordon. For, however accepted Nell had felt by Hallie, that was how Hallie saw her children's spouses. At least Gordon had the Princeton degree.

"What about her?" Hallie asked, frowning.

"Gordon hurts her. I saw him." Maria, recognizing Hallie's talent for seeing things not as they were but as she wished they would be, spoke bluntly.

"That's ridiculous. What did you see?"

Knowing what she was about to say, Maria suddenly felt tender toward her mother. "You'd better sit down," she said. Taking Hallie's arm, Nell led her to the kitchen table. The three of them sat in a semicircle, Andy playing on the floor.

"It happened after dinner the other night—when we were all together at their house," Maria said. "I went back afterward, it doesn't really matter why. . . . They were in the bedroom. I heard him talking about her funeral, about scattering her ashes. He had a rope tied around her neck."

Hallie shook her head violently, refusing to look up. "It's none of our business," she said. "Whatever games people want to play in their bedrooms, it's not our concern."

Maria reached for her hand, but Hallie pulled away. "Mom, I saw the bruises."

"Gordon wouldn't do that," Hallie said.

"Have you seen Sophie lately without a turtleneck or a scarf on?" Nell asked in a gentle tone.

"As a matter of fact, we went shopping yesterday. We had a really lovely time in Blackwood, poking around all the shops, then having lunch," Hallie said, neatly avoiding the question.

"I'm worried about Flo and Simon," Maria said. "Sophie was pretty horrible to Flo at the library last week. And they both saw what was happening the other night."

"Gordon is a wonderful son-in-law," Hallie said. "He wouldn't do that."

Not a wonderful father, not a wonderful husband, but a wonderful son-in-law, Maria thought, hating her mother. She would rather preserve her notion of the Littlefields (a branch of the Darks, after all) as a happy family than get Sophie help. "He's a *monster*," Maria said, starting to cry. "Can't you see what he's doing to her? He's breaking her. She'll never be the same after all this. She'll wind up dead . . . or a zombie. She already *is* a zombie. She lies, she steals to buy him caviar. She doesn't care about anything but pleasing Gordon."

"Do you have any idea how good Gordon was to her after the miscarriage?" Hallie said, her voice rising and breaking. "He held her through the whole awful thing, and then he picked up the little baby, all bloody, in his hands, and carried it outside to bury it in the garden." Hallie was sobbing now. "I'm sorry, Nell. I know you asked me not to, but I had to tell Sophie I knew about it. And thank heavens I did. She might never have told me otherwise . . ."

"Told you what?" Nell asked.

"That the baby was a girl. They were planning on naming her Hathaway and calling her Hallie, after me."

"But—" Nell began, frowning. She held herself back, and Maria wondered whether Sophie had told her they were planning to name the baby Nell.

"Mom," Maria said, grasping Hallie's forearm. "There was no miscarriage. I told Gordon how sorry I was, and he didn't know anything about it. Sophie made the whole thing up. It's how all this started, the reason I went back to their house."

The truth was starting to dawn on Hallie. Maria could see it in her eyes, full of despair. Her face looked ancient, all lines and shadows. *This is the year my mother got old,* Maria thought, looking away.

"She had such talent," Hallie said without expression. "She could have been a great singer. I used to imagine seeing her at the Met—as Lucia di Lammermoor."

"I know," Maria said.

"I didn't have such a bad singing voice myself," Hallie said. "Though it certainly wasn't operatic. Torch songs were what I did best. Many nights when you children were asleep, I'd sing for Malcolm." She brightened for a moment at the memory, then her face fell, and she laid her head on the table. She breathed a small moan.

"What can we do?" Maria asked Nell.

"We have to talk to Sophie."

"She'll defend him to the death," Hallie said, raising her head.

"She won't answer my calls," Maria said.

"When I tell her I know about this," Hallie said, "she will stop talking to me. She has never been able to bear any criticism whatsoever of Gordon. I mentioned something about his Bermuda shorts one time—they were a little too long, I think—and I spent the next two weeks trying to win back her favor."

"Why does she do that?" Nell asked.

No one spoke. Maria wondered why Sophie had invested so much in the myth of her husband's perfection.

"I'm so worried for those children," Nell said. "Even if he's not *hurting* them, how can this not affect them for the rest of their lives?"

"Children are very resilient—don't forget that," Hallie said, assuming a vestige of her usual blind optimism.

"I'm afraid Sophie's hurting them," Maria said slowly. "Not physically, necessarily. But certainly psychologically."

"It may not even be intentional," Nell said.

"Maybe she's passing on to them what's being done to her."

Hallie covered her ears. "I can't listen to one more word of this—not one more word!" she said, her voice dwindling to nothing.

The three of them sat there mute, unable to comfort each other. Hallie's frown, her suddenly erect posture, warned Maria and Nell that she wanted to be alone. It occurred to Maria that Hallie's call for silence was tyrannical and imperious, but she kissed her mother anyway, leaning down to give her as hard a hug as Hallie would permit, because Maria knew Hallie was in the throes of losing a child and she couldn't for anything imagine how that must feel.

11

AT FIRST MARIA THOUGHT IT WAS A PROMOTIONAL gimmick, but on closer inspection the card imprinted with seven primary-colored balloons and the words WE'VE DONE IT! proved to be an invitation to Gordon's parents' fiftieth-anniversary party. Ed and Gwen Littlefield were throwing themselves a bash at the Masonic Temple the following Saturday. In Gwen's back-slanted handwriting was a personal note: "Now that you're back from far-off lands, hope you won't miss *this* very special family occasion!" Maria wondered if the dig at Maria's having missed Sophie and Gordon's wedding was intentional. She called Hallie.

"Did you get one?" Hallie asked right away.

"Yes," Maria said.

"Well, Sophie will be very unhappy about it," Hallie said. "She asked Gwen not to invite you, but the invitations had already gone out. It was very hard for Sophie to do that—she and Gwen aren't close, and she doesn't want to let on she's having trouble with her family. Gwen always thinks everything is Sophie's fault. Sometimes I'd like to bop her one."

"I take it you didn't talk to Sophie about what I told you," Maria said dryly.

"No, I didn't. And the more I think about it, I'm *positive* you're mistaken."

"How did Sophie explain to you that she doesn't want me invited?"

"As a matter of fact, she said you've been pursuing Gordon. Something about hanging around Kathy's, hoping to have breakfast with him," Hallie said with just enough disapproval in her voice to make Maria furious.

"You can't possibly believe her," she said.

"No, I don't. But this is just what I was trying to tell you about Duncan Murdoch: you're the glamorous divorcée, and people are going to talk. Even your own sister is liable to misinterpret."

Maria couldn't even summon a rebuttal. She knew exactly what Hallie was doing: it was easier to think Maria was a husband-snatcher than admit Sophie was involved with Gordon in something terrible.

"Were Peter and Nell invited?"

"She didn't mention them."

Peter and Nell hadn't actually seen anything, after all, Maria thought. "I think you're making a mistake, not confronting Sophie with what you know. You're not doing her any favor. She needs help," Maria said.

"Assuming what you've told me is true," Hallie said, sounding tired again, "how will my confronting her help? It will only alienate her, and she'll have no one left to talk to."

Everything between you is false, Maria wanted to say. Sophie had played the role of the happy wife and mother for so long that when people asked her questions, Sophie would respond in character: the adoring mother, Gordon's devoted wife. Maria wondered what Sophie was really like, what someone would see if she ripped off the mask. Maria thought of the painting *The Scream,* of the huge-headed baby, its toothless mouth gaping blood-red and veined down to its bottomless black throat.

"For Sophie's sake," Hallie said, "I think you should skip the party."

"Why? So she can keep up the act?" Maria asked. "I don't see that as helping her. I'm going."

"Oh dear," Hallie said.

*   *   *

Maria knew gold was the gift for fiftieth anniversaries. Finding some in Peru would be no problem; she could bargain with Anselmo Ramis, the local goldsmith, for a pendant or a llama figurine. Hatuquitit had only one jewelry store, and the gold in it was mass-produced and boring: charms for high school girls, pierced earrings, pins shaped like flowers with pearls for the centers. Also, it was expensive. Maria decided to buy Gordon's parents a watercolor instead.

She drove to Blackwood, once known as an import center for mahogany, rosewood, and teak brought from the Far East by Connecticut sea captains. Now it was famous for its turn-of-the-century hotel, its restaurants, the antique shops and art galleries lining Main Street. Even on a weekday in early spring Blackwood was crowded with tourists left over from the weekend or vacationers taking advantage of the hotel's off-season weeklong packages. Maria parked on Crooked Street, just north of the center.

She passed by the sea captains' white center-chimney houses, separated by privet hedges. Gale Parsons, a girl Maria's age who had sailed for the Blackwood High team, used to live in one. Maria remembered that Gale's father had owned Blackwood Motors and had sold Malcolm his Mustang. Now Gale's windows were curtained in damask; a sticker on the door proclaimed that the premises were protected by Alert Security. Maria figured the house had been bought as a weekend place by New Yorkers, the only people who could afford it. Locals had long since moved out of Blackwood to subdivisions or less fashionable towns like Hatuquitit.

Hyacinths and daffodils ringed flowering trees planted in sidewalk wells. It felt pleasantly unreal, to be shopping for Gordon's parents' anniversary present. Maria felt high and removed, like the one time she had chewed coca leaves with Carmen Puño. She walked in and out of galleries specializing mainly in marine art or paintings of the same scene at different times in history: Blackwood's Main Street before settlement, in the days of the wood trade, as it looked today. Everything seemed too quaint and wistful for Gordon's parents, whom she remembered being determinedly upbeat and contemporary.

She came upon a new shop—an oddity in Blackwood. The sign said CAPE OF GOOD HOPE and showed a barkentine chasing a white whale. Its windows were full of totem poles, fish carved from wood, pressed tin candleholders, Native American jewelry, Muslim prayer rugs. Bells tinkled when she opened the door. Maria walked slowly through the dark, cluttered space, examining things; everything seemed imported from India, the Philippines, Mexico, and Peru.

"Let me know if I can help," a voice said. Maria turned, expecting to see someone swathed in muslin. But the woman had been plucked straight out of the Blackwood Garden Club: frosted blond hair, understated eye makeup, pink cable-knit sweater, full khaki skirt.

"I will, thanks," Maria said, stunned because she had just found a plaque depicting the principal Chavín god—a fanged human-looking creature who served as a guardian of cosmic harmony. It hit her with a blast of good luck, and she decided to buy it for the Littlefields.

"Isn't he splendid?" the shopkeeper said when Maria placed the plaque on the counter. The woman's long pink fingernail tracing the figure echoed his fangs.

"He is," Maria agreed. "Do you have any more Chavín things?"

"Chavín?"

"Well, Peruvian," Maria said, not really wanting to get into a discussion.

"We have some lovely South American gold things in the case," the woman said, pointing at a locked glass-front showcase along the wall.

Maria wasn't about to pay U.S. prices for gold, even if she did need a fiftieth-anniversary present. She wrote a check for the plaque, thanked the woman, and started for the door. On the way out, she glanced into the case. There were lapis beads, a topaz ring, Mercury dimes and Kennedy half-dollars, silver necklaces, and there, under a tiny spotlight, the gold Chavín goddess Maria had given Sophie.

She gazed at it for a long time. She remembered buying it from Anselmo Ramis. His shop stood in a dusty street behind the massive Spanish Colonial church; she had visited him one day after shopping at the town market. Anselmo also operated a one-man black market, buying Chavín artifacts from grave robbers and selling them to collectors who contacted him from the United States and Europe. Aldo, wishing to preserve the few remaining unpilfered graves, constantly lobbied the police to have Anselmo arrested. While Maria disapproved of Anselmo's activities as a fence, she appreciated his talent as a goldsmith. Without telling Aldo, she had commissioned him to forge the little goddess for Sophie.

"Where did you get this?" she asked the owner of Cape of Good Hope.

Coming around the counter to see which object Maria meant, the owner peered into the case. "Oh, from a customer," she said. "Isn't it exquisite?"

"She sold it to you?" Maria asked.

"Yes, she did."

"Do you know where she got it?" Maria asked, her heart pounding.

"I really don't know. She must be a collector, because she often brings me things."

Maria almost couldn't bear to know what those other nifty things were, but she found herself looking through the case for Hallie's gravy ladle, Grandmother Dark's jewelry, anything familiar. "What's her name?" Maria asked.

The shopkeeper laughed, a nervous trill, as if Maria had just burped at a dinner party. "I can't tell you," she said. "That's confidential."

Maria stared at the goddess a few seconds more. The statue glinted in the spotlight. "How much is she?" Maria asked.

"Two thousand dollars," the woman said. "She's pre-Columbian. Probably made in Bolivia, nine hundred or so years ago. She really belongs in a museum."

Maria had paid Anselmo Ramis the equivalent of three hundred U.S. dollars. "That's a little steep for me," she said, thanking the woman and closing the shop door behind her.

12

"IS THAT WHAT SHE DID WITH THE MONEY?" MARIA asked Peter, watching Sophie dance with Gordon. Sophie's dress, made from a generous amount of beaded fabric, must have cost a mint and reminded Maria of exactly the sort of thing she, Sophie, and Nell had called "old lady dresses" when they were young.

"If the statue was selling for two thousand, Sophie must have gotten at least six hundred for it," Peter said.

"That dress cost six hundred, believe me," Maria said, watching the rainbow of bugle beads shimmer under the dim lights. She herself wore a narrow black dress of soft wool. It rode low on her shoulders, making them look very pale, and it was her favorite in spite of the bittersweet memories it brought back of shopping for it with Aldo on the Rue du Faubourg St. Honoré. She had pinned to it a crested eagle of hammered gold, bought from Anselmo Ramis the same day she had picked up Sophie's goddess.

"She's ignoring you, isn't she?" Peter asked. That was about as direct as Peter ever got on matters of emotional importance, and Maria felt touched by his gentle tone.

"She won't even look at me."

"Well, if it makes you feel any better, she's been pretty cool to me and downright rude to Nell."

"That doesn't make me feel any better," Maria said. The Littlefields had filled the Masonic Temple with all their friends and relatives. The Porch Swing, a five-man band made up of Ed's cronies, played forties music with an occasional Neil Diamond tune thrown in. Maria noticed Gwen smoking at her table, look-ing vaguely sullen except when the bandleader belted out "I Am . . . I Said" and "Forever in Blue Jeans." Both times she leapt to her feet to drag Ed onto the dance floor. When the band launched into "Sweet Caroline," the singer substituted "Gwen-dolyn" for "Caroline," and Gwen stood by her table crying for joy.

"What a show-off," Hallie muttered. She and Julian came to stand with Peter and Maria. Peter kept craning his neck to spot Nell, who had taken Andy with her to the bathroom.

"Gwen's enjoying herself," Maria said, knowing her mother felt miffed because, for once, she wasn't the center of attention. Julian stood at Hallie's elbow, an enormous smile on his face.

"Heavens, wouldn't Malcolm and Elizabeth just love those old songs?" Hallie asked him, holding both his wrists and looking up into his eyes.

"They would, they surely would," Julian said, obviously intox-icated by Hallie. He took her hands and held them until she turned back to Maria.

"The only reason they keep playing this junk is because Gwen thinks we'll all forget she's the same age as the rest of us if she flits around like a teenager. Will you look at her getup!" Hallie said, clucking her tongue, looking regal as ever in her vintage Chanel suit.

Gwen wore a floor-length lavender velour sheath that compli-mented her pretty figure. Maria glanced from Gwen to Sophie, her head resting on Gordon's shoulder as they both gazed at Gwen with patent devotion. It was as if, for this night, Gwen was dressed like the young woman and Sophie like the matronly one. Sophie's dress looked like something Olivia de Havilland would wear to the Oscars. Maria's eyes were drawn to its tall collar; but wondering what the collar hid, she had to look away.

"Come on, Peter," Hallie said, holding out her hand. "Dance with your old mother."

Peter smiled and bowed, and he led Hallie onto the floor. Julian gave Maria an apologetic glance. "Bum wheels," he said.

"Excuse me?" Maria asked.

"I have a problem with bunions," he said. "Can't dance."

Maria suppressed a big laugh. She smiled instead. "Oh, that's okay. I haven't danced in so long, I've forgotten how."

"Guess they don't have the big-band sound down in Peru," Julian said, fingering the buttons on his blue blazer. They were brass, inlaid with an enamel version of the Hatuquitit Yacht Club's burgee. He adjusted his pocket square—blue and white, the club's colors. "I think I'll freshen up your mother's drink," he said. "May I get you something? You'll be all right alone?"

"I'll be fine," Maria said, feeling delighted by his gallantry. She would have given anything to have Sophie hear it. But then she turned instantly sad, knowing that Sophie didn't even want her at the party.

"Hello, Aunt Maria," Flo said solemnly. She stood several feet away, her hands folded. Maria could hardly hear her voice over the music, but the sight of her made her gasp. Was it possible Flo could have grown so much since Maria had last seen her?

"You look at least an inch taller!" Maria exclaimed, crouching to hug her. "I didn't know you and Simon were coming tonight. Isn't it past your bedtime?"

"Way past," Flo said, sounding excited. Maria's hug had stripped away the formality. "But Simon had to stay home. Only one of us could come."

Maria let that pass. Flo wore a pink party dress with white bows covering the buttons. Her lacy white socks looked neat with her black patent leather shoes. The braids were gone; Sophie had used a curling iron on Flo's hair, and the curls were now falling down. Flo kept touching them, her forehead furrowed with worry. She had little purple half-moons under her eyes that Maria at first thought could be bruises but quickly realized were shadows from not sleeping.

"Your curls are pretty," Maria said.

"They're failing," Flo said.

"You mean falling?" Maria asked.

"No, failing," Flo said simply.

"Well, they're pretty anyway," Maria said, not wanting to push it. "I've missed you," she said. She wondered how much Sophie had told Flo about why they never saw Maria anymore.

"I miss you too." Flo followed her parents around the dance floor with her eyes.

"Your mommy looks . . . beautiful," Maria said doubtfully.

"Do you think Daddy looks handsome?" Flo asked, more urgently than usual. She stuck her face two inches from Maria's.

"Very," Maria said.

"I know you like him," Flo said.

"He's nice," Maria said, on guard.

"A lot, right?"

"Well, he's married to your mother, and I love her. So yes, I like him a lot."

"Mommy said you did," Flo said, sounding satisfied, as if Maria had just answered all her questions.

"Why couldn't Simon come tonight?" Maria asked bluntly.

"Because I was the best one this week." Flo smiled with pride. "Daddy said only one of us could come, whoever was best."

"Hello there, Flo. Hello, Maria," Gwen said, tapping Flo's head.

"Happy anniversary, Gwen," Maria said.

"We're glad you could make it." Gwen's tone was cool; holding Flo's hand, she leaned back from Maria, as if she were trying to tug Flo away. A couple Maria had seen in town stopped by to congratulate Gwen. Gwen half-turned away from Maria.

"What a beautiful child!" the woman said. "Is she your granddaughter?"

"Yes, she is. Gordon's daughter."

"She's a chip off the old block," the man said. "The spitting image of her father."

"She's a doll," Gwen said.

"Stopped in to see Gordon the other day," the man said. "He's taking good care of his father's business. In fact, he gave me a nice price on a top-of-the-line Black & Decker hedge clipper just because he knows I pal around with you and Ed."

"That's Gordon," Gwen said, beaming. "I've often said most mothers get gems, but I got a jewel."

The couple said good-bye and moved off. Lighting a cigarette, Gwen stared at their backs. "I can't for the life of me remember their names," she said. "He used to play cards with Ed Thursday nights. Tad and Helen? Or is it Dora? It doesn't matter—they're dreary. They had a daughter who was mad for Gordon and he wouldn't give her the time of day."

"I like your earrings, Gwen," Flo said.

"Flo!" Maria said, laughing. She smiled at Gwen, whose expression remained untouched. "Is that what you call your grandmother?"

"Of course it is," Gwen said.

"Oh," Maria said. Watching Gwen run one hand down her slim left hip, Maria felt she was stretching the youth angle a bit. She saw Sophie standing across the room, trying to look nonchalant. But every so often Sophie would glance nervously over at Maria, Gwen, and Flo, as if wondering what they were saying.

"So, you and your sister have had a falling-out," Gwen said, so sympathetically it surprised Maria.

"Yes," Maria said.

"I love Sophie like my own daughter," Gwen said matter-of-factly. "So you know I don't say this maliciously. But I really think if she lost some weight she'd have less to worry about in the jealousy department."

"Mommy's jealous?" Flo asked.

"I think she tends to make a lot out of nothing," Gwen said, as if she hadn't heard Flo. "When Ed ran the store, wives were always popping in for stupid things their husbands couldn't possibly have use for. Ed saw straight through it, and he flirted a little just to keep their business. Sophie has never quite understood that. In fact, once or twice I've seen her turning into the green-eyed monster looking at me!"

"Mommy isn't a monster!" Flo said, sounding very anxious. Her chin began to wobble.

"No, she's not," Maria said, lifting her up. She couldn't think of a decent reply to Gwen. If Maria wasn't careful, she'd tell her off. Sophie had once tearfully confided that whenever Gordon visited his parents, Gwen would parade from her bedroom to the bathroom in lacy underwear and Gordon would whistle. Once after a party, drying dishes, Gwen had wiped each shallow champagne glass on her sweater-clad 38D breasts before putting it away.

"What's wrong, sweetie?" Sophie asked in a stony tone, coming up behind them.

"Mommy!" Flo said, sobbing as soon as she heard Sophie's voice. She held out her arms, and Sophie ripped her away from Maria. Sophie's proximity made Maria tremble; she felt choked with all the things she wanted to say.

"It'll be okay," Sophie said, patting her daughter's back. "What happened?"

"You're not a monster, are you?" Flo asked fretfully.

Sophie glared at Maria, and Gwen said nothing to get Maria off the hook. Maria saw exactly how this was going. "I didn't say that," she said calmly.

"Here're my girls," Ed said, slinging his arms around Gwen and Sophie. He nuzzled Flo's nose. "Hi there, Maria."

"Hi, Ed. Can I talk to you, Sophie?" Maria asked, not taking her eyes off Sophie's.

Sophie just shook her head, still staring at Maria. Maria nearly squirmed under the gaze, but she made herself stand taller. She knew if she caved in, Sophie would consider it an admission of guilt.

"Where's the lunkhead?" Ed asked. Both Sophie and Gwen's expressions turned hard, but they said nothing. "Where is he? I caught him loafing down at the store today. You tell him, Sophie. Every time I drove by, I caught him standing outside jawboning with Earl Marsden. The big loafer."

"Earl is building a new house," Sophie said in a voice so stately it reminded Maria of Hallie. She felt proud in spite of herself, allied with Sophie against Ed. He wore a suit of maroon polyester and a wide tie imprinted with tiny cruise ships. In different circumstances Maria would have whispered "Experimental fabrics" to Sophie when he walked away.

"Earl Marsden, the big shot," Ed said. "Country club clientele—

sucking up to country club clientele has always been Ticky's downfall."

"Don't call him Ticky, Ed," Gwen said quietly.

"Ticky, Ticky, Ticky," Ed said, laughing. "Big Princeton man. Where the hell is he, anyway?"

"Does he mean Daddy?" Flo asked. "Daddy went to Princeton." But Sophie didn't answer. She stood still, staring over the top of Flo's head into the distance. Maria felt spellbound by Gordon's father calling him lunkhead and Ticky, by Sophie and Gwen's inability to defend him. Spying his son across the dance floor, Ed shot one arm into the air. "Hey, Ticky!" he bellowed. "Come over here and dance with your wife!"

Gordon approached sheepishly, his big shoulders hunched, like a boy who'd been caught misbehaving. He grinned at his parents; he only had eyes for them. Sophie leaned toward him, but he hugged Gwen instead. "Great party, Mom, Dad," Gordon said.

"Have you had enough to eat, honey?" Gwen asked. "Did you try those little kielbasas?"

"In the barbecue sauce?" Gordon asked. "Yeah, I've had about a ton so far. They're my favorite."

"I knew they would be," Gwen said. "They're mine, too." Gordon's presence seemed to change her whole demeanor. She appeared uplifted, radiant. If Maria had been asked to describe Gwen's aura, she would have used the word *reverent*.

"Caught you loafing today, Ticky," Ed said.

"No, Pop," Gordon said, frowning as if he were trying to place whoever it might have been that Ed saw. "I was busy all day. I'm trying to make a deal with Dutch Boy."

"Dutch Boy!" Ed said. "What's wrong with Cover-Brite? We've always carried Cover-Brite. Customers expect it."

"They have a new supplier, Pop," Gordon said earnestly, his Adam's apple bobbing. "He can't deliver on time. Orders are up, but I don't have the stock. This is a really great move."

Ed grinned. "Ticky, you and your great moves. That's all I'm going to say—you and your great moves."

"Why does Ed call Daddy Ticky?" Flo asked, placing her hands, flat as paddles, on Sophie's cheeks. "Because of tick-tock?"

"No, because he got bit by a tick once," Ed said. "When he was ten years old, he had a big, ugly tick hanging off his neck. Who was it started that nickname? Paulie Conklin?"

"Paulie, I think," Gordon said. Maria felt ashamed for Gordon, embarrassed for herself, listening to such an awful Littlefield family episode. In spite of her feelings for Gordon, she wished she could throw her arms around Sophie and Flo, dance them away, spare them having to see him humiliated, and spare him having them see it.

"Paulie Conklin," Ed said. "A great hitter. What'd he hit your senior year? Three sixty?"

"I think it was three sixty," Gordon said, idiotically repeating everything his father said.

"No wonder he made it to the pros," Ed said. "What is he now, an announcer for the White Sox?"

"I think so," Gordon said.

"I love Chicago," Maria said, hoping to change the subject. "I've only been there twice, but—"

"Gordon's high school buddy's announcing baseball out there now," Ed interrupted. "After playing ball professionally, now he's on the radio. Last spring he came back to Hatuquitit to dedicate the new field. He's no big-shot Princeton grad either. Nothing fancy about Paulie. He's just a good, honest ballplayer. Right, Ticky?"

"Right, Pop," Gordon said. His face was red; the veins in his temples were throbbing. Sophie, on the other hand, looked pale, a million miles away. Maria strained to hear; she thought Sophie was humming under her breath.

"Dance with your wife, son," Ed said. "Come on—Mom and I will look after Flo. Wouldn't you like that, honey?" He took Flo from Sophie, and Sophie beamed at him.

"Oh, thank you, Ed," she gushed. "A chance to dance with my husband again!" Maria couldn't believe the transformation, the way Sophie was thanking Ed after what he had just said. It seemed as if Sophie, by humming, had blocked out everything except Ed's offer to baby-sit.

Gordon held Sophie's hand, led her into the crowd. The band was playing "Moon River." Maria stood there, watching Sophie lean against Gordon, swaying to the music. Across the floor Hallie stood with Julian and Peter stood with Nell and Andy. All of their eyes were on Sophie.

"Too bad it wasn't a fast dance," Ed said. "Then she could shake some of that weight off."

"You let yourself go, you lose the prize," Gwen said. Maria walked away from them without looking back, without even kissing Flo good-bye. She walked straight out the door into the clear spring night, and she stood there gulping fresh air. She found herself humming "Moon River" under her breath, but she was thinking about what would happen later, when Gordon and Sophie got home. She wondered what Gordon would do. She had seen the pain in his eyes, the color of his skin. She knew that someone would have to pay retribution for what Ed had done to him, and she knew it was going to be Sophie.

13

MARIA HEADED FOR THE HAUNTED ISLES, SPEEDING across the waves in her new boat. Salt spray stung her eyes. The day, balmy for April, was breezy. Her boat, newly painted, had been left at her dock that morning, a neatly typed Bold and Intrepid Boatworks bill tucked beside the wheel, along with a handwritten note from Duncan: "Have fun in your new boat. I'll be thinking of you." She held the note for a long time, feeling strength from the connection, disappointment that he hadn't come to the door.

Driving into Lookout's shallow cove, she hopped into knee-deep water and tugged the bow onto the pebbly beach. The cold sea hurt then numbed her feet. She had a rucksack full of tools, sneakers, and a sandwich. Sitting on the beach, she dried her feet. She concentrated on wiping all the sand off, and tied on her sneakers. She refused to think of Sophie and Gordon.

Pacing the island, Maria reviewed what she had been reading lately and tried to imagine where a trading post might have stood, where the Pequots might have dumped the quarried stone. She had read that various New England tribes had had a thriving stone bowl industry: stone was quarried in Massachusetts or eastern New York, then brought down the Connecticut River to trading posts throughout Long Island Sound. She imagined the Pequots setting up a station on Lookout where they carved the rough stone into cooking kettles, nut mortars, plates, and platters.

Against all rules of archaeology, she scuffed a patch of earth. She knew that once she decided where to dig, she would rope off sections, then begin meticulously troweling the ground. She had learned the methods in college and with Aldo, and she knew that they worked. But here on Lookout she felt liberated; this was her excavation, and for the first time in her career she didn't have a pack of Aldo's devotees looking over her shoulder.

She estimated the island was half a mile long and a quarter mile wide. Except for the one pebbly beach, the shore was granite rising to a plain of sandy soil. Straggly oaks and scrub pines grew right down to the rocks, with several relatively clear patches of silvery beach grass. Maria knew the canoes would have come ashore at the beach, so she walked inland from there, stopping at the point where the vegetation really took hold.

Removing her trowel, she decided to dig a sample section. Aldo always instructed his students to remove the uppermost layer of soil—he was so interested in getting to the bottom of things. Because of his impatience, he would take the top layer straight down to the clay below. On her knees, Maria followed her own rule, scraping gently until she came upon a change, anything at all different—pebbles turning to clay or clay to sand, for instance.

The work, slow-going and methodical, lulled her. She moved backward across the site to avoid kneeling on the freshly troweled surface, watching for soil color and texture changes. The sun beat down on her head. She found her first artifact, a used condom, and her second, an aluminum flip top. They pleased her; she had always gotten pleasure from removing layers of artifacts one by one in the reverse order in which they were deposited—moving from the new to the old, backward in time.

Coming upon the first clear change in soil quality, a layer of pebbles, she felt an absurd rush of excitement. She pulled out her brush to flick dirt from between the stones. Here were two smooth clamshell fragments. She examined them, wondering whether they'd been dropped by seagulls or left by picnickers. She recorded the find in her notebook and set them aside. She continued brushing and did so for nearly an hour before her knees got stiff and her palm began to blister.

She was just about to quit when she came upon a stone, different from any other she had found so far, its long side protruding from the ground. It was perhaps two and a half inches long, its edges fluted like a piecrust, with a sharp point and a tapered stem. She recognized the stone as flint, the object as a spear point. If she had to estimate, she would say it had been made by a Pequot during the late Ceramic period, around 1600, after the English settlers had arrived.

She held the point, running her fingers along its sharp edges. Right then, she believed that no archaeological find had ever made her so happy, and she was shocked to find herself wishing Duncan were here.

Her old friend Duncan. Not Aldo . . .

But then, as if from guilt or habit, her thoughts turned to Aldo.

He had acknowledged that Maria, growing up in Hatuquitit with its Native American name and local legends, would have to dig there someday. Rome had exerted a similar hold on him: walking to school along the Aurelian Wall, playing in the Colosseum and the Forum, receiving his first communion in a church one thousand years old, had made him want to discover the past. Thinking of Aldo, she turned the point, hafted by a New England Indian, over and over in her hand.

She remembered that cold night in his tent, telling him she was going to leave. He had leaned on his desk, his hands in the pockets of his khaki jacket, half-turned away from her. He had seemed to be studying an aerial photograph of the site propped on an easel; his Roman profile, silhouetted in lantern light, had looked tense with anger.

"You want this? For our marriage to be over?" he asked after the long silence that followed a stretch in which Maria had done all the talking.

"Don't you?" Maria asked, wondering why, after all the nights he'd left her alone and all the days when he'd surveyed her work with a detached, professorial eye, her decision seemed to take him by surprise. This wasn't the first time they'd discussed separation.

It was simply the first time she had told him she'd be returning to Hatuquitit and not coming back.

He shrugged, then began pacing the tent, his eyes on the floor, the walls, anything but Maria. "After so much time, so many years," Aldo had said.

Look at me, Maria thought. She'd had the feeling he was going to cry, carry on about all the good times they had had—make it seem as though Maria's decision to leave was unilateral, as if he had played no part in it. "Are you telling me that you still love me?" she asked.

Then Aldo looked into her eyes. "I will always love you," he said. But by his sad smile Maria knew he was admitting that their marriage was over, that he loved her the way she loved him: with a bittersweet edge of loss for what they'd thought they had.

"I'm going to leave next week," she said. "I want things to run smoothly when I'm gone, there's a lot Carmen can take over when I—"

Aldo put a finger to his lips, shushing her. "Let's not talk about that," he said. "Not right now. My wife has just told me that she wants to leave me, and that's all I want to think about tonight. You are the brave one, to put into words what we have both been thinking."

He spoke with loving sadness, but Maria felt angry to think of how much hurt might have been avoided if he could have told her how he felt instead of avoiding her, insulting her by his distance. Their bed sat in the tent's corner; Maria's gaze shifted toward it. Every night when Aldo was done working he would come into bed. She wondered whether he would continue to sleep beside her; she wondered whether she wanted him to.

But Aldo took that brave step. Crossing the tent, he kissed the top of Maria's head. *"Buona notte, bella,"* he said. "I'll sleep on the cot in my office."

Sitting beside her new dig on Lookout, Maria sighed. She ran her thumb along the spear point's edge. She tried to remember the Pequot legend she had read, the one of love and betrayal, where the Pequot brave had followed his spirit wife to the Land of the Dead. Feeling that she had just conjured something from her own past, Maria could believe the legend.

A gentle chugging noise made her turn, and she saw the *Alicia* coming into Lookout Cove, its wake a ruffle in the calm water. Duncan stood at the wheel, waving as soon as he saw her. Maria's hand shot up—shocked with excitement that he was actually here. She stepped carefully out of her excavated ground and crossed the granite ledge toward the beach, the spear point in hand.

"Take a look at this," she called even before he had beached the boat. But as he came toward her, his mouth unsmiling and his hazel eyes grim, she knew something had happened. "What is it? Tell me," she said.

"Peter asked me to come out here and find you," Duncan said. "Sophie's hurt. She's in the hospital."

"What happened?" Maria cried out. Her mind spun with images: the cord around Sophie's neck, the veins throbbing in Gordon's temples, Flo and Simon tearing around the yard. She heard Ed's voice calling "Ticky, Ticky, Ticky." At the back of it all was the thought that she had known something was going to happen, that she should have done something to stop it.

"She fell down some stairs."

Maria walked numbly toward her boat but Duncan caught her arm. "Come on," he said. "I'm taking you back. I don't think you'd better drive." His hands were blue with bottom paint, and there was a streak of it across his tan cheek.

Wordlessly, Maria climbed into the *Alicia* and watched Duncan secure her boat to shore. He wedged a Danforth anchor into the sand above the high-water mark. She would have to name the boat one of these days. She thought of the Native Americans, how they had no family names, only individual ones. In *Pequot Tales* she had read that boys were named for dead ancestors or a phenomenon of the heavens. Fleeing Cloud, for example, or Eagle of the Sky. Girls were named for the earth, a vegetable, or water, such as The Woman of Corn, She Who Lives in the Valley, or The Woman Swimming for Shore. That made Maria think of Sophie—shipwrecked, half-drowned, swimming for shore, with no one to save her—and she groaned.

Duncan climbed into the boat beside her. He started *Alicia*'s engine, glanced over his left shoulder as he prepared to back into the cove. He threw the engine into reverse, hesitated, shifted back to neutral. Rising from the battered wooden seat, he walked across the deck to Maria. He pulled her out of her seat and hugged her so tightly his jacket zipper dug into her cheek. They stood there for a few seconds. Duncan was trying to give her strength; she had a feeling he knew that Sophie hadn't fallen down any stairs.

"You okay?" he asked. Maria nodded, not wanting to let go yet. But she did, and he eased her back into her seat and drove *Alicia* as fast as she could go away from the Haunted Isles, past Squaw's Landing, toward the town of Hatuquitit.

Peter met Maria at the hospital waiting room. "She has a concussion and a broken wrist, but she'll be okay," he said, kissing Maria's cheek. "They're saying she fell down the cellar stairs carrying a load of laundry."

"Have you seen her yet?" Maria asked, looking into her brother's eyes and seeing signs of Sophie. The flecks of gold around the pupils, the long, straight lashes, the insistent sadness Maria always saw in their eyes at times of family pain, like when their father died.

"No. Gordon's with her."

"He did it, you know," Maria said.

"I want to kill him," Peter replied. Maria, with her dirt-rimmed fingernails and digging clothes, felt grubby beside him in his glen plaid suit and wingtips.

"I—" Maria gulped, almost crying. "Peter, I knew he was going to hurt her." The idea was even harder to speak aloud than it had been to think to herself.

"What do you mean?"

"Last night, at his parents' party, I saw Ed humiliate Gordon," Maria said, the horrible memory filling her mind. "I watched Gordon getting madder and madder—he was turning red he was so angry—" She broke off.

"You couldn't have done anything," Peter said in a monotone. He gazed down the hospital corridor lined with patients' rooms, one of which was Sophie's.

Maria didn't respond. What could she have done, after all? Told Sophie that Gordon was mad when she'd obviously seen it before? Called the police before the fact? Snuck into their house to spy, waiting for him to erupt? Still, the nagging thought that she could have stopped him clung to her.

"Listen, Maria," Peter said, holding her wrists, looking straight into her eyes, commanding her undivided attention. "I wanted you to come. Nell said you'd be out digging, that Duncan Murdoch would know where to find you. The only reason I'm here is that Dr. Salter called me. He says Sophie's been here before. None of us knew about it, but she's been treated for cuts and bruises several times. Once she was admitted for a burn. He called my office to tell me he suspects Gordon's hurting her. There's nothing he can do, officially, because Sophie won't press charges. She won't even talk to the social worker. But this time . . ." Peter's voice trailed off because he was choked with tears. Maria had never seen her brother cry. She patted his hand, focusing on his neat white shirt cuffs peeking out from under the glen plaid.

"It's okay," Maria whispered. He was trying so hard to control himself, to keep the sobs inside, his body was quaking. Maria wondered whether the strong emotion, so unusual for Peter, frightened or embarrassed him. The flock of interns standing around the nurses' station hardly seemed to notice.

"This time," he said, able to talk again, "when the ambulance went to pick her up, the paramedic saw something on Flo."

"Something on Flo?" Maria asked, her skin prickling. "Like what?"

"Bruises. Up and down her arm."

"Where is she now? Where's Simon?"

"With Gordon's parents," Peter said. "Legally, Dr. Salter is obliged to report any suspected child abuse to the state. There will be an investigation." Speaking about form and legalities, Peter seemed to collect himself. He removed his glasses, wiped them on a linen handkerchief, put them back on.

"Have you told Mom?"

Peter shook his head. "Nell was going to drive over to tell her."

"How can Sophie let this happen?" Maria asked, feeling empty. "I've loved her so much for so long, but you know what?"

"What?" Peter asked. As if he knew what Maria was about to say, that it was killing her, he put his arm around her.

"I hate her for this. For letting Gordon hurt her and Flo."

"Don't hate her," Peter said in a voice heavy with sadness. "She's going to need you."

And the wish that Sophie *would* need her was so mighty, Maria closed her eyes hard, squeezing her eyelids tightly together, so that when she opened them she saw spangles.

Gordon came down the hall toward them. He looked surprised to see Maria. "She's resting comfortably," he said, like an old family doctor.

Peter shoved him against a wall. "You fucking bastard," he said. Gordon threw up his hands to protect his face. Peter ripped them away, but Gordon jabbed back, giving Peter a bloody nose. Peter punched him in the stomach, swinging back for another hit when two of the male interns pulled him away. Blood streamed down Peter's face, staining his white shirt and Gordon's windbreaker.

"He broke your nose," one doctor said.

Maria stood apart, watching doctors and security guards surround the two men; she backed away, then turned and walked toward Sophie's room.

Sophie, lying still in white sheets, her eyes closed, her head wrapped in gauze, looked serene as a Memling madonna. She had purple bruises on her cheek. Maria stood close to the bed, wanting to touch her. "Hey, Sophie?" she said in a low voice.

Sophie's left eye fluttered open; the right one seemed glued shut. But when she saw Maria, the left one closed too.

"What happened?" Maria asked.

"I fell down the stairs," Sophie said in a dead voice.

"Sophie, you can tell me," Maria pleaded. "I can help. You need it, I know you do. You need it for Flo and Simon's sakes."

"Go away."

"He did this, didn't he?" Maria asked. "He hurt Flo, too."

"He would never hurt Flo. He's her father. Flo got hurt trying to block my fall. She was standing at the foot of the stairs." Sophie's recitation had a rote quality, like lines spoken by a child in a Christmas play.

"That might fool the social worker," Maria said, "but I know the truth. I saw what he did to you before."

"No one will believe you. Everyone knows you're jealous of what Gordon and I have." Smug, Sophie gave a little smile, as if she believed what she was saying. The idea of such terrible self-delusion made Maria feel sick to her stomach.

"Save yourself, Sophie," she said.

"I'm fine," Sophie said. "I'm happy."

Maria stared at her for a long time, trying to make up her mind. She had the impulse to walk out the door and not look back. But she had to try one last thing. "Don't say anything," she said. "I just want you to think: think about what happened. Try to remember how much it hurt. Then think of Flo. Peter says her arm is bruised."

At that, Sophie's face twisted. She seemed to be at war with herself, as if she were trying to get control of herself or decide what to say next. Still, her eyes remained shut.

"Sophie?" Maria said.

"Leave us alone," Sophie begged. "We're a family."

"I'm your family, too," Maria said. Sophie didn't reply but lay there, her eyes tighter than ever. Her uninjured hand was clenched in a fist.

"Why won't you look at me?" Maria asked, already knowing the answer: Sophie, deeply under Gordon's spell, realized the one person who might pull her out of it was her sister. Maria had the feeling that if she could get Sophie to open her eyes and gaze into Maria's for just a few seconds, Maria would have her back. Sophie must have felt it too because she started groping in panic for the buzzer hanging from the bed's guardrail. Finding it, she pressed the button.

"I'm calling the nurse," Sophie said. "I'm going to ask her to make you leave."

Maria didn't say anything. She planted a kiss on Sophie's moist forehead and, without waiting for the nurse to tell her, she left.

Peter's nose was broken; it was being set. He sent word via an intern that he would be there for a while, that Maria should get a ride home, where he would call her later that afternoon. She walked out the hospital door, amazed to discover it was still a beautiful day. Duncan stood at the curb, leaning against the Bold and Intrepid Boatworks pickup truck. He walked toward Maria. "Is she all right?" he asked.

"She'll recover," Maria said quietly. "Why aren't you at work?" She felt taken aback by his presence; her heart ached, her insides were melting, it took everything she had to hold herself together.

"It's my coffee break," he said. "I knew you didn't have your boat or your car, so I figured you'd need a ride."

Ordinarily such kindness might seem merely unexpected, but after the horror she'd just witnessed, Maria felt her knees go weak.

"The question is," Duncan continued, "do you want a ride home or back to your boat?"

"I forgot about the boat," Maria said. She had forgotten, also, about the spear point in her pocket. She reached for it, holding it like a worry stone.

"You shouldn't leave it there past low tide," Duncan said. "You'll never get it off the beach."

"Then I guess I'd like you to take me to Lookout," Maria said, unsure of everything. They rode through town in silence. She looked out the window, feeling no pressure to make small talk, the way she usually did with people outside her family. She glanced across the seat, wondering why he had come—the real reason. Glancing down at his hand on the gearshift, she imagined it touching her cheek, and she looked away.

"Where's *Alicia*?" Duncan called to Jim, parking next to the vacant slip.

"Tory took her out to set the Morgans' mooring," Jim called back.

"Oh, well," Maria said, disappointed because she would have liked to start digging again. And, she admitted to herself, she would have liked to take another boat ride with Duncan.

"Don't worry," Duncan said. "We'll sail. I just put my boat in the water, and I've only had one chance to test her out this year. The day's fine, the wind's steady. Want to give it a try?" He was gazing toward a sleek boat tied to the dock, her hull white and glistening. Stenciled on the transom was the name *Arcturus*.

"I love to sail," Maria said.

Twenty minutes later, her hand on the tiller, Maria wondered how it was possible to go from despair to exhilaration in such a short time. Sun glanced off the sea's calm surface, laying a path of diamonds from Hatuquitit Harbor to the Haunted Isles.

Maria felt more at home in a sailboat than a motorboat. She'd set off from the dock on a broad reach, then, rounding the red nun at the harbor's mouth, started tacking into the wind. They flew across the water. Duncan sat beside her on the windward rail; heeling so far over, they could look straight down their legs, feet braced against the centerboard housing, into the water where she had dipped the starboard rail.

"Ready, about," she said. Ducking, they let the boom swing over their heads. The jib and main luffed, then cracked as the wind filled them; the bow veered left, and Duncan and Maria settled themselves on the dripping rail.

"Why didn't you sell me a boat like this instead of that tub?" Maria yelled over the wind.

"She's a nice tub," Duncan called back. "Much more practical for getting back and forth to Lookout than a sailboat. Did you find anything this morning?"

"Yes." Their fingers brushed as she pressed the spear point into his hand.

He examined it, smiled as their eyes met, and handed it back to her. As they approached the shoal water of Tautog Reef, Maria made a slight course change. The boat headed off, and their speed reduced by half.

"You're a good sailor," Duncan said.

"I haven't done too much since high school," Maria said, absurdly pleased at the praise. Her thoughts flashed on the last time she had sailed: with Aldo, in Lake Titicaca, two and a half miles above sea level, surrounded by glittering snow mountains.

"I'd sail all day if they'd let me," Duncan said. "Of course, I'm the boss, so sometimes I get away with it."

They sailed through the channel between Lookout and Little Shell and veered into the cove. Maria's boat lolled in the water, shallower now. Maria released the halyard, lowering the mainsail. On shore, she remembered how happy she had been, digging, seeing Duncan arrive. Then she thought of Sophie.

"I'm so worried about Sophie's kids," she said.

"Flossie and—what's her brother's name?" Duncan asked.

"Simon. I guess Flo has some bruises," Maria said. "What will happen if they're taken away? Where will they go?"

"Foster homes, I think," Duncan said hesitantly.

"That would kill Sophie," Maria said. What would Sophie have left without Simon and Flo? Maria thought of Sophie and Gordon all alone, with no one depending on them and no one to account to, and she tried to imagine how far things could go. Until today, seeing Sophie in the hospital, she would never have imagined they could go this far.

"If he's hurting Flossie," Duncan said, "taking her away would be the best thing. She's just a little girl. It wouldn't take much to hurt her badly."

"I know," Maria said. She buried her face in her hands. She felt

Duncan put his arms around her, and she let him hold her. After a moment she eased away. "You're married," she said quietly.

He nodded his head. "It's . . ." he began. "It's not good. She's unhappy . . . so am I. I've stopped even thinking that it will ever . . ."

Maria wanted to hear more about it, but instead she reached up to hold the back of his neck and kissed him. Closing her eyes, Maria tasted salt on his lips. He smelled like a mixture of the sea wind and machine oil.

When the kiss ended, Duncan was staring down at her. "Well . . . ," he said.

"We're both married," she said.

"I don't feel married," he said. "Is that hard to believe? I haven't for a long time. We live together, but that's about all."

"I can believe it," Maria said, thinking of herself and Aldo. She wanted to touch Duncan, to have him hold her in his arms and kiss her again. "When you stop loving someone, and you stop living together the way you think a husband and wife are supposed to, it's already undone."

Duncan shook his head. "She feels it too. My wife, Alicia. We just pass each other. We're hardly even polite about it anymore."

"You named your boat for her," Maria said.

"I did," Duncan said. "I never wanted to hurt her, and I still don't. We have a kid, and I don't want to hurt him either."

Maria said nothing, suddenly thinking how much better it would be for Simon and Flo if their parents had gotten divorced instead of playing this game of control.

Duncan reached for Maria and kissed her again. This kiss was different from the last one. It made Maria tingle all over; it made her want Duncan to ease her onto the cockpit's deck. "I don't want to go back," Duncan said after a minute.

Neither did Maria. She looked at her watch. She knew that Peter was going to call when he got home from the hospital. "I have to," she said.

"I figured you did," Duncan said, not letting go of her. She didn't move. There was something bewitching about this spot, Lookout's shallow cove, and she wondered whether she and Duncan would have kissed anywhere else.

"Call me if you need anything," he said, holding her hand for a long time before letting go.

"I will," she said. But climbing into her boat and starting the engine, she felt sad. She knew that she would not. Away from this spot, things would return to normal. Leaving the Pequots' Land of the Dead, Maria was about to return to a town founded by Puritans. She herself was a descendant of them, and old scruples die hard.

14

SOPHIE STAYED IN THE HOSPITAL FOR OVER A WEEK. Eight days there seemed a long time for a concussion; it worried all the Darks, especially since Sophie had left word at the nurses' desk that she didn't want visitors. Even Hallie wasn't allowed to see her. But Dr. Salter, who had delivered both of Sophie's children and their cousin Andy, called Peter every night with news. He said the first CT scan had shown a shadow around blood vessels in the brain; a subsequent scan, however, seemed clear, and Sophie was allowed to go home.

"No one believes she fell down the stairs, but they can't do anything anyway," Peter said. He sat at the head of Hallie's table, where the family had gathered.

"What if I told the police about that night Gordon tied the rope around her neck?" Maria asked. "Couldn't they arrest him then?"

Peter shook his head. "Only Sophie can file a complaint against him. If there were proof he's been hurting the kids, that would be another story."

"I'm so angry at Ed and Gwen I could just scream," Hallie said, her voice thin and strained. "Keeping those children all to themselves. Who do they think they are? I'm Simon and Flo's grandmother, too."

"What gives them the right?" Nell asked. "When I called Gwen to ask the kids over to play, she said they were just settling in to her house, that they were extremely upset with their mother in the hospital and their new routine shouldn't be disturbed. And what's Gordon doing staying with his parents? Why doesn't he just take the kids back home? I never knew he was such a mama's boy."

"Gwen's protecting Gordon," Maria said. "She doesn't want us to see Flo's bruises." Never mind that the state social worker had confirmed that Flo's right arm was black and blue, marked in five spots that corresponded with fingerprints. Dr. Salter had said the social worker could do nothing unless she actually saw Gordon hurting Flo. Flo was going along with her parents' story, that Sophie had crashed into her falling down the stairs. That made Maria feel worse than the rest of it: that Flo, at the age of six, would be coached to lie by the people she trusted most in the world.

"What are we going to do?" asked Nell, sounding bleak. "It's just getting worse. We can't just sit here and wait for him to *kill* her."

"Oh, no," Hallie shrieked, covering her ears. "Don't let me hear you say that."

"I'm really sorry, Hallie," Nell said, but Hallie just sat there, her ears covered and her eyes shut.

Maria watched her mother dispassionately. She wore all her regular jewelry: the Roman coin dangling from the bracelet of heavy gold links, her big diamond and the ruby anniversary ring from Malcolm, the gold bangles. Her wrists jingled, catching the lamplight, as she held her hands over her ears. The bigness of her jewelry made her wrists seem even more delicate, childlike. *All right,* Maria thought, losing her patience: *If you want to be treated like a child . . .*

Maria reached over and pulled Hallie's left hand down. Hallie's eyes flew open, surprised. "Knock it off," Maria said.

"Maria," Peter said warningly. Since everything with Sophie had started, he seemed to have loosened up. His plaid flannel shirt was open at the collar; his hair looked uncombed and possibly not even washed this morning.

"Knock what off?" Hallie asked, her tone imperious.

"The 'poor me' business," Maria said. "Sophie is in serious trouble. Gordon put her in the hospital—do you understand that?"

Hallie nodded and lowered her head. Tears squeezed out the corners of her eyes. Maria stared; she had never made her mother cry before. She forgot what she had been about to say.

"When I was a little girl," Hallie said, "I just adored my father. He could do absolutely no wrong. It just... *pains* me to think of Gordon hurting Flo. To think she won't be able to grow up loving her father the way I did. It makes me so sad."

"She'll manage," Nell said. "If we can get him some help, she'll find a way to love him. In fact, when she's grown up, she'll respect him more for saving himself." She pushed the fine reddish hair out of her eyes. Maria had never really credited Nell for her role as family peacemaker. She watched Hallie stare wide-eyed at Nell, as if she hung on every word.

Maria continued to stare angrily at Hallie. She wanted more from her mother, and she always had. She didn't doubt that Hallie felt terrified by what was happening to Sophie. But by some subtle shift, Hallie's need for comfort overrode everything else. There was Peter stroking her shoulder, Nell gazing at her with sympathy. Why not? Hallie was Sophie's mother, after all. And with a guilty shock, Maria realized that she was really angry at Hallie for taking the comfort that was rightfully hers—Maria's. Because all through their lives no one had loved Sophie more than Maria, and no one could imagine how bad she felt right now.

"I've been selfish," Hallie said miserably. "If only I'd spent more time with them, I could have seen this coming. I've always loved Gordon, but honestly—I'm not very close to him. He's going to have to get help—for all of their sakes."

"Who cares about Gordon?" Maria asked. She could see she had hurt her mother's feelings, but she felt overwhelmed by a vast, undisciplined rage. "Do you really care if he reforms or not? I just want him to get the hell out of Sophie and the kids' lives."

"He *is* her husband," Hallie said.

"So what?" Maria asked. "She's my sister. I'm really afraid—" she hesitated, "that he's going to kill her," she finished.

"Don't say that," Hallie said again. But this time her voice was quiet and she didn't put her hands over her ears.

No one had a solution. They sat around the table in silence, staring into the oak grain for familiar patterns. Maria recognized the Indian sachem. She had reclaimed her place from Gordon. She could never imagine him coming to Hallie's house again. Then she imagined never seeing Sophie again, and she shivered.

"Is that Andy?" Peter asked, and everyone strained to listen. He pushed back his chair, its legs gently scraping the wood floor, and headed down the hall to the guest room where Hallie had stashed a Portacrib for her grandchildren. Without speaking, everyone followed him.

Peter eased open the guest room door and stepped inside. He, Nell, Hallie, and Maria fanned into a semicircle around the sleeping child. Yellow light from the hallway slanted into the room, stopping just short of the crib where Andy slept peacefully.

They stood watching him for a long time. He slept on his stomach, his thumbs tucked into his fists, his bottom sticking up and his legs drawn in like a frog about to leap. His hair—red and fine as his mother's—stuck damply to his round head. He breathed through his mouth, open slightly. Maria heard a whippoorwill, calling from somewhere down by Bell Stream. She wondered whether Duncan, across town, could hear its call. She caught herself breathing along with Andy, and she had the sense of the others doing it too: the easy rhythm of a child sweetly dreaming, hidden from danger, safe in his crib.

15

LOOKOUT ISLAND ROSE HIGHER OUT OF THE SEA
than the other Haunted Isles. Oaks and pines covered its crest; if
not for the trees and small rise, one could easily see from one side
of the island to the other. The soil was deepest just above the
sand beach where Maria anchored her boat. And that was where
she decided to concentrate her dig.

Maria uncovered pennies, a black button, the remains of a
Styrofoam lobster buoy, and one side-notched arrow point. Although she tried several different spots, she found no other
traces of Native Americans. She considered moving her dig to
one of the other islands, but on the thirteenth day of sifting carefully through the earth, she found a grave.

It contained the bones of one human. The skeleton lay on its
back, its hands drawn up to cover its face. The rim of what appeared to be a stone bowl showed through the dirt. That would
be for food in the next life, a custom Maria knew the Pequots
shared with the Chavíns. She was excited, exhilarated by her
find, but years of training made her careful and deliberate. As she
gently brushed away soil, she discovered some beads and badly
tarnished metal disks among the bones—jewelry, as if someone
had lovingly dressed this body for burial. And an arrowhead, perhaps for protection in the Land of the Dead.

It took Maria hours to partially uncover the skeleton. On her
knees, the sun warming her back, she took notes of the bones'
depth, condition, and placement. Care had been taken to place

the body in extreme flexion, with hands over the face. She took several black-and-white photographs, then several in color to show verdigris staining on bones where a bronze ornament rested. She analyzed the bones: two ribs that appeared to be broken, long fingers, a broad pelvis, which led Maria to deduce it was the body of a squaw.

At the end of the day Maria stood and stretched. She felt stiff from so much crouching. It puzzled her, that a Pequot would be buried alone out here. Cemeteries were usually close to where the Pequots lived, because they liked to pay frequent visits to their dead. Though the sky was still light, the crescent moon hung in the west. Maria went to her bag for stakes, twine, and a polyethylene sheet. She pounded the stakes into the ground and fashioned a tent over the grave. In Lookout Cove a fish broke the surface and disappeared. Maria had not intended to stay so late.

Shivering, she climbed into her boat. She backed out, setting a course for Squaw's Landing. Lights twinkled in town and darkness billowed over the land. Maria drove slowly over the waves, leaving the Haunted Isles in her wake, thinking all the way home about the grave she had found.

In the days since Sophie had left the hospital, Maria had fought the urge to call Duncan. But tonight, with a fire burning in her fireplace and a glass of wine in her hand, she dialed his number at the boatyard. The line rang and rang, leaving her time to imagine what she would say if he answered: she would tell him about her day, about the grave on Lookout.

Holding the empty phone to her ear, the ringing noise provided a sort of company. It became apparent that Duncan was not going to answer. Maria pictured him at home, seated on a sofa beside Alicia—what did she look like, anyway?—helping their son do his homework. The image made her bang down the receiver, feeling guilty for calling him in the first place.

But she had the urge to talk. She decided to call the Archaeology

Club at Chavín de Huántar on the off chance Aldo was dining there. Or maybe Carmen Puño would be around. Speaking rusty Spanish, she asked for Aldo and was told that he was in the bar.

"Maria!" came Aldo's voice. The way he said her name in his Italian accent always sounded so lovely; she sipped her wine and smiled before saying, "Hello, Aldo."

"You are well? I have not received letters from you in so long."

"I'm okay." She hadn't told him about Sophie, and debated about it now. The words could have spilled out, taken up an hour or so on the phone. But it was just as easy, even easier, to hold them back. "I'm digging on the Haunted Isles," she said instead.

"And finding something?"

"Today I found a grave." She described it: the body's placement, the condition of the bones, her sense the bones were that of a squaw.

"Grave goods?" Aldo asked thoughtfully, wanting the full picture. Maria knew that grave goods—the objects buried with a body—were Aldo's great interest.

"I haven't removed them yet. There's a stone bowl, an arrowhead, some jewelry. But they're still too deep."

"Are there other graves nearby?" Aldo asked.

"Not that I've seen," Maria said. "I never expected to find this one. I'd sort of hoped to find evidence of a trading post, but not a grave."

"Very interesting," Aldo said. Maria could see him, forefinger pressed to his temple, making deductions all the way from Peru about a site he had never seen. He was brilliant at it. Aldo treated every archaeological find as a mystery to be solved. He had taught Maria to learn the story about every ruin, every skeleton, and because of him she still considered personal details as important as the larger context.

"Any clues as to how she died?" Aldo asked.

"Not so far."

"There were no apparent injuries? No bones missing?"

Maria tried to remember. "Two broken ribs," she said.

"Could have been an injury," Aldo said. "Or perhaps the weight of the soil cracked them after burial. Any weapons?"

"None that I've discovered," Maria said. "I'm not very deep yet."

"Send me your field notes, *bella*," Aldo said. He spoke more quickly, as if he were preparing to end the conversation. Maria wondered if he had a girlfriend, if she was standing impatiently beside him. The thought of it made Maria jealous.

"I'll make copies," she said. "And I'll send photos."

"Maria," Aldo said, his voice now very serious. "I have heard from the cardinal."

"What cardinal?" Maria asked.

"Giovanni," Aldo said, meaning his uncle, the pride of the Giordanos, one of the most powerful cardinals in Italy. "I have been granted an annulment."

"But we were talking about divorce," Maria said, shocked. "Divorce, not annulment. Annulment, doesn't that imply that we were never actually married? Did you have to say the marriage was never *consummated* or something?" The idea filled her with fury.

"No, no, of course not," Aldo said hastily. "My annulment comes straight from His Holiness, the Pope. As a favor to the cardinal."

"But why?"

"So that we may marry again someday," Aldo said.

"Have you already found someone?" Maria asked, picturing Phillippa, a beautiful graduate student from Cambridge.

"No, I have not. I thought this would make everything easier, *bella*. Why would we want to mess up our lives with lawyers and courts? We are not the types. I would cry to think of you suffering through a divorce."

"Aldo, you are full of shit," Maria said.

"I know," Aldo said sadly.

"Don't ever call me *bella* again," Maria said.

"That I cannot promise."

"I hate you right now," Maria said.

"That is only natural," Aldo said.

"Annulment," Maria repeated dully.

"In the long run it's best," Aldo said. "I'm sure you will see this."

"Maybe," Maria said sadly. "I'd better go now."

"Good night, Maria," Aldo said. Maria said good night, and they hung up.

I am not married, Maria thought, drinking the rest of her wine. *I never was.* The conversation was typical of times with Aldo: unstructured, exciting, full of surprises. He was right—annulment was easier than divorce. She had known for a long time that the marriage was over, so what difference did it make how it officially ended? She pictured the Pope saying a few prayers, ripping up her marriage certificate. The image made her laugh out loud. She wanted to talk to Sophie.

She clapped her hand on the receiver, dialed the Littlefields' number. "Guess what?" she said when she heard Sophie's voice. "I'm annulled. My husband's close personal friend the Pope has declared Aldo and I were never married."

She thought she heard a giggle. "Sophie?" Maria said, smiling broadly. "Did you hear what I said? His Holiness called the whole thing off. I guess that means you were never my maid of honor."

Sophie didn't say anything, but she didn't hang up either. Maria gripped the telephone, hearing nothing but a television playing somewhere in the Littlefields' house. She sat there a long time, attached to her sister by a phone wire, until Sophie gently broke the connection and the line began to hum.

16

IT POURED RAIN FOR FOUR DAYS STRAIGHT, turning yards to swamps and streets to rivers. Bell Stream swelled and overflowed, as it did every spring. Shopkeepers laid newspapers and sheets of corrugated cardboard at the entrances to their stores in a futile attempt to keep their floors clean; customers wearing rubber boots tracked over them, trailing shreds of newsprint in their muddy wakes. "It's mud season" replaced "Hello, how are you?" as the common greeting.

Maria felt depressed, the aftermath of her nonconversation with Sophie. At the time it had seemed better than nothing, but now it just made Maria yearn for the way things used to be between them. Every morning she sat in her window, staring at the fog. Sometimes it would lift just enough to see an outline of the Haunted Isles. She ached to return to the grave, but it was too wet to dig.

She wanted to find out more about Pequot cemeteries, so she called Reverend Hawkes, the Episcopalian minister and a local historian. He suggested she come to his rectory office.

Shaking water off her black umbrella, she left it outside the white clapboard church. She hadn't set foot in St. Luke's since the Christmas after Flo was born, when all the Darks and Littlefields, feeling festive, had decided to attend church and give thanks for the new baby girl. Flo had cried all through the service, and Sophie had had to leave early.

Cool gray light came through the tall windows. Maria blinked, staring at the pew in which they'd sat for her father's funeral.

Maria had sat between Hallie and Sophie, and she remembered being surprised by how Hallie wept silently all through the service. When she took Hallie's hand and squeezed it, Hallie's hand just lay there, limp. Hallie was beyond comfort. Maria felt sad, and she knew Sophie and Peter did too. But they hadn't really known their father. He'd been too old and too sick all their lives. At that moment Maria realized that Hallie had done more than take care of an elderly man: she had been devoted because she really loved him.

Now, gazing at the pew where she'd had that revelation, Maria knew that Malcolm had been Hallie's only true love, that after he died there had been no one left to see her as a child. That Hallie had realized she had three children herself and didn't know what the hell to do about it.

"Maria?" Reverend Hawkes stood at his office door. Maria shook his hand. She felt embarrassed, coming to church to talk about archaeology when she hadn't been to Sunday mass in years.

"How is your family?" he asked.

"They're fine," she said. Her mind flicked to Sophie. But she had come here on business.

"Come on in," he said.

"Thank you for seeing me on short notice," she said. She had always thought he looked hawklike, with a long crooked nose that curved down and a chin that curved up; he had small, piercing blue eyes. He stood over six feet tall, and he hunched so that his neck disappeared into his collar. He'd always frightened Maria, but so did the church. It seemed as austere and unforgiving as the bleak New England weather outside. But then he gave her an outrageous, toothy smile.

"It's my pleasure," he said, gesturing for her to take the black Windsor chair across from his desk. "I've always thought someone should make an archaeological study of this area. Strange that one hasn't, considering that this was such an important center of Pequot life."

"It's not a full-fledged study," Maria said. "I'm working by myself, digging on one of the Haunted Isles."

"We have some money in the pot," he said. "The Historical Society has a fund; we've never spent a bit of it. I'm the chairman, you see."

Maria wondered whether he was offering it to her. Since yesterday, she had started thinking of applying to the Archaeological Foundation for a grant to study the grave she'd found. "Yesterday I uncovered a grave," she said, relaxing.

"Out there?" he asked, frowning. "That surprises me. We know of one Pequot burial ground in town here and one out on Squaw's Landing. I've never heard of one out there on the islands." He went to a long harvest table between two windows, brought back a large black volume called *Historical Cemeteries in the State of Connecticut,* and opened to a map of Hatuquitit. Maria recognized it; the same map appeared in the book of Pequot legends she'd taken out of the library.

"I live here," she said, pointing to the spot on Squaw's Landing where her house stood.

"Your house may be built over Pequot graves," he said sternly.

On the map, the cemetery closest to her was located in an open field between two houses. She had walked through it, but none of the graves were marked. "Not there," she said, pointing at the cemetery, thinking he had misunderstood her. "I live west of that."

"There are Pequot graves all over Squaw's Landing," Reverend Hawkes said. "The Pequots made a deal with an Englishman, sold Squaw's Landing to him, including the cemeteries, with the provision he'd move the graves."

"I've read about that," Maria said. "He was killed before he had the chance, right?"

The minister nodded. "It's really terrible. Native American groups still say they want their dead moved to sacred ground. But no one knows exactly where the bodies are located. Every so often someone digs a new foundation and they find another skeleton."

Maria, thinking of the grave she had found, felt excited by the idea of such archaeological richness literally in her own backyard.

Reverend Hawkes checked his watch. "Maria, this has been great, talking with you. I'm absolutely thrilled you're making this study. Will you keep me posted?"

"I will," she said, rising, wondering if he was sincere.

"And I'll see to it you get some of the study fund, to cover some of your expenses. We're not big-time, now. But still . . ."

She smiled. "Thank you," she said. "That would help a lot. I have a big gas-guzzling boat."

"Take it to the local boatyard, they have a gas dock," he said. "The owner is married to my niece."

"Alicia Murdoch?" Maria asked.

"She used to be Alicia Hawkes before she married Duncan," Reverend Hawkes said.

"Oh," Maria said, shaking his hand and leaving.

Instead of heading straight home, Maria decided to go out to lunch at Kathy's. She ordered a "cheese dream"—grilled cheese with a pickle and potato chips on the side. Kathy stood behind the counter, keeping up a conversation with whoever felt like talking while scraping her spatula across the big black grill. Maria sat at a table along the wall, reading about Pequot burial customs. Outside, rain pelted the window boxes, bruising the primroses and tossing dirt against the glass. Cheese dreams sizzled on the grill. Maria glanced up every time the door opened, hoping to see Duncan and dreading Gordon.

Nancy Grunwald ran in wearing a shiny red raincoat and matching boots. "Nancy!" Maria called, hoping for company.

"How's the house working out?" Nancy asked, shaking water off her sleeves.

"It's terrific. Can you sit down?"

"I'd love to," Nancy said, "but I'm just grabbing a sandwich to take back to the office. I'm alone there today."

"Rats," Maria said.

The door swung open and Duncan and Jim walked in.

"The whole world comes to Kathy's on a rainy day," Nancy said when Duncan and Jim walked over.

"It's miserable out there," Duncan said, looking straight at Maria.

"Oh, have you met?" Nancy said, ready to make introductions.

"Yes, we have," Maria said, blushing. "Hi, Duncan. Hi, Jim."

Water dripped off Nancy, Duncan, and Jim, and gathered in a puddle under Maria's table. She felt it soaking through her sneakers. Nancy was saying how awful it was to take house-hunters around in this weather, they all felt so bad about tracking mud into the houses.

"The town's a puddle," Jim said.

"The Big Pond," Duncan said. "That's what we used to call the Atlantic Ocean; now it's what we call the boatyard."

"What kind of sandwich do you want, Duncan?" Jim asked.

"Maybe I'll eat here. Would you mind if I joined you?" he asked Maria.

"No, I'd like it," she said, hoping he couldn't see how much.

"Back to work," Nancy said. "Nice seeing you, Maria."

"You, too," Maria said. She watched Nancy and Jim walk to the counter and order their sandwiches before looking straight at Duncan. Shaking off his slicker, he didn't notice her watching. His shirt stuck to his back; she wanted to smooth it down, but held herself still.

The waitress, on duty only during lunch hour, cleared Maria's plate and took Duncan's order: sliced turkey on rye. Maria ordered tea with lemon.

"What are you reading?" he asked, picking up her book.

"I tried to call you the other night," she said. "I tried the boatyard."

"Usually we close up at five-thirty. You should have tried me at home." He looked vacantly toward Kathy as he spoke; Maria knew he didn't mean it.

"How could I try you at home?" Maria asked.

"I won't be there much longer," Duncan said. "I'm going to

move into that little cottage at the boatyard this weekend, after we have a chance to tell Jamey."

His words hung in the air; her pulse thundered in her ears. Was this because of her? She couldn't ask.

"It was hard for me to leave Aldo," Maria said slowly, instead. "You know, since I couldn't get you the other night, I called my husband in Peru and he told me he's had our marriage annulled." Maria tried to make it sound like a joke. But as funny as it had struck her the other night, now she couldn't even smile about it. How strange it felt to be talking about Aldo, anyway, when all Maria wanted was to be with Duncan. His hand moved across the table and touched hers for a second. Their eyes met, and they smiled, and her heart cracked a little.

"I just met with Reverend Hawkes," Maria said.

"Alicia's uncle," Duncan said. "He married us." His voice was low, his eyes full of pain.

Several nights when she couldn't sleep she had lain awake imagining conversations with Duncan. They always led to a kiss, nothing more. But in these fantasies he was loving, and he told her things that he told no one else. Right now, in the middle of Kathy's, she reached tentatively across the table and lightly touched his hand.

"Look out," Duncan said suddenly. Glancing up, Maria saw Gordon come in. He wiped his feet, shook water off his back like a retriever. Maria wanted him to see her, so he could beat a hasty retreat. But he passed the point of no return; he had started taking off his jacket when he finally spotted her. They stared at each other for five long seconds. Gordon twitched, then walked straight to a table without acknowledging her.

Maria felt so consumed by Sophie and Gordon's strange passions, it seemed odd to her that the rest of the town didn't know their family's terrible secrets. She half-expected the lunch crowd to turn on him, cast him out of Kathy's, leave him coatless in the rain.

"I've never wanted to kill anyone before," she said in a low, even voice. "But I can imagine killing him." She pictured Gordon dying at her hands for what he had done to Sophie. She wouldn't want to stand back; shooting him would require too much distance; she imagined stabbing him with a knife or strangling him with her bare hands.

"Alicia says Flossie's been pretty subdued lately," Duncan said.

"Really? Did you tell Alicia about what happened?" Maria asked, knowing it was absurd to expect Duncan to have kept her family's troubles from his wife.

"No," he said. "She noticed on her own. Usually Flossie is so happy and outgoing. It's not hard to pick up on how quiet she's been."

"That's true," Maria said, picturing Flo's smiling face, her enthusiasm when she told one of her long, involved stories. Everything interested her. Maria's eyes slid to Gordon. He was reading a newspaper with such intensity, she thought he might rip it apart. "My being here makes him uncomfortable," she said.

"It must," Duncan said. "He thinks you're the only person in here who knows what he's done."

"Did Alicia say anything else about Flo? Did she see the bruises?"

"She didn't mention it. Did you see them?"

"I haven't seen the children for weeks," Maria said. "No one in my family has. Gordon and Sophie won't let us."

"Really?" Duncan asked, sounding alarmed. "I would have thought you'd want to see for yourselves. I mean, you know Gordon's, uh, violent and Sophie's, well . . ." He paused, looking straight into Maria's eyes. The longer he waited, the more she felt fear growing. "Sick," he said finally.

Suddenly Maria *needed* to see Flo and Simon, to make sure they were safe. She checked her watch; it was one-fifteen. They would still be at school. "What time is recess?" she asked.

"At the elementary school? I don't know," he said. "Come on, I'll drive you over."

He had a spark in his eyes that caught Maria, held her still for a minute. Duncan's gaze didn't waver, and she saw in it her own terror of what was happening in Sophie's family. Maria rose, feeling suddenly calmed by the connection between them. "I want you with me, but we can't walk into Jamey's school together," she said.

He nodded, squeezed her hand. The spark of fear was gone, replaced by something else—the power and strength that comes from having a true friend. Then she left.

She parked the Mustang in the teachers' parking lot and ran through the rain to the north door. Only fifth and sixth graders, teachers, and visitors were allowed to enter here; little kids had to use the south door. It was part of the hierarchy Maria remembered from her days at Covey School. The worst part had been when Maria entered fifth grade and had to use a different door from Sophie, Peter, and Nell. But by sixth grade she had grown to like the distinction and privilege of being the oldest.

The first grade classrooms were all the way down the hall. She peered into the door of one, then the other: both were empty. Crayon drawings covered the bulletin boards; a shallow stone well stood in the middle of one room. Maria couldn't resist looking into it for plants and turtles, but it had been drained. The sight left her feeling sad and disoriented. The turtle well had been one of her favorite things.

She smelled popcorn and remembered the rain-or-snow-day tradition of making popcorn and letting the whole school eat it during recess in the gym. The stairway she had thought massive seemed tiny now. She took three stairs at a time. The echo of children's voices reverberated eerily through the corridor; for a spooky instant Maria feared walking into the gymnasium and finding the ghosts of her own teachers and classmates. Miss Laird, Miss MacMorris, Miss Rosen, Patty Schaller, Helene Warble, Jeffrey Clay, Beau Stanton.

But the kids were jubilantly alive and playing. Dressed in warm, bright clothes, they ran after balls, tumbled on mats, danced to Madonna, as if driven wild by the smell of fresh popcorn. The teachers hadn't brought it out yet, and as always Maria wondered where they made it. Most of her classmates had thought they used the office or the nurse's room, but no one really knew. Covey School had no kitchen the kids had ever seen: if it had one, why did they have to bring their own lunches instead of eating hot meals the way they did at Hatuquitit High?

"May I help you?" a teacher asked. She looked so young, Maria could hardly believe she had graduated from college.

"Yes, I'm looking for Florence Littlefield," Maria said pleasantly.

The teacher's expression turned suspicious. "You're not her mother," she said.

"No, I'm her aunt. Maria Dark." She shook the teacher's hand.

"Now I recognize you. I've seen you in *National Geographic,*" the teacher said, smiling. "A lot of the kids know you went to school here, so they all want your pictures on the bulletin board. Flo is over there, with her brother." The teacher pointed toward the windows. In the gray light, Maria made out two small shapes.

"Thank you," Maria said. She started to walk away, then paused. "Can you tell me where they make the popcorn?" she asked.

"In the teachers' lounge," the teacher said. "We have a little stove in there."

"Oh," Maria said, thinking it strange that after all these years she should learn the answer to the question that had burned in her mind every rainy day of her childhood from a woman who hadn't even been born then.

Flo and Simon stood together, their backs to the wall, watching the other children play. Although they saw Maria approaching, they did not move. "Hello, Aunt Maria," Simon said when she stood directly in front of them.

"Hi, sweeties," she said, not hugging them. She didn't want to embarrass them in front of their friends. She thought they might think something was wrong, and she wanted to reassure them. "I just stopped by to visit my old school. They still have rainy-day popcorn, I see."

"Yes," Simon said.

Flo did not speak. She stared into the distance, studiously avoiding Maria's gaze.

"Flo?" Maria said. "Can you say hi?"

Flo's eyes traveled slowly to Maria and regarded her for a few seconds. Her skin looked pale, as if she had a cold. Sophie had dressed her neatly, as always: red corduroy overalls and a navy blue turtleneck. Her braids were tied with bows of yellow yarn. "Hi," Flo said, then looked away again.

"Why aren't you playing?" Maria asked. Neither child answered. "How come?" she pressed.

"We don't want to," Simon said.

"How about you, Flo?"

"We don't want to," she said.

"Oh, rats. Recess was always my favorite part of the day," she said, even though it wasn't, in an attempt to hide the alarm she felt.

"Mommy doesn't want us to talk to you. Daddy doesn't either," Simon said forcefully.

"I don't understand that," Maria said. "I love you. Did they say why?"

"Because you are mean to our family," Simon said. "You've done things to try to take us away from our parents," he finished solemnly.

"Simon, no—" Maria said.

"We have to go. We can't talk to you anymore." Simon gave Flo a push, and she stumbled. Maria caught her, and for one instant Flo clung to her.

"Keep your hands to yourself, you cunt," Simon said.

"Simon!" Maria said, reaching toward her ten-year-old nephew. But he stepped back, pulling Flo with him.

All at once, almost without thinking, Maria reached for Flo.

She pushed up the child's long sleeve and there in the pearly skin of her arm was a field of bruises. Flo started to cry.

"Nice." Simon spat the word at Maria, sounding just like his father. "See what you've done?" He and Flo ran away.

Maria stood perfectly still, watching them go. She knew she should find Flo's teacher or the principal or the school nurse, but instead she hurried downstairs, out the north door, into the parking lot, where she stood between two cars, throwing up in the rain.

17

STORM CLOUDS DARKENED THE SKY AFTER
Hatuquitit's week of rain; they refused to lift. The low pressure
gave Maria a headache, and she saw the clouds as ominous por-
tents of something terrible about to happen. She called the elementary school and spoke to Flo's teacher and the principal.
They seemed relieved to hear from her.

"We're glad to know the family is concerned," the principal,
Mrs. Cannon, said. "We've been worried about Flo and Simon for
a long time."

"Then why can't you do something?" Maria asked. The principal's soothing, friendly tone set her teeth on edge. She wanted
the woman to sputter with fury, to join Maria in her outrage.

"We've reported our suspicions to the state authority on child
abuse. They've sent social workers to the Littlefields' house, but
they didn't find anything."

"They didn't? But what about the bruises?" Maria asked. "And
their personalities? Flo used to be so happy and sweet. Simon
was so polite." Maria couldn't get Simon out of her mind, the
scornful expression in his eyes when he called her a cunt.

"We've tried to get both children to talk to Miss Calderone, our
school social worker. But they say the same thing: everything is
fine at home, they love their parents and their parents love them."

It seemed a cruel contradiction, but Maria believed that their
parents did love them. She had seen the way the family banded
together, shutting everything else out. She imagined that Gordon

had created a universe populated by his wife and children and ruled by him. "What happens next?" she asked.

"We hope the children will confide in someone," Mrs. Cannon said.

"Otherwise you have to catch Gordon in the act?" Maria said.

"We have to catch one of them in the act. Of course, we don't know for sure that it's him."

Maria was struck dumb for a moment. She'd been under the impression that she'd found an ally, someone who cared about protecting the children and Sophie against Gordon, and now the principal was saying that maybe Sophie had done it. "We know it's Gordon," Maria said icily.

As she hung up the phone, she had the feeling she was settling down to wait, to sit out the storm, to maintain a vigil that could promise no happy conclusion.

But solitude was driving her crazy, so Maria dropped in to visit her mother. Hallie sat on the living room sofa, doing needlepoint; she held up the canvas for Maria to see. "It's an eyeglass case for Julian's birthday present," Hallie said. "I designed it."

Maria admired her mother's design, executed in tiny stitches, of golf clubs and the Hatuquitit Country Club's crest. "I'm sure he'll love it," she said. She gazed at her mother, pulling the canvas into shape. It seemed like a labor of love, a lot of effort for Hallie to put into a gift. "Are you and Julian serious?" Maria asked, suddenly alerted.

"No," Hallie said in a tone intended to squash that possibility.

"I went to church the other day, to talk to Reverend Hawkes, and I thought of Dad's funeral."

Hallie's gaze snapped to Maria. "I suppose you went there to talk about Sophie," she said.

"No, we talked about local history."

"Sophie was such a friend to me after your father died," Hallie said, staring at the needlepoint. "I thought my world was coming to an end, and Sophie just wanted to take care of me. She was such a good girl."

"It must have been hard, being left alone with three kids," Maria said tentatively.

"It was," Hallie said. "I can hardly believe all those years have gone by. I'm sixty-seven, and I feel exactly the way I did when I was sixteen." Hallie didn't bother trying to hide the gray in her hair. She had just been to the hairdresser; Maria thought Hallie's hair looked stiff with hair spray and made her look more matronly than usual. But her expression was slightly bewildered, childlike.

"I can imagine," Maria said without irony. She sat beside Hallie and took her hand. "I've come to talk to you about Simon and Flo," she said.

"Okay," Hallie said. "But first let me make us some tea."

So Hallie went into the kitchen to put the kettle on, and Maria followed. Hallie threw some towels into the washing machine. Then the telephone rang, and it was Ginger Talisker. Maria watched her mother settle into the chair beside the wall phone in the kitchen, the spot where Hallie always sat when she was getting ready for a nice long chat. Maria glared at her for a few minutes, but Hallie didn't look her way. So after a while, Maria left.

The sun came out late that afternoon. Maria grabbed her digging tools, ran down the yard to her boat, and steered for the Haunted Isles. The breeze turned warm; it pushed the storm's last clouds over the horizon. Zooming over the waves, she shook off her frustration with Hallie. For the first time in many days Maria felt free of her family, and she began to think about the woman whose grave she hadn't visited since the rain began.

One flap of the low tent sheltering the grave had torn free in the storm; Maria looked inside. The bones were exactly as she had left them. Now Maria rolled back the polyethylene tent. One night, lying awake, Maria had reminded herself to check the squaw's pelvis for ridges that might indicate whether she'd given birth.

She crouched down, using her supple brush to clean the pelvis's surface. She noticed the discoloration, the lacy edges of the porous brown bones. Touching one rough spot with her finger, she traced the pelvis's curve to the spine. At one point the bone flared; the separation might have been caused by a baby passing through the birth canal. Childbirth could have cracked it; centuries of dampness, earthworms, and soil deposits might have widened the crack. The skeleton was remarkably well preserved; Maria was sure whoever buried the body had first wrapped it carefully in skins, furs, and mats.

She sat on her heels, her knees making dents in the wet earth. Like a magpie, her eyes traveled from the once-bright objects to the bones, and remembering Aldo's question about injuries, she checked the tibia and femurs for signs of breaks or ossification.

Maria concentrated on removing some of the small grave goods mingled among the bones. The gifts had probably been placed in the shroud, and once the body had decomposed everything shifted, mixing bones and talismans together. Maria brushed away soil from three beads, clustered in a group. Moss and dirt had stained them brown, but holding them to the light she could see they were deep purple, made from the insides of clamshells.

Uncovering the arrowhead was more difficult. It lay beside one rib, weighted down by a second. Maria glanced at the sky; in an hour it would be too dark to dig, and she wanted to retrieve the arrow point before then. She worked at it painstakingly with her brush and a small pick, thinking it odd that the arrowhead would lie so close to where the heart had been. Suddenly the realization washed over her like a cold wave: the woman had been shot through the heart.

Maria recoiled. Upright on her knees, she stared down at the woman, trembling. Maria had always believed that archaeologists owed love, or at least compassion, to the people whose bones they uncovered.

In her earliest digs she had cried every time she saw a skeleton: they all had in common teeth that were clenched and bared, as if in pain. They all seemed to be begging for help. Even then she had realized the sentimentality of her fantasy, and over the years she had stopped crying, had gained distance from her subjects, had traded grief for a scientist's objectivity.

But this grave was different. It was so close to her home, Maria could easily believe its occupants had walked the same ground that she and those she loved walked every day. This woman had probably set off on her final journey, alive or dead, from Squaw's Landing.

The sun was beginning to set, filling the sky with golden light. Maria stayed on her knees a long while, gazing at the murdered squaw. She wondered how she had died, who had shot the arrow, whether someone could have saved her. Thinking of the power to protect, the power to save, Maria realized that she was thinking of Sophie. Maria rose and brushed dirt from her knees. Then she stood and pulled the polyethylene cover over the grave.

Walking along the rocks, she found herself thinking of Duncan Murdoch, wanting to kiss him beside the sea, his favorite place in the world. And at that moment a chuffing sound made her turn toward the bay, where she saw the *Alicia* rounding the headland. She felt like a wish had been granted, and her heart started to pound; heading toward the beach, she stood waiting for Duncan.

They waved to each other but didn't speak. Maria watched him cast the anchor onto the beach, then haul on the anchor line to bring the boat's bow close to shore. The sun had gone behind Lookout's pines; the bay, flat calm, glistened like black ice. But the windows in the houses across the water at Squaw's Landing glowed orange with fire, reflecting the setting sun.

Maria remembered the last time Duncan had found her here. Somehow she knew he hadn't come with bad news this time; she felt her heart beating fast in her throat. She wished she could watch him on his boat a little longer, until her heart calmed down. But he jumped off *Alicia*'s bow and walked across the wet sand to where she stood. His light hair, damp with salt spray, fell across his eyes; Maria wanted to push it back.

"Hi," he said. "I saw your boat. I knew you'd be here."

"How'd you know?"

"It's the first nice day in a while. I was on my way out to the Race to fish."

"Oh," Maria said.

Duncan's face was glowing. "I had to stop. I've been fishing five hundred times when you haven't been here, but today I saw your boat."

"I'm glad," Maria said.

"I thought you might be hungry," Duncan said. "It's dinner-time."

"It is, isn't it?" Maria asked.

"Yeah. Want something to eat? All the comforts of home—well, almost."

"I've found something incredible," Maria said, staring at Duncan's midnight blue sweater, speckled with dots of white wool.

"What did you find?" he asked, moving toward her.

"A murdered squaw." She wanted to tell him about it, but she was mesmerized by his eyes, which were dancing, alive with longing. They were happy, Maria and Duncan, just standing there, knowing what was going to come next. He pulled her toward him, right against his sweater, and she tipped her head back to let him kiss her.

His sweater felt as scratchy as she had known it would; it felt as rough as his hands. She rubbed her cheek on it and grabbed a clump of sleeve with her left hand.

"You came all the way out here to bring me dinner?" she asked, wanting to climb aboard his boat. Perhaps it was the ghostliness of talking to a mother who didn't listen, or the hours spent on her knees prying an arrowhead from the rib cage of the woman it had killed, but Maria wanted to feel Duncan's warm body against hers, to run her hands down his back, to feel him shiver beneath her and feel that they were both alive.

"I had to see you," he said. Maria let him take her hand and lead her toward his boat. She hoisted herself onto the bow where fish scales glittered in the last light. They eased past a stack of green wire-mesh lobster pots, an empty bucket, and the cabin top, down into the cockpit. Duncan reached through the door leading into the cabin and switched on a light inside. Maria climbed down the ladder and glanced around. There was a tiny galley, a dining table, two bunks covered with red plaid, racks filled with boating magazines and mystery novels lining the bright wood bulkheads. Two small lamps cast a rosy light.

He lit the alcohol stove, and almost instantly the cabin filled with heat. Pawing through the cupboard, he pulled out can after can and examined them in the light. "How about clam chowder?" he asked.

"Sure," Maria said.

He opened the can, poured the contents into a saucepan, added bottled water, and adjusted the flame.

"So," Maria said, sitting on one bunk.

Duncan sat opposite her and stared at his hands, folded on the table. They were quite tan; he had three skinned knuckles. He looked up, smiling. "I've been wanting you to come into this cabin for about two months now."

"I've been wanting it, too," Maria said. She knew how it sounded; she didn't care about the double entendre. The chowder began to bubble.

Duncan came around the table. For a big man in such a small space, he moved with surprising grace. He sat on the bunk beside Maria; she felt his arm close around her shoulder, and she held the back of his neck and kissed him. His hand traced her throat, slid under her sweater, rested on her collarbone.

They leaned back into the bunk, shyly unbuttoning each other's shirts, stopping to hold each other close. It felt strange, lying beside someone other than Aldo, and she wondered if Duncan felt the same way. Maria felt his heart beating against her own chest. His muscular shoulders and chest felt soft compared to his rough hands; he ran his hands down Maria's white throat, down her arms, so tenderly she had to close her eyes.

"You're so smooth," he whispered. "I never thought anyone could be so smooth."

Her eyelids opened, and his gold-flecked hazel eyes were right there, smiling at her. She smiled back, tracing his lips with her finger, feeling warm and alive. She said his name out loud, just for the pleasure of it, and he said hers back.

"I'm falling in love with you," he whispered, and she believed it.

Duncan turned off the stove, and then he kissed her again. Their lips parted, and she felt his hands slide up to cup her breasts. His fingers excited one nipple, then the other, while Maria worked on loosening his belt. It reminded her of high school, fumbling for love in such a small space; all that was missing was the awkwardness.

She didn't feel awkward now. She unzipped his pants, and he unzipped hers, and then she reached down and freed his penis, hard as ivory, from his white shorts. He held himself over her, propped on his elbows; he looked into her eyes, and they smiled at each other.

The bunk smelled musty, but sea wind whistled through openings in the boat. "I've never made love in here," Duncan said.

"I'm glad," Maria whispered, locking her arms around his neck.

And then she pulled him down on top of her, into her, and it could have been the motion of the boat licked by the tiny waves in Lookout Cove, but they moved together with the rhythm of the sea. Maria held herself against him, tight, as if she were trying to press her body into his, wanting never to come up for air.

They headed home in their separate boats. Maria followed in Duncan's wake until they hit the black can buoy at the mouth of Lookout Bay and Duncan swung left, toward town. He blasted twice on his air horn, and Maria blasted back. This was the first time she had driven her boat in the dark; she steered toward the light on her next-door neighbors' porch. Constellations blazed overhead: Orion, the Pleiades, the Big Dipper, and Cassiopeia. Maria could still feel Duncan's arms around her shoulders, and the light wind blowing reminded her of his breath on her hair.

Turning on her bright searchlight, she held it above her head and guided the boat into shore. She walked slowly through the rough grass toward her house. With her feet on dry land, her thoughts veered from Duncan to Sophie to the squaw in her grave on Lookout. Glancing up at the sky, she realized with a shock that her feelings for the two women were strangely similar: she grieved for them, but the horror they'd experienced was as closed to her as knowledge of the grave.

Inside, Maria made herself a cup of tea. She sat in the living room, her curtains drawn. She imagined keeping Simon and Flo with her while Sophie and Gordon went far away to work things out. Maria could pretend the children were upstairs now, asleep, while Duncan, their step-uncle, waited for Maria in the barn room. Maria smiled at the thought. Was it possible that after all her years of traveling the world, the thing Maria had wanted most was a husband, kids, and a house in Hatuquitit?

But right away reality rushed back: Flo and Simon were not her kids, Duncan was not her husband. He was married to another woman. She carried her cup to the kitchen, and was starting up the stairs when the phone rang.

"Hello?" Maria said.

"It's me." Sophie's voice came thinly through the wire.

"I've just been thinking about you," Maria said. But Sophie did not respond. She was breathing hard into the phone.

"Sophie?" Maria said, alarmed. "What is it?"

"Please calm down," Sophie said quietly. "Can you come over here? Right now? I've just killed Gordon."

Sophie met Maria in the driveway. The house looked cheery; most of the first-floor lights had been turned on. The sisters stood three feet apart for a few seconds, staring at each other. Maria could see streaks of blood, like war paint, across Sophie's cheeks and on her chest. The right side of her sweater was soaked with it. Sophie seemed frozen as Maria grabbed her in a hug.

"Everything will be okay," Sophie said, stepping out of the embrace and rubbing her right arm and shoulder.

"Are you cut?" Maria asked.

"I'm not hurt," Sophie said.

"What happened?" Maria asked.

"I've just called the police," Sophie said, as if she had not heard Maria, as if she were ticking off a mental checklist. "I wanted to make sure you were on the way, so you could take Flo and Simon home with you. They're upstairs packing their things now. They shouldn't go to school tomorrow."

"What happened?" Maria repeated.

Sophie glanced toward the garage, then back at Maria. "Tell me!" Maria said, shaking Sophie's forearm. The contact made Sophie shrink back, and suddenly she collapsed to the driveway, where she remained crouched in a ball. The shake had perhaps reminded Sophie of things Gordon had done to her; Maria wished she could take it back. She leaned over Sophie, holding her with both arms. Sophie flinched again when Maria touched her right side.

"You told me on the phone that you killed Gordon," Maria said.

"I did," Sophie said, starting to sob. "It was an accident. He walked right in front of my car."

Maria felt hope building; if it wasn't murder, Sophie wouldn't have to go to jail. "Then you didn't mean to do it? Where did it happen?"

"Right there," Sophie said, pointing. Maria saw Sophie's car parked in its usual spot in front of the garage. Light from the first floor threw it into shadow. But what Maria had at first taken for the shadow of a Chinese maple was really Gordon's leg.

"Oh, Gordon," Maria heard Sophie moan. Maria walked slowly across the driveway to Gordon's body. Its upper half was hidden under the car. His legs protruded, and when Maria bent down, she could see that the front left tire had driven over his torso. Hearing voices, Maria glanced up at the house. Simon's head disappeared from the window of his parents' second-floor bedroom, directly above.

"He's dead, isn't he?" Sophie asked.

Maria wondered if a pulse could be found in the leg, the only part of Gordon's body she could reach. "I think so," she said, not wanting to touch him, hurrying back to Sophie.

"We were having a fight," Sophie said woodenly. "A very bad one. I decided to leave him, so I jumped into my car. I gunned the engine, and Gordon walked right in front of me. He just . . . went down."

"Sophie, how did you get his blood all over you?" Maria asked, touching her cheek.

"I have blood . . ." Sophie said, very disorientedly, her fingertips brushing the exact spot Maria had touched. "I crawled under the car to be with him," she said after a moment.

"Did the children see? Were they in the car with you?" Maria asked.

"They were sleeping," Sophie said.

That was how Maria decided that Sophie was lying: Sophie would never have tried to escape without Flo and Simon. Maria took Sophie's hand; she thought she heard the sirens, but it was only a television inside the house. "I'm going to call Peter," Maria said. "You need a lawyer. I don't want you to say anything to the police until Peter gets here."

Sophie nodded. In the semidarkness she looked like a young girl: blushing, lovely, terrified. The streaks on her cheek could be mud from sliding into second base instead of her husband's blood. "You meant to do it, didn't you?" Maria whispered.

"*Yes,*" Sophie said, gripping Maria's hand. Her eyes gazed fiercely into Maria's, and Maria thought she saw a glimmer of triumph.

"Why tonight?" Maria asked. Now the sirens were real; they were coming fast, getting louder as they turned off Cove Road into the Littlefields' long driveway. "What did he do tonight?"

"Someday I'll tell you," Sophie said. She relaxed her grip on Maria's hand and turned to face the oncoming police cars. The loom of their blue strobe lights flickered eerily through the trees.

"I'm going in to call Peter," Maria said. She ran into the kitchen, but the telephone had been yanked out of the wall. Taking stairs two at a time, she flew up to Sophie and Gordon's bedroom. Simon and Flo huddled in their parents' bed. Flo whimpered when she saw Maria and held out her arms so Maria would pick her up.

"Hi, sweeties," Maria said, cradling Flo and kissing Simon's forehead. She saw that Flo had bitten her lip. She peered at the lip, but outside police cars were screeching into the driveway. "I have to call Uncle Peter," she said.

She reached for the phone but stopped short when she saw the big bloody handprint on the receiver. She had no choice; it was the only working telephone in the house. Lifting it, trying not to blur the sticky handprint, she dialed Peter's number. "Get over to Sophie's right now," she said as soon as he answered. "She just killed Gordon."

Neither Simon nor Flo moved or in any way reacted to the words, spoken aloud, that their mother had just killed their father. They seemed paralyzed, asleep with their eyes wide open. They were staring into space, little dreamers in the middle of the same nightmare. Maria rocked Flo and, following her gaze, saw what the children were staring at and what they would carry with them all their lives: a wall splattered with blood and hair, an off-white thick-pile carpet soaked with their father's blood, an open window. Maria, glancing around the room, realized that she was looking for a gun or a knife or a club.

Maria lifted Flo. Simon didn't want to get out of his parents' bed. "I told Mommy to wash her face," he said dully. He hunched with despair and wouldn't look at Maria. Thinking of his cruel defiance at Covey School, Maria could hardly believe this was the same child. Because he refused to move, Maria had to lift him with her other arm. She felt desperate to get the children out of that room, away from the blood. She wanted to hurry downstairs, to make sure Sophie wasn't saying too much. A police officer met them in the hallway. "Hi, kids," he said kindly.

Maria held on to Flo, but she lowered Simon to the floor. Free of his weight, her shoulder throbbed with pain, and suddenly she knew why Sophie's right side hurt: she had strained it lifting Gordon's body, pushing it out the window. She thought of what Sophie had said just before the police arrived: "Someday I'll tell you," and Maria wondered if she ever would.

PART TWO

CAPITAL OF THE UNIVERSE

18

THEY'RE READY TO EXCUSE ME, TO LET ME OUT OF here. They peer at my bruises, the black eye, the ugly sore on my leg. "Why did you kill your husband?" one matron asks me. I've seen her in her uniform at Caldwell's buying groceries. She asked the question so easily, just as if she were asking about how I planned to cook the chicken in my grocery cart.

"I don't know," I say, because I consider it none of her business. I just want her to leave me alone.

"You must have hated him very much," she says, her voice loaded with sympathy. Then she tells me about the protesters marching along Route 11A, just outside the prison grounds. "They're mainly feminists who care about issues like yours, and they want you out of here."

I can picture the protesters, carrying those sad little signs made of cardboard stuck to yardsticks. Mom always complains about how they block traffic, especially during the hot months when all the summer people are here. I never minded them; I actually enjoy turning on the television at night and seeing our jail, all red brick and white columns—so colonial-looking—the site of anything as interesting as a protest.

It seems like the protesters always want the state to release a person they consider unjustly accused. On TV they look so passionate about it, it never occurs to me that the person might actually be guilty. So it bothers me to imagine them hiking around with signs that say FREE SOPHIE. LET HER GO HOME. PUNISH THE ABUSERS, NOT THE ABUSED. I haven't been unjustly accused.

I don't want to be freed. I'm afraid to go home. How can I walk into our house and not see Gordon?

Last night I dreamed he was there. It seemed as real as being awake; more real, even. Simon and Flo had grown up, flown the coop. We were cooking lobsters in the speckled black enamel pot, listening to WGBH on the radio. We didn't have to talk because we could read each other's minds. Gordon was thinking *I love you,* and I was thinking *These lobsters are almost done.* He took a stick of unsalted butter out of the refrigerator and put it in the tiny copper pot Maria brought us from Paris. I was thinking *Wouldn't it be fun if we had lobster bibs?* That cracked Gordon up. He stood there laughing, and then he grabbed a pillowcase out of the dryer, drew a lobster on it with Flo's Magic Marker, and tied it around my neck. He tied it too tight, like in his game with the cord, but in the dream I knew he didn't mean to hurt me. Then I woke up.

I felt so lonely and depressed as soon as the dream dissolved. In the dream I was happy and alive; awake, I can imagine how it feels to be dead. This really is a cell. I am in solitary confinement, under observation. I asked if they would let me keep pictures of Simon and Flo; the matron said I couldn't tonight but she'd give them back as soon as possible. I have a narrow bed, a toilet, and a sink. Nothing to read, no paper, no music. My body and the dress they gave me to wear are the only things in this room not bolted down. I think they expect me to try suicide.

I can't stop thinking of Gordon: I hear his voice, I relive times we spent together. Last Christmas, planting the apple trees last spring, shopping for the children's school shoes at Jewel Box Mall, the night we met. That was the night I fell in love with him.

I had gone to the Labor Day dance with Billy Walker. Billy and I and John Finnigan and Polly Crawford didn't have dates, so we went with each other. The whole way to the yacht club Polly was testing us on Kentucky Derby winners because her parents had those stupid highball glasses featuring all the great horses: Man O'War, Secretariat, Seattle Slew, Northern Dancer.

I spotted Gordon as soon as I walked in, and I felt an electric charge, the kind I hadn't felt since Jack. Gordon stood alone at the bar in his blue blazer, with that wonderful posture of his, towering about six inches over everyone else there. He had just come home from Princeton; I had read that in the *Hatuquitit Inquirer,* in a write-up on how he had taken over his father's hardware business. I made the mistake of telling Billy how wonderful I thought it was of Gordon to take over the family business when he was, after all, a Princeton graduate with the world at his feet.

"What's so great about selling hardware?" Billy asked.

"That's not the point," I tried to explain.

"Go tell him you want a screw," Billy said. He thought he was so hilarious, but we're not talking about a high school boy here. He and I had finished UConn by that time. Of course I realized his feelings for me were deeper than mine for him, so I just laughed as if I thought he was a real wit.

Once I told Maria that I knew in the middle of our first date that I wanted to marry Gordon, but in fact I knew it that night at the yacht club, even before I talked to him. He had everything: looks, position, a good business, and the sweetest eyes I'd ever seen. They were eyes I could trust. They looked so sad; he stood all by himself half the night, not even paying attention to the girls who stood beside him, taking their time ordering drinks. But his eyes told me he needed someone as much as I did, so finally I got up my nerve. I walked over to the bar and cleared my throat. I wanted to seem shy, and I didn't have to try very hard.

"I'm about to ask a stupid question," I said to him.

That made him smile. "I'm sure it won't be," he said.

"Did you happen to find a driver's license on the sidewalk outside your hardware store?" I asked. "I got stopped for inspection, and I remember the cop handing me back my license, but when I got home, I couldn't find it."

He frowned. I could see him picturing the motor-vehicle inspection—two police cars and a line of traffic—right outside his store, and I felt so bad about duping him. But I'd been watching him a little while, and I could see he wasn't the type to respond to a typical flirt. "No, I didn't," he said.

"Rats," I said. "Well, if you do find it, will you let me know?"

"Sure—what's your name?" he asked, taking out a little notepad. I remember it perfectly: it had an orange cover with the Princeton seal stamped in black.

"Sophie Dark," I said. Then I told him my number and said good-bye.

Billy had cut in on Peter and was dancing with Nell, so I got John to drive me home, and on the way I told him to head through town where I wedged my license under a Coke can in the street outside Gordon's store. John was laughing like crazy. I made him promise never to tell anyone.

The next day Gordon called. "I found it," he said.

"Great!" I said. "I'll come pick it up."

"Would you like to have dinner?" he asked. "I could give it to you then."

"I'd love to," I said.

He took me to the Sea Shanty. We sat at a table right by the window, the one he said his parents always reserved for birthdays and anniversaries; how happy I would have been that night to know it was the table Gordon and I would occupy every anniversary for the next twelve years! He wouldn't even let me look at the menu; he ordered clams casino, then lobster bisque, then baked stuffed lobsters. I started to say I liked my clams raw and my lobster boiled, but the look on his face stopped me.

I could cry, just remembering it. It took practically nothing to hurt Gordon's feelings. You could say the wrong thing and not even realize it for an hour, when he would finally get up the nerve to tell you how awful he felt. I blame the whole thing on Ed and Gwen, who raised him to have no self-confidence whatsoever.

"I'd love clams casino and a baked stuffed lobby," I said right away, as soon as I realized I was spoiling his plans. It pleased him a lot, ordering such a special dinner for both of us. I couldn't stop grinning at him, he seemed so proud. Jack had taken me to nice places, but it felt different with Gordon: serious and grown-up. I knew, even though he didn't come right out and say it, that he was ready to settle down.

As we drank our whiskey sours, he told me all about Princeton, where he'd majored in economics and rowed on the crew team and where he'd shunned the big eating clubs—Ivy, Cottage, and Tiger Inn—for being too elitist. He told me he'd had a steady girl-friend at Bryn Mawr, but that he broke up with her just before her senior ball. She had been pressuring him to propose. But some-thing in the breezy way he spoke—a little too fast, as if he didn't want his feelings to leak out—made me wonder if she'd broken up with him, not the other way around. Anyway, he told me about job offers from IBM, Merrill Lynch, and Chase Manhattan Bank. And then he asked me about myself.

I hate this part.

Just because I couldn't imagine a Princeton man wanting to marry a woman who had never left Hatuquitit except to go to the state university, I gave myself Maria's credentials.

"I went to Radcliffe," I said. "I spent my junior year in Rome, studying archaeology. I was supposed to go do graduate work at Cambridge, on a Fulbright, but I decided not to." How would I have answered if he'd asked me why I hadn't gone? It still embar-rasses me to think of what I would have said: "I decided I wanted to stay here, in Hatuquitit, because I want a simpler life. I've left the rat race to my sister." It was a response custom-tailored to the man who would shun certain Princeton eating clubs for being elitist and who would return home to run the family business; like him, I would have turned down an opportunity many would envy. But he didn't even ask.

"I'm glad you decided not to go," he said, covering my hand with his own. His smile made me go weak, as it would so many times through the years. But the night was spoiled because of the lie I'd told; the minute I told it I began worrying how to undo it. I sat at the table rehearsing retractions.

I found myself thinking in terms of how much of the truth I could get away with. What if I told him I'd starred in UConn's presentation of *Aïda*? What if I told him I'd had a poem published in the *Yale Review*? What if I told him I'd broken up with Jack be-cause I thought him too artificial? I stripped away those three lies and was left with the truth: that I was an English major at UConn where I'd sung in opera club, that the boy I'd loved and was going to marry had recently left me for someone else.

Sitting next to Gordon, listening to him apply the economic principles he'd learned at Princeton to the hardware business, I felt ashamed of my truths and glad I hadn't told them. I leaned forward, to rest my chin on my hand, so my eyes would sparkle in the candlelight. I imagined him thanking his lucky stars for sending him a woman so talented she could have made it big in the outside world but had instead returned home to Hatuquitit.

I counted my own blessings. Gordon had so many things Jack lacked: a solid family, a good business, a calm, easy way about him. I told myself that life with Jack would have been a roller coaster, that Jack loved fun more than anything—more than me, anyway—and sooner or later he'd get tired of his new girlfriend and leave her just the way he'd left me. I knew that that would never happen with Gordon. Somehow I knew right from the start how loyal Gordon was, how much love he required and how much he'd give in return.

Our wedding came as a big surprise to everyone except me and Gordon. God, how his mother tried to talk him out of it! He used to tell me the things she'd say, mimicking her voice perfectly: "Are you *sure,* baby?" "You know her mother's such an awful snob and you know how you feel about snobs...." "Her sister's such a big shot." Thank heavens Gordon never told her I'd said I went to Radcliffe, because naturally Felicia Woods, my freshman suitemate, was Gwen's goddamned goddaughter and she told Gwen every detail of my college career, including my breakup with Jack and the fact I spent all those days in bed and had to be dragged by Felicia and Carol to the infirmary. Gordon never said even one word about my lie; at least, not until about two years ago.

I'm probably the only person in the world to go to jail next door to her mother's house. Poor Mom, just through those trees. She's probably trying to do her best to forget I'm in here, but of course that won't work. It's like the game Simon and Flo play, where Simon forbids Flo to think of lima beans, and then all she can think of is lima beans.

Last night when they brought me in here I tried not to think of Gordon. I tried tricking myself; "You do not have to think of him anymore," I told myself. But Gordon is all I want to think about. All the while they were washing his blood off me, clucking like mother hens, telling me what a nightmare my life has been, assuring me that they approved of what I did, I kept my hand clenched, to save a few specks of his blood under my fingernails. I know it's pathetic, but it's all I have left of him.

19

"*CHARLOTTE'S WEB* IS MY FAVORITE BOOK," FLO said. "I guess."

"What about you, Simon?" Maria asked. "What's your favorite book?"

"I don't know," Simon said sullenly.

"You're a little old for *Charlotte's Web,* right?" Maria asked, wracking her brains for a solution. If only she could think of a book they would both enjoy, she could read to them for an hour and then everyone would be tired and go to bed. It had been this way all day: the children sitting quietly in her living room or walking around her yard while Maria tried to entertain them. Every so often the phone would ring and it would be Hallie, Peter, or Nell, with the latest news about Sophie, Gordon's funeral arrangements, or the police investigation, everyone full of advice and inquiries about the children. Duncan had called, just to tell her he was thinking of her. That was the only time she had let herself cry.

"Can we watch TV?" Simon asked.

"I told you—I don't have one," Maria said. "We'll buy one . . ." She trailed off; she had been about to say "tomorrow," but Gordon's funeral was tomorrow.

"Can we get a Sony?" Simon asked, seeming more alert than he had all day.

"Sure," Maria said.

"But I want to go home," Flo said, her lip starting to quiver. "We have a TV at home."

"We can't go home," Simon said sharply.

"I miss Mommy and Daddy!" Flo wailed.

"Shut up," Simon said.

Maria put her arm around Flo. She held her hand out toward Simon, but he ignored it, scowling. Maria felt powerless to comfort them. A policewoman had spent the morning questioning them and both claimed they had been watching television when their mother came in to tell them she had accidentally hit their father with the car.

"I know you miss them," Maria said. She felt physically aware of the words that she could not say: "But they'll be home soon."

"It's, like, kiss Mommy *good-bye*," Simon said, tossing his hair out of his eyes in a manner bizarrely reminiscent of Gordon.

"What do you mean?" Maria said.

"She won't be coming home," Simon said. "She's one of those ladies at the jail now."

"It's true that she's there right now," Maria said slowly, "but we don't know for how long."

"What's going to happen?" Flo asked anxiously. She had twisted a strand of her hair onto her index finger, tight as thread on a spindle, and now it was knotted. Maria eased it off, pretending to concentrate on the tangle instead of answering.

"What *is* going to happen?" Simon asked, his tone insistent.

"Well, Uncle Peter hired Mr. Grunwald to be your mommy's lawyer. Mr. Grunwald is going to talk to the police, some other lawyers, and a judge, and they'll decide how long she has to stay there."

"How can they make her stay there at all?" Flo asked. "She has little kids to take care of."

"Daddy said she'd be going there someday," Simon said fliply.

"What do you mean?" Maria asked, her voice sharper than she'd intended. She could see she'd scared Simon; he shrank into himself and looked down. "Tell me, okay?" she asked gently.

"He always said it," Simon said.

"He did," Flo said. "Poor Daddy."

"I wonder why he said such a strange thing," Maria said, not wanting to pressure them, but wanting to hear the details.

"What's so strange about it?" Simon asked. "He was right—she's there now, isn't she?"

"She loves you very much," Maria said.

"Yeah, sure," Simon said, gazing down at his knee. Everyone wore pajamas; Simon's were flannel covered with dinosaurs, and he picked at a small hole starting in a stegosaurus's head.

"She does!" Maria said, choked with frustration.

But Simon turned his head, gave her a wily smile. "I know," he said. "I *said* 'Yeah, sure.'"

His message confused Maria and sent a chill down her spine. She couldn't imagine what these children had witnessed. Bob Frederickson, the district attorney who had been in Sophie's class at school, had told Peter that Gordon had been shot five times by a .38 revolver, pushed out the window, and run over and over by the station wagon. The police had not yet found the gun, but they believed it was the one registered to Gordon and usually kept in his bedside table. Sophie had admitted nothing but had been treated in the prison infirmary for a dislocated shoulder, lacerations, and a sprained wrist.

"I wish we had a TV here," Simon said again.

"You guys like TV, don't you?" Maria asked, wanting to lead them as close as she dared to what had happened the night before. She had the feeling of playing with fire: she knew it might be dangerous for them to start remembering too close to their bedtime, but she couldn't stop.

"We love it," Flo said.

"What were you watching last night?" Maria asked.

"Reruns," Simon said. "Just good old reruns."

"Reruns of what?"

"*Kate and Allie,*" Simon said. "Then *Cosby,* I guess."

"Don't you love that little girl on *Cosby*?" Flo asked, tugging on Maria's sleeve. "Isn't she cute? Mommy always braids my hair just like hers."

"Can we go to bed now?" Simon asked.

"Are you tired?"

"Kind of," Simon said. "If you don't have a TV."

"Okay," Maria said, wondering what their bedtime ritual was like. She hadn't baby-sat overnight for them since they were very small, one weekend when she and Aldo were staying in Hatuquitit and Sophie and Gordon wanted to go to Nantucket. She knew that she should talk to them about their father's funeral tomorrow, explain what they should expect. But she didn't have any idea of what to say. She wished Duncan could tell her what a good parent—or aunt—would do.

"Should you brush your teeth?" Maria asked, trying to remember what her bedtime routine had been as a child. "Should we kneel down and say our prayers?"

"We have to have a bedtime snack," Flo said helpfully. "Like graham crackers or cereal."

"How about cinnamon toast?" Maria asked.

"That would be fine," Simon said.

"This is absolutely horrible. It's mortifying," Hallie whispered to Maria. All the Darks, the Littlefield children, and Julian Porter stood in St. Luke's, in the same pew from which the family had buried Malcolm. Ed and Gwen Littlefield stood just across the aisle. Friends of Sophie and Gordon, townspeople, police, and reporters from all over the region filled the rest of the church.

"The funeral of First Selectman Brown didn't draw such a crowd, and he died in *office*," Hallie whispered.

"Shhhh," Maria said. Flo wouldn't let go of her hand. Peter, holding Andy, sat between Flo and Simon; Nell sat at the pew's end, just six feet away from Gwen Littlefield. Gwen wore an opaque veil that covered her face down to her upper lip. She wept constantly; when Maria glanced over, she saw tears dripping off Gwen's chin.

"I wish she would *stop* that," Hallie whispered.

"Try to remember: Gordon was her only child," Julian said gently.

"Oh, will you please *shut up*," Hallie said between clenched teeth. Hallie's distress was so great, Maria and Peter felt worried she'd have a heart attack. She was sick with worry for Sophie. At the same time she mourned Gordon, whom she had loved, and she felt deeply ashamed of the entire situation.

Entering the church, the Darks had been blocked by reporters and photographers. Hallie had stood stock-still until the throng fell silent. "We have no comment," she said with cold dignity. Then the photographers had started clicking, focusing on Simon and Flo, adorable in their Easter clothes, and Hallie, elegant in her black bouclé suit, black kid gloves, and high-heeled Italian boots.

Reverend Hawkes entered; the congregation rose. Gordon's coffin was carried forward by his uncle and cousins; it rested in the aisle between the Darks and Littlefields. Maria kept her eyes on the children. Simon stared at the coffin, leaning toward it as if it exerted a physical pull. Then his head snapped forward, and Maria could see his profile, frowning at the minister.

Flo glanced at Gordon's coffin, looked away, glanced back. Hallie leaned across Maria to pat Flo's knee. "The angels are taking your daddy to heaven," Hallie whispered. "Tell your brother that."

"The angels are taking Daddy to heaven," Flo said to Simon in a normal voice. Simon nodded, still frowning.

Reverend Hawkes began to talk, and Maria felt tears slipping from her eyes. She wanted to wipe them, but Flo was holding one hand and Hallie the other. Maria imagined how Sophie must be feeling at that moment. She pictured her alone in her cell, aware that Gordon's funeral was going on without her.

The prison was just a few miles down the road. The funeral procession would have to pass it on the way to the cemetery. Maria imagined that Sophie would look out the window, watching for the hearse bearing the body of her husband, the limousines carrying her family, to pass by. She wondered whether Sophie would cry or whether the relief of being free of Gordon would block grief. All the evidence indicated that Sophie had killed Gordon intentionally, but Sophie had admitted it to no one.

Except to Maria. Maria remembered asking Sophie if she had

meant to do it and Sophie answering yes. Still, Sophie and Gordon had been married for twelve years, had had two wonderful children, and Maria realized that on some level Sophie must have loved him.

A great sob filled the church. Maria glanced around. She saw Duncan standing with his wife a few pews back. Duncan's eyes met hers for an instant. She had to turn away. She heard the sob again. Craning her neck to look across Gordon's coffin, she saw Ed weeping, his mouth wide open, spit running down his chin. Maria remembered Ed calling Gordon Ticky at the anniversary party, the night Gordon had put Sophie in the hospital. Maria, who had been crying quietly, felt her tears dry up. Stone-faced, she stared straight ahead. Suddenly she realized that she, Flo, and Simon were the only three people in the Dark and Littlefield families not crying, and she knew it was because they were the three people closest to the truth.

"I just can't get over how they ignored us!" Hallie whispered an hour later, back at her house. Under the circumstances, they had decided not to invite other mourners over for the customary coffee and pastries. "You'd think we're *happy* about all this."

"Gordon was their son, after all," Peter said.

"That's what I've been telling her," Julian said. As usual, he was no more than a foot away from Hallie. "It can't be easy to lose your only child."

Nell cast a furtive glance into the den, where Simon and Flo watched a game show and Andy played with blocks. "I can't get over Simon and Flo not showing any emotion," she said. "I'm worried about them."

"I think they're very brave," Hallie said.

"They don't know what to feel," Maria said. "They must be very confused. They loved their father, but they saw what he did to their mother. I'm sure they know what was going on."

"How can they?" Hallie said. "We don't know what went on, and we're adults."

"They lived there," Maria said, looking Hallie straight in the eye.

"They must have seen Sophie shoot Gordon," Peter said in a low voice. "Or at least heard the shots."

"We don't know that that happened!" Hallie cried. "Good God! Where's the *gun* if she shot him?"

Everyone regarded her with sympathy and didn't bother to argue. "Come, dear," Julian said after a while. "Let's sit down and have a drink."

"A drink?" Hallie said disdainfully. Her sense of propriety was offended by the mere mention of a drink before noon.

"I'm going to insist," Julian said, leading her away.

"Do you believe that?" Maria asked, as her mother left the room. "Sophie's in jail for shooting Gordon, and Mom's so goddamn upset about what people think that someone has to force a drink down her throat?"

"Calm down," Peter said.

"Maybe if she'd been paying attention, none of this would have happened. Gordon's been beating Sophie for years, and Sophie couldn't even go to Mom for help," Maria said, thinking of how lonely Sophie must have been, how afraid to confide in anyone. Then she felt a flash of anger for Peter and Nell, especially Nell. Why couldn't she have seen what was going on?

"Sophie has always protected your mother," Nell said softly. "Going all the way back to when we were kids. You remember, don't you, Maria? Don't you?"

"Of course I remember." Maria's spine was stiff.

"Maybe Sophie didn't want to burden Hallie, maybe she thought she couldn't take it."

"Maybe she thought Mom would be ashamed," Maria said. "Mom has never left any doubt about what she'll accept and what she won't. She sure as hell wouldn't accept Sophie getting hit by Gordon."

"You mean she wouldn't accept Gordon hitting Sophie," Peter corrected gently.

"That's not what I mean at all," Maria said, her voice rising. "Don't put words into my mouth, Peter. I mean the first person Mom would criticize is Sophie."

"Don't hate Mom," Peter said, sitting down, holding his head in his hands. "Isn't it bad enough without all of us starting to hate each other? I know you think I should have seen this coming and taken care of Sophie."

"Why didn't you?" Maria asked, her voice breaking with the panic she felt inside.

"God, Maria!" Nell said, her translucent skin turning feverishly pink. "Peter loves Sophie just as much as you do, and so do I. We didn't know anything. As a matter of fact, I think you'd better accept the fact that things have gotten about a hundred times worse since you got back." Nell gasped the last words, as if she hadn't intended to say so much.

Maria exhaled with a shudder and sat beside Peter, her knee touching his. Nell's words had echoed a feeling Maria herself couldn't shake: how things between Sophie and Gordon had deteriorated after Maria came home to Hatuquitit. Was it just that no one had noticed it before? "We were too close," Maria said, breaking down. Suddenly all the anger turned to grief, and she sobbed. "She couldn't hide the truth from me." And Maria reminded herself it was she Sophie had called after killing Gordon, she to whom Sophie had admitted intending to kill him.

"*We* were close, too," Nell said, the pitch of her voice calling Andy the way a high-pitched whistle summons a dog. Andy toddled into the kitchen, whimpering in the doorway until his mother scooped him into her arms. "Before you came home we used to go out together twice a month."

"I know you were close," Maria said. She no longer wanted to blame anyone: she only wanted to understand. "But Nell, why didn't you tell her you knew she was stealing? That would have helped her, wouldn't it? That night she stole your money at the airport, why didn't you confront her then and there?"

"I don't know," Nell said bleakly, tears falling down her blank face. She held Andy against her breast. "I would have done any-thing to help her. But I knew she'd be ashamed if I knew she was stealing."

"Nell loves Sophie," Peter said, smiling at Nell, gazing at her as if he wanted to send her strength. "I know that, and so does Sophie."

"Dada, Dada," Andy said, and Peter held out his arms to take him.

"I think we should take it easier on Mom," Peter said, turning toward Maria. "She's going through hell. You guys haven't gotten along since you've come home, and you're putting me in the middle."

"All this news about Sophie and Gordon has hit her incredibly hard. She thought they had such a perfect marriage," Nell said gently.

"But is it our responsibility to help her lie to herself?" Maria asked softly. "I don't see it that way at all."

"Would it have been so horrible to let her go on thinking Sophie had miscarried a baby she had intended to name Hathaway?"

"No, you're wrong," Maria said, confused, thinking that every-one in her family would rather preserve the status quo than seek the truth and perhaps save Sophie in the process. If everyone had acted earlier, maybe Gordon would be alive and Sophie would be free. The thought of it made Maria moan.

"I can't believe this!" Nell said, beginning to sob. The grief and madness of what had happened filled the room. Andy's expres-sion changed from worry to terror, and he began to wail.

"Don't fight!" Simon yelled. He and Flo stood in the doorway, not touching, tears streaming down their faces.

Maria turned toward the children, not speaking, hardly daring to breathe, not wanting to cause them any more pain than they'd already felt.

"We hate fights," Flo sobbed.

"Finally she's crying," Maria heard Nell whisper to Peter. "She had to cry for her father sometime." And perhaps the relief of see-ing Flo act like a normal child made Nell dry her own tears.

But holding on to her nephew and niece, their rib cages quaking as they gulped air, Maria doubted that they were crying only tears of grief for Gordon. Simon and Flo couldn't stand to see Maria, Nell, and Peter fight, because they knew where fights between people who supposedly loved each other could lead.

20

MARIA MET SOPHIE FACE-TO-FACE IN A PRISON anteroom generally reserved for conferences between prisoners and their lawyers. Steve Grunwald had spent the previous hour with Sophie; toward the end, he had called Maria in, then left them alone together.

"He seems thorough," Maria said of Steve.

"He's nice," Sophie said. "It's strange to think my fate rests in the hands of a guy I've played volleyball with. A guy I've served planked shad to."

"Your fate?" Maria said.

"People get the death penalty for doing what I did," Sophie said. "Or deserve to."

"Sophie, stop," Maria said, unconsciously feeling under the table, along the arms of her chair. She realized she was checking for a listening device. "Don't talk that way."

"Why not?" Sophie said, without a trace of zip in her voice. She had about her the air of someone who had given up. Her shapeless prison dress was lilac, the color of those endless towels on rollers in restaurant bathrooms. It fit her loosely; Maria thought Sophie had lost weight in the days she had been here.

"I want, I . . . ," Sophie stammered. Maria said nothing; she waited for Sophie to go on. Sophie bowed her head and picked at the threads of her shift, and Maria recognized where Simon had acquired the habit. Maria stared at the top of Sophie's head while Sophie fiddled with a loose button on her sleeve.

"I want to know about the children," Sophie said finally, still not looking at Maria.

"They're having a hard time," Maria said.

"Tell me. How . . . ," Sophie began, then interrupted herself with a guffaw. "As if I didn't know."

"They're both sad. They won't tell anyone what happened. Flo acts a little like a baby. She sucks her thumb all the time; she wet her bed last night. Simon's belligerent."

"Flo loves to be a baby," Sophie said, smiling for the first time. "She loves to cuddle up on your lap and have you play with her hair. Has she told you that?"

"Yes," Maria said. Although it had happened without either of them saying a word: Maria had been reading on the sofa one night when Flo, in her pink rayon nightgown, had lain down beside her, wriggled onto Maria's lap, taken Maria's left hand from the book and placed it onto Flo's head. Maria had gotten the idea and had begun twirling the fine strands of hair.

Sophie was frowning now. Maria wondered whether she was jealous that Flo would let Maria play with her hair. "They miss you," Maria said.

"They're better off without me," Sophie said with a hard edge to her voice.

"That's not true."

"Flo's been wetting her bed for months now," Sophie said briskly, as if taking care of business. "It embarrasses her terribly. Do you let her know you know about it?"

"Of course I do," Maria said, confused.

"You shouldn't. That only upsets her more. Just change the sheets and don't say anything."

"Why does everyone in this family love secrets so much?" Maria exploded. "Hallie's the same way. Don't let Nell know Hallie's mad at her, don't tell you we know Gordon hits you." Maria stared at Sophie, waiting for a reaction.

"He hardly ever hit me," Sophie said after a long silence but in a disturbingly conversational tone. "I can count the times he did on the fingers of one hand. Strange, but it didn't bother me as much as the other stuff."

"What other stuff?" Maria asked.

"I guess I didn't mean to start talking about this," Sophie said, smiling at Maria. "Steve actually seemed upset when I said that Gordon was rarely violent. He said that could wreck my defense."

"What was worse than being hit?" Maria pressed.

"Lots of things," Sophie said, looking down. Then, seeming to regroup, she said, "But it wasn't all bad. Not at all. You may not believe this, but our family had more love than any other family I know."

Maria nodded, taking Sophie's plump hand across the table. She could see that Sophie believed it, and at various times Maria had even thought so herself, a fact that now left her incredulous. She had envied Sophie and Gordon their closeness, their beautiful children.

"So, you'll keep the kids for a while?" Sophie asked, regaining her composure.

"As long as it takes."

"For what? For me to get out of here?" Sophie asked, her voice shaking again.

"What's it like?" Maria asked. "Is it terrible here?"

"It's not too bad. There's no privacy. They treat me like, like . . ." She frowned, searching for the word.

"Shit?" Maria said.

"The opposite," Sophie said. "Like a cult hero. Not only the prisoners—the matrons, too. A lot of the prisoners have husbands who beat them up. Violence is nothing new to them. They keep asking me if I've seen *The Burning Bed*. I tell them what happened to me isn't so black and white, but it doesn't matter. They think I'm very cool for having . . . killed Gordon."

"Why couldn't we have talked like this before anything happened?" Maria asked, feeling bleak.

"Like what?"

"Why couldn't you have told me what was going on?" Maria asked. "I know I could have helped you get away."

"I didn't want to get away," Sophie said, suddenly frosty. "What do you mean 'talked like this,' anyway? I hate to say it, but I'm not telling you anything. Why are you so desperate?"

Maria cringed, as if Sophie had slapped her. She tried to make sense of her sister's attack, but Sophie's tirade had left her speechless. "I want you to talk to me," Maria said after a solid minute, "because you're my sister and I love you."

"Are you sure it's not because you want to know the grubby details?" Sophie asked, sounding disgusted, and at that moment Maria saw that she was filled with self-loathing.

"I'm sure that's not the reason," Maria said.

"I'm not saying I'm a goner," Sophie said, "but I'm in bad shape."

It sounded like Sophie calling for help, but Maria, still stinging from Sophie calling her desperate, held back from promising anything. At the back of her mind was the idea that Sophie should be *thanking* her for her love and support, for taking care of her children, for letting Simon and Flo turn her entire life upside down.

"You need someone," Sophie said. "Now that His Holiness has declared that you and Aldo are no longer as one."

Maria smiled. "I'm getting by."

"I hear they have fabulous singles dances at the VFW hall," Sophie said, grinning. "Why don't you go? You might meet a nice man."

Maria could picture it. She had the feeling she was sharing Sophie's vision of men in plaid shirts. "I have been seeing someone, sort of," Maria said.

"Duncan Murdoch, right?" Sophie asked.

Maria nodded. "Did Mom tell you? Or Nell? They think I'm pretty terrible."

"No, I just knew. You've been crazy about him forever. Since school, right? Tell me you haven't."

"You're right," Maria said, glowing as she remembered making love in his boat. It returned to her in a flash: darkness falling over Lookout Cove, the warm cabin, the feeling of Duncan's arms around her.

"His wife's a little . . . odd," Sophie said.

"What's she like?" Maria asked.

"Flighty. Thinks she ought to be performing at Lincoln Center. Two or three times a year she tries to get some musician moms together. Herself on cello, Anne Drake playing piano, me singing." Sophie rested her elbows on the Formica table. The conversation had taken a turn that transcended the prison setting; now Maria and Sophie were two sisters chatting. They could have been anywhere.

"What's so awful about that?" Maria asked. "It sounds great."

"She wants the town to sponsor a concert series and advertise all over the country. She wants us to be famous and, believe me, we don't have the talent."

"Yes, you do," Maria said. Talking about Duncan's wife made her depressed; Maria knew herself how awful it was when a marriage was over. So far her romance with Duncan had taken place on the water, out of town, which had made it possible for Maria to ignore what was happening to Duncan's family. Maria's own separation had been painful, and she didn't even have a child. She wondered when Duncan would tell Alicia and his son. "He's leaving her," Maria said quietly.

"Are you in love with him?" Sophie asked.

"Yes," Maria said, blushing as she smiled. "But he's not leaving her for me. He told me they'd been in trouble for a long time." She thought of the last time she had seen him: at Gordon's funeral, with Alicia beside him. Alicia had surprised Maria by her delicacy. She was no taller than a child and just as slight. She had large, beautiful doe eyes. Silky silver hair fell to her shoulders.

"I'm sure he's not leaving her for you," Sophie said encouragingly. "Everyone knows the Murdochs would have gotten divorced sooner or later. They were never right for each other. In fact, she told me once. Like you and Aldo." At Maria's expression, Sophie flashed a soothing smile. "Well, I'm right, aren't I? Otherwise you'd still be in Peru."

"That's true," Maria agreed, feeling sad.

"Duncan's sexy," Sophie said. "And smart. You've got to clinch the romance. Here's what to do: Hire a limousine. Make sure you use an out-of-state company. Try to get a car with New York plates. Tell them to drive it to the boatyard and park right outside the gates at a predetermined time. Make it late in the day. Cocktail hour would be perfect."

"Why?" Maria asked, feeling confused.

"Arrange to be at the boatyard. Talking to Duncan about . . . I don't know, tell him you lost your anchor. You need to buy a new one. The limo will drive up. Everyone will notice: Who takes limos in Hatuquitit? Duncan will send someone over to ask the driver what he wants. Have the driver say 'Mr. Clooney is waiting for Miss Dark.' Make sure the car has black windows, so no one can see into the backseat." Sophie chuckled at her own scheme. "Duncan will fall dead at your feet. Imagine how much he'll want you if he thinks you've got George Clooney sending cars for you."

Prickles raced across Maria's forehead, the shock of realizing that Sophie was serious. She squeezed Sophie's hand, unable to reply.

"I think you should do it," Sophie said. Maria could see that she had forgotten she was in jail.

"I'm doing okay, stealing him without the help of George Clooney," Maria said, thinking that if she could let Sophie in on the guilt she'd been feeling, she could bring her back to reality.

"Did they sing any hymns?" Sophie asked suddenly.

Maria didn't understand. "When?" she asked.

"At Gordon's funeral."

"No," Maria said, shocked by the sudden change of subject. "They didn't."

Sophie didn't try to stop the tears from spilling down her cheeks. "That would have been Gwen's doing," she said. "Anyone singing would have made her think of me. So by keeping music out of the church, she was keeping me out."

"Would she really do that?" Maria asked, thinking it far-fetched.

"Yes. Will you promise me one thing?" Sophie asked plaintively.

"What?" Maria asked, ready to promise anything. She wanted Sophie to talk and not stop, to tell Maria everything Gordon had done to her and how her feelings had finally tunneled deep into the part of her that had let her kill him.

"Don't let Gwen get ahold of Flo and Simon."

"You mean custody?" Maria asked. "Of course I won't."

"I mean not at all. I don't want them to visit her, I don't want her to see them or talk to them."

"Sophie," Maria said. "How can I stop that? She's their grandmother. Wouldn't it provide stability, to let them see people they know and love?"

"So, your answer is no. You won't give me your promise."

"Tell me how I can," Maria pleaded, wanting to be convinced. "I understand how you must hate Gwen and Ed. I heard the way they talked to Gordon at their party. I know how you must feel—"

"No one knows how I feel," Sophie said, her voice shaking.

"Sophie," Maria said.

But Sophie just stared straight ahead, as if she had said everything she needed to say. Her refusal to speak, to meet Maria's eye, reminded Maria of that time in the hospital, just after Ed and Gwen's party, when Sophie had lain hurt in her bed, refusing Maria's help. Now Sophie had asked for help, and Maria had declined to give it. Maria stared at Sophie for a few moments, watching her try to gain control of something.

After a while Sophie spoke in a low voice. "I'm giving you my children," she said.

"No, you'll be back soon . . ." Maria's voice trailed off.

Sophie held Maria's gaze. "Did you hear what I said? Don't you know what I'm saying? Simon and Flo . . ."

"I know," Maria said, on the edge of her seat.

"I'm giving them to you, no one else. Not Peter and Nell, not Mom."

"Can you imagine Mom . . . ?" Maria was about to say, "with a ten- and a six-year-old," but Sophie's calm eyes made her stop.

"You're the only one I trust them with. I know you'll love them because you love me. I know that, Maria." Tears slid down Sophie's cheeks, and Maria's.

"I'll take care of them," Maria said.

Sophie nodded. "I don't want them spending any time with Gwen, because she's the one who hurt Gordon. She had a little boy and she turned him into—" Sophie's voice faltered and her body started to tremble.

"Into what?" Maria asked, mesmerized.

"Into a monster," Sophie said.

"What did she do?" Maria asked.

"What did she do?" Sophie echoed, her voice rising. "She locked him in the cellar. She made him wear . . ." Sophie held up one hand, as if she couldn't go on. "Oh, forget it. It doesn't even sound like anything."

"I think it does," Maria said. "I think it sounds horrible." There was something chilling in Sophie's tone; she was leaving out more than she could bring herself to say.

"I want you to keep them away from Gwen," Sophie said, sounding exhausted.

"Okay," Maria said. "I will." She and Sophie rose and stood still, not wanting to part. Then Sophie kissed her hard on the lips and they held on to each other for a minute, until the matron came in. She whisked Sophie into an inner room, and Maria left the prison through the front door.

21

PETER HAD ALWAYS WANTED TO BE THE STRONG one in the family. He encouraged his sisters to lean on him; he wanted Hallie to summon him any time she needed anything. That the Dark women were strong and willful, not easily given to asking for help, thwarted his fantasy. At Gordon's funeral and afterward, Maria had seen how upset Peter was over Sophie. He couldn't understand why Sophie hadn't called him to defend her against Gordon; he felt hurt that Sophie had entrusted her children to Maria instead of to him; his role in her legal defense was peripheral. Maria could see that Peter was wounded, but she believed his pain had been born years ago, when they were children. In a family full of women, Peter was odd man out.

On her way home from the jail, Maria swung by Peter's law office. She parked on Summer Street and walked into a white-columned stone house, home in the eighteenth century to a whaling captain, now converted into office space for lawyers, accountants, a photography studio, and a dermatologist.

Peter's receptionist, a cheerful young woman who was visibly pregnant, showed Maria into Peter's office.

"Hope you don't mind my just stopping by," Maria said, looking out the plate-glass window at Hatuquitit Harbor and the colorful fleet of fishing boats on their moorings. Maria strained to see the boatyard, but it was just out of sight.

Peter came around his desk to give Maria a kiss. He touched his lips to her cheek and started to step back, but she caught him with a hug and pressed her cheek to his shoulder. He had taken off his jacket; his white shirt smelled like aftershave.

"Shit," he said after a few seconds.

"She's okay," Maria said, pulling away.

"I know how okay she is," Peter said, sitting down. "I've had clients in that jail before. Sophie won't make it there."

"She'll make it," Maria said, feeling scared.

"She won't let us bail her out," Peter said. "She refuses."

"Why?"

"She says she doesn't deserve to be free."

When Maria didn't reply, Peter continued. "How are the kids doing?" he asked.

"Not great. They don't understand why Sophie won't come home. I'm not really sure they understand why Gordon won't."

Peter stared intently at a pencil on his desk. "I remember Gordon explaining death to Simon. It was years ago—I don't think Flo was even born yet. A robin fell out of its nest and broke its wing. Sophie tried to keep it alive, digging worms in the backyard and feeding it water with an eyedropper. Simon called it 'the baby.' "

"And it died?" Maria asked.

"Yeah. One morning we were all over there for Sunday breakfast or something, and Simon wanted to know where the baby was. So Gordon took him outside and showed him the dead bird, and tried to explain death was like going to sleep. And Simon just kept saying 'He's sleeping,' or 'The baby's sleeping,' with this terrible, confused look on his face all day."

"Simon's terrified," Maria said. "Or furious, I can't tell. He never stops scowling. He's mean to Flo. When I try to comfort him, he looks at me like I'm an idiot."

"His mother just shot his father," Peter said, running fingers through his hair. "Shit."

"Do you remember when Dad died?" Maria asked. "You were about Simon's age."

"That's different, Maria," Peter said. "Dad died of old age."

"I know it was different," Maria said quietly. "We hardly knew it had happened. He was never there before he died, and he was never there after."

"He was there before," Peter said. "I used to visit him in his room and he'd tell me about court. About how he'd make his expression disapproving and lower his voice to intimidate witnesses for the other side. I do that myself now."

Maria cocked her head, gazed at her brother. "It was much worse for you than for me and Sophie. You're the only one he'd ever talk to. You and Mom."

"Yeah," Peter said. "And after he died, Mom latched onto Sophie and that was that."

Maria had never really considered how bad it must have been for Peter after Malcolm's death. Maria and Sophie had always been close, had always relied on each other; Maria hadn't really minded sharing Sophie with Hallie. But who did Peter have? His mother and sisters indulged him as Man of the Family, amused by—sometimes grateful for—his efforts to keep the lawn mowed, the books in order, the shutters painted. Now Maria saw how hard he must have tried to win their love.

"You're so good to Mom," Maria said. "Sometimes I try to be, but it's like she's in a fog all by herself. I don't think she really wants anyone there."

"She wants us *present*," Peter said, "but she doesn't want to tell us anything real. She's completely denying what's happened to Sophie."

"I know," Maria said. "She's ashamed. She can't stand the TV reporters, the articles . . ."

Peter shook his head. "That's not it. She hates the publicity, but it's not the main thing."

"What is?" Maria asked, doubting him.

"Once Mom admits what's happened to Sophie, she has to admit the part she played. She has to admit to herself that Sophie couldn't go to her and ask for help about Gordon because Sophie never *could* go to her."

"Mom will never blame herself for anything," Maria said. "She and Sophie had a cozy thing going as long as Sophie listened to Mom reminisce about her childhood and as long as Sophie pretended to want to sing at Carnegie Hall."

"You sound so bitter, Maria," Peter said, shocked.

"Well, I'm not. It's just the way I see her. It's the way I see the family." Her tone softened. "I've been away a long time, and you've stayed here, keeping things together."

"Thanks," Peter said, accepting Maria's words as a compliment, the way she'd intended them.

Maria rose, brushed the wrinkles out of her skirt. She wished she were going to Duncan. The thought of him hit her hard—a sweet and clear image—and she felt herself sway. "I'd better go. I wanted to buy a TV on the way home—any idea where I can get one?"

"Go to Ernie's Electronics," Peter said. "It's on the road to Blackwood."

"Okay," Maria said, kissing her brother good-bye.

An hour later, backing her car to Ernie's delivery door, Maria spotted Reverend Hawkes walking through the parking lot. He waved and headed toward her. Handing her keys to the stock boy, she told him to put the TV in back, and walked to meet Reverend Hawkes. She'd felt uncomfortable seeing him since she'd learned he was Alicia's uncle, that he had officiated at the Murdochs' wedding ceremony.

"Hello, Maria," he said. His sharp eyes searched her face; he had last seen her at Gordon's funeral. "How is your family?"

She shrugged. "We're managing," she said. "I visited Sophie today."

"She doesn't want to see me," he said.

Maria could understand that; Sophie, like Maria, had never been terribly religious. The recent events weren't likely to change that. But she didn't know what to say to him. "Simon and Flo are living with me," she said.

"That must complicate your work," he said.

"I haven't done any since . . ." Maria cast around for the words. "Well, since the kids came to my house."

"It might help if you found a counselor for them."

She opened her mouth to protest—the last thing Sophie would want was for Simon and Flo to spend a lot of time with Reverend Hawkes—but he continued talking. "I know people who say good things about Dr. Middleton. She specializes in children."

"A psychiatrist?"

"A clinical psychologist," Reverend Hawkes said, patting his pockets. He removed a notepad and wrote down, *Dr. Elizabeth Middleton, Slocum, CT.* "I don't have her phone number, but I'm sure she's listed. Walk with me to my car, Maria," he said, smiling at her. "I've been meaning to give you something."

Heading across the parking lot, they chatted carefully. Maria told him Hallie was coping, Peter was taking care of family business, Nell was delivering hot meals to Maria and the children every day or so. Then she remembered the grave. She started to tell Reverend Hawkes about her discovery of the arrowhead, her sense that the woman had been murdered, but she didn't want to talk about murder. She thought of Sophie in her cell, and her mind went blank.

Reverend Hawkes unlocked the front passenger door of his navy blue Buick. Rummaging through a leather briefcase, he found what he was looking for. He handed Maria a Xerox copy of a document executed in spidery handwriting.

"It's from the Hatuquitit land records," he explained. "A copy of the deed between the Pequot sachem and Charles Slocum, the Englishman who bought the land out at Squaw's Landing."

"The one who didn't move the graves," Maria said, reading the paper:

These present Testifie that I, Nasseequidgeon, Sachem of Hatuquitit, have bargained and Sold to Charles Slocum of AdamsVille on Connecticott, all my Right, Title and Interest in a parcel of land called by the Indian name Squam Lying on a point of land in the sea.

Being in quantity Thirty Acres more or Less, including the burial Land of Hatuquitit, and I do hereby Engage to make Good my sale of the Said parcell of Land, and to Secure it from the Claim or Calling of any other Indian or Indians Whatsoever, except those who are buried there, and whose remains Shall be removed to other Ground, and own hereby that I am alred payd. Witness my hand or mark Anno: 1665. Aug. 5

> *Witness by John Chester, registrar.*
> *Matthew Walker.*
> *The Mark of Nasseequidgeon.*

"Squaw's Landing used to be called 'Squam,'" Reverend Hawkes said thoughtfully. "Never knew that before. I looked it up, and it means 'Pleasant Water Place.' The English settlers must have corrupted the name when they developed the land."

"Thank you for this," Maria said, tapping the paper.

Reverend Hawkes smiled, gave her a knowing look. "I know the good that work can do at a time like this," he said. "It might help you."

"It might," Maria said, moved by his kindness. Yet, shaking his hand, she couldn't help thinking: this is the man who married Duncan and his wife.

The children weren't home from school yet, and Maria was relieved. She tried to do what Reverend Hawkes had suggested—to work. Spread across her desk were photographs of the grave, her field notes, books about local Native Americans. But they blurred in front of her; she couldn't concentrate. The phone rang, and she reached for it.

"Hello?" she said.

"Are you okay?" Duncan asked.

"I'm okay," she said. "I miss you."

"You have no idea," Duncan said. Then, after a long silence, "I saw you in church. I wished I could have been with you."

"I'm glad," she said.

"I was watching you between your mother and Flo, and I knew what you must be feeling. All those times you talked to me about her, Sophie. You saw something coming, didn't you?"

"Not this," Maria said, her voice tightening. "I never thought it would get this bad. All I could think was that Sophie needed help." She paused a few seconds, holding onto the receiver. "You know what, Duncan? I'm glad it was him, and not her. When I found out he was hurting her, I was afraid he'd kill her."

"You've been thinking that all along?"

"In the back of my mind . . . I miss you," Maria said again, feeling empty.

"Alicia wanted to go to the funeral—she knew Gordon from the shop."

"I saw her," Maria said. "Does she know about us?"

"No. This weekend we're going to tell Jamey that—" he paused, "we're getting a divorce. I'm moving out on Monday."

"Really?" Maria asked. "I'm glad. I mean I'm sorry for your family, but—I'm glad for me. I just saw her uncle. We talked about some old land records, and I felt bad about what's going to happen. He doesn't know yet."

"He's known about me and Alicia for a long time," Duncan said. "And, believe it or not, I don't think he'd take sides."

Maria heard the doubt in Duncan's voice and wondered whether he believed what he was saying or was just trying to talk himself into it. "It'll be okay," she said.

"I know." He paused. "I want this to be over soon so I can see you. It feels like exile."

"I know," Maria said.

"Why didn't we find each other a long time ago?" Duncan asked. "Before we met other people?"

Maria held the phone in silence, her heart racing. "Because we had so many mistakes to make," she whispered. "We didn't want to make them with each other."

22

"I NEED A BIRTHDAY PRESENT FOR TOBY JENKINS'S party," Flo said at breakfast on Saturday.

"When is it?" Maria asked, standing by the toaster, waiting for more frozen waffles to pop up.

"Next week," Flo said. "After school."

"She means which *day,* stupid," Simon said.

"Don't say 'stupid,'" Flo said. Her voice threatened to become a whine.

"She's right, Simon," Maria said. "Look, let's all go to the mall. We can buy Toby a present and you can both get new sneakers."

"Nikes?" Simon asked.

"Sure," Maria said, relieved at having averted another argument. She served waffles to the children; while they were busy mashing hunks of butter and pouring syrup into the waffles' wells, Maria took her coffee to the far end of the table and tried to read the *Hatuquitit Inquirer.*

She feared finding stories about Sophie, so she skipped the news sections and went straight for her horoscope, "Doonesbury," and the weather report. These days the newspaper was mainly an excuse to stave off conversation with Simon and Flo until after she had her coffee and mentally prepared herself to talk to children aged six and ten. They demanded more truth and logic, even at such an early hour, than any adult Maria had ever known.

Sometimes Maria longed for the mountain, where she and Aldo would spend an hour at the breakfast table discussing world events, the day's agenda, rival archaeological teams. She glanced over her newspaper at Flo, who frowned as she concentrated on cutting her waffle into small squares.

"Need some help?" Maria asked.

"No, thank you," Flo said, not even looking up.

Maria resumed staring at the paper. She thought of Duncan. This was the weekend he and Alicia were going to tell their son about the divorce, about how their lives were going to change.

Maria wondered whether she would hear from Aldo again—soon or ever. When she had been planning to divorce him, the notion of a waiting period imposed by the State of Connecticut had seemed an outrage, a throwback to the Puritans, a paternalistic ploy in which Connecticut would send both spouses to their rooms, as it were, instructing them to think long and hard about the irrevocable act they were about to commit.

She hated to think of Duncan going through it. She wondered what role she would play: how openly they could see each other, when Duncan would decide she should meet Jamey. She thought of the waiting period as a time when the Murdochs' resentments would fester, when they'd turn into adversaries on opposite sides of a legal battle. Her stomach hurt as she thought of the part she played.

On the other hand, the suddenness of Maria's annulment seemed too hasty, like an unexpected death in the family, compared to Connecticut's dolorous ninety-day waiting period. Maria had felt unable to call Aldo, to hear his voice as she told him what Sophie had done; she had written him a long letter, complete with her field notes concerning the squaw's grave, instead.

"Can I ride shotgun?" Simon asked.

"What?" Maria asked, feeling disoriented.

"On the way to the mall. 'Shotgun' means the front seat. Daddy told me guys with shotguns rode next to the drivers of covered wagons, to protect the wagon train."

"I want to ride shotgun!" Flo cried.

"How about if Simon rides in front on the way over and you on the way back?" Maria asked.

"That's fair," Simon said, nodding.

But an hour later, when they were standing in the driveway, the children began to squabble again. "Mommy always lets me ride in front on the way to the mall," Flo said, starting to cry.

"Crybaby," Simon said.

Maria, standing on the opposite side of the car, saw Simon pinch Flo's upper arm. Flo screamed in pain. She covered the spot with one hand and hung her head, sobbing.

"I saw that," Maria said calmly, walking around the car. Saturday morning fights among herself, Sophie, and Peter had been common and harmless. She and Sophie would pinch Peter as often as they could get away with it, and he would throw gravel at their clean canvas sneakers. But somehow any hostility between Simon and Flo seemed sinister, because of the possibility they had learned it directly from their parents.

"She's a little brat," Simon said, his voice thinning.

Flo continued to cry, and Maria observed her small hands clenched into fists. "She's not a brat," Maria said. "Can you tell her you're sorry?"

"I'm sorry," Simon said reluctantly.

"No you're not," Flo said.

"*Ride* in front, for all I care," Simon exploded. "It's the death seat, anyway." He yanked open the car door, pushed the front seat forward, and tripped trying to climb into the back. He bumped his nose on the doorframe. Both children stood there crying. Maria gazed down at them, both of them awash in misery, unable to turn to each other or to her for comfort.

"What does he mean, 'the death seat'?" Flo asked. Now that Simon was in tears, she seemed to compose herself slightly.

"Most people who die in car crashes were riding in the front passenger seat," Simon said, sounding like a statistician. "When I rode there, Daddy said it was the shotgun seat. When Mommy rode there, he said it was the death seat."

"Let's just call it the front seat," Maria said, deliberately keeping her voice steady. "And let's have Simon ride in it on the way over and Flo on the way back. Okay?"

The children nodded. Simon held the seat forward as Flo

climbed into the back. Then he and Maria got in front. Maria waited until they buckled their seatbelts, then started the car and drove out of her driveway.

"I just love this place," Flo said, the sparkle in her eyes reminding Maria of Judy Garland's upon her first sight of the Emerald City.

"It's neat here," Simon said avidly. Maria had never been to the Jewel Box Mall, and the kids were eager to show it to her. On the way over they had told her it was named for the different colors given to each section of the mall: the Ruby Court, the Diamond Promenade, Sapphire Walk, the Gold and Silver Way. The idea seemed magical to them. Even Simon seemed captivated by the romance of a mall named for something as splendid as precious jewels.

They parked a long way from the entrance and traversed acres of cars. It was a sunny May day. Shopping in a mall wasn't Maria's idea of fun, and she thought fleetingly of Sophie freed from prison, shopping with her own children for sneakers and Toby Jenkins's birthday present while Maria excavated the grave on Lookout. She wished it were true.

"Gwen takes us here sometimes," Flo said.

"She does?" Maria asked, pausing as she remembered promising Sophie that she would keep the children away from Gwen. But how likely was it that Gwen would be shopping today? Or that, of the hundreds of people who must be here, Maria and the kids would bump into her? "What stores does she like?" Maria asked, so that they could avoid them, just in case.

"She likes Jeannie's," Simon said.

"Not as much as the candle shop," Flo said. "Gwen loves candles. Also perfume and girdles."

"How can anyone love girdles?" Maria asked, laughing.

"Gwen does," Flo said confidently.

Inside the mall, people moved like cars on a highway. The westbound lane headed for Jeannie's; the eastbound lane passed the Ruby Court on its way to Raphael's. Banners of scarlet, azure, and gold hung from the ceiling. A crystal chandelier glittered high overhead, but the children were more dazzled by window displays at Tuneville and Foxcroft Tweeds. People passing by watched them curiously. Maria assumed they had seen pictures of the children in the newspapers; she was glad the children didn't seem to notice.

"Can I get a Metallica CD?" Simon asked.

"Icky," Flo said. "Don't let him, Aunt Maria."

"Why not? Why is it icky?" Maria asked, willing to spring for the CD.

"It's heavy metal," Flo said sadly.

"It's awesome," Simon said. "Can I have it?"

"Okay," Maria said, handing him a twenty-dollar bill. He bolted into the store. Flo stood beside Maria, shaking her head. Maria, gazing down at her, smiled. "If you don't like that music, you don't have to listen to it. Simon can play it in his room and you and I can sit downstairs listening to *The Phantom of the Opera*," Maria said, knowing Flo loved it.

"Mommy wouldn't like it," Flo said.

"What do you mean?" Maria asked.

"She wouldn't let Simon buy it. She doesn't approve of heavy metal."

Maria grabbed Flo's hand and pulled her into Tuneville. A clash of tastes was one thing, but defying Sophie's wishes was another. Simon stood at the counter, clutching the plastic bag, waiting for the man to count out his change.

"Uh, Simon," Maria said, wondering whether he'd willingly exchange the Metallica CD for one by another group. He gazed expectantly into her eyes. He looked happy. The corners of his mouth quivered upward, then set in a definite smile. "Never mind," Maria said.

"Aunt Maria!" Flo said.

When they had left the store and reentered the flow of mall traffic, Maria put one hand on Simon's shoulder. "Next time I'd like you to stick to the rules. I don't like buying you things your mom wouldn't approve of. Okay?"

"Do I have to return the CD?" Simon asked.

"No," Maria said, hating to go against Sophie but hating more the idea of unhappiness returning to Simon's face.

Flo wanted to buy Toby a pink tutu for her birthday. It hung in the window of Penny Violet, a children's store named for the owner's daughters. The bodice, of white cloth so silky Maria could hardly believe it was nylon, had silver sequins along all its edges. Rhinestones sparkled throughout the pink tulle skirt.

"Does Toby like ballet?" Maria asked.

"I don't know," Flo said, mesmerized by the garment.

"It would never fit Toby," Simon said, hanging back, pretending to be uninterested in the transaction. "She's way too big."

"She's a second grader," Flo said. "But she would love that tutu. She would look beautiful in it."

"But if we don't know whether she likes ballet or not, maybe we should buy her something else," Maria said. "Let's look through the store."

Maria remembered giving painting kits, baseball gloves, and friendship rings as birthday presents, but Flo insisted that she had to give Toby clothes. Flo and Maria looked through racks of dresses that seemed much too expensive to buy a child who would outgrow them in no time. Sweaters were stacked on one shelf. Maria touched a pullover, noting the swirl of colors: red, blue, yellow, green, pink, orange, and lavender. It reminded her of the Christmas she was seven, when she asked Santa for a "skirt of all colors" and got one of black and purple paisley instead.

Flo drifted back to the tutu. "How about this sweater?" Maria asked.

Flo nodded. "I guess," she said. "If you want."

"That way," Maria said, her mind made up by the grim memory of the skirt, "we can buy the tutu for *you*. Would you like that?"

"Oh, yes!" Flo exclaimed, clapping her hands, then throwing her arms up in the air.

"Can we go now?" Simon asked.

"As soon as I pay," Maria said. "We'll buy sneakers at Sports Loft on the way home." Standing in line, Maria felt absurd relief. She realized that she had been looking over her shoulder for Gwen ever since they'd arrived at the mall, and she had the sense that she and the children were about to make a clean getaway. Mainly, she felt outrageously happy for having found a way to make Sophie's children smile.

But later that night, when Flo and Simon were asleep, Gwen called.

"Ed and I were wondering if the kids could come over for Sunday dinner," Gwen said. "It's sort of a tradition, and I'll bet you could use some space."

"Actually, we're already invited to my mother's," Maria said, her voice warmer than she wanted it to be. It was difficult, being civil to the mother of the man who had abused Sophie, especially after Sophie had told Maria about the role Gwen had played. But Maria also realized how hard it must be for Gwen to have a normal conversation with Sophie's sister.

"I see," Gwen said. She paused a moment, and when Maria didn't fill the silence, she went on. "How are they, anyway?"

"They're very upset," Maria said.

"I can understand that," Gwen said, and although the line was silent, Maria knew Gwen was crying hard at the other end.

"It's an awful time," Maria said feebly.

"I can't believe he's gone," Gwen said, her words making Maria's stomach tighten. Maria had been thinking of Sophie in prison. She felt sympathy for Gwen, losing her son, but she couldn't bring herself to say so.

"Well, I'll tell the kids you called," Maria said.

"When can we see them?" Gwen asked, sniffling. "I would have called before, but honestly, I didn't think Ed could bear having them visit. Simon is just the spitting image of Gordon. Ed is a total wreck."

"I can imagine," Maria said, stalling.

"So, when would be convenient?" Gwen asked.

"I don't think it's a good idea, them seeing you quite yet," Maria said.

"Why not?" Gwen asked, her tone suddenly cold.

"For the same reason you didn't think Ed should see them: the sad memories it's going to bring up."

"I don't like the sound of this," Gwen snapped, more like her brittle self. "I don't know where you got this idea, but I'll ask you one thing: Have you heard of grandparents' rights?"

"Yes," Maria said.

"Because if you try to keep Gordon's children from me and Ed, we'll take you to court. Have you got that?"

"Yes," Maria said, and softly hung up. She stared at the black window, not even seeing her own reflection; she thought of Sophie, and she closed her eyes.

23

MARIA AND PETER SAT OPPOSITE SOPHIE AT A LONG table in the prison law library, waiting for her to finish flipping through Polaroids taken that day of her children. Sophie's cheekbones, collarbone, even her nose seemed more prominent, as if pounds were dropping away, and Maria worried that Sophie was austerely depriving herself of food as punishment for her crime. When Sophie smiled sadly, Maria imagined her thinking about what she was missing: her children, the fine May weather, freedom.

"'Tell me she won't take it off," Sophie said, grinning suddenly, holding up a picture of Flo wearing her tutu.

"How did you guess?" Maria asked.

"Because that's Flo. Latches on to things and won't let go till something even more wonderful comes along. Has she worn it to school yet?"

"She asked," Maria said, "but I wouldn't let her. I mean, a tutu? To school?"

"Let her!" Sophie squealed. "God, Maria, are you a stick-in-the-mud."

"Sophie, I wouldn't let her either," Peter said.

Sophie's eyes flicked over her brother: his neatly clipped mustache, his foulard tie held in place by their father's gold monogrammed tie clip, the matching silk pocket square poking out of his suit's breast pocket. "No kidding," Sophie said, deadpan, and Maria laughed.

"Very funny, Maria," Peter said in the solemn way of a reasonable man, but Maria could see that his feelings were hurt.

"Last year Gordon and I gave Flo jodhpurs and a little velvet hunt cap to wear when she rode her friend Emma's pony, and she absolutely refused to take them off except to sleep. Her teacher didn't mind her wearing them to school."

"Sophie . . . ," Peter said.

"She was so cute," Sophie said. "You're only little once, you know. Definitely let her wear her tutu to school."

"If you say so," Maria said.

"They're fine, though?" Sophie asked.

"Yes," Maria said.

Maria and Peter fell silent, wanting Sophie to arrive, on her own, at the moment when she would begin to talk about Gordon.

"Come on, Sophie," Peter said after a long minute.

"What?" Sophie asked, uncooperative.

"Steve says you won't talk to him. He says you won't tell him any details, and he needs to know more in order to build your defense."

"So, this is our brother the lawyer," Sophie said indulgently.

"Could you try taking this seriously?" Maria asked.

"Mind your own business," Sophie said in a voice as affectionate, as singsong, as the one in which she had just spoken to Peter. Maria felt crazed by the discrepancy between Sophie's tone and her words. The desire to shake Sophie was so strong, Maria had to close her eyes and clench her teeth.

"Did you shoot Gordon?" Peter asked. When Sophie didn't answer, he pressed. "Did you shoot Gordon five times?"

Sophie nodded.

"You're saying yes?" Peter asked, but Sophie merely nodded again.

Maria's urge to shake Sophie was transformed into a need, no less urgent, to take her hand. She held it across the table. "Remember that night? When you told me that someday you'd tell me why you did it?"

"Today's not that day," Sophie said.

"Telling us will help you," Peter said. "Don't you want to get out of here? And go home?"

"No," Sophie said. "I don't."

Maria couldn't believe what she was hearing. "You're kidding, right?" she asked.

"No, I'm not," Sophie said, looking Maria straight in the eye. And Maria, although she couldn't imagine what Sophie was thinking, believed her.

Peter had read and reread the police report. Maria knew that it stated that Gordon had been shot with five bullets, one of which had killed him; that his body had been pushed out the bedroom window; that the Littlefields' car had driven back and forth across his body. Peter had told Maria the police were saying Gordon had been "overkilled."

"How's your shoulder?" Maria asked.

"It's fine," Sophie said. But she flexed it, as if testing for pain, as she spoke.

"Did he do something to Flo that night? Or to Simon?" Maria asked, thinking that Gordon harming the children could have pushed Sophie to kill her husband.

Sophie shook her head.

Peter exhaled. "Okay, if you won't talk about Gordon, we'll talk about his parents. Their lawyer sent me a letter. Not Steve— me. If you don't permit them visitation, they'll sue for custody."

At that, Sophie's face collapsed, and she pulled her hand out of Maria's grip. "I hate them," she said.

"Tell me what they did," Maria said.

"They used to lock Gordon up for hours in the cellar. When he was little. If you could see the place . . . dark, with cobwebs. A horrible artificial Christmas tree they leave decorated all year."

"How bad was that compared with what Gordon did to you?" Maria asked.

"Shush, Maria," Peter said. "At least she's talking."

But Sophie seemed not to hear. "Ed used to call him 'coward' and 'woman' for not going to Vietnam. Ed doesn't give a damn about the fact Gordon had a high lottery number, and that's the reason he didn't go."

Peter frowned and tapped his pencil on the table. "I'd think Ed would be glad Gordon wasn't drafted."

"Ed's lucky Gordon didn't have to go," Maria said after a long pause. She thought of Hallie—who loved to tell of her father's heroism at the Marne and of Malcolm's as a pilot over Normandy—saying how glad she was that Peter was too young to fight in Vietnam.

"Ed," Sophie said, shaking her head.

"If you let him and Gwen see the kids, they won't try for custody," Peter said.

"Is there any chance they could get it?" Sophie asked.

Peter shrugged. "I doubt they could, but it would depend on the judge. Maria's not married, she's never raised kids of her own. Some judges might consider the Littlefields better qualified."

"That would be a disaster," Sophie said.

"Are you saying that Gordon's parents treated him badly and you think that made him treat you and the kids badly?" Maria asked.

Sophie nodded, white-faced.

"How?"

Sophie frayed a hole in her sleeve. "One time they caught him peeling wallpaper off his bedroom wall. So, to punish him, they put him on a leash," Sophie said. "In the basement, with no lights on. They put a dog collar around his neck and leashed him to Ed's workbench." She looked up at Peter and Maria. "Have you ever heard of anything so terrible?"

Maria, thinking of the cord Gordon had tied around Sophie's neck, said nothing.

"Why didn't he take it off?" Peter said.

"Because the only time he took it off, Gwen held a burning cigarette to his bottom and said the next time she'd touch him with it. So he never disobeyed again. He was only eight."

"Oh, God," Peter said.

"So you can see why I don't want them trying to get custody of Simon and Flo," Sophie said calmly, deep in thought, as if—for the first time—she was thinking of legal strategy. "I can put up with the kids visiting them if Gwen understands that if the kids say anything—anything at all—about her or Ed hurting them, she'll never lay eyes on them again."

"Okay," Peter said, nodding, making notes on a yellow pad.

"I want you to get out of here," Maria said. "So you can have Simon and Flo all to yourself."

"Are they wearing you down?" Sophie asked, smiling.

"That's not the reason," Maria said. "But they miss you so much. I'm so worried about them. I've made an appointment for them with that psychologist Reverend Hawkes told me about."

"That's good," Sophie said.

"Tell us a little more," Peter said. "Something about that night."

"That night?" Sophie asked. "The night I killed Gordon?"

"Yes," Peter said. "Tell us where you put the gun."

"I threw it into Bell Stream," Sophie said, her voice and eyes totally empty of expression.

The police had been searching Bell Stream for hours. Maria, Simon, Flo, Peter, Nell, and Andy had gathered at Hallie's for a picnic. Peter hunched over Simon, teaching him how to grip a horseshoe properly. Hallie was bothering everyone with mosquito repellent. Maria sat in a lawn chair, listening to the distant squawk of police radios. The squad cars were parked in a clearing just out of sight near the Littlefields' house, but Maria knew it well; high school kids used it as a place to park, and Maria had spent a pleasant interlude or two there with boys whose names she could now barely remember.

Nell sat beside her, sipping a gin and tonic. Horseshoes thudded in the pit, then clanged as Peter threw a ringer. Hallie and Julian cheered from the sidelines. "Bravo!" Hallie called, sounding more like an opera-goer than a sports fan. No one had told her that Sophie had admitted throwing the gun into Bell Stream, so the sound of police radios held no significance for her.

Maria glanced under the brim of her straw hat at Nell. Nell caught her looking, and smiled. "They're not even close," Maria said.

"No," Nell said.

A jet flying from Europe to New York passed high overhead; they saw its vapor trail before they heard its drone. Most airlines' routes took them from Rome, Geneva, Paris, or London straight over Hatuquitit on the way to JFK. Maria shivered, remembering how excited she would feel, sitting beside Aldo, when the familiar contours of Narragansett Bay, Point Judith, Westerly, Squaw's Landing, and finally Hatuquitit would come into view. She had learned to recognize Bell Stream, trickling into Long Island Sound.

"Want to walk down there?" Maria asked.

"Let's," Nell said.

Maria and Nell headed barefoot through tall grass toward the stream. Maria's faded, sea-green cotton sundress, retrieved from the closet of her old room in Hallie's house, left her arms and ankles bare. Fabric and grasses swished against her calves; she slowed but didn't break her stride as she leaned down to scratch a bug bite.

Maple and oak trees grew along the stream's banks. The grass grew stubby in the shade, then turned to mud. Maria felt it squish through her toes. Sophie's house stood two hundred yards ahead, on the opposite side of the stream; that was the stretch of water where the police were searching. Water burbled along, blocking the noise of the police radios.

"I haven't been down here in ages," Nell said.

"Neither have I," Maria said. "I wonder if we can find it."

Both women kept their eyes trained on the ground, sweeping from the water's edge to a spot ten or so feet into the Darks' meadow. When they came to a small grove of pines, Maria slowed down. "It's right around here," she said.

Nell looked up, triumphant. "The stones!" she said. "Oh, God, can you believe they're still here?"

Maria walked over to where Nell stood and there, nearly buried in soil and covered with whiskery grass, were the stones Sophie had arranged in the shape of a heart over twenty years ago to commemorate the time the church bells had rung until the storm stopped, allowing a newly married couple to reunite, giving Bell Stream its name. Crouching, Maria used her fingers to brush dirt from their edges. Embedded in the earth, they were artifacts. Another archaeologist would wonder how stones washed smooth by the sea had found their way three miles inland and formed a heart, but Maria knew.

"It seems like yesterday," Nell said. "You were standing over there. Sophie was crouching down just the way you are now, wedging the rocks into the soil."

"You were complaining that she made you carry more than your share home from the beach."

"I remember a piece of pink quartz," Nell said, kneeling beside Maria. "Is it still there?"

Maria brushed dirt away from one rough stone near the heart's cleavage; it might have been pink quartz, but dirt and moss had stained it brownish green. "I can't say for sure, but I think this is it," she said.

"Oh, Sophie," Nell whispered.

Maria said nothing, but tears burned her eyes. The stone heart blurred. She could no longer remember how Sophie had determined this was the most likely spot for the famous wedding to have taken place, but she did remember how convinced Sophie was of it. "It happened right here," Sophie had insisted. "I know it. I'm positive."

Maria and Nell had willingly entered Sophie's world, trusted her instincts. Sophie, though younger than Maria, had been their heart and soul. That was why Maria, still staring at the stone heart, found it impossible to understand how Sophie had abandoned her convictions and become Gordon's victim. That Sophie finally escaped by killing him made more sense to Maria than the fact that she had endured his harm.

"It's shallow here," Maria said, rising. Nell followed her to the stream's edge. They leaned over the water, just four inches deep, gazing down to the pebbly bottom. Water bugs Sophie had called daddy-O's skittered across its surface. Bubbles rose, maybe from a frog hiding in the shallows. Green weeds swayed in the current and pebbles lay on the bottom. And amid them, washed by Bell Stream, was the revolver Sophie had used to kill Gordon.

24

I CAN'T IMAGINE WHAT KIND OF MOTHER WOULD want her kids to visit here. Bess, my cellmate, has three sons, and they come every other Saturday. I just hate to think of them leaving with a mental picture of their mother in a uniform, looking just like everyone else, living in the midst of criminals because she is one too. She talks about them constantly: Benjamin, Dougie, and Lance. She cries because they live so far away, at the other end of the state, and can't visit more often. I tell her she's lucky. I tell her to imagine how awful it would be if they lived in Hatuquitit and had to pass this place on the school bus every day, knowing their mother was inside.

Of course, mothers often have a cockeyed view of what's best for their children. Look at Mom. When we were little she saw me and Maria as miniature debutantes and Peter as a very short escort. Maria was obviously too brainy to join Mom's dog-and-pony show, so I got the singing lessons. Peter took clarinet; the instrument was as tall as he was and just about as skinny, and he never once hit a right note on it. It was supposed to be for fun. There's nothing wrong with music lessons, but Mom really hoped we'd make it to Juilliard.

She hasn't visited me here. "It's hard for her," Peter keeps telling me. He's so understanding of her, a quality I consider dishonest. I mean, it's okay to understand what a person is going through, but you have the right to let them know what you think. If Mom let it be known that she was planning to come here, I'd send her the message *Don't bother.* Why would I want her to put herself through it? I'm sure she never thought she'd have a daughter in here. Radcliffe, yes. Carnegie Hall, yes. Jail, no.

Though maybe I'm being unfair. Mom's not big on visiting. When she went to Slocum General for her hysterectomy, she wouldn't let anyone visit her. "I'm coming tonight at six," I said. Six sounds about right—it was the middle of evening visiting hours anyway. But she wouldn't let me. "The traffic will be horrible, dear," she said. Or "Stay home with your little family and send flowers instead. I adore dahlias."

It used to *get* me, the way she said "your little family." As if hers was so enormous! She only had one child more than I did. Of course, back when she had her hysterectomy, I only had Simon. Maybe that explains it. Anyway, it took me years to figure out why she didn't want visitors: it was so she wouldn't be obliged to return the visit. She'd always come to see a new baby, but when I checked into Slocum to have my disc operation, she didn't come once. Hospitals depress her.

Gwen, on the other hand, makes a career of visiting friends in the hospital. Her friends are always in for something terrible: rectal cancer or nose removal or toe amputation due to complications from diabetes. She knows all the best florists and she belongs to a craft club so she can make her sick friends cheery little gifts to keep at their bedsides. You'd think this was something that started recently, since her friends became elderly, but it dates way back.

She used to take Gordon with her. Children weren't even allowed on the surgical floor back then, when he was a kid, but Gwen was such a regular the nurses would make an exception for her son. She'd teach him the things she'd learned in craft class, and he'd do them at home. She kept some of his best things: a crocheted top hat to cover an extra toilet paper roll, a crèche made entirely of pipe cleaners, a centerpiece formed by stretching a wire coat hanger into a circle and twisting strips of tinfoil around it. He did a bust of his fourth-grade teacher by inverting a saucer and gluing the inverted cup to it. The cup's handle was her nose; then he painted on blue eyes and a smile and glued on yellow yarn for hair and strips of lace for a frilly collar on the upside-down saucer's rim.

Mainly Gordon gave his crafts to his mother's sick friends. Pomander apples and oranges, potpourri made from Gwen's roses and wisteria, felt cigarette cases. I get so angry when I think of Gwen dragging him into the surgical ward to visit poor nose-less Mr. Peabody. What the hell was Mr. Peabody to Gordon? No-body! Just because he delivered dry cleaning for Clean-More and Gwen had more of her clothes dry-cleaned than anyone else in Slocum.

Don't get me started. There's not much else to do but remi-nisce. There's no point thinking about the good times, so I've been feeding my grudges. I do admit that. I lie here thinking about how much I hate Ed and Gwen. Gordon could have been such a wonderful man. He could have been so happy. Sometimes I admit what I've always known: that Gordon never had one happy day in his life.

His parents wanted so much from him. He gave them many things, but they were the wrong things. Ed can hardly live with the knowledge that Gordon didn't become a sports professional. "Which sport?" I used to ask. "It doesn't matter," Gordon would say. "Any sport." He was good at track, golf, and swimming. He played in golf tournaments at Princeton, and Ed hoped that Gordon would come home and become the Hatuquitit Country Club's golf pro. At first we used to laugh when Ed would say that if Gordon hadn't married me and had a family to support he could have been great. But after a while we stopped laughing and I could see that Gordon had started to believe it.

All the women here gripe about their mothers-in-law. It is such a common topic of conversation. Mostly they say that they haven't lived up to the expectations of what the mothers-in-law wanted for their sons. Sometimes they complain that the mothers-in-law can't mind their own business, that they intrude, that they criti-cize. They're dying for me to talk about Gwen, because they think she must have been a real number to have raised a son like Gordon. They're right, but they wouldn't understand why. They would see Gwen as a wicked woman who raised a villain, but I see her as a stupid woman who raised a confused, lonely boy.

Bess is the only one I talk to. She hears me cry at night, and sometimes she reaches down and we hold hands. There's so little comfort here. It's easy to talk tough about mothers-in-law, about what bitches they are, about the control they still have over the grown men we love. Last night Bess and I stayed awake a long time talking about our husbands and their mothers. Twice the matron told us to go to sleep, but we couldn't stop. Once we got started, the thoughts kept coming.

Bess said Jimmy, her husband, was hit by his parents and then he hit his own children. She said it was known as a "chain of abuse," and she asked if Gordon's parents had abused him. I said, "They didn't beat him. There are worse ways," I told her. "Like what?" she asked. "Like locking a kid in the basement," I said. "Or never praising him. Or pretending not to hear him, as if he wasn't there." "Well, hitting was Jimmy's worst problem, and it still is," Bess said. She asked me what was the worst thing Gordon ever did to me. I had to think a long time, and I never did come up with the answer. But one thing popped into my head and stayed there, a subtle thing that Gordon never used to do but did all the time the last few months, and it really used to bother me. Bess is the only person I've ever told.

Whenever I entered a room, Gordon would leave it. If he was reading a book and I walked in with a pile of clean laundry to put away, he would close his book and walk out the door. He'd whisper something under his breath just as he passed me. "What?" I'd ask. But he'd just keep going.

A month ago, he started saying it louder. I could catch the words "I wish . . ." Getting ready for bed, I'd hear Gordon whisper "I wish," just before he locked himself into the bathroom. "What do you wish?" I'd ask through the door. "Please tell me." He never would. I tried to imagine what Gordon wished. That we were happier? That he loved me and the kids more? That none of this had ever started?

One night I had just put Simon and Flo to bed, and I walked

down to the kitchen for a cup of tea. Gordon stood at the counter, measuring coffee into Mr. Coffee for the next morning. It was a special blend of Viennese and French Roast I'd bought mail-order from Dean & Deluca. Gordon stood in our kitchen, frowning as he concentrated on filling the coffee scoop just right. I watched him for a while, and I couldn't help thinking about our first years of marriage, when we were so happy. When I thought we had the real thing.

"I love you," I said to Gordon. He glanced up; he seemed surprised to see me, as if he'd been thinking of something far from home. He dropped the scoop back into the bag, and he walked out of the room. "I wish . . . ," he said, in a louder voice than usual, as he passed me.

"What do you wish?" I asked. I ran after him. I would have begged him to tell me, but I didn't have to. He stopped short in the front hall, just before the coat closet. The lights were off; I fumbled for the switch, so I could see his face, but he caught my hand. His grip wasn't particularly tight. He had held it that way many times when we danced. We stood there so long, my eyes got used to the dark and I could see him clearly. His beautiful eyes, his slightly receding hairline, his high cheekbones. This was the man I had married. This was the father of my children. Standing in the hallway of the house we had chosen and decorated together, I could feel his warm breath on my hair.

"I wish you would die," Gordon said to me. And then he walked upstairs.

"Are you ready for a boat ride?" Maria asked. Simon and Flo slouched on the sofa, watching music videos on TV; neither child seemed to hear her. They had walked straight into the house after school, dropped their books on Maria's desk, grabbed a snack, and settled down in front of the television. Maria, dressed for digging, stared at them and fought to control her impatience. This was the first reasonably dry day after several days of drizzle.

"I said, is anyone ready for a boat ride?" Maria asked slowly.

"I don't want to go," Simon said.

"Neither do I," Flo said. She had dropped chocolate cookie crumbs on the front of her tutu but didn't seem to notice. Maria wondered if there was some special way to wash a tutu without crushing the tulle skirt, and she added it to the long and unwelcome list of chores she had taken on since the children had arrived. She switched off the television.

"Hey!" Simon protested.

"Change your clothes," Maria said. "We're going for a boat ride."

"To where?" Simon asked. He remained where he was, staring at Maria with a skeptical expression, as if her answer would determine whether he would decide to go or not.

"We're going digging. On the Haunted Isles. Now hurry!" she said. The children's eyes widened at her tone, and they ran upstairs.

While they changed, Maria walked down to her boat to make sure everything was in order. She tried to isolate her resentment and decided that it came from being trapped. She liked to work late in the day, just as the children were coming home from school. There were groceries to buy, laundry to wash, homework to check. Maria hadn't seen Duncan since the children had moved in. She missed him. Sometimes she felt angry with Peter and Nell, even with Hallie, for not taking a turn keeping the children. But she knew that the children needed her, needed stability, that moving from house to house was the last thing they needed. Yet she looked forward to Friday, when she'd reluctantly arranged for them to stay at Ed and Gwen's.

"Is this okay to wear, Aunt Maria?" Flo asked. Maria smiled, noticing that she had pulled on a windbreaker over the tutu and tucked the full skirt into her jeans.

"It's fine," Maria said. "Where's your brother?"

Flo shrugged. She let Maria hoist her into the boat and fasten an orange life preserver around her neck. Waiting for Simon, they gazed through mist across the placid bay toward the Haunted Isles, shimmering like a mirage.

At the sound of a screen door slamming, Maria glanced at the house. Simon came sullenly down the path, eyes cast down, taking his time. Maria pretended not to notice. Whenever she asked him what was wrong, he would snap, "Nothing." She fought the urge to help him into the boat. With much difficulty, he climbed over the rail. Maria told him to put on his life jacket. He slipped it over his head, but left it unfastened. Maria let it pass.

As they crossed the channel, Maria glanced back at the kids. She wanted them to be delighted by the boat ride, as she would have been at their ages, but they seemed bored. "Look at that!" she yelled over the engine. Terns were dive-bombing a school of fish; silver tails flapped, churning up a rough patch of water.

"They're blues," Simon called back, suddenly interested. He gripped the rail, watching the fish until Maria rounded the red nun buoy and cut the throttle. She wished she had a fishing pole aboard.

They beached the boat. "Want to see the excavation?" Maria asked.

"Maybe we'd rather play now," Simon said.

"That's a much better idea," Maria agreed, and the children scrambled across rocks in search of a tidal pool. Maria watched them go. Suddenly they seemed willing to have fun, and she felt grateful. Most of the time they seemed so solemn. They ate their food in measured bites. They stared at the television without smiling. Sometimes they told mean jokes. Listening to them squeal as they made their way across slippery rocks, Maria smiled. For once they sounded like little kids.

But Maria herself turned solemn as she carried her pack up the small rise. She hadn't visited the grave in days. At the crest she stopped and stared at it. Rain had pocked the earth around the tent; a fine layer of dust had settled on the surfaces she had so scrupulously cleaned the week before. A bird or something larger had been scratching the area, perhaps in search of sandworms. Long clawmarks scored the dirt. Maria stared dully at the site for a few minutes, plotting how she would proceed. Returning to a dig after time away always felt awkward. Maria was never quite sure whether the theories she had formed in a previous spate of digging would hold.

Shaking off the polyethylene tent, Maria examined the woman's bones. She thought of the Pequot cemetery at Squaw's Landing, and she wondered why this woman hadn't been buried there. Crouching on her heels, she located the broken rib. Were murdered tribe members cast out? In some cultures she and Aldo had studied, murder was as shameful for the victim as for the killer.

Yet there were plenty of grave goods here, indicating that the woman had been beloved at the time of her burial, sent away on her three-day journey to the Land of the Dead with plenty of gifts. Maria tried to remember the Pequot legend of a brave chasing his spirit wife across the water to the Land of the Dead, somewhere on the Haunted Isles. These bones could belong to that woman, Maria thought, using her stiff brush to clear soil away from a metal disk.

"Is that a skeleton?" Simon asked. Maria jumped at the sound of his voice. He and Flo stood on the hill's crest.

"Yes," Maria said. "This is the skeleton of a Native American woman. Want to see?"

The children stepped forward. Maria shifted left, to let them look. "I'm trying to uncover these beads and stones," she said. "Living Indians always buried the dead ones with presents."

"When did this Indian die?" Flo asked. She reached out to touch the woman's tibia; Maria didn't stop her.

"Three hundred years ago."

"Will Daddy look like this?" Simon asked. Crouched on his heels, he was staring at the woman's skull.

"Well," Maria said after a small silence.

"Yeah, he will," Simon said, exhaling angrily.

"Daddy won't look like that," Flo said, her voice starting to quaver.

Maria reached over to pull her close. She was so used to a matter-of-fact approach to archaeology, she hadn't considered that this was possibly the first time these children had seen a skeleton. "We all will," Maria said quietly. "But it's okay. If we're loved when we're alive, we'll be loved after we die. See how much someone loved this person? See how she was buried with a bowl and some jewelry?"

"I still love Daddy," Flo said.

"See what I mean?" Maria asked.

"I still love him, too," Simon said. Tears slipped down his cheeks, and he licked them off his lips. "It's not fair he's going to look like that. Do you think he does already?"

"No," Maria said.

"If he looks like that, how will I find him when I get to heaven?" Flo asked.

"People don't change in heaven," Maria said. "Everyone looks exactly the way you remember them looking."

"Only happy," Simon said. "They have the same faces they had when they were alive, but in heaven they're happy."

Maria's heart quickened, waiting for Simon to go on. When he did not, she touched his shoulder, to encourage him. "Why, honey?" she asked. "Wasn't your daddy happy?"

Simon shook his head.

"He was not happy," Flo said, also shaking her head.

"Do you know why?" Maria asked. "Do you have any idea why he wasn't?"

"Because of Mommy," Simon said.

"Mommy *tried* to make him happy, though," Flo said, her voice thin and strained. "She knew his favorite things. Remember the fish eggs?"

"Caviar from Russia," Simon said. "Some people just have it for special occasions, but we had it all the time."

"And she bought him lots of presents," Flo said, sounding like an old person reminiscing about the good times. "She sent away for things. They came from all over the world. Daddy had the softest pajamas and scarves and ties of anyone."

"Then why do you say he was unhappy because of your mommy? What did he do?" Maria asked. She wanted to prod them, to make sure they kept going. She had the feeling they were finally ready to talk, that she was about to learn what Gordon had done to them; every nerve in her body tingled.

"It made him unhappy when Mommy hit us," Flo said.

"Daddy always said she'd go to jail for what she did to us," Simon said, his voice turning sullen and bitter again. "He said she'd wind up there."

Maria felt dizzy. She could hear her own heart in her own ears. "But Sophie could never hit you," she said.

Flo nodded. "Oh yes she could. She always did."

They're lying, Maria thought. *Just like their parents.* She felt like taking off in her boat, leaving them on the island. But she forced herself to stay, to keep her voice steady. "That time Sophie was in the hospital, when she said she fell down the stairs?" Maria began. "And you had bruises all over you, Flo? You said she fell into you. Did she? Is that what happened?"

Flo's hands were clenched into fists. She shook her head; she was crying too hard to talk.

"Mommy gave Flo a good pounding that day," Simon said.

Maria's mind spun back to winter, to the time she had over-heard Sophie and Flo in the Hatuquitit Library, and she knew the children were telling the truth. "Then what happened to your mommy?" Maria asked, suddenly calm. "How did she wind up in the hospital?"

"Daddy pushed her down the cellar stairs," Simon said. "To punish her for hurting Flo. He pushed her, then he closed the door on her and he said we had to leave her there for a long time to make sure she had time to think about what she'd done."

Flo cried harder now, and Maria held her tight and rocked her, wanting somehow to make up to them a fraction of what had been done by their parents. She knew she should be shocked by what Simon had told her, but she was beyond shock. She was thinking of Sophie's impassioned speech to her and Peter, about how Gordon's parents had locked him in the cellar for hours at a stretch; Maria found herself wondering whether Sophie and Gordon kept an artificial Christmas tree decorated all year in their basement.

"I wonder if Daddy was buried with things for his last journey," Simon said after a while.

"It's not done much these days," Maria said.

"Why not? It's a good idea," Simon said. "I'd want my skateboard. And a TV."

"I'd want my tutu," Flo said. The sobs had stopped, but she continued to silently cry, sucking her thumb.

"I'll bet Daddy has things with him," Simon said confidently. "You said people who were loved in life were buried with things. And we all loved him."

"What about your mommy?" Maria asked, afraid to hear the answer. "Would she have things with her?"

"Of course," Simon said. "We love her, too."

"Yes, we do," Flo said.

25

ON FRIDAY AFTERNOON MARIA HAD TO DROP FLO at Toby Jenkins's house for the birthday party, take Simon downtown for his first appointment with Dr. Middleton, shop for groceries, pick up both children, and have them ready by six o'clock, when Ed and Gwen would take them to their house for the night. Duncan was coming for dinner—it would be the first time they'd seen each other since he'd moved out of his house.

The moment Maria awakened, the schedule closed in on her. She tried to map it out in her mind, like an agenda with columns of hours and corresponding appointments. But all she could think about was that it was Sophie, not Gordon, who had hit the children. Maria had told no one, and she wanted to find some way to tell the children that they should keep it a secret from Ed and Gwen.

Simon waited in the car while Maria and Flo walked, hand in hand, up the flagstone walk to Toby Jenkins's house. Toby's mother, prematurely gray with a dazzling smile, answered the door.

"You must be Maria," she said, shaking Maria's hand. "I'm Olivia Jenkins."

"Hi," Maria said.

"Run inside, Flo," Olivia said, fluttering one of Flo's braids with her fingers. "The party can't start without you."

Clutching Toby's present, wrapped in paper printed with lavender teddy bears, Flo hesitated in the doorway.

"Go on, honey," Maria said. But she kept her hand protectively on Flo's shoulder. Maria knew how Flo felt, entering a roomful of kids who knew about what Sophie had done, and Maria's stomach tensed. Mrs. Cannon had told Maria that Simon and Flo were being teased at school.

"Why don't you stay for coffee?" Olivia said. "Some of the other mothers are here."

"Simon's waiting outside, but thanks anyway," Maria said, noting "other mothers."

She walked with Flo as far as the living room, where a group of noisy six-year-olds were playing with balloons. Several young women sat talking around a low table. Alicia Murdoch was one of them. She glanced at Maria. Her gaze seemed quizzical, and it lingered, as if Alicia were trying to place her. Perhaps she remembered seeing Maria at Gordon's funeral. Maria, shaken, complimented Olivia on the small landscape hanging near the door. She watched Flo hand Toby the present and ease into the party, and then with one backward glance at the woman whose husband she loved, Maria said good-bye to Olivia and left.

Feeling like she'd made a quick getaway, Maria jumped into the car. Simon didn't look over at her; he sat staring out the car window. The sight of him—sullen and silent—made Maria's heart sink. His hair had fallen into his eyes, and he tossed his head in a manner that conjured Gordon exactly. Maria kept glancing at him, trying to tell what he was thinking.

She felt a blast of anger. She hadn't bargained for all this: Simon's silence, Flo's bedwetting, the fact that other kids were mean to them. She couldn't wait till six o'clock, when Ed and Gwen would take the kids and Duncan would come to Squaw's Landing.

"You must have a lot to tell Dr. Middleton," Maria said.

"Not really," Simon said, frowning out the window.

"You can tell her anything. She'll keep it secret."

Simon said nothing; he worked his finger into a small ragged hole on the knee of his maroon denim pants. "What does she know about me?" he asked finally.

"She knows about your parents," Maria said.

"Then what's there to tell?" Simon asked, his voice straining.

"You can talk to her, Simon. Tell her how you feel."

"Feel?"

"Yeah. If you feel sad, or worried. When you miss your parents. When you get mad at me. Anything."

"It sounds stupid. Talking about things just makes them worse," he said bitterly.

"That's not true. You might think it's easier to watch TV and pretend the bad things are fine, but you know they come back when the program is over."

"No, because there's always another program," he said.

And what could Maria say to that? The way Simon could sit for hours in front of the television made her want to smash the damn set. "Maybe you could talk about the kids teasing you."

"It's all because Mom's in jail, and I just want to *forget* about it!" The strain in his voice set loose in Maria a wave of hatred for Sophie. She hadn't visited Sophie since the children's revelation; she couldn't stand to see her.

Maria parked the car. She and Simon stared for a few seconds at Dr. Middleton's building, a big white house with a widow's walk. Wordlessly they walked up the sidewalk. Inside, the waiting room had posters of boats and flowers. Maria thumbed through *Highlights,* and Simon played with an Etch-a-Sketch.

An inner door opened, and a tall, beautiful woman stepped out. Maria guessed Dr. Middleton was about her own age.

"Hello, Maria?" she said.

Maria shook her hand, and then the doctor focused on Simon. "Hello, Simon," she said, smiling into his eyes.

"Hi," Simon said, slouching.

"Would you like to come in?" the doctor asked.

Simon shrugged. Maria started to follow, but the doctor stopped her. "I thought Simon and I would talk alone today, if that's okay with him."

"With me?" Simon asked, surprised, looking at Maria.

"Would that be okay?" Maria asked.

"Sure," Simon said. And without waving good-bye to Maria, he walked into Dr. Middleton's office and she closed the door behind them.

Maria bought lettuce and tomatoes, potatoes, swordfish for the grill, and a chocolate cake. She shopped in a hurry because she wanted to be outside Dr. Middleton's office when Simon finished. Waiting in the car, she watched people walking down the street. Every so often someone would recognize her or the car, glance back for another furtive look, and keep walking. Maria had been buying her groceries at the shopping center near Blackwood, just to avoid the town's prying eyes. The story wasn't nearly as big outside Hatuquitit.

Hallie and Nell came ambling along. Nell pushed Andy in a stroller. Hallie wore a large sun hat and dark glasses. They were deep in conversation. Maria climbed out of the car.

"Where have you been?" Hallie asked. "I was calling you all morning."

"Errands," Maria said.

Hallie glanced around. This stretch of Summer Street was mainly residential. Many of the large houses had been divided into apartments or condominiums, or converted into doctors' offices. "What are you doing here?" Hallie asked.

"Simon's in there, seeing Dr. Middleton—a psychologist."

Hallie thinned her lips. "I don't like that," she said.

"I think it's a great idea," Nell said.

"Things are bad enough without people thinking the kids are all mixed up."

"Mom, you've got to be kidding," Maria said, not believing that even Hallie could be so ridiculous.

Hallie's sunglasses slid down her nose. Behind them her eyes were wild, confused. "It's a stigma the kids will carry their whole lives. The fact they had to get psychiatric help. It might even keep them out of college."

"Mom!" Maria said, shocked by her mother's skewed logic.

"I know I'm old-fashioned, but when I was young, families took care of their own problems. They didn't go running to psychiatrists."

"I think this is too big for us to handle alone," Maria said with exaggerated steadiness to hide the alarm she felt. She thought of Peter's theory, that Hallie was denying how awful things were to preserve her own equilibrium.

"Notice all the people who walk past without speaking to me," Hallie said. "I never thought the day would come when I'd have to hang my head in Hatuquitit."

Maria, who had been feeling the same thing, stared at Nell, hoping for support.

"It won't last forever," Nell said. "People don't know what to say. I'd been thinking the other mothers who take their kids to day care were snubbing me, but yesterday when I picked up Andy one of them told me how sorry she was about Sophie and everything. I think she really meant it."

Hallie glanced at Dr. Middleton's building. "They like to blame the mothers. I'm sure he's in there telling Simon that Sophie's problems are all because of me."

"Dr. Middleton is a woman, and I'm sure she knows that nothing is as simple as that," Maria said, though sometimes she wondered whether it wasn't. A UPS truck had parked beside them, and its driver began unloading cartons. His presence made everyone conscious of how their voices had risen.

"Are you coming for Sunday dinner?" Hallie asked less shrilly, trying to compose herself.

"Yes," Maria said.

"And tonight is the night?" Hallie pressed. Maria knew she was referring to Ed and Gwen taking the kids. Maria nodded.

"She must be going crazy over it," Nell said, referring to Sophie.

Maria had the sense they were talking in code. She imagined the seventeenth century, when Charles Slocum had bought land from Nasseequidgeon. Three women discussing trouble on

Hatuquitit's Summer Street could easily have been taken for witches.

"I'd better go inside and wait for Simon," Maria said.

"Good-bye, dear," Hallie said. "We'll see you Sunday."

"Have fun tonight," Nell said, waving.

"What are you talking about?" Hallie asked as they walked away. Maria turned her back and headed up the walk, leaving Nell to explain.

Simon seemed more relaxed when he came out of the doctor's office. If he didn't exactly smile, he nodded easily when Maria told him she had seen Hallie, Nell, and Andy. When they stopped to pick up Flo, he got out of the car to pet the Jenkinses' collie.

"Carol and Alicia are still here," Olivia said. "Would you like to have a glass of wine with us?"

"Thanks," Maria said quickly. "But I have to get the kids ready to spend tonight with their grandparents." Seeing Alicia again only hours before Duncan arrived was more than she could face.

Olivia smiled. "I know how you feel. I get into a state every time I send Toby to her father's for the weekend. I care more about her making a good impression on him than I ever did when he and I were married."

"I'm afraid I'll forget to pack something stupid, like their toothbrushes, and they'll say I'm not a fit aunt."

"How long are they staying?" Olivia asked.

"Just tonight."

"That's a cinch. Just stand in their room with the bag in your hand, and run through every single thing they're likely to need in a twenty-four-hour period. Pajamas, robe, slippers, books, the toys they sleep with, play clothes for tomorrow, extra socks, bathing suits if their grandparents like the beach . . . you'll do fine."

"Thanks, Olivia," Maria said, craning her neck to see into the house. She heard kids running down the hall.

"We had a little trouble," Olivia said in a low voice. "Patty asked Flo why her mother was in jail—believe it or not, I don't think she meant to be cruel. But Flo acted as if she didn't know what Patty meant, said her mother was at home. Then they forgot all about it. Here she is!" Olivia said, touching Flo's back as she ran past.

Maria nodded gratefully and said good-bye. But her mind was already on something else. Walking toward Simon and the collie, with Flo's little hand in hers, she was rehearsing how she would tell these children to protect the mother who had failed to protect them.

Simon's anxiety increased by the minute. Waiting for the Littlefields by Maria's front door, he and Flo squashed their duffle bags by sitting on them. Simon kept glancing at Maria, a frown on his face.

"What's the matter?" Maria asked.

"Do Ed and Gwen hate Mommy?" he asked.

"I don't know," Maria answered.

"They must," he said. "Because she killed Daddy. I mean, wouldn't Mommy hate someone who killed me or Flo?"

Maria wanted to hug him for his logic. She wondered whether he'd discussed this with Dr. Middleton. "I'm sure she would."

"They wouldn't understand," Simon said. "They weren't there."

"That's true," Maria said neutrally, wanting Simon to keep talking.

"I don't want them knowing the bad stuff Mommy did," Simon said. "Because they'll just blame her for everything."

"Blame her for what?" Flo asked.

"For everything," Simon said. He gazed at Flo for a few seconds. Maria could see him wrestling with the same dilemma she had confronted an hour earlier: how to tell Flo to keep her mouth shut. "You don't want Mommy in jail forever, do you?" he asked.

Flo said nothing, but shook her head solemnly.

"Then don't tell about the hitting," he said.

"Why did you tell me about it?" Maria asked, sitting on the floor between the children, amazed that he had come to this decision on his own.

"Because you're her sister. You know she's not a bad person," Simon said simply.

Too moved to speak, Maria hugged him because she hadn't known Simon realized that.

Ed and Gwen pulled into the driveway and sat in their car until the children ran out to them. Maria watched them leave. The children waved at her out the back window, but Ed and Gwen stared straight ahead. Abstractedly Maria wandered after the car, down the driveway, and stood by her mailbox watching the Littlefields disappear down the road. Opening the mailbox, she discovered a letter from Aldo.

The timing was bad. Maria didn't feel like reading a letter from Aldo when Duncan was about to show up. She stuffed it into her back pocket, strolled around her house to the front porch. Settling into a woven metal chair, she faced the Haunted Isles. In spite of herself, she nearly opened Aldo's letter. She wanted to know what he would say about her theory of the murdered Pequot woman. But then Duncan appeared.

She heard him knock at the back door. "I'm out here," she called, and he came around the house. The sight of him after such a long time apart—when so much had happened—brought tears to her eyes. She wiped them away, smiled as he approached.

"Boy, is it great to see you," he said, taking her in his arms. He had changed after work from his summer-weight Bold and Intrepid Boatworks T-shirt into a red polo shirt; his hair was wet from the shower, but he still smelled faintly of teak polish and diesel oil, and she closed her eyes as he rocked her back and forth, and took it all in.

"All day long I've been running errands like crazy, but I kept thinking that tonight I'd see you."

"I brought some wine," Duncan said, letting go of her just enough to hold up a brown bag.

"Have a seat," Maria said, easing away, thinking he'd like to stare at the sea after a hard day at work, "and I'll open the bottle."

"No way, I'm coming with you," he said, throwing his arms around her again. He kissed her on the mouth, and she felt flooded with desire and emotion. *Don't let me cry,* she thought, steadying herself. Then they walked into the house.

"Well, this is where you live," Duncan said.

"It's hard to believe you haven't been inside before," Maria said.

Since he had his arm around her and didn't seem inclined to let go, he couldn't explore very well. But he seemed to take notice of the big windows, the furniture, photographs on the mantel of Maria's family. Maria got the wineglasses down, and Duncan took his arm away long enough to open the bottle of white wine.

"Duncan, did you . . ." Maria began, unable to wait any longer.

Duncan frowned, working on the cork, pain just behind his eyes. "God, telling Jamey was horrible. Alicia made me say it's just a trial separation, to let him hold out hope that I might be coming back. We had a huge fight about it—I told her we should tell Jamey the truth, that we're filing for divorce. But she wanted to break it to him gently."

"Maybe it's Alicia who wants to hold out hope," Maria said, watching Duncan's face.

He nodded, looking away. "It's possible. She didn't seem unhappy when I left. She was in the kitchen, talking on the phone with her friend. She yelled good-bye to me, just as if I were leaving for work. But she's called me every night since."

Maria took Duncan's arm. "Let's go outside and drink wine and talk about my husband and your wife. I just got a letter from Aldo." She wanted to make light of it, but her heart felt heavy.

They settled their chairs side by side, so that their elbows could touch. Maria was barefoot. Duncan kicked off his sneakers and gently rested his foot on Maria's. They stared at the sun, bright orange-yellow, about an hour from going down.

"Would you put it back together if you could?" Maria asked, almost afraid to hear.

"I can't remember how it felt when it was together," Duncan said, squeezing her hand as they fell silent. "I'm not sure it ever really was . . . together."

Maria closed her eyes—*together* . . . What did it mean, anyway? She thought of Sophie and winced.

"How is your sister?" Duncan asked.

Maria tried to reply, but she had a lump in her throat.

As if Duncan realized the question was too big for her to answer, he took her hand and changed tacks. "How's her defense going? I saw Steve coming out of the jail on my way here."

"Whenever I see Steve Grunwald, I think of him managing the baseball team, lugging burlap bags full of bats and bases through the halls. It scares me to think of him in charge of Sophie's case."

"Next to Peter, he's probably the best lawyer in town," Duncan said.

"I don't know," Maria said. "Maybe we should have hired someone with more experience in criminal cases."

Duncan held her hand tighter. "Steve's fine. He'll take care of her. How's she doing with it?"

Maria shook her head. "She's not really cooperating. I thought she'd be going crazy, wanting to get out. But she refuses to let us post bail. She's in a daze or something."

"That doesn't surprise me," Duncan said. "It must be hell, not seeing her kids. It's only been since Monday and I . . ." He trailed off.

"You miss Jamey?"

He nodded. "I hate being away from him. It's the worst part. You never had kids." It was a statement, not a question, but he looked up for her response.

"No, we never did. Keeping Flo and Simon with me, sometimes I wonder how Sophie . . . They're relentless—they're always *there*." She paused, thinking. "And other times, I'll be reading a story to Flo and she'll fall asleep against me. She cuddles like a puppy. Or Simon will come out of the doctor's looking calmer, less upset, and I'll really have the feeling I did something good by sending him . . ."

"You're right," Duncan said. "They're relentless. They need so much, and you're the only one who can give it to them."

"Their parents, you mean?"

"Or whoever takes care of them. For Simon and Flo right now, you're it."

That's true, Maria thought, but suddenly she found herself thinking of Hallie. After Malcolm died, Hallie had sort of disappeared with him. Maria had been old enough to take care of herself, but maybe Sophie had suffered more than Maria knew. Maybe Sophie had just pretended to be strong enough to look after Hallie. Who knew? Maria placed her glass on the slatted floor.

"I'm going to light the charcoal," she said, standing. "We're having swordfish."

"I'll help," Duncan said. "I cook swordfish nearly as well as I make canned chowder."

"That was the best meal I've ever had," Maria said, hiding her face in Duncan's shoulder. And both of them laughed, remembering that meal on the boat when neither of them had eaten a bite.

Waiting for the coals to turn white, Duncan and Maria watched the sun, glowing like fire, go down behind Lookout.

"Once my father and I saw a sunset like that," Maria said, "and he said, 'Tomorrow's going to be a scorcher.'" The memory came out of nowhere. She was two, standing on the front seat of her father's car, her arm crooked around his neck as he drove home from the beach one July night when Hallie, pregnant with Sophie, had been too hot to cook. Maria remembered digging a pit in the sand, gathering driftwood for a fire, and roasting hot dogs on sticks.

"Your father died when we were in high school, didn't he?" Duncan asked.

"Eighth grade," Maria said.

"My father died the year before," Duncan said.

"Really? I didn't know—"

"Yeah. I remember feeling sorry for you when it happened. You always acted so happy, taking part in all those school activities, but I knew how sad you really felt. Because it had happened to me."

"I don't know," Maria said. She remembered how it had been, waiting for Malcolm to die. One night she had stared at the ceiling in terror, knowing that soon—perhaps at that instant—his breathing would stop. "He was old and very sick," Maria said. "When he finally died, it felt like a relief. Isn't that awful? It made me so guilty, feeling that way. Especially because everyone else in the house was a wreck. My mother practically fell apart. So did my brother and sister. The strange part is, I'd always thought Peter and Sophie felt the same way I did."

"It must be terrible, watching someone you love die slowly," Duncan said.

"Did your father—"

"A car crash," Duncan said. "Late one night, on his way home. He died right there, and we never saw him again."

They stood on the porch, staring out to sea, remembering. After a minute Maria turned her back on the sunset. "I want to kiss you," she said.

Duncan pulled her against him, kissing the top of her head, her forehead, her cheeks, finally her lips. She trailed her finger down his spine until she came to his belt, and then she slipped her hand into the back of his pants. Duncan pulled away, surprise in his eyes.

"Do we have a few minutes before the charcoal is ready?" Maria asked. "Can we go upstairs?" Her eyes darted from Duncan's to the screen door. She wanted to dispel the feelings sweeping over her—love and sorrow for Malcolm, Sophie's children, her entire family. She fought down panic and tried to breathe evenly.

"It's all right," Duncan whispered in her ear. "We can do

anything you want." Then, lifting her, he walked across the porch with Maria in his arms. She held on to his neck as he opened the door with a gentle kick and carried her up the stairs to the barn room.

A cool breeze ruffled curtains at the open windows, and the beacon at Little Harbor flashed across the Sound. Duncan laid Maria on the bed; she smiled up at him.

"No one's ever carried me to bed," she said.

"You're light as a feather," he said, panting quietly.

"Need a minute to catch your breath?" she asked.

He touched his heart. "Not from carrying you."

They wiggled out of their clothes, kissing on the bed. Every so often Maria pulled back to look down at their bodies together. In the evening light their tans looked darker. Her breasts and hips, Duncan's ass—the parts protected from the sun—were white as pearls, and Maria felt oddly excited to look at them.

She lay on her back while Duncan kissed her, starting with her toes. When he reached her calves, he rolled her over and tickled the back of her knees with his tongue. Maria felt a tingle shoot through her body. Turning over, tugging on Duncan's shoulders, she moaned. "Come up here," she said. "Hold me."

He seemed not to hear but continued up her legs inch by inch, kissing and licking with infinite leisure. Maria felt wild, exquisitely excited in the strangest spots—her ankles, nipples, the hairs on her head. Her head tossed back and forth on the pillow; she felt like a prisoner of Duncan and her own desire, and she thought she might scream. When she thought she couldn't stand it anymore, she sat half-upright. "Please," she said. She was going to beg him to stop when he took her hand and smiled at her.

"Do you trust me?" Duncan said. "I love you. I want to do this for you."

Maria studied his eyes, searching for what was familiar in them. She knew why she wanted reassurance: because she felt like someone new, she had never gone this far before. She felt thrilled, not only by what Duncan was doing but by the way he felt about her. She could see it in his eyes, shining in the darkness. Maria nodded. Then she lay back on the pillow. The sensations came back as strong as before, and Maria knew that she was going to lose control, and knew that that was okay.

26

IT WASN'T UNTIL THE NEXT MORNING, AFTER A
midnight supper of swordfish and a night full of making love,
that Maria reluctantly opened Aldo's letter while Duncan slept
beside her.

Dear Maria,

> *Your letter disturbs me—for so many reasons! First,
> especially, poor Sophie. Poor Gordon. I pray for them, for
> their children, above all for you, bella. I know this time
> cannot be easy for you. I think of all the Christmas holidays
> we passed with your family, of the happiness it gave you to
> be among them. I would see the sadness in your smile—
> with the Darks you were always smiling, but often sadly. I
> know the pain I caused you, taking you away from them.
> You will be frowning as you read this, angry with me for
> imagining I could make you do something you did not
> want to do. I know, Maria, that you wanted to come with
> me. I know, too, that you did it for love. That I did not love
> you properly back is something I must live with.*

> *You were never happy. Admit that someday. In England,
> in Peru, in Paris: never happy. Only when we boarded the
> plane for New York would I see the real sparks. Sparks on
> the plane, contentment in your mother's house. Then,
> finally, sadness because soon it would be time to leave.*

How are you holding up? What a strong one you are!
Sophie is in jail. Perhaps it gives her comfort to look out her
window and see your mother's lights through the trees. All
the times I saw that jail, I never imagined your sister would
be a prisoner there. She is lucky to have you taking care of
Simon and Flo, but do not imagine she is grateful.

Maria, you will not want to hear this: Sophie is envious
of you. Yes, she has the locally prominent husband, the
adorable children, the pretty house. But think: Would that
be enough for you if your sister was successful and you were
not? Remember, bella, *what ambitions your mother had*
for Sophie. In her darkest heart, Sophie must feel like a
failure for not meeting them, especially in light of your
success.

And now you have her children, too.

I do not say you should give them up. I'm sure it is best
for all that they stay with you. Poor Simon and Flo, it is
impossible to think of their parents hurting them. Just as I
find it crazy to think of Gordon harming Sophie. To me,
Gordon seemed merely shy and harmless, totally without
passion. Yes, those children must stay with you. (I think of
you kissing their foreheads in bed every night, and I cry to
think that you are not kissing the foreheads of your own
children.)

Now, a warning about your field notes. Often you have
brought much imagination, much of yourself, to the
excavation. I have watched you do it before, over and over
again at Chavín de Huántar, and it is your great gift. But
this time, practically nothing! So you've found a murdered
Pequot woman, buried on an island where there was no
known burial ground. Why is she there? Examine the grave
goods carefully, with an eye open for clues. Certainly the
person who buried her would have left something for you to
find. Remember that talismans for the last journey say
more about a culture or individuals within it than any

*other artifacts. Usually you would see this. That you have
not is due to your emotional state and because I am not
there to set you straight.*

*If I had known what was going to happen, I would have
postponed our annulment. I know that it is for the best,
that you will be happier within the bosom of your family,
nearby your beloved Long Island Sound. But I still, and will
always, love you.*

*With tender kisses,
Aldo*

Maria felt Duncan touch her leg with his toe. "Good morning," he said.

"I probably shouldn't have read this with you sleeping right there," she said. "But I've been awake for ages."

"Did it upset you?"

"Well, a little. Aldo writes exactly the way he talks, and now I feel like he's right here in the room with us."

"He's not," Duncan said.

"I know."

"On the other hand, I woke up a few hours ago and thought I heard Alicia and Jamey downstairs making breakfast."

"Do you wish they were?" Maria asked.

"No," Duncan said.

They hugged. She had once had the naive notion that love affairs were supposed to be carefree. Theirs had started out that way—on the water. But Aldo had brought up things from their past that Duncan couldn't possibly know yet—perhaps would never know. Aldo was familiar. And now, lying in bed on a sunny summer morning, Maria felt a little scared for the amount of power she'd let Duncan have over her last night.

"That's not to say I don't wish for breakfast," Duncan said, kissing her, climbing out of bed. "I'm going to make us coffee and toast, and I'll bring it back to bed—how's that?"

"Sounds great, but I'm coming with you," Maria said, following him, not wanting to be alone with Aldo's letter.

*   *   *

The Bold and Intrepid Boatworks did land-office business on early summer Saturdays, so Duncan had to leave right after breakfast. He stood by the door, dressed for work in his red polo shirt and khakis, and not only because it was a weekend. Maria had put on white trousers and a loose white shirt to reflect the sun. Her forecast last night had been right: the day was going to be hot and muggy, unusual so early in the season.

"Will I see you tonight?" Duncan asked.

"The kids will be here," Maria said.

"That's right." Duncan gave her a hug, rocked her back and forth. They smiled at each other, not wanting to part. "The thing is, I don't want you to go through this alone. I want to be with you."

"I don't know," Maria said, fighting a gut feeling that told her that seeing their aunt with Jamey's father might upset Simon and Flo.

"Well, you're not married anymore, and I'm officially separated . . ."

"I'll ask their mother," Maria said.

Duncan kissed her good-bye, a long kiss that ended in an even longer hug, and when he finally walked down the path to his truck, Maria hated to see him go.

There were plenty of things Maria could have done with her day: return to the grave, join Nell at the beach, write back to Aldo, examine the grave goods she had already excavated. But as soon as Duncan's truck pulled out of her driveway, she climbed into her car and drove to the jail.

It seemed that all Sophie wanted to talk about was Bess, her cellmate. Maria listened, frustrated at first, but then lulled because Sophie's monologue gave her the chance to rehearse how she would bring up what the children had told her about Sophie.

"She's a character!" Sophie was saying. "I mean it! We stay up half the night talking—the matron is threatening to separate us, just like Mom when you and I refused to sleep. She's had such an interesting life. She was born in Jacksonville, and her mother died when she was eleven. Her mother was murdered by a robber. So Bess was sent to a foster home, and the *same night* she arrived, her foster mother was attacked by her foster brother. Can you imagine that?"

"No, that's horrible," Maria said.

"So then she came up here to live with her grandmother, who sounds so wonderful. She loves Bess just like a daughter, but they don't have the normal mother-daughter bullshit you and I have with Hallie."

"What do you mean?" Maria asked.

"Oh, you know," Sophie said. "The complications . . . Hating Mom. Anyway, Bess had Benjamin when she was fourteen. She never married his father. . . ."

"What's happening with your defense?" Maria interrupted.

"Why are you being like that? Aren't you happy I have a friend here?" Sophie asked, her expression bruised.

"I'm thrilled," Maria said, boiling over. "But meanwhile your kids are trying to patch their lives together, I'm with them night and day and I don't have a clue about what to do, and you haven't even asked about them."

"Oh, Maria," Sophie said, her face falling.

Maria instantly regretted her outburst. Now she wanted to hold Sophie's hand, but she didn't dare take it. Sophie was too obviously trying to compose herself.

"I'm sorry," Maria said. "I'm really sorry, Sophie."

Sophie nodded.

"I'm just so frustrated, listening to you talk about life here, about your cellmate, as if you really fit in here."

"I do," Sophie said. "Believe it or not, I like it here."

"Why?" Maria asked. "Why won't you let Steve try to get you out?"

"I don't know," Sophie replied. But Maria had the feeling that she did know and just didn't want to tell her. Was it because she felt safe? Because she believed she deserved punishment?

"Tell me what Steve says," Maria said. "What's going to happen? How's your defense coming?"

"Oh, I don't know," Sophie said. "The whole thing has to do with intent. If Gordon died in the bedroom, from gunshot wounds, it's a lesser charge because then I didn't have time to form intent. I just grabbed the gun and shot. But if he died in the driveway, it's worse. That's the part that's complicating things. The fact that I pushed him out the window and ran over him with the car. Considering that I dislocated my shoulder doing it, you can't say I didn't plan to push him out the window. But I know he died in the bedroom."

"Sophie," Maria said gently. "Try to remember that I saw what he did to you. I saw the cord he tied around your neck. I'm going to be a witness for you."

"The cord," Sophie said in a dreamy voice that frightened Maria. "Have you ever let someone take you past your limit?"

"What do you mean?"

"I mean you put yourself—your life, even—in someone else's hands. You trust them that much."

Maria stared. Was that what she had done last night with Duncan? But she shook herself out of it; she could hardly compare Duncan's eroticism with what Sophie had let herself endure. "Are you telling me you liked that thing with the cord?" she asked.

"It's all relative," Sophie said. "It was a game I played to please Gordon. I liked making him happy."

"He hurt you that night," Maria said. "I could see . . ."

Sophie's hand trailed across her collarbone, then dropped into her lap. She frowned at the Formica tabletop. "A trial will be terrible for the kids. The things that will come out."

"Tell me," Maria said. "Help me prepare them."

"I deserved a lot of what I got," Sophie said.

"Are you talking about . . . hitting the kids?" Maria asked.

Sophie's head snapped up. "They told you?"

"Yes, but no matter what you did, you didn't deserve the things Gordon did to you. They told me he pushed you down the stairs. And I saw him hurting you that night in your bedroom."

"I started off spanking them," Sophie said, sounding distant. "When they were naughty. The books say to punish kids by giving them time-outs—ten-minute intervals in solitary confinement, so they have a chance to know they've done bad. Nell does it with Andy. But it never worked with Simon or Flo. So I'd spank them."

Maria frowned. She could understand how children could misconstrue, how they could confuse spanking and hitting. Especially if their father was coaching them. "So you were just disciplining them?" she asked, wanting it to be the answer.

"No, Maria." Sophie's eyes were piercing. "I was hurting them."

"How could you hurt Simon and Flo?"

"'How could you hurt Simon and Flo?'" Sophie repeated, mocking Maria with an expression so cruel that Maria could imagine how frightened the children must have been. "Do you think I wanted to? You think I *set out* to hurt them? I love my kids." Now her voice fell. "Sometimes I didn't know where to stop. I really did spank them to make them stop misbehaving. But their misbehavior frustrated me so much sometimes . . . it used to drive Gordon completely crazy when they'd act like wild animals before bed every night."

"What do you mean?"

"Gordon used to say I couldn't control my own kids."

"They were his kids, too," Maria said, stopping short of blaming Gordon for what Sophie had done. Although she wanted to curse him for it, she knew that the responsibility was her sister's.

"Gordon meant everything to me," Sophie said, almost absently. "Even now, even after what I've done. He was a perfectionist, and I tried to be perfect."

Maria wanted to ask how stealing from her family and hurting her children had fit into Sophie's idea of perfection, but she couldn't bear to do it. Staring at her, Maria tried to calculate how many pounds Sophie had lost since coming to jail. Ten? Twelve? She pictured Sophie as a thin teenager. She had sometimes wondered whether Sophie had had anorexia nervosa. She had seemed so perfect, as if she'd never wanted to lose control.

"You've lost a lot of weight," Maria said.

"I'd let myself go . . ." Sophie said.

"You must have been so unhappy," Maria said, thinking of the wedding pictures. Sophie's dress was a copy of Jacqueline Kennedy's, with little cap sleeves tilting off her shoulders, and Maria remembered how slight Sophie had looked, how pretty and happy.

"Would you mind if we talked about something other than my rotundity?" Sophie asked. "Tell me about Simon and Flo."

"They're having a hard time," Maria said gently. "Simon saw Dr. Middleton on Friday, and Flo's going on Monday. I'm sure you know that they spent last night with Ed and Gwen."

"I know."

The children would be at her house in less than two hours. Maria knew she should get home to wait for them. She gazed at Sophie and saw her lip quivering. *How much more can she take?* Maria wondered, suddenly afraid. "You haven't asked," Maria said, "but I'm sure you wonder how they feel about you. They love you."

"Have they said that?" Sophie asked, staring down at the table as if she feared seeing the truth in Maria's eyes.

"Yes, they have. They told me. But they're overwhelmed. They want you to come home."

"Thank you for telling me," Sophie said, finally looking up. She and Maria stared into each other's eyes for a few seconds, not smiling, but exchanging something as strong as an embrace.

Maria stood to leave. "You look good in white," Sophie said.

"It's hot out."

"Will you wear white at your second wedding?"

Maria laughed. "Sophie," she said, shaking her head.

"So, it's going well," Sophie said, smiling back.

"It's fine. Duncan . . ."

"Duncan—what?"

"He's good to me," Maria whispered. Her throat ached, to be having this conversation with Sophie *here.*

"You deserve that. You do, Maria."

"Thank you. He moved out," Maria said. "We spent last night together. But I don't want to when the kids are there."

"Maybe not, but at least have him over for a meal. Make him something fabulous." She paused. "I like Duncan. It would be good for the kids to have him around."

Maria nodded gratefully.

"Don't let Mom find out, that's all," Sophie said, sounding suddenly bitter.

"About Duncan? I already know she doesn't approve," Maria said.

"Duncan has nothing to do with it," Sophie said. "It's your being happy that she minds."

"Sophie!" Maria said, stunned.

"Wait till you've lived in Hatuquitit a while longer," Sophie said. "You'll see what I mean."

Maria left then. Driving home, she was shaking—she'd never get over seeing Sophie in there, and she felt shocked and sickened by the way her sister was talking. But it wasn't until she reached the Lovecraft Wildlife Refuge that she remembered what Sophie had said earlier, at the beginning of the visit: that she hated Hallie.

27

SUNDAY SUPPER AT THE DARKS' WAS USUALLY ROAST beef in the winter and fish on the grill in the summer. Peter, Simon, and Maria stood in the driveway, cleaning a striped bass Peter and Simon had caught that morning. Nell and Hallie were making a salad in the kitchen. Julian had taken Flo and Andy for a walk to Bell Stream.

"What a great fish," Maria said.

"It's forty inches long," Simon said, watching Peter clean it. "The biggest fish I've ever caught."

"What did you use?"

"A Kastmaster," Peter said. "We were standing out on the point, casting into a school of blues, getting nothing. No luck at all till Simon threw it way out, beyond the blues, and caught this guy."

"I was good, right, Uncle Peter?"

"Right, Simon."

"Flo caught one, too. I'm going to run and find her, okay?"

"Okay," Maria said, patting his head and watching him run off. Then she turned to her brother.

"What does Steve say about Sophie's case?" she asked.

"The good news—if you can call it good—is that Gordon was dead before she pushed him out the window." Peter lowered his voice and glanced furtively around. "I just can't picture her doing it, can you?"

"No," Maria said. She couldn't, any of it: the rage in Sophie's eyes, the gun firing again and again, Gordon's bloody body tumbling out the bedroom window, Sophie starting the car.

"She's so damned little," Peter said, "compared to him. He was dead weight—literally. How the hell did she lift him up and throw him out the window?"

"Can't Steve try an insanity plea?" Maria asked.

"He may not have to. It's definitely not first-degree murder." He shook his head. "I can't be objective about this. I know she's going to have to serve some time, and I can't stand it."

"I visited her yesterday," Maria said.

"So did I," Peter said. "She told me you'd been there. She . . . told me what you'd talked about."

"She did?"

"About hitting the children. That she's the one who did it, not Gordon."

Maria was silent for a few seconds, sliding the fillet knife between the fish's flesh and its bones. She washed off the blood with a hose. "Did you ever suspect?" she asked quietly.

"Yeah."

"How?" Maria asked, noticing how easily she accepted Peter's words, how incapable she was of feeling shock anymore.

"Thinking back, things that used to seem innocent. Sophie always spanked her kids, and we never agreed on that. Nell and I wouldn't spank Andy. I'd see Sophie hit Simon, really whack him. . . ." Peter grimaced at the memory. "When I'd ask her about it, she'd get defensive and say it was just her way of punishing him. But when I think back, I probably realized she was hitting him much too hard."

"Do you think you should have done something?" Maria asked, her voice rising. "To protect them?"

"Of course I should have done something. I believed her because I wanted to—all of us bought her story because we couldn't stand the alternative." His face was etched with the agony of a brother who had let his sister ruin her life.

"I'd have believed her, too," Maria agreed loyally. But if she had been here, would she have seen what none of the others could bring themselves to see?

"Fucking Gordon," Peter said. "I used to think Sophie pushed him around. You know Sophie—she's such a sparkplug. I used to think she ran the show. She took care of the house, the kids, him. I had no idea what was going on, not even after she started to change."

"I can understand believing her," Maria said. "But I can't understand how you didn't notice the changes. Or how Nell noticed but didn't do anything."

"Maria, you weren't even here. You say you care so much about Sophie, and you crucify the rest of us for not doing enough, for letting her go down the drain, but you weren't even *here.* Except for the army and law school, I've been here the whole time, and I've done whatever I could to help the family."

"Except you *didn't* help Sophie," Maria said, suddenly furious at her brother. His accusations stung, and she wanted to fight back.

"Will you guys please stop?" Nell said, coming out the back door, drying her hands on the skirt of her sundress. "Why don't you make up, and let's walk down to the brook and find everyone. Don't let the kids see you fighting."

Maria closed her eyes. Did Nell think she could just walk over and make everything all right? But she forced herself to calm down. "Hi, Nell," she said.

"Nell's right," Peter said. "Those poor kids."

"You were so good to take Simon fishing," Maria said, trying to make peace.

"Guy stuff. Very important," Nell said, wanting to exchange a smile with Maria.

Maria hosed the fish blood off her hands. "Have a nice walk," she said, and smiled sadly. "I'm staying *here.*" Accenting the *here* for Peter's sake.

Standing at the sink in Hallie's kitchen, shucking the first corn of the season, Maria felt her fury gathering. She kept glancing at her mother, who was meticulously pulling threads of corn silk from the ears Maria had already done.

"Corn has changed so," Hallie said. "When I was a tiny child, we ate Golden Bantam. It was just delicious, yellow as melted butter. My father adored it. No one knew anything about Butter and Sugar or Silver Queen."

"Why haven't you been to see Sophie?" Maria asked, breaking up Hallie's monologue.

Hallie didn't look up; she collected the silvery threads into a gossamer ponytail and smoothed it with her fingers. "Maria," she said, sounding exhausted.

"Would it be very hard for you?" Maria asked, feeling like an eagle going in for the kill.

"Yes, it would."

"Well, imagine how Sophie feels. She's right through those trees over there." Coming around the kitchen island, Maria put her arm around Hallie's shoulders and pointed at the thicket of pines. "She's right there."

"I know that," Hallie said. "I live with that every moment of the day."

"How would it be worse to see her?" Maria asked. "What you imagine may be worse than the reality."

"It couldn't possibly be," Hallie said. Her tone opened up a mysterious possibility in Maria's mind; it gave Maria the feeling that Hallie knew much more about Sophie's situation than anyone else. Maria felt alerted by the tone in her mother's voice, somewhere between resignation and incredulity.

"Tell me what you imagine," Maria said, trying to be gentle.

Hallie was a silhouette; light from the kitchen window surrounded her and made her features dark, hard to read. But when she turned her face toward Maria, her eyes were pools of sorrow. "I imagine that I have lost a daughter," Hallie said.

"Oh, Mom," Maria said. "Sophie needs you. She's as much your daughter in jail as she was before. I want you to go see her."

"I don't want to," Hallie said. "I've never been in that place. I've hated living next door to it all this time, and I hate knowing I have a child there. I can't stand thinking of her living among criminals." Hallie's voice caught. "I saw a picture of her in the

Hatuquitit Inquirer—wearing one of those baggy prison dresses. It was horrible."

"Then don't read it," Maria said.

"But I want to read about her," Hallie said. "I want to know what's happening."

Maria shook her head, to clear it. How could Hallie subject herself to the endless articles, the interviews with psychiatrists, professors, and other abused women, Dark and Littlefield family photos supplied by turncoat friends of Sophie's, when she wouldn't even visit Sophie in person? "Why don't you take a walk over someday and ask her? She's exactly the same—do you think she's become a different person?"

"I don't know," Hallie said, sounding haunted. "She had such *talent*. When she sang, you'd want to cry. Just cry. She would sing with such . . . such *heart*."

It was true. One July night when it was too hot to sleep, Maria and Sophie had snuck into the backyard to try to find some moving air, and they had walked through the dry, dewless grass toward the stream. They must have been thirteen and sixteen. They sat with their feet in the water for a while, singing songs that reminded them of boys they liked. School was out for the summer, and when Sophie sang "Moon River," Maria's heart had flooded with emotion, her eyes with tears.

"Do you think that all this happened just because Sophie didn't want to sing professionally?" Maria asked.

"I think she threw quite a lot away. She made some bad choices," Hallie said bitterly.

"You sound like you can't forgive her for them," Maria said.

"I can't, entirely," Hallie said, looking at Maria. "I'll never know how she could have squandered that talent. She didn't use it, and it started to fester inside her. This isn't only my opinion. One psychologist believes that Sophie let Gordon hit her because she considered herself worthless."

"Did you read that in the paper?"

"Yes."

"And you believe it," Maria said, feeling the breath go out of her. She had to hold herself back from telling Hallie that Sophie hated her.

"It makes sense."

"Go see Sophie," Maria said stonily. "That's what you need. Sophie needs it too; she's going through the worst time of her life."

"So am I," Hallie said. Watching her brush stray corn silk into her open palm, Maria knew that the subject was closed.

"Mom, I think you're wrong," Maria said quietly. "I think you're making a big mistake, not going to see her. I'm afraid of what's going to happen."

"What more can happen?" Hallie asked.

"She may never come home," Maria said. She'd noticed Sophie's spirit slipping away by degrees. "She doesn't care when she gets out of jail. Maybe you're right—maybe she does think she's worthless. I think she needs us to convince her she's not."

Hallie seemed to listen, but at the sound of the family returning, she turned away. Watching Hallie hurry to the back door, to tell everyone to wipe the grass clippings off their feet and to greet her grandchildren with hugs, Maria felt her eyes fill with tears, and she wondered exactly what had made the girl who used to sing with heart turn to stone.

28

WELL, IT'S BORING. I'VE BEEN TRYING TO OCCUPY my mind, remembering old stories to tell Bess and the others, but except for Bess all anyone wants to hear about is Gordon, and I just can't stand talking about him. I know they want to hear the bad parts. Any time I've told those, except to Bess, I've felt horrible afterward, as if I'd desecrated him.

But the other day, I started talking about Gordon and couldn't stop—there were women sitting there I hardly know, and I showed everyone the scars on my back and thighs. I can still hear my voice—it was disgusting, shrill. I felt like someone had cast a spell over me. I was laughing and crying.

Oh, well. Except for times like that, I'm pretty bored. A visitor comes, and they trot me out. Maria, Peter, Nell, Steve. None of my neighbors, no one from town. Women from Bainbridge—far away—get more visitors than I do. It's just as well. Would I really want to sit around with Nancy Grunwald or Alicia Murdoch gossiping about the other inmates?

I suppose the most interesting thing happening is the "creative rehab" program. Not because I think it will be fun, or even that I plan to try it: just because it's bringing people with a little pizzazz here. Forget those two sociologists from New York—I'm sick of that sad little head-tilt they've all perfected. I'm talking about the choreographer and actors from Whitehall Repertory.

At the assembly last Wednesday, for the first time since I came here, I wanted someone to know that I'm different, not one of "them." All the inmates were in the auditorium, listening to the sociologists talking about the show we're supposed to put on in August. I was about to fall asleep, but then they brought two guys from Whitehall onstage to do a scene from *A Chorus Line*.

I was on the edge of my seat. I really was. I remembered one of them from last summer: he did such a magnificent job in Linden Mobley's play. I can't remember its title. Gordon and I saw it at Whitehall in Adamsville one night last spring. This actor had me laughing my head off, even if the rest of the play wasn't that funny. He had the greatest timing. He'd get halfway across the stage and stop, as if he'd forgotten something. Then he'd turn and give the audience the cutest quizzical little look. Gordon wasn't impressed, but I loved him.

After the play, some customer of Gordon's insisted we join him and his wife for a drink at that bar around the block. It's all a ploy, the way they bill it as a spot for theatergoers to mingle with the actors, but it's fun anyway.

About an hour after the final curtain, Gordon and I were just getting ready to leave when that actor walked in. I caught his eye in the doorway. We smiled at each other. "I loved it," I said, meaning his performance, and he thanked me. I know Gordon didn't hear, because he never said anything about it, and he would have.

It was weird, seeing him on the prison stage. I thought maybe I was the only person in the audience who'd seen him perform at Whitehall. A few of the other inmates were doing wolf whistles, the way they do whenever a man gets inside, and it really pissed me off. I'd never heard the actor—his name is James Court—sing before. Finally they did quiet down, and I could hear. He doesn't have a really great voice, but he has the kind of spirit that makes you want to listen.

Afterward I tried to speak to him. He was talking to the matron, the sociologists, and a couple of women in business suits. He was right there! I explained the situation to Etta, one of my favorite guards—that we'd met before at a play in Adamsville—but she wouldn't let me get close. What did I expect?

Bess is thrilled about the show. She does card tricks, so she wants to dress up like a magician and do a few for the audience. She says her boys will come; she wants them to be proud of her. Marla Gericault tap-dances and she's trying to get me to sing along with her in some number from *Forty-Second Street*. She has incredible delusions about wearing leotards and high-heeled spangled tap shoes, dancing her little heart out on a monster-sized snare drum while I sing background. Doesn't she ever look in the mirror? Can you imagine a two-hundred-pound woman tap-dancing in a leotard?

According to the matron, no one is required to participate, so I won't. It's pathetic, if you think about it, encouraging people to take the stage and make fools of themselves. It's like Hallie used to say about school pageants: you'd suffer through forty children with off-key voices just to hear your own kid for three seconds.

It's not fair to the kids. I still cringe when I remember Maria standing on stage, reciting Coleridge's "Kubla Khan," and she forgot the words. She'd rehearsed it a hundred times at home. Stage fright is a strange thing; I've never had it myself, but I can imagine how it feels.

She was standing there, her hands clasped in front of her, all dressed up in a velvet jumper, patent leather shoes, and bows in her hair. That only made it worse. It wouldn't have been so humiliating if she'd looked nonchalant. She just stopped speaking. Silence. She found me in the audience, and she stared at me. I'd heard her rehearsing so often, I knew the poem myself. I tried mouthing the next line, but she couldn't read my lips. So I said it out loud. Mom gave me a look like pure ice, but I'm glad I did it. It gave Maria a jump start, and she finished the poem.

I wonder if she remembers.

Gordon wouldn't let Flo sing in the Christmas concert. He told her teacher it was because the songs were all commercial—not real carols. "Frosty the Snowman," "Silver Bells," "Rudolf the Red-Nosed Reindeer." He told the teacher he'd let Flo sing if they did "Hark, the Herald Angels Sing" or "Adeste Fidelis" instead. I wonder what he'd have done if the teacher had changed the program. Gordon loved making people bend to his will. Still, I doubt he would have let Flo sing. He told me he didn't want her turning into a show-off like me.

Flo was heartbroken. Her part in the show was to shake the jingle bells when Rudolf came on stage. I never found a way to explain to her why she couldn't do it. I just held her on my lap and let her cry.

Every time I remember something like that, I ask myself how I could have done it. How I could have wasted so much time with them. How I could have hurt them. Their little faces, twisted with pain. Caused by me. Yes, it was. It was. It was.

Bess is teaching me to pray. She's extremely religious. By that I mean that she is a spiritual person. She isn't showy, the way a lot of the born-again inmates are. They go around trying to convert everyone, saying "Praise the Lord" for trivial things, like getting waffles for breakfast. Bess really believes. She believes in atonement, and she believes in redemption.

"My sins are so great," I whispered to her last night.

"Yes, they are," she agreed.

"But what are they?" I asked. I need her to tell me. The things I thought were worst possibly aren't. I have lied, stolen, and killed. I have harmed my children.

"Your worst sin is a failure to love yourself," Bess told me. "If you loved yourself, none of the rest would have happened. You have to take things from the beginning. God loves you, so you must love yourself. You must take God's example. God loves all of us."

"Even Gordon?" I asked.

Bess paused. "Why, yes," she said. She held me close, and I thought her neck smelled sweeter than any skin I'd ever known. We were drinking from a bottle of vodka her husband Jimmy had brought her.

"Say a prayer," I said.

"Our Father, who art in heaven, hallowed be thy name," she began, but I started to laugh and could not stop.

"What is it?" she asked, not at all huffy, the way I would have been.

"I was thinking of Simon," I said. "When he was little, he used to think God's name was Howard. He thought the prayer went 'Howard be thy name.'"

"God bless Simon," Bess said, and we were laughing so hard at how cute he was, the guard came to tell her to get back into her own bunk.

"I'll say a real prayer," Bess whispered after the guard passed by. "Dear God, please protect everyone I love. Keep a special eye on Grandma, 'cause she is old. Help my friend Sophie make amends for her sins and find her way. Watch over Simon and Flo, and the soul of Gordon. Give Sophie's sister Maria the guidance it takes to care for two little kids, because you know she is going to need it. Help Sophie's mother become a better person. Bless our lawyers and guards. Have mercy on us, Lord, and keep all of us safe from harm. Amen."

"Amen," I whispered.

29

SIMON BEGAN TO SCREAM IN THE MIDDLE OF THE night. Maria, sound asleep, heard it at first as part of her dream. Jumping out of bed, she met Flo, who had come to get her, in the hallway.

"He's having a bad nightmare," Flo said, her eyes wide and afraid.

Together Maria and Flo hurried to Simon's bed. Thrashing, he was wrapped like a mummy in his bedclothes, his hair soaked with sweat. He screamed without stopping, with his mouth open as wide as it would go.

"Simon," Maria said sharply, her pulse racing. She pounced at him, smoothing his wet hair back from his eyes. "Simon, honey. Wake up. You're safe in bed. Here I am; here's Flo."

"Here I am," Flo said in a squeaky voice.

Simon freed his arms from the tangle of sheets and beat the air above his head. He hit Maria's cheek with one fist, and at that moment he stopped screaming and opened his eyes.

Maria, her cheek stinging, kissed his forehead. "Hi, Simon," she whispered.

"He was choking her," Simon said dully. "Or they were choking me."

"It was just a dream," Maria said. "It's all over now."

"I couldn't tell who was me and who was Mommy," Simon said. "At first I knew, but after a while we were the same." He began to cry.

Maria trembled as she held Simon in her arms. His eyes were open wide, but he didn't seem to recognize her or Flo. Flo wiggled into their embrace. "You're awake now, right? Aren't you, Simon?" Flo asked.

Simon didn't answer. His body was stiff as a plank. Maria sang him a lullaby and rubbed his back, and finally he relaxed. When she saw that he was asleep, she laid him down gently and straightened out his sheets, her heart still pounding.

"Can I sleep with you?" Flo whispered.

"Wouldn't you be more comfortable in your own bed?" Maria asked.

Flo looked up, her eyes pleading. "What if his nightmare comes into my head while I'm sleeping?"

"That doesn't happen," Maria said. "Everyone has their own dreams."

"Sometimes it happens," Flo said. "I've had the choking nightmare before. Maybe I gave it to Simon."

"I don't think you did, but maybe you'd like to talk with Dr. Middleton about it next time you see her," Maria said. Still, she let Flo come into bed with her anyway. Maria didn't get back to sleep that night, with her face hurting and the memory of Simon's screams in her ears, and she was glad to have Flo snuggling beside her, breathing evenly, seeming to dream sweet dreams, until close to dawn when Flo began to toss and Maria was afraid she, too, was having a bad dream; instead, Flo wet the bed.

Simon didn't remember his nightmare. When Maria and Flo asked him, he said no; he was fascinated by the possibility that he could have done anything as dramatic as give his aunt a shiner and not remember it.

"Does it hurt?" he asked, frowning with concern.

"Not too much," Maria said, touching it. She hadn't had a black eye since elementary school, when Sophie had caught her under the eye with a jump rope.

"I'm sorry," Simon said.

"I know," Maria said. "That's okay."

She felt peculiar, close to crying. She wanted to escape the Littlefield children, their nightmares and bedwetting, their psychologist, their constant need. She wanted someone to reassure her that she was doing a good job, that they were better off with than without her. Then, she wished they would just disappear. She felt deeply ashamed of her feelings, but she couldn't help them.

The children rigged their poles. They were going fishing with Duncan. Simon had pulled the tackle box from the back of Maria's kitchen closet. It held a treasure of hooks; lead sinkers; red-and-white bobbers; wire leaders; lures of shiny silver metal and hot pink bristles or slimy green plastic squiggles meant to resemble worms; previously used line flaky with dried seaweed; a fillet knife covered with lusterless scales. Simon and Flo had spread the entire contents across the front porch, trying to decide which lures to use.

"If we catch a fish, can we cook it for dinner?" Flo asked.

"Of course," Maria said. "We'll build a fire and grill it."

"We caught it with a Kastmaster, that flat silvery lure there," Simon said.

"This one?" Flo asked doubtfully. He held up a two-inch-long lure, trapezoid-shaped, silver on one side and metallic blue on the other. Compared to the gaudier bright ones, it had a functional elegance.

"Yes, that's it," Simon said.

"It looks like a minnow," Flo said.

"That's right," Maria said, proud of her niece's Darwinian sense. "Big fish like blues and bass like to eat minnows, so the Kastmaster is usually a good bet around here. Do you know what the food chain is?"

"No," Flo said.

"When you bring cans of food to school for the poor at Thanksgiving?" Simon asked.

"That's a food *bank,*" Maria said, smiling, wishing Sophie had been there to hear that. "The food chain starts with plankton—microscopic plants and animals in the sea. They feed the tiniest fish, which are then eaten by minnows. Then big fish eat the minnows."

"Then we eat the big fish," Flo said.

"Then sharks eat us!" Simon said.

"Daddy saw a great white one time," Flo said, slinging one arm across Maria's crossed legs. She lowered her head toward Maria's lap, so Maria would play with her hair.

"He did?" Maria asked. "Was he fishing off Montauk?"

"No, he saw it right at Hatuquitit Beach," Simon said eagerly. "Right while we were swimming! We were on this raft, me and Flo and Mommy, and Daddy was standing on the beach, yelling for us to come in. And when we got there, he told us a great white was swimming all around us!"

"It almost ate us," Flo said, sucking her thumb.

Maria didn't know what to say. She could envision the scene: Sophie and her children lolling happily in the water, Gordon standing on shore, feeling left out, needing to spoil their fun. She bet it had happened in September or October, when the beach was nearly deserted, when there wouldn't have been anyone outside the family around to hear him. When only Sophie, the other adult present, would know what he was doing.

"How come we can't see Mommy?" Simon asked with sudden fierceness.

"I *want* my Mommy!" Flo said, starting to cry.

"She loves you," Maria said carefully. "But she's afraid it would be hard for you to visit her at the jail."

"She doesn't want to see us anymore," Simon said. "Just forget it."

"Yes, she does," Maria said, not believing it.

The children abandoned the tackle box and sat separately, their legs dangling off the porch. Glancing up, Maria saw *Alicia* chugging into the cove and felt a tingle of relief run down her spine. Duncan brought her broadside to the jetty and cut her diesels. Maria and the children watched as he made her fast.

Simon turned to give Maria a curious glance over his shoulder.

"What's the matter?" she asked.

"Why is he here?" he asked, looking worried.

"I invited him," Maria said.

"Is he taking us fishing in that boat?" Simon asked.

"I think so," Maria said.

"Well, I'm not going." Getting to his feet, Simon strode toward the porch door.

"Simon," Maria said, "tell me what's on your mind."

"I just don't feel like fishing," Simon said.

"He's afraid of going far out in a boat and seeing sharks," Flo squeaked. "He's afraid it'll give him nightmares."

"That's not true," Simon said. Duncan approached the house and waved. "I just don't feel like fishing."

"Neither do I," Flo said.

"Hey, Simon. Hey, Flossie," Duncan said. Standing beside Maria, he frowned at her bruised cheek. "What happened?" he asked.

"I hit her in my sleep," Simon said, sounding scared. "I didn't mean to!"

"No, of course you didn't," Maria said, trying to soothe him.

"I'm sure it was an accident," Duncan said.

"I'm fine," Maria said, her voice shaking.

Duncan looked long and hard into her eyes, saw how upset she felt. He gave her a wink that seemed to promise he'd take over for a while.

"What's this rig?" Duncan asked, crouching over the lures. When no one answered, he held it toward the sun.

"We were planning on using Kastmasters," Simon said hesitantly. "But I don't think we should go out in the boat."

"Good thinking," Duncan said. "As I was coming in here, I saw snapper blues feeding in the cove. What do you say we fish off the jetty?"

Simon's eyes brightened. He watched Duncan gather the

poles, a few lures, and a bucket. Then he stepped forward, took his pole out of Duncan's hand. He walked toward the jetty.

"You coming, Flossie?" Duncan asked.

"Okay," Flo said.

"Aren't you coming, Aunt Maria?" Simon asked.

Maria knew she should join the fishing party and make sure everyone got along. But the thought of fishing when what she wanted to do was work—fix up her field notes, examine the grave goods she'd extracted—made her dull with resentment.

"Maybe we should let Aunt Maria finish her work," Duncan said with the authority of a good father. "What do you say we go catch her a fish?"

"If she says so," Simon said, watching her.

"I think it would be great," Maria said, smiling, encouraging him to follow Duncan. After a second, Simon smiled back and hurried to catch up with Duncan and Flo.

But Maria couldn't concentrate. She knew she had to see her sister, and so she drove to the jail.

"I'm having a problem with the kids," Maria said to Sophie when she entered the visiting area.

Sophie looked disoriented, as if she had just wakened from a nap.

"Simon had a terrible nightmare last night. I've never heard anyone scream like that before." Maria touched her own face. "It was so violent. Simon hit me in his sleep."

"What was the nightmare about?"

"You and Gordon."

They were silent, trying to wait each other out. "Aren't you going to say anything?" Maria asked after a while.

"Did he say more than that? What were we doing?"

"Choking each other." Maria paused, her gaze steady. "I think you not seeing them makes it worse."

"I don't want them picturing me in here," Sophie said.

"God, you're just like Hallie," Maria said. "She hates picturing you here, you hate picturing your kids picturing you here. The problem is, you're here."

"Choking each other," Sophie said slowly, as if she were feeling it.

"I'm not sure I can take much more of this." Maria felt like she was about to hyperventilate. "I have no idea what to do for them. They're seeing Dr. Middleton, but who knows if she's helping? I can't do my own work, and I feel like I'm failing your kids."

"Take a deep breath, Maria," Sophie said kindly. "Put your head between your knees."

Maria did; the blood rushed behind her eyes. She jerked her head up, to face Sophie. "Tell me what to do."

"You're doing fine," Sophie said. "They're better off with you than they would be anywhere else."

"They need to see you," Maria said.

"I thought of them coming to see me in the show," Sophie said, her gaze drifting off.

"What show?"

"Oh, some stupid thing the prison's putting on. I guess it's meant to make us feel worthwhile, discovering our hidden talents. Bess is going to do card tricks."

"You could sing," Maria said.

"I'm not going to sing," Sophie said, and her eyes filled with tears. She wiped them with her index fingers, but tears continued to spill down her cheeks. "I dream of my kids every night. We're a happy family, all together, in a town like Hatuquitit only in Australia or somewhere."

"Listen to me! Listen!" Maria's voice rose. "*That* isn't real. Neither are your dreams. You have two wonderful children who need you. That's what's real. They're too much for me. Do you hear me, Sophie?"

"I hear you," she said, still crying.

"Then tell me, so I know what I'm up against. Did they know what was going on? Did they see anything?"

"They know everything," Sophie said.

"Everything?" Maria asked, her stomach twisting.

"Everything."

The two sisters stared at each other; their silence went on and on until it seemed like noise. Sophie looked down at her hands, examining her bitten fingernails. She twisted a loose thread on her left sleeve. Then she looked up. "They saw me shoot Gordon," she said.

"Sophie?" Maria said, when Sophie didn't continue.

"I knew they were there. They'd been watching TV, but they heard us yelling. Usually I didn't yell back. Usually I just took it. So maybe it was the sound of my voice that made the children come to our room. I had the gun in my hand. Gordon was standing against the wall near the window, in front of that picture of Hatuquitit in the twenties."

She glanced at Maria, to see if she knew the exact spot she meant. Maria nodded.

"I told the kids to stand back, and I fired the gun. I knew they were right there, but I didn't care. I fired five times. Simon was screaming for me to stop. Flo had hold of my knees—she was crying. As soon as I did stop, they didn't say another word. They were mute as swans. They climbed into our bed—it was all messed up because Gordon and I had been lying in it. We had made love an hour before." She started to laugh but moaned instead. "And they watched me crying and grunting, pushing their father out the window."

Maria remembered finding them in bed, staring at the streaks of Gordon's blood and hair on the wall. "Why did you do it, Sophie?" she whispered.

Sophie shook her head impatiently. "Then I took a walk to the stream. I left my children alone, in that room where I had killed their father, for half an hour. Maybe I was out of my mind. I must have been—I wanted to get rid of the gun, hide the evidence. You know where I threw it?"

"I know. By the stone heart."

"Then I came home and found Gordon lying in the driveway.

That's the last thing I remember until you got there. I don't even remember calling you."

"Why did you do it?" Maria asked again.

Sophie ignored her. "Can you understand why I don't want to see my children? After what I put them through?"

Maria nodded. "I understand. But doesn't it change things, the fact that they want to see you?"

Sophie shrugged. "Sometimes I imagine they forgive me, because they knew what I was going through. But I know that's not realistic."

"It might be," Maria said.

Sophie laughed through her nose. "What a joke, the prison show. We're a bunch of killers and robbers, and they want us to sing and dance."

"The other day I was thinking of you singing 'Moon River,'" Maria said. "One night when it was too hot to sleep."

"That was a long time ago," Sophie said, but she smiled a little.

Maria didn't want Sophie to stop talking. She wanted to know everything.

"I have to confess something to you," Sophie said. "That beautiful little goddess you gave me? I sold it."

"I know." Sophie looked up, surprised. Maria continued. "I came across it in Blackwood. I figured you used the money to buy that dress you wore to Ed and Gwen's party," Maria said, impatient to steer Sophie back to the night of Gordon's death.

"No," Sophie said. "I used it to buy the gun."

Maria sat, silent and still, for a few seconds, taking it in.

"Didn't you hear me?" Sophie asked.

"Have you told Peter?" Maria asked. "Or Steve?"

"You're the only one who knows," Sophie said softly. "And you can't tell anyone. . . ."

"Where did you buy it?" Maria asked.

"From a guy I know in Stamford. An antique dealer."

"Was it old?" Maria asked, sensing an evasiveness in Sophie's expression, a desire to skip over this part.

"No, it was new. He sold it to me as a favor, without papers. The police assume it belonged to Gordon, that he kept it in the bedside table in case of robbers. But Gordon never owned a gun in his life."

"Why would some guy sell you an unregistered gun?" Maria asked.

Sophie's lips were set in a thin, almost mocking line. "Because we've done business before. I've sold him things."

"Things you stole?"

"Yes, Maria. Things I *stole*," Sophie said, her voice cracking. "God, you're so perfect. You've never done anything wrong, you've always landed on your feet. Why don't you go home and cook some incredibly nutritious dinner for *my* kids?"

"What do you mean, cook them dinner?" Maria asked, confused and furious. "*You're* the great homemaker, aren't you? Why else would you sell Hallie's gravy ladle, if it wasn't to buy a truffle or something to serve for dinner? Do you think that was *right*?"

"No, as a matter of fact, I don't," Sophie said. She held her head up and wouldn't look away. She stared Maria down. "I don't care what you think of me."

Maria didn't say anything.

"Go ahead—tell me what you think of me. Get it off your chest. You'll feel better. Speak for Hallie and Peter and Nell, too— all the rest of the perfect people."

Maria stared with amazement. "How can you think we're against you?"

"You'd better go now," Sophie said. "Duncan's probably pretty tired of baby-sitting."

"Will you tell me one thing? What made you buy the gun?" Maria asked. "Were you planning . . . ?"

Sophie shook her head. "I just wanted to have one. I thought it would be a good idea—for protection. That's all. That night when I grabbed the gun and went into our room, it was like a dream. At least, that's how I felt."

"You said you bought the gun for protection," Maria said,

wanting but not entirely able to believe her. "What did he do to you that night? Why did you suddenly need to protect yourself like that?"

"He hurt me, Maria," Sophie said wearily. "Let it go at that." She gazed toward the door, as if willing the guard to walk through it and take her away.

"You said you'd just made love. Is that when he hurt you?"

Sophie was quiet a long time. "How did I get into it?" she asked, as if to herself. She looked up. "You'd never let a man hurt you, would you?"

"No," Maria said.

"It didn't seem bad at first. It was kind of exciting. He'd tie me up and say he was going to torture me, but all that meant was he'd drive me crazy before he let me come. It was kind of wonderful. I know you can't understand."

Maria said nothing, thinking of making love with Duncan, the way he'd told her to lie still while he kissed her all over.

"But after a while he'd leave me tied up for longer and longer, and he'd pinch me, insult me. I have this scar . . . he said he wanted to brand me, so no other man . . ."

Maria was horrified. "That's what he did, the night you killed him? He branded you?"

Sophie shook her head. "No, a long time ago. He didn't lay a finger on me that night."

"But you said he hurt you. . . ." Maria knew that Sophie sometimes lied, but this felt more sinister. She felt sick to her stomach, light-headed.

Sophie just stared at her. Her arms folded across her chest, she wasn't going to say anything more.

"I'd better go," Maria said awkwardly, rising. "Will you let me bring the kids tomorrow? Please?"

"Not tomorrow," Sophie said, visibly relieved that Maria was leaving. "But I'd like you to kiss them for me. And send them my love."

"I always do," Maria said, wondering what Gordon could have

done that night that was worse than what Sophie had ever lived through before.

Maria felt distracted, split in two, walking out the jetty, as if she had left half of herself back at the prison. Simon and Flo flanked Duncan, who was gazing intently into the water beneath their feet. Maria looked down and saw it seething with fish. They were striped with silver, black tigers flashing past.

"We haven't caught any," Simon said sorrowfully.

"We got skunked," Duncan said, looking up at Maria, trying to read her eyes. He got to his feet and put his arm around her. "The biggest school of mackerel I've ever seen, and we can't catch one. The lures are too big."

He and Maria walked back to the porch, leaving the children to hold their poles, waiting for fish to bite.

Walking with Duncan, Maria suddenly thought of Aldo. He had a historical sense of the Dark family; he had been a member of it through Sophie's marriage to Gordon and the births of their children. After all the horror and violence and lying, nothing shocked her more than the fact that Gordon had branded Sophie, and she had let him. Maria's thoughts were buzzing: how had he done it? How had Sophie stood the pain? She couldn't stop imagining the details, and she couldn't bring herself to tell Duncan.

"What did she say?" Duncan asked.

"She won't see them," Maria said, feeling desolate. His arm across her shoulders felt like an intrusion. She walked out from under it, then couldn't look into his eyes.

"What else did she say?" Duncan asked.

"I can't talk about it," she said. "I want to, and at the same time I want us all to get into your boat, head out to sea, and never talk about it again."

"We can do that," Duncan said, holding her. "But I think you'd feel better if you talked to me."

Maria glanced at him. His eyes crinkled, gazing into the sun; he reminded her of a sea captain. "I talk to you," she said.

"No, you don't. You tell me you're upset, but you don't really tell me why. You don't tell me the details. You say the kids are a handful, but you let it go at that. You say you're upset because your sister used to be such a great girl and now she's in jail."

"What else am I supposed to say?" Maria asked, shaking. She watched a lobsterman pulling pots in the channel between Lookout and Little Shell and imagined returning to the grave. How satisfying it would be to start digging again, to do it right this time: to set up grids, to record each discovery with precision, to solve the mystery.

"Start with the kids," Duncan said, stroking her hair. "Tell me how worried you are that Simon never smiles and Flossie sucks her thumb constantly. That Simon's only ten and he likes to pull the legs off live crabs."

"He did that?" Maria asked, her stomach flipping as she pulled away.

Duncan nodded. "I caught one, to try using it for bait, and before I could kill it, Simon began pulling all its legs off."

"God, the nightmare he had last night . . . ," Maria said.

Duncan reached across the space between their chairs to take her hand. "Maria—I want to help you."

The Darks had been taught that feelings were dangerous, that keeping them inside was best for everyone. Maria trembled now, unable to contain them anymore. "Today Sophie told me the children saw her kill Gordon," Maria said, the words pouring out. "Flo was hanging onto her leg while she fired the gun."

"Oh my God," Duncan said, holding her again.

"They saw everything. If Simon tortures crabs, it's because he saw his father torturing his mother," Maria said. "I saw it once. I walked into their bedroom one night and found Sophie with a cord tied around her neck. And today she told me . . . she told me . . ." Maria couldn't say it out loud, the part about Gordon marking her. She thought of what Sophie had said about being tied up, how it had been exciting at first, and she wondered at what point they had crossed the line.

"No wonder . . . ," Duncan said.

"No wonder what? No wonder she killed him?" Maria asked. "She loved him. That's the strangest thing of all. After everything he did to her."

"And you couldn't help her," Duncan said in a voice so tender it made Maria's heart break wide open.

"No," she said, and she began to cry.

Duncan drove into town to buy some mackerel fillets, and Maria sautéed them with cider—a recipe she had learned from a French archaeologist on the dig at Hastings. The children seemed pleased to be eating the fish that—while they hadn't exactly caught them—they had at least seen swimming around their jetty an hour before. But the fishing had exhausted them, and they went to bed before it got dark, with just one bedtime story.

"Are you okay?" Duncan asked. Maria tried to smile, and he saw, and reached out his hand to touch her lips. "Don't answer that," he said. "I know you're not."

"I'm not," she whispered.

He stared at her, his hazel eyes filled with deep concern. She swayed, knowing no one had ever looked at her that way. Her family loved each other—the problem was, none of them had ever learned how to show it.

Duncan took a step toward her; her eyes filled with tears.

"Let me hold you," he said.

"I don't think I can," she said. She closed her eyes, feeling life moving so fast. The world was spinning, right under her feet. How did people manage to keep from flying off into space? Tears squeezed out from her eyelids. Sorrow for her family washed over her. She loved them so much, but did she know them at all? Had she ever let them know her? Had she ever let anyone?

"So much has happened since you came home," Duncan said. "And it's not your fault."

"Some of it is," she said.

"Like what?" he asked.

"I haven't given enough value to things," she said. "The things that matter...I didn't realize what secrets were doing to our family. And I..." She stared up at him. "I've been so free about taking you away..."

"You didn't do that," he said. "It was over long before..."

Maria's heart ached—she wanted to believe him. Now that she was starting to see the destruction in her own family, she couldn't bear to think she was responsible for hurting another.

"We're a lot alike," Duncan said, his voice as serious as she'd ever heard.

"In what way?"

"Neither one of us has a clue on how to get close to people. My whole marriage..."

"And mine," she whispered.

Just then, she felt Duncan take her hand.

Maria swallowed. His fingers laced with hers, he led her down the porch steps. The grass felt cool and damp under her bare feet. She heard the leaves rustling overhead in a cool breeze, blowing in from the Haunted Isles. Duncan stood so near, she felt the heat of his body. He took her hand, placed it on his heart; she felt the soft beating rhythm under her fingertips.

"That's how close I want to be to you," he said.

"How do we do it?" she asked.

"We'll figure it out."

Staring up at him, Maria glimpsed a shooting star. It flashed through the black velvet sky, but she couldn't look away from his eyes. They were wild, passionate, filled with desire. Standing in the quiet yard, Maria thought of how she had come halfway around the world to find this man she had known forever. His heart beat steadily under her hand.

"How can we figure out something we've both done so badly before?"

"This time we have each other," he whispered.

And she knew that that was true.

They walked into the house and up the stairs. But when she checked the children, Maria found them sleeping so soundly she couldn't resist bending over to kiss their foreheads. They didn't even stir.

In the barn room, Duncan eased her down on the bed. "I love you, Maria," he whispered.

"I love you, Duncan," she whispered back.

"You need someone to take care of you for a change," he said. He began to unbutton her shirt. She tried, but she couldn't stay still. She slid her hands along his back, pulling his shoulders toward her. He arched with pleasure at her touch, and they kissed, smiling. Kissing Duncan, Maria thought how good they were for each other: he wanted her to relax and let him take care of her, and she, who had never felt taken care of, wanted to ravish Duncan, who twisted and grinned like a man who had never been ravished.

The trick of a good archaeologist is to leave no evidence of herself behind at an excavation. A good archaeologist must slip through the dust of civilizations like a cat burglar: clad in black, trailing no threads, in stocking feet. Duncan dozed, but Maria lay awake, her head on his chest, watching the rising moon turn the old walls silvery, wondering whether it was too late to leave something behind.

30

ONE AFTERNOON WHEN NELL TOOK SIMON AND
Flo to the beach with Andy, Maria invited Hallie over for a boat
ride. Hallie showed up looking like Katharine Hepburn in *The
African Queen:* she wore a wide-brimmed straw hat held down by
a chiffon scarf and a smocklike cotton shirt to cover her summer
shirt and pants. She might as well have carried a parasol.

"I love boating," Hallie said, settling herself in the bow. "I
should do it more often."

Maria started the engine and cast off the spring lines. She
knew Hallie was gently reproving her for not having invited her
sooner. "Shall we cruise the Haunted Isles?" she called.

"Let's take a spin through Lovecraft—I want to wave to Ginger
Talisker. She's waiting for the new cygnets to hatch."

Maria drove the boat slowly, leaving almost no wake as they
passed through a reedy channel into the Lovecraft Wildlife
Refuge. Coming around the first bend, they surprised a gray
heron standing on one knobby leg: it beat its great wings, taking
slow flight. Maria glanced down, into shallow water full of eel-
grass. The engine throbbed, making conversation moot. A pair of
osprey circled overhead, and plovers scooted across a muddy
sandbar. The boat hit a small wave; Maria held tight to thoughts
of Duncan.

Hallie wrinkled her nose. "Let's get *out* of here!" she called. "I
don't like the smell of low tide."

Maria felt oddly like a mother taking an elderly child out for
the day. Low tide . . . Hallie could never accept or forgive nature.

Wheeling the boat around, Maria left the marsh and headed for Lookout.

"This is where I've been digging," Maria said, tossing the anchor into Lookout Cove.

"That Indian grave you found?" Hallie asked, pretending to shiver. "No wonder they say these islands are haunted."

"Would you like to see it?" Maria asked, knowing as she did so that the answer would be no.

"I don't like bones," Hallie said. "Can we just sit in the boat? It's lovely, the way we're rocking in the waves."

Maria leaned on a gunwale, gazing toward the grave. She had covered it with a polyethylene sheet, the corner of which was just visible.

"How's your sister?" Hallie asked hesitantly.

"Sophie? She's okay," Maria said.

"That's good," Hallie said after a long pause.

But she had raised the subject, and Maria continued. "Actually, she's a mess. She won't let the children visit her, and they're devastated. But I guess you understand that, right?"

"Why would I understand it?" Hallie asked.

"Because you won't visit Sophie. You're afraid it might be too 'hard.' Which it is, of course."

"It is too hard?" Hallie asked. "Then why do you go?"

"The fact that you can ask that question means I can't even try to answer it," Maria replied quietly. She wanted this boat ride to be over; she began to haul on the anchor line. Life with Hallie was a slippery glide over black ice—an ice-skating lark until someone fell through. Then it was terrible for them, but not enough to keep Hallie from skating along her elegant way.

"Let go of that rope and tell me what you need to say," Hallie said.

"I tried to explain it that Sunday in your kitchen. Sophie needs you—how much simpler can it get?"

"I've been thinking about that," Hallie said with queenly dignity that disappeared the next instant. She slumped, covering her eyes with trembling fingers. She began to sob. Perhaps their isolation made it possible for Hallie to cry without reserve, without stifling the sound.

"Mom?" Maria said after a while. She stood beside her mother but did not touch her. "Mom?"

Hallie's sobs subsided; gulls crying on the Little Shell rookery echoed them eerily. She looked up at Maria with old eyes. "What did I do wrong?" she asked.

"I don't know," Maria said. She knew Hallie wanted absolution, but Maria couldn't give it.

"Will you take me?" Hallie asked in a low voice. "To see her?"

"Her?" Maria asked, her heart skipping.

"Sophie," her mother said.

"Yes," Maria said, dropping the anchor in the bow and hurrying midships to start the engine.

"Greetings, friends, and welcome!" Sophie said when she caught sight of Hallie.

"Hello, dear," Hallie said, seeming to physically restrain herself from lurching across the prison table to embrace Sophie, or possibly to check her head for gray hairs, signs that she'd aged in here. "You look so thin!"

"We have a Weight Watchers program here," Sophie said. "Sensible diet coupled with exercise."

"You *do* look thin," Maria said, as if she felt that piping up would give Hallie's comments, naturally suspect, credibility.

"Why use a scale when I have Maria?" Sophie asked with brittle fondness. "I can always count on her for an up-to-the-minute assessment of my diet."

"Are you being well treated?" Hallie asked.

"I'm fine," Sophie said.

"The papers say you're something of a celebrity here," Hallie said, though not precisely with pride.

"I'm a cause célèbre," Sophie said. "The beaten wife who did something about it."

Hallie's gaze lowered disapprovingly. In the ensuing silence, Sophie caught Maria's eye. "How are they?" she asked.

"They're at the beach with Nell and Andy. I do have something I'd like to talk over with you—about Simon."

"I suppose you don't want me to hear," Hallie said, hurt.

"No, Mom—stay," Sophie said. "If you want to."

Hallie hesitated, as though she were not quite sure whether she dared to stay or not. Then she seemed to settle back in her chair.

"Duncan took them fishing the other day," Maria said with a warning glance at Hallie, who pulled herself up at the sound of his name. "And he told me Simon was pulling the legs off a crab."

"Simon was?" Sophie asked. The color began to drain from her face. "Pulling the legs off?"

"That's what Duncan said. It worries me . . ." Maria felt distracted by Hallie's presence, yet vaguely exhilarated by it. She wanted Hallie to know the messy details of what she and Sophie were going through.

"He's never done that," Sophie said. "Simon loves animals. Last year he found a caterpillar on a milkweed pod, and he kept it in a milk bottle until it spun a chrysalis and turned into a monarch butterfly. He was holding it on his finger when it made its first flight."

"I can't believe Simon would do anything cruel," Hallie said, casting clear aspersions on Duncan's version of the events.

"Well, if Duncan *says* he did," Sophie said.

Maria felt grateful for Sophie's support, even if it came, in a way, at Simon's expense. "When I asked Simon about it the next day, why he had pulled the crab's legs off, he said it was because the crab was going to die anyway. Duncan'd caught it to use it for bait."

"That's no good," Sophie said, now truly pale. "Have you told Dr. Middleton?"

"No, but we have a meeting on Tuesday."

"Well, tell her," Sophie said. She played with the hem of her violet-blue dress and seemed to grow more tense by the second. "About his nightmares, too. Oh God . . ."

"Don't fiddle, dear," Hallie said helplessly, and Sophie stopped. She smiled at her mother with gratitude. For the attention? Maria wondered. For her concern? Because she was certain that Sophie had appreciated Hallie's critical comment.

"What else should I tell her?" Maria asked.

"It's up to you," Sophie said, the stiffness returning. "You know more about them than I do. I don't even have the right . . ." Sophie sounded hostile and miserable.

"Maria is taking such good care of them," Hallie said. "You don't need to worry."

"Is that supposed to make me feel better? That my kids don't need me anymore?" Sophie asked in a low, dangerous voice.

"Of course they need you, dear," Hallie said, inadvertently breaking the ice. "Children always need their mother. No one loves a child more than its mother."

Sophie and Maria, thinking of their childhoods, exchanged tentative, knowing smiles.

"Have you read about the show?" Sophie asked.

"What show?" Hallie asked.

"The show here. We're putting it on with actors from Whitehall. You know—James Court."

"He was marvelous in that Mobley play last summer," Hallie said. "A regular stitch."

"Yes, Gordon and I saw that," Sophie said in a voice so normal it carried Maria straight out of the prison, over the trees, to Hallie's kitchen. She, her mother, and her sister might as well be sitting at the big oak table drinking tea. "Anyway," Sophie continued, "he's helping us put on a variety show. Singing, dancing, card tricks, the whole bit."

"*Card* tricks? In a variety show?" Hallie asked, her nose crinkling with distaste. "I'm not too sure about *that*."

"They're amazing tricks," Sophie said, bubbling over. "Wait'll you see."

"What do you mean, 'Wait'll I see'?" Hallie asked, sounding suspicious.

"I don't mean anything," Sophie said. "You're invited, that's all. The whole family is."

"I thought you weren't performing," Maria said.

"Oh, I'm not," Sophie said. "I'm wardrobe manager."

"You're not *singing*?" Hallie asked.

Sophie leaned forward, her elbows on the table. "Would you come if I were?" she asked.

"I would," Maria said.

Hallie shrugged. She stared at a painting on the far wall, at the barred window, at her own wrist. But Sophie's unrelenting gaze pulled her back. Finally she looked Sophie in the eye.

"Come on," Sophie said. "Tell me—would you come hear me if I sang?"

"I suppose I would," Hallie said.

It worried Maria that Sophie might consider this her big chance to make Hallie proud. "I don't believe you," Sophie said.

"You're both going to jump down my throat," Hallie said, "but there's something unseemly about a group of convicts putting on a show. I'm sorry, but there is."

"No kidding," Sophie said.

"I didn't mean you!" Hallie said, hitting her brow with an open palm. Her expression appeared to be one of genuine anguish. "Sophie, I don't group you together with them. I pray for you every night."

"This is going back a ways," Sophie said, trying to keep her voice light, "but you never came to hear me sing before. When I was in school, I mean."

"Never came to hear you?" Hallie asked, a blank look in her eyes. "I always did. I couldn't wait for your concerts."

"No," Maria said. "You never did. You always said you had to take care of Dad. I'd go instead and sit in the parents' row. . . ."

"You're wrong," Hallie said resolutely. Maria could see she truly believed what she was saying. "I don't know why you're both so mistaken about the same thing. I remember it so clearly, how proud I was. I remember the songs—that Gershwin medley, the Puccini arias . . ."

"I think maybe you remember me rehearsing at home," Sophie said. "It's okay, I'm not blaming you. I've just been wondering why . . ." Her voice trailed off wistfully.

Sophie was letting their mother off the hook too easily, but Maria said nothing. She saw the pain in Hallie's eyes, saw her clouding her vision of the past because the truth was shameful.

"My Sophie," Hallie said. "No one ever took better care of me than you did after your father died."

"No one *ever*? Not even your mother?" Maria asked, remembering Hallie's earlier speech. Hallie and Sophie were staring at each other so intensely, Maria felt jealous. Sophie was soaking up Hallie's love like a sponge, and sympathy was flowing from Hallie.

"My mother adored me," Hallie said, "but she was very busy all the time. People said she gave the best parties in New England. And you know she was a leader in rights for women."

"Really? I didn't know that," Maria said, interested.

"Yes, it's true. She never wanted to see a woman stuck at home with kids and boring housework. I think she would have turned in her grave if she knew what I gave up for Malcolm. It turned me right into a drudge. My mother loved him when we married, of course—both my parents adored him for the simple reason that he loved me. That's how I felt about Gordon and Aldo, you know. I was so happy you'd found men who loved you."

Maria couldn't bear to look at Sophie as Hallie continued in a throaty voice. "I blame myself for not seeing what was happening to you, Sophie. I—I almost hate to say this. I hope you won't take it the wrong way, but I loved Gordon as a son. I truly did."

"I know," Sophie said, a little color returning to her cheeks. She touched her throat and could not take her eyes off her mother.

"Which is why it makes this a hundred times harder. I gave that boy my love all the time he was . . . he was . . ."

"I know," Sophie said, reaching for Hallie's hand. For the second time that day, Hallie wept. Maria thought how revolting it was, talking fondly about Gordon. But she knew how hard Hallie was trying, talking about deep and difficult feelings. She reached for Hallie's other hand, and Hallie squeezed it.

"My girls," Hallie said.

Maria and Sophie exchanged small smiles.

"So," Hallie said. "Can we expect to hear you singing something from Puccini in the show?"

Sophie just shook her head, smiling a little. "I'm not going to sing," she said. "I just had to know you'd come to hear me if I was."

"I would," Hallie said with certainty.

But even if Hallie meant what she said now, when the moment came, Maria doubted she would be there.

PART THREE

BELL
STREAM

31

SITTING IN DR. MIDDLETON'S WAITING ROOM, MARIA felt nervous. This time she had dressed in a black gabardine suit to impress upon the doctor that she was a neat, responsible woman; that she, like the doctor, was professional. People waiting to see other therapists read magazines or stared into space. No one exchanged tentative smiles, the way they did at dentists' or family doctors' offices. Coming up the stairs, Maria had heard traffic whizzing past on Hatuquitit's Summer Street and the drone of motorboats in the harbor. But a little machine on the windowless waiting room's floor replaced real noise; it made the sound of a wind tunnel or of a radio left between stations. Maria found that it distracted her from thinking.

"Maria?" said a voice. Glancing up, Maria saw that the therapist wore a cotton print dress; a tortoiseshell headband held back her hair, blonder since summer started.

"Hello, Dr. Middleton," Maria said, and they shook hands. Maria preceded her into a sunny office. They sat in chairs upholstered with tan cotton, facing each other. Tall windows overlooked a gravel-strewn parking lot with the Bold and Intrepid Boatworks in the distance. A print from Richard Diebenkorn's Ocean Park series hung on the wall. A tattered hooked rug covered the hardwood floor, and baskets of dried grasses and bayberry nestled in the corners. Maria had instant feelings of coziness and friendliness.

"My sister was very anxious for me to come here. She's worried about her children," Maria began. She felt slightly like a poseur, someone pretending to be Simon and Flo's mother, and she wanted the situation to be clear from the outset.

"I was wondering whether *you* have any questions," Dr. Middleton said, surprising Maria. "Is there anything you'd like to ask me?"

"About the children? Yes, there is," Maria said, but suddenly her mind went blank. There followed a silence that at first felt comfortable but turned awkward; Maria shrugged and raised her eyebrows.

"Let me ask you a couple of things," the doctor said, breaking the ice. "How do the children seem at your house?"

"They like to stay inside more than I think they should. Simon, especially, would watch TV all day if I let him."

"What do you think they should be doing instead?"

"Well, I don't know . . . ," Maria said, although she did: children should spend summer days playing and having fun outside. She suddenly feared giving a wrong answer. "I guess I wish they liked the beach more. Being outside in general."

"When kids come from an unstable home," the doctor said, "it's not unusual for them to be afraid of leaving the house. When they do leave, they're afraid of what they'll find when they get home. There are no boundaries in their home, so there's no safety."

"So I should let them stay inside?" Maria asked.

"I wouldn't push them out just now," Dr. Middleton said. "I know that you're not used to children, that it must be hard for you."

"I want to do what's best for them," Maria said. The air conditioner hummed. Through the window she could see Duncan driving the Travelift toward the docks.

"Have you been particularly worried about anything?" Dr. Middleton asked.

"I take it you know the situation," Maria said, referring, she supposed, to the fact that Sophie had killed Gordon. When the doctor nodded, Maria continued. "And did you know that Gordon regularly beat Sophie or—at least—he did things to degrade and humiliate her? I don't know how you define abuse."

"There are plenty of ways to define it, including constant

criticism or a lack of respect. But from what I understand, there was physical abuse as well."

"Did Flo and Simon tell you that?" Maria asked.

Dr. Middleton paused for several seconds. "I've promised them I wouldn't tell anyone—not even you—the specifics of what they've told me, but yes—they were aware of physical abuse."

"Sophie told me they saw her kill him," Maria blurted out. From the doctor's steady expression, she knew that the news didn't surprise her, that the children had already told her. "What's that going to do to them—in the long run? How can they grow up and have normal lives after everything they've seen and heard? I mean—the other day, Simon pulled the legs off a crab." Maria felt herself starting to cry.

"Children learn values quite young—before the age of three—through observations and feelings, not through words," the doctor began slowly. "The things they see bring on feelings that they don't have words for. It doesn't matter if you tell them everything will be fine or 'Daddy didn't mean to do that.' Their feelings tell them that everything isn't fine, that Daddy does the same thing over and over again."

"So what will happen to them?" Maria asked, feeling bleak.

"We're all working together," Dr. Middleton said. "They need to put words to their feelings, and to feel safe enough to express them."

"How can I help?" Maria asked.

"By being patient with them, not expecting them to conform to your timetable. By not making them go outside if they can't."

"Did Simon say I do that?"

Dr. Middleton just smiled. In a way, Maria resented her for not telling Maria every shred of information that might matter, but the doctor's smile was kind, not smug; it made Maria smile back.

"Can you tell me what to do?" Maria asked bluntly. "Is there anything I'm doing wrong?"

"Just do your best. You can't take the place of their mother, of course, but the children know you care about them. It would be good if you kept up your own interests."

"I try," Maria said, thinking at once of Duncan and of the dig at Lookout. "But the children take a lot of time."

"It's important," Dr. Middleton said.

After the appointment ended, Maria walked straight to the boat-yard. She wondered whether people already knew about her and Duncan. She remembered when, as a child, she had overheard Hallie and her friend Ginger talking about Mrs. Brown, the librarian, and Patty Winograd's father. Separations and divorces might be more common now, but Maria had no illusions about Hatuquitit's Puritanical roots.

Duncan stood shirtless at the helm of a lobster boat, moving it from one dock to another. Sun glared off the calm harbor. He hadn't seen her yet, so Maria stood in the shade watching him. She knew he would be glad to see her, glad to stop and listen to what Dr. Middleton had said. She couldn't imagine telling the same thing to Aldo in the middle of a workday.

As he made the boat fast to a floating dock, he spied her. He waved. Perhaps he called her name because suddenly two men standing on the dock turned to look at her. At the same time, a small head popped up, peering over the gunwale. Duncan climbed out of the boat, then turned to help a little boy climb out after him. He came toward Maria with long strides as his son ran all-out to keep up.

"Jamey, this is Maria—Flossie's aunt," Duncan said.

"Hi," Maria said, reaching out to shake Jamey's hand. Jamey grinned—more into the air, perhaps with the pleasure of being greeted as an adult, than at Maria. His eyes looked like Duncan's; he wore his reddish brown hair long and a little shaggy. But even in these first seconds Maria sensed a difference between this child and Simon or Flo: Jamey's expression was happy.

"Hi," Jamey said. Now he scanned Maria intensely—from head to toe—possibly comparing her to his mother, taking in the details of her shoes, hem length, belt buckle, lack of makeup, hair color, facial expression. When he was finished, he smiled broadly.

"So, this is your son," Maria said to Duncan, blushing.

"Yep," Duncan said proudly, observing the scene avidly; Maria imagined him gauging the possibilities for happy alternate weekends, school vacations, Christmases à trois into the future.

"Do you have a boat?" Jamey asked.

"I do, but not here. I keep it at my house."

"Did you buy it from my dad?"

"Yes," Maria said.

"How much did it cost?" Jamey asked.

Maria, who had been taught it was impolite to discuss money, waited for Duncan to admonish Jamey. When he didn't, she felt slightly flustered and just smiled wildly.

"Hey, Duncan!" Jim called, gesturing at an engine block swinging from a derrick.

"Can you guys wait here a second?" Duncan asked. "I'll be right back."

Maria and Jamey watched him go. After half a minute, Jamey cleared his throat. "Want to sit down?" he asked. "I know a spot."

"Sure," Maria said, letting Jamey lead her to an overturned Boston Whaler. They sat down. Maria wondered whether the back of her black skirt would be chalky-white when she stood up. She was about to ask Jamey what he liked to do in the summer, but she had the feeling he was working up to something. He kept glancing at Maria, smiling brilliantly, then looking away; he slid a little closer.

"So, how old are you?" Maria asked.

"Six," he said solemnly.

Maria was going to ask if he liked sailing, but Jamey spoke first.

"Do you know about—the divorce?" he asked, his tone intimate.

"Which . . . ," Maria began, confused.

"My mom and my dad," Jamey said. "They're getting a divorce." Now he looked mildly worried, as if he thought maybe Maria would walk away upon hearing this news.

"I did know about that," Maria said solemnly.

"But my uncle's divorced," Jamey said. "Lots of people are."

"In fact, so am I," Maria said, not wanting to explain about the annulment.

"Some people take it hard," Jamey said. "But I don't." By his vehemence, Maria was pretty sure he meant the opposite.

"Are you having a nice summer?" Maria asked. She wished the breeze would pick up.

"Yes," Jamey said.

"That's good," Maria said.

"You're Flo Littlefield's aunt?"

"Yes, I am," Maria said, half-turning toward Jamey. "Is she in your class?"

"She came to my party," Jamey said. "Dr. Kaufman gave her and my cousin the exact same ring—it has a big ruby."

Maria remembered Flo had gone to Dr. Kaufman's the day Sophie had left her in the library. "It must be pretty," Maria said.

"Flo must be so sad," Jamey said. For the first time Maria sensed a high-pitched anxiety that reminded her of Flo's own.

"Yes, she is," Maria said, waiting for Jamey to continue by himself; she didn't know how much the child knew.

"'Cause her mommy's in jail," Jamey said. "She's never at home with Flo anymore."

"Her mommy is my sister," Maria said.

"Oh, you must be so sad," Jamey said. His little hand slid close to Maria's on the boat, but stopped just short of touching it.

"I am, sometimes," Maria said. All at once, smiling down at Jamey, Maria was overtaken with the vision she had imagined Duncan having earlier: Maria, Duncan, and Jamey decorating a Christmas tree with the same ornaments every year, Jamey in third grade, then sixth grade, then high school, then college. The words son and stepson filled her mind. Alicia lurked out of sight, sorry and alone. But still Maria found it a simpler vision than her usual, more troubling one: she, Simon, and Flo living out their lives with the specter of Sophie in prison down the road.

32

LAST NIGHT I LAY IN BED WITH MY SHEET UP TO my chin. I remembered back when I was little, under the covers, when I would feel as though I were trapped in a very narrow rock crevice. I would throw off the blankets and breathe and breathe and sometimes wake up Maria and convince her to climb out on the roof with me. Last night I tried throwing off the sheet and feeling the air move across me, but it was air-conditioned, not fresh, and I felt more trapped than ever.

I'm trapped by where I am, that's true, but that's nothing compared to being trapped by what I did. I can't bring him back. Last night I had a dream—no pictures, just his voice. "I'm coming for you," it said, just a voice in the night. That's when I woke up sweating, feeling trapped in the rock crevice.

Would I bring him back if I could? It's a stupid, worthless game, but I play it. I think of ways. What if I hadn't killed him, what if he just went away? What if he'd just died of a heart attack? Then I'd have his life insurance, the house, the cars, money in the bank to send the kids to college, the freedom to get on with things. Then I think: get *on* with things? Who do I think I'm kidding? I had choices—I didn't *have* to let things get so bad, go to hell the way they did. The first time it happened I could have called the police. I could have told Peter and Nell. I could have just walked out the door.

The other day, telling Maria about the time Gordon branded me, I caught her looking like she didn't want to hear. Didn't want to know me. She probably pictures a hot branding iron and a lasso, which in a way I guess it was. The rope around my neck was sort of a lasso, but really it was more like the dog collar Gwen used to make him wear. I felt like telling Maria it didn't even hurt at the time. It felt like a pencil, the razor blade, just tracing his initials in my skin. It hurt later, it seared like a branding iron for days afterward, and I couldn't sit down. Through all the pain I hated myself for letting him do it, and now I'll have Gordon's mark on me for the rest of my life.

Some nights I lie awake wondering if I could have been happy with Jack. If we had stayed together, I mean. Some nights I wonder whether I would have let things get so bad with Gordon if it hadn't been for Jack. When Jack left me, I thought my life was over. He loved me more than anyone ever did—more than my parents, my brother, maybe even more than Maria. And he just got tired of me! That was it—he just met someone new. That was all the explanation he gave. I never expected to find another love like that. I thought I did, with Gordon, but then I was so afraid of losing it.

He could get me to do anything just by looking hurt. So *terribly* hurt. As if I'd just slapped, insulted, and laughed at him all at once. Every time he'd push a little farther, until all those years went by and I couldn't remember where we'd been when we started.

Again and again. If it was Christmas and I wanted to spend it with my family instead of his: that face, the face of a sad little boy on a big strong man, always got me. If it was Saturday and I wanted to go to Lord & Taylor's with Mom instead of waiting for him to get home from golf with Ed: that face. God, it comes to me now and I can't stand it. But before, all I could ever feel was sympathy. Even when I realized it came between me and everyone who ever loved me and I ever loved: Mom, Maria, Peter, Nell, even Simon and Flo. I'd hold Simon on my lap, singing in his little ear, so happy and proud to have such a lovely son, and I'd catch Gordon looking *so* sad because I was giving my love to Simon, not him.

"I love him because he's our son," I'd say at the beginning. "Part you and part me."

But that wore out. Gordon didn't buy it. If I was holding Simon, I wasn't holding Gordon. If I was occupied with Flo, I loved her, not Gordon. Maybe if I had held my ground, proved to him that the more you love the more love you have, this wouldn't have happened. I've thought that so often: if only. If only I hadn't tried to outsmart him, to tell him what I thought he needed to hear. All I did was give him a foot in the door.

Maybe I remember this because it was so dramatic, but I think it was the real beginning: when I was breast-feeding Simon. It hurt, the way he'd suck so fiercely with his eyes closed, but it filled me with joy. It's taken me all this time to be able to admit that to myself again, when at the time it was just so normal and obvious. Gordon would stare at us, so proud and sweet, telling me what a beautiful mother I was. Then one time he and I were making love, and he began sucking my breast and he wouldn't let go of it. I mean *would not.* I began to feel afraid I would dry up. And from then on Gordon didn't think it was normal for me to enjoy feeding Simon. He'd always find a reason to interrupt us; he'd ask me where I put his car keys, or he'd say he had a splinter in his foot and he couldn't wait another minute for it to come out. He'd glare at us, me and Simon.

"Does that feel good?" he asked me one time, and from then on it was one innuendo after another about how turned on I was getting by my son taking milk from my breast. Well, it *did* feel good, which made me feel incredibly guilty. That plus the fact I'd probably moaned with pleasure or something the time Gordon did it when we were making love.

But I wasn't going to stop. All the books said the best-adjusted babies were breast-fed. I'd hold Simon in my arms and give him my breast and think: this is natural, this is how animals feed their young. I'd think of cows and horses and dogs and prehistoric women before bottles were invented. But of course that wouldn't last and I'd be back to thinking of me and *my* baby, Simon, my beautiful child.

And one day it must have been too much for Gordon to bear, watching us. I remember I was wearing my nursing bra and one of Gordon's old shirts unbuttoned; Simon and I were sitting on the screened porch, his last feeding before bedtime. The crickets were chirping and I could hear kids playing in Bell Stream. Gordon was sitting in that big wicker chair, staring at us with the meanest look on his face. I could feel my arms getting stiff and tense, like a cage around Simon.

"What is it?" I asked finally. "What's wrong?"

"It's time he started using a bottle," Gordon said. "It's time you weaned him."

That made me giggle; I could almost believe Gordon was kidding. "He's only sixteen weeks old!" I said.

Who knows? Maybe it was because I laughed, but Gordon came charging across the porch and ripped Simon off my breast. God, I'll never forget how they looked. My baby with his mouth open like a baby bird and my husband crazy with rage. I nearly couldn't breathe; I thought Gordon was going to smash Simon against the wall.

He didn't. He very calmly carried Simon, who was by this time wailing, out to the car, and he put him on the front seat and drove away. Just drove away. I didn't have a car of my own then or I'd have gone after them. Instead I just paced in the driveway and wondered whether I should call Mom or Peter. But they weren't gone long—maybe fifteen minutes. And when they got out of the car, Simon had stopped crying and Gordon was smiling for forgiveness. He handed me Simon and embraced us. We stood like that a long time, a family of three, with Gordon whispering "I'm sorry, I'm sorry" in my ear. At that moment, I wasn't sure I'd *ever* forgive him, but I did, eventually.

He handed me a brown paper bag he'd bought at the drugstore containing a bottle and some cans of formula. "Please," he said. "Do this for me."

I didn't want to feed Simon formula, but after that I was afraid to keep breast-feeding him. For Simon's sake, I did what Gordon wanted.

That's probably the moment I should have walked out. There've been other moments, too. I should have walked out after he stopped teasing and began to torture me. I should never have let him humiliate me. I shouldn't have let him carve his initials into my skin. It makes me sick, the way I believed him saying he wanted to mark me so no other man would have me, because he loved me so much. When all he wanted was to hurt me. I should have walked out, but I never could. We were a family: me and Gordon and Simon and Flo. Up until that last instant, we were stuck with each other. We were *it*. And through it all, maybe not when it was actually happening, when he was hurting me, but before and after, I loved him.

I wish Bess wasn't mad at me. I wouldn't mind waking her up and telling her about how I decided to stop breast-feeding Simon. She's hurt because I couldn't pretend to think her card tricks were any great shakes. She'd built them up to sound really magical; I guess my expectations were way out of proportion. She can't even shuffle very well. She did a couple of stupid ones, then that one where the ace of spades keeps turning up. "What next?" I asked.

"That's the grand finale," she said. Her eyes turned incredibly sullen, and she just stared at me.

"Oh," I said, wishing I could redeem the situation. But could I ooh and aah just because she wanted me to? I mean, she's always telling me how important honesty is, and to tell the truth, I felt a little pissed off that she seems to have a slight double standard. I mean, she's always urging me to tell my mother or Maria off, yet she expects me to give her crummy card tricks a standing ovation.

Sometimes I wish I could get the hell out of here. Just because Bess and I are cellmates thanks to the State of Connecticut doesn't mean we're destined to be friends for life. I'm glad I didn't get Rhonda or Marla or Peggy, but that doesn't mean I can't be mad at Bess. I guess I'm a little disappointed in her. That's probably all it is, though: disappointed. We're still friends. Of course we are.

33

ONE NIGHT A BLAST OF AIR SO CHILLY IT FELT LIKE October swept across Squaw's Landing and Maria decided to light a fire. "We need some kindling," she said.

Simon and Flo followed her into the yard. They stared at the ground, gathering bundles of twigs. "Don't pick up any pine," Simon warned. "Daddy said if you burn pine you get tar in your chimney."

"That's right," Maria said. "Creosote."

"I hate those pine-flavored cough drops, don't you?" Flo asked. She reached for Maria's hand, making twig-gathering close to impossible. The sun, which had nearly set, fired orange and purple streaks into the western sky and the bay below. When they had enough kindling, they ran inside.

Maria piled crumpled-up newspapers, twigs, and three split logs in the fieldstone fireplace. She imagined the stone had been quarried up the Hatuquitit River. The upriver Pequots had traded the local tribe stone like this for fish and clamshells.

"Can we cook something?" Simon asked.

"Like what?" Maria asked, wishing she had some marsh-mallows.

"Hot dogs!" Flo said. "On sticks."

"But we've already had dinner," Maria said, thinking of the mustard-honey chicken they had seemed to enjoy.

"We'd love to cook hot dogs," Simon said.

So Maria took three hot dogs out of the freezer while Simon

whittled the ends of three forsythia branches, stripped of leaves, into sharp points.

They sat cross-legged on the floor, facing the fire. Except for the flame, the room was dark. No one spoke; they concentrated on keeping the hot dogs on the sticks, roasting them to a perfect golden brown.

"Oh no," Flo said when her hot dog fell into the fire.

"That figures," Simon said.

"Here, take mine," Maria said, putting her arms around Flo to show her how to point the stick slightly up. Then Maria ran into the kitchen for another hot dog.

"Point it up, that's the way," she heard Simon saying. His tone of voice was surprisingly kind and warm; she hung back in the dark passageway between the kitchen and living room, watching them.

Their backs were hunched and relaxed, not tense, for once, so limber that sitting cross-legged came easily to them; Simon's knee rested comfortably against Flo's.

"How can you tell when it's done?" Flo asked.

"You keep turning it and turning it till it's all the same color," Simon said.

"Mine looks black," Flo said. But as she pulled the hot dog toward her for a closer look, it fell into the embers. "Oh no!" she said again.

This time Simon started to laugh, which made Flo start to laugh. Were they always so relaxed alone together? Maria wondered. When she walked into the living room with more hot dogs, the kids were rolling on the carpet in great hilarity. Simon held the one successfully cooked hot dog aloft.

"Should we roast a couple more?" Maria asked.

"Sure," Simon said, straightening up, still grinning. The three of them held their sticks into the fire, passing the cooked hot dog down the line and taking bites.

"Oh no!" Maria exclaimed as her new hot dog went up in flames and fell into the coals, and all three of them laughed so hard Simon got hiccups.

*   *   *

"You sure you don't have stomachaches?" Maria asked when she put them to bed.

"No, that was fun," Simon said.

"I could eat at least two more," Flo said.

"What should I read to you tonight?" Maria asked, perusing the bookshelf.

"Let's tell ghost stories," Simon said.

Maria had heard some hair-raising ones from the locals in Peru, but they weren't for children. She remembered a few from her own childhood—"The Sunken Canoe," "The Midnight Campfire," and "Buried Wampum"—all of which had supposedly taken place on the Haunted Isles. But they were pretty violent, and she wouldn't tell them to Simon and Flo.

"I know a good one," Simon said. "But it's scary, Flo."

"That's all right," Flo said eagerly.

"Okay," Simon said. "Turn off the lights, Aunt Maria."

Maria obeyed.

"One night these kids were camping out without their parents," Simon began. "It was really dark, without a moon or lanterns or anything. They were in the tent, and it was quiet. They were way out in the country, miles from anywhere. There were definitely wild animals like wolves, foxes, and bobcats. It was near that place near Cornwall where people keep sighting panthers. All of a sudden, the kids heard footsteps . . ."

Flo shivered with appreciation, pressing closer to Maria. Simon saw this and seemed pleased. "Then what happened?" Maria asked.

"The footsteps were getting closer. Crunch, crunch!" Simon said.

"Was it eating something?" Flo asked.

"No, it was coming through tall grass. Closer and closer. The kids were really scared. All of a sudden, they heard it calling 'Bloody fingers . . . bloody fingers . . .'"

"Oh my God," Flo said.

"Its voice was getting louder," Simon said. " 'Bloody fingers! Bloody fingers!' The kids were imagining it had really long finger-nails dripping with blood 'cause it had just killed something with its bare hands."

Maria wondered if she should stop the story. But Simon was telling it with gory relish and Flo was enthralled.

"The kids huddled together. They were shivering with fright! The girl wet her pants because she was so scared. Suddenly the Thing was right outside the tent. They could hear it walking around and around, looking for the zipper. Now it was whisper-ing . . . 'Bloody fingers, bloody fingers.' The girl grabbed hold of the boy. 'Do something!' she said. 'You have to!' 'Okay,' the boy said. He grabbed a frying pan." Here Simon climbed off the bed and grabbed a book, holding it over his head and advancing cau-tiously, just the way the brave boy in his story might have ap-proached the Thing.

"He had to protect her," Simon said with great drama. "The Thing wouldn't stop whispering 'Bloody fingers.' So the boy very slowly unzipped the tent's door. 'Be careful!' the girl whispered. 'I will,' the boy said. He stepped outside, and there—right in front of him—was the Thing! It was tall and hairy with big feet and fangs, like Bigfoot. When it saw the boy, it ran toward him, holding out one bloody finger! The blood was dripping right off! The boy was just about to hit him with the frying pan, and the Thing stopped short and said, 'Excuse me, mister, you got a Band-Aid?' "

Simon finished the story in a voice that sounded like Donald Duck's, looking immensely pleased at the fact that Maria and Flo were both laughing and shaking their heads with relief.

"What a good story!" Maria said.

"The Thing wasn't ever going to hurt them, was it?" Flo asked, relief mingled with anxiety in her voice.

"No, it just had a cut finger," Simon said.

"It just needed a Band-Aid, it wasn't going to kill them or any-thing, right?" Flo pressed.

"Right," Simon said.

"That's good," Flo said. "That was an excellent story. I'm glad it wasn't a real ghost story, about someone dead."

"Come on, you guys," Maria said. "Time for bed." She tucked them in.

"I'm going to tell about the dead baby," Flo said in a voice full of mystery.

"Is that a ghost story?" Maria asked.

"Shut up, Flo," Simon said.

"Shut up yourself!" Flo said.

"Oh, do you have to start fighting after we've had such a nice time?" Maria cajoled. "Let's just say good night and have sweet dreams."

"It was just a little baby," Flo began, as if she hadn't heard Maria. "A girl as cute as could be, who never cried or wore diapers. She never even ate or drank. She wasn't even born."

"Was she magical?" Maria asked, going along with Flo.

"Very," Flo said. "She didn't come along the usual way. She just *was*."

"We're not supposed to talk about this," Simon said, the familiar sullenness returning to his voice. "When I see Mommy, I'm going to tell her you did."

"I don't care," Flo said. "I love that dead baby, and I'm going to talk about her."

"Tell me," Maria said.

"Well, she was like a fairy," Flo said. "With silky wings, pretty curls, and tiny hands and feet. She could fly."

"You're thinking of the angel," Simon said.

"She *is* an angel," Flo said.

"What are you two talking about?" Maria asked. "Is this a ghost story?"

"Yes, but a real one," Flo said happily. "A nice one."

"A *nice* ghost story—fat chance!" Simon said.

"Who was the dead baby?" Maria asked.

"Mommy and Daddy's other baby," Flo said. "The one who died. Do you know what happened to it?"

"There wasn't another baby," Maria said. "You and Simon are your parents' only children."

"There was too!" Flo said, her voice growing strained.

"Flo!" Maria said with affectionate exasperation. Flo was fretting now, tossing her head as if she wanted to work it into the pillow. Maria put her hand on Flo's damp forehead and began playing with her hair. After a moment, Flo quieted down. "We buried her, all of us together," Flo said.

"Honey, there wasn't . . . ," Maria began, but a chill came over her, the way it always did in the middle of a really good ghost story, as if the spirit had been conjured.

"She's right, Flo," Simon said. "There wasn't."

Maria kissed Flo good night, then Simon. She sat on the end of Flo's bed for a long time, until the children were breathing steadily in their sleep. Then she walked out, leaving their door open a crack. And suddenly she knew that Simon had been lying when he said "There wasn't." She could feel the cold presence of a third Littlefield child as surely as if she were holding it on her lap.

Maria lived with that feeling for a few days. Perhaps that was what sent her back to Lookout. Pulling back the polyethylene sheet, she found the grave exactly as she had left it. She set to work with her trowel and stiff brush, cataloguing each small bone, amulet, and stone. She thought of Aldo telling her to solve the archaeological mystery, and she set to it. Applying the familiar rules of science, Maria felt far from the Haunted Isles of her childhood's ghost stories.

She made a list of each item in the grave:

> *steatite bowl, four inches in diameter*
> *a beaver incisor*
> *forty-one shell fragments, including scallop,*
> *channeled whelk, clam, mussel, and periwinkle shells*

ninety-six shell beads, drilled with symmetrically
*   placed holes, possibly once having comprised*
*   a necklace*
metal disk
side-notched arrowhead, two inches long
one adult female skeleton

While not allowing herself to ponder the indisputable evidence that the squaw's rib cage had been shattered with the arrowhead and wonder about possible reasons for her murder, Maria found herself thinking about the Pequots' religion. It was a form of prayer, kneeling on the hard ground, brushing soil from the bones, thinking of Cautantowit.

Cautantowit was the Pequots' great god. They believed that he lived in a mountaintop house. At the dawn of time, evil spirits undammed the lakes and rivers, flooding all the earth but Cautantowit's house. Many birds and animals escaped by taking refuge there; those who did so absorbed godlike qualities.

Cautantowit dried the earth. First he made a man and a woman from stone, with whom he was displeased. He made others from a tree. He gave the people gifts of wisdom, bravery, goodness. Each Pequot chose one animal, bird, or fish—endowed with godliness by Cautantowit at the time of their sojourn in his home—as his or her personal god, or manito. This creature would guard the Pequot during life and beyond.

With her naked eyes, Maria examined the metal disk and stone bowl for evidence of a fish or bird—a manito for the dead woman. She knew that if the squaw used Cautantowit's spiritual gifts during her life, she would make her three-day journey after death to the Land of the Dead. There she would lie peacefully for eternity.

Otherwise, if she was a robber, liar, or murderer, she would be doomed forever to wander the earth without resting. And, in spite of Maria's determination to dig for scholarship and for no other reason, she found herself filled with horror for this squaw, and for Sophie and the third baby of Flo's ghost story.

*   *   *

When she got home, Maria spread the grave goods over her worktable. The sentimental flush she'd felt at the grave had passed, and she set about discovering why the woman had been buried so far from the Pequot cemetery. Maria pulled the gooseneck lamp over her shoulder, rummaged through a drawer for her big magnifying glass.

She examined all the objects that appeared to have been worked by hand: the tiny hole in each bead through which a gut strand had passed to form a necklace, the arrow point's symmetrical side notches, the smooth stone bowl. Then, holding it with forceps, she focused on the metal disk. Upon close inspection, she saw that it was an alloy containing gold. Vaguely oval-shaped, it had two thin edges suggesting it might once have been a ring.

Maria's pulse quickened. The Pequots had no gold source. If this was jewelry, perhaps it had been part of a trade with the English settlers. She turned the object over in her hand and examined it with her naked eye. There were faint scratchings in the gold.

Pulling the light even closer, she held it under the glass, tilting it until the magnification turned clear. The scratches were shallow, hardly visible, but they had a uniform height and width. She couldn't be sure, but it seemed possible to Maria that they were initials. And if she had to guess, she would say that they were *C.S.*

34

"COULD IT BE A SIGNET RING?" MARIA ASKED. She leaned over Reverend Hawkes, who sat at his desk, examining the metal disk.

"It's terribly thin," he said. "Of course, they would have used considerably less gold in their alloys back then, and the nickel and copper might have worn away."

He ran a forcep around the disk's edge, and a greenish black crumb of metal fell to the desk. "It's not a coin or medallion," he said. "Too convex."

Maria pointed with her finger at the two sections, directly opposite each other, where the metal curved down, then tapered into thinness. "That's where the band was," she said.

Maria had called Reverend Hawkes, and he'd told her to come right over. She wanted a witness, corroboration for what could be an exciting discovery. Beside her, on the desk, sat *Pequot Tales*.

"I think you're right," he said after a moment.

"And the initials? Are they his?"

"They look like *C.S.* to me."

Maria's imagination took her spinning through the Pequot legend, where the English settler Charles Slocum had fallen in love with the Pequot woman and her jealous husband had killed first his wife and then the Englishman—before he could move the graves on Squaw's Landing.

"It's far-fetched," she said.

"Some of those old myths are grounded in truth," he said

thoughtfully, and the fact that he didn't dismiss her outright loosened her tongue.

"What if Charles Slocum saw the Indian kill his wife, or came upon her body sometime later? What if he took her body away and buried it himself—on Lookout?"

Reverend Hawkes continued to gaze through a magnifying glass at the gold's surface. "I'm sure this is a C, and if this isn't an S, it's an F."

What if she was right? Knowing he would have to move the Pequot graves anyway, Slocum would have wanted to bury the woman he loved in a final resting place, somewhere permanent, a place he could visit without the tribe watching him. She pictured him rowing her body to the Haunted Isles, digging her grave, laying her body on hides and fur, surrounding it with grave gifts, including his gold signet ring, and covering her with soil.

"In the Pequot legend," Reverend Hawkes said, blinking his birdlike eyes, as if the close work had strained them, "the brave follows his spirit wife to the Land of the Dead. If it's more than a myth, and Charles Slocum did bury his lover on Lookout, maybe her husband followed them, and that's how the legend was born."

"If that's true, maybe the husband killed Charles Slocum on the island, and maybe there's another grave."

Now Reverend Hawkes shook his head and smiled widely, as if they'd just spent the last half hour indulging themselves in a fairy tale. "No, Maria. That I'm sure isn't the case, because he's buried right outside, in our churchyard." He walked to the door, and Maria followed him into the shady cemetery along the church's north wall.

There were only twenty or so headstones. Maria walked along the mossy stone path, noticing the names and dates. The engravings on many were nearly worn away. She read the names Brown, Honeyman, Fowler. Several were from the 1700s and were crowned with winged angels of death.

"Charles Slocum is buried here," Reverend Hawkes said, stopping before a short headstone, no thicker than a small-town telephone book. Crouching beside it, Maria could distinguish several letters in the name Charles, but only *S* and *L* in Slocum. His dates were blurred. "You're sure it's his?" she asked.

"One of the first things they told me when I came to this church was that Charles Slocum lies buried in our graveyard. We're proud of it—he played as great a role as anyone in the settlement of Hatuquitit."

Kneeling before it, Maria felt an archaeologist's desire to excavate, to open the Englishman's coffin and see if she'd find an arrowhead in his rib cage, a signet ring on one of the bones that had been a finger. If she dug, she was convinced that she would find the arrowhead but not the ring.

"It's a romantic idea, isn't it?" Reverend Hawkes asked. "Parish records say Charles Slocum died of fever, but 'fever' could have been a euphemism for something less seemly."

"Like being killed by his lover's husband."

"Exactly."

At the sound of someone coming through the gate, they looked up. Alicia and Jamey Murdoch were walking into the churchyard, carrying a basket of tomatoes.

"Hi, Jonathan," Alicia said. Sun coming through the leaves dappled her silvery hair. She gave Maria a curious smile. "Jamey wanted to bring you our first tomatoes."

So far Jamey hadn't noticed Maria. He darted from headstone to headstone. "Where's the oldest one, Uncle Jonathan?" he asked. "That one you showed me last time?"

"You mean Sidney Starr? He's right here," Reverend Hawkes said.

"That's the oldest grave . . . ," Jamey began, delighted. He glanced up, to make sure everyone was paying attention. At the sight of Maria, his mouth fell open, and then he smiled. "Hi," he said.

"Hi, Jamey," Maria said, her chest tightening.

"Oh, you know each other?" Alicia said, coming forward to be introduced. "Didn't I see you at Olivia Jenkins's?"

"She's Daddy's girlfriend," Jamey said happily.

Alicia's face crumbled; her eyes went blank. She stood still, her arms at her sides. Her uncle had taken the basket of tomatoes from her.

"Hello," Maria said, knowing at that instant that no matter what Duncan had told her, Alicia didn't want their marriage to be over.

"Hello," Alicia said.

They stood there, face-to-face, for several long, awkward seconds, until Reverend Hawkes tapped Maria's shoulder. "Let me pack that ring in a plastic bag or something, all right?"

"That would be great," Maria said, grateful. They walked into his office, leaving Alicia and Jamey outside.

"I'm sorry about . . . ," Maria began, but Reverend Hawkes stopped her with one raised hand. Whether he meant that it didn't matter or that he didn't want to talk about it, she didn't know. She felt her face redden.

"Your theory is fascinating," he said. "I'm so glad you brought the ring to me. Maybe you'll give a talk on the subject for our historical society."

"I'd be happy to," Maria said. "I'll try to learn more."

And she left his office through an interior door, the one that would take her through the church instead of the graveyard where Charles Slocum lay buried and Duncan's wife and son waited for the reverend to come out and tell them she had gone.

Maria felt jumpy anyway, and it didn't help matters when Hallie was late getting the kids back from Mystic Seaport. She wanted to work out her hypothesis, go over the evidence again, but Gwen had pulled into the driveway at five o'clock—on the nose, as they'd discussed over the phone last week. She was sitting there now, in the driver's seat, eyes straight ahead, waiting for the children to come out. A heat wave had drifted in, blurring the crisp clearness of the previous week. Watching her from the living room, Maria figured Gwen must be very hot. Gwen had parked in the shade of a maple. She had all four windows open, fanning herself, glancing now and then at the front door. After ten minutes, Maria went out.

"Simon and Flo are late," Maria said. "Would you like to come in and wait for them?"

Gwen checked her watch doubtfully. "I thought we *said* five o'clock," she said.

"We did," Maria said. "But my mother took them to Mystic . . ." With someone else she might have added "And you know Hallie," but not with Gwen.

"Okay. I'll come in," Gwen said in a forceful tone that implied she was complying under duress. She climbed out of her car wearing a two-piece bathing suit and a white lace thigh-length cover-up. As she preceded Maria into the house, Maria noticed that she had great legs. Her toenails, like her fingernails, were lacquered a frosty shade somewhere between salmon and rose, and she wore open-toed strapless sandals. They slapped her soles gently as she walked. They were of a sort much favored in Milan; Aldo would have called them "fuck-me shoes."

Inside, Gwen looked around pointedly, noticing the view, then turning her back on it. She sat in a Boston rocker, facing into the room. "Doesn't it get lonely in the winter out here?" she asked.

"No, I like it," Maria said. "It's taken me a while to get used to all the summer people."

"You've always been one for those lonely spots," Gwen said. "Mind if I smoke?"

Maria handed her a small brass ashtray. Gwen held it up, examining it, then dropped the match in. Maria noticed a slight shake in Gwen's hand, and dark half-moons skillfully hidden with makeup under her eyes. Maria so accepted Sophie's view of Gwen that she sometimes forgot what Gwen had endured. But now, sitting with Gwen in her living room, she felt a rush of sympathy.

"How have you and Ed been?" Maria asked in a smooth tone that didn't give away too much.

Gwen shrugged. "We're coping," she said. An awkward silence passed. "We look forward to seeing our grandchildren," she said.

"I know they enjoy seeing you," Maria said.

"I'm so worried about them," Gwen said. "What they must be going through. When I start feeling too sorry for myself, I just think of Simon and Flo."

"They're seeing a therapist," Maria said.

"The shame of it all is what a beautiful family they were, all of them," Gwen said, her voice thin and full of wonder. "Gordon adored your sister. Just adored her."

At this, Maria's spine stiffened; she was ready to speak up, but Gwen continued.

"I'll never forget when they first met. It was 'Sophie, Sophie, Sophie' all the time. 'If I hear that name once more. . . !' I'd say to Ed. Gordon had had a lovely girlfriend in college, terribly sweet and polished. Went to some finishing school in Virginia—she graduated from Bryn Mawr. I was crazy about her. 'Marry her,' I'd say to Gordon. This girl understood a man's needs—that was clear from the start. She was pretty and unassuming—very shy, but the only time she visited us in Slocum she surprised us all by cooking a marvelous four-course meal. I thought she was perfect for him.

"Anyway, it didn't work out. Whatever. When he met your sister, I had my reservations—the rebound thing. Also, the fact she was local, hadn't been out of state to college. I wasn't sure she was his . . . intellectual equal . . . and I was afraid they'd grow apart after a while. But my God! Gordon was mad for her. He told me she was smart as a whip, knew how to cook like a chef, that she left Shelley—that was her name—in the dust. And you know: I really had to agree."

"You did?" Maria said, surprised that Gwen would make such a concession. She had been expecting Gwen to say "I knew it all along, I knew she was bad for him." Maria felt disloyal, talking about Sophie, but she wanted Gwen to finish.

"Yes. I did. She was lovely. That porcelain skin women kill for, that gorgeous hair, wonderful figure. She was exquisite. Gordon would go all starry-eyed when he saw her. I'd raised him to look for three things in a woman: brains, devotion, and beauty. In that order."

"That's Sophie," Maria agreed. Her brains and, before she got fat, her beauty were unmistakable. Her devotion was selective, but once she singled someone out she was relentless.

"I taught her all Gordon's favorite foods, and she picked up the recipes like *that*. Such a quick study. Plus, she was very inventive in the kitchen. I saw that right away. She could whip up lunch from leftovers and you'd think you were eating a feast." Gwen shook her head and put out her cigarette. "Gordon *idolized* her. He bragged constantly. Ed used to tease him, ask him if he could start a sentence with something other than 'My wife.' Gordon put her right on a pedestal . . ." Gwen trailed off wistfully.

He didn't marry a woman, he hired a goddess, Maria thought. "It must have been hard to live up to . . . those expectations," Maria said.

"Apparently," Gwen said, snorting. "Apparently. Don't you think that's strange? I mean, I know she's your sister, but don't you think it's a little odd that she'd have so much trouble being adored?"

"I'd rather be loved than adored," Maria said.

Gwen flapped her hand in the air. "Whatever," she said. She frowned into space for a few seconds. "The point is," she began heatedly, "that Sophie let him down. He gave her everything. That boy could have done anything with his life. He could have run for office, been a golf pro, anything. Instead, he runs his father's prosperous business in order to support his wife and children. And she lets herself go—I've never seen anything like it. Greasy hair, old clothes . . . she looks like the fat lady in the circus."

"Gwen, he abused her," Maria said steadily, but ready to explode.

"Gordon abused her?" Gwen asked with the aplomb of a cabaret singer onstage.

"Yes. He did. He put her in the hospital. He tortured her, and he didn't care if Simon and Flo saw. He took away all her self-confidence," Maria said, her anger flooding out.

"You and your family make me sick," Gwen said. "You all think you're so much better than everyone else, and if you want to make up lies to cover what your sick sister did, that's fine by me. I'm *above* all that."

"But you weren't above locking Gordon in the basement with a *dog* collar around his neck!" Maria shouted.

All the color drained out of Gwen's face. She stared at Maria incredulously, with her mouth ajar. "What are you talking about?" she asked, shaking.

Maria couldn't drop it. "You know what I'm talking about. Gordon told Sophie all about it. Do you want to know what it turned him into? He hurt my sister . . . If you want to talk about *sick*—" For one moment, Maria thought she was going to hit Gwen. But then Gwen twisted out of her chair.

"I'm not going to stay here and listen to this garbage," Gwen said, flying toward the door.

Maria heard car doors slamming. Hallie, Julian, and the kids had pulled into the driveway at the same time as Duncan. Maria checked her watch: five forty-five. Duncan would have figured the kids would be long gone by now. She heard Hallie making charming small talk with him. "And I think that white flagpole you've put in adds so much to the boatyard," she was saying. Maria watched Gwen sweep into everyone's midst to claim her grandchildren, and she looked away, to avoid catching Hallie's expression when the children ran to hug Gwen.

"Well, *she's* ready for the beach," Hallie said after Gwen and the children had driven away. "What a getup."

Taking deep breaths, Maria had walked into the driveway to

join them. She figured that by talking to Hallie and Julian outside, she might avoid having to invite them in. She was dying to ask Hallie if she had ever suspected Sophie had been pregnant a third time, but more than that, she wanted Hallie to leave. Maria wasn't in the mood for her mother.

"Did you have fun at the seaport?" Maria asked.

"Yes, it was great," Hallie said. "Can you imagine, they'd never been aboard the whalers there? Simon was quite taken by the whole thing. He wants to be a whaling captain when he grows up."

"Now, he didn't quite say that," Julian said, chuckling. "As I recall, you said you thought he'd make a fine whaling captain."

Maria smiled at the way Julian was brave enough to call Hallie on her version of the truth.

"Jim saw a minke whale on his way back from fishing at the Race last week," Duncan said.

"A whale in Long Island Sound?" Julian asked.

"Oh, when I was a little girl the Sound was *full* of them," Hallie said. "Whales and porpoises. Whole flocks—is that what you say of whales?" she asked.

"I believe the word is *pods,*" Duncan said.

"Thank you, dear. How's your mother, anyway?"

"She's fine, thanks."

"Just tell me one thing," Hallie said, lowering her voice, turning toward Maria. "What did she have to say about Sophie? Anything?"

"Quite a lot," Maria said.

"I'll just bet," Hallie said. "Was she completely up in arms about that prison show?"

"She didn't even mention it," Maria said, feeling off-balance. "What are you talking about?"

"I'm sure she thinks it's a scandal, prisoners putting on a variety show," Hallie said, seemingly disdainful of Gwen.

"She didn't say a word about it," Maria said. "I know it's you who thinks it's a scandal."

"If it's good for Sophie, I'm all for it," Hallie said.

*   *   *

When she was alone with Duncan, Maria lay on the sofa with her head in his lap staring at the ceiling. She was trying to calm down; her heart was still pounding from screaming at Gwen.

"I got a call from Alicia," Duncan said.

"Did she tell you we met?"

"Yes."

"Does that upset you?"

He hesitated, and she pushed herself up to look into his eyes. His expression looked so sad, she felt her stomach fall.

"What's wrong?" she asked.

"It's hard," he said.

"In what way?" she asked. "I thought you said that you felt close to me, that we . . ."

"I do," he said. "Closer than I've ever felt to anyone. But it's hard. We were married a long time, Maria."

"I know," she said, nodding, touching his hand. "Just because you don't want to be married to her doesn't mean you don't care how she feels. And I think . . ."

"What?"

"I think she's still in love with you."

"The separation is harder on her than on me. She's left in the house where we lived together, with all our furniture, everything that reminds her of when we were happy. I haven't wanted to tell you, but she called me, asking me if we can try to work it out."

"Really?" Maria asked, feeling cold and scared. "Do you want to?"

"When she said that, I asked her what she thought we'd been doing the last five years. Maybe longer. I'm not even sure how it started. All of a sudden I noticed we weren't paying attention to each other—not at all. It was okay, at first. I had the boatyard, she had her friends. Later, Jamey. We were on different schedules. I'd come home late, she'd be on the phone. She would have eaten with Jamey, so I'd heat up whatever was left and eat in the kitchen while she did . . . other things."

"Did you still love each other?"

"I don't remember—but not for a long time. We shared a

house, that's all. We hardly ever touched. Sometimes I'd want to make love, and she'd give in." He was quiet, remembering. "After a while, I realized I just wanted to have sex. It had nothing to do with Alicia. She didn't want me, and I didn't want her. It seemed kind of dispiriting."

"Would you fix it if you could? Would you go back five years and make it better this time?"

Duncan took Maria's hand. He held it gently, balancing it on his knee. "I couldn't do that. I've met you."

"But not counting that," Maria persisted, remembering Alicia's devastated expression. "If you could get back to what you had when you were in love with Alicia, would you do it?"

"I *have* to count that," Duncan said. "I can't pretend the last five years haven't happened, and I can't pretend I haven't fallen in love with you."

"But I saw her face," Maria said. "She's still in love with you."

"She's not," Duncan said. "She couldn't be. She misses the idea of something we had a long time ago."

Maria nodded, knowing what he meant.

"We'll get through this," Duncan said. "I promise you."

Maria rested her head on his shoulder, tracing his callused index finger with her thumb. She felt the ambiguity of knowing that there were no easy answers, the peace and hope of having the man she loved beside her. Looking at their hands made her think of the gold ring.

And sitting in her house at Squaw's Landing, she told Duncan the story of a Pequot woman who was murdered for loving an Englishman, of how the Englishman had buried her with his gold ring in a grave on an island in the sea.

35

"WHERE ARE YOU GOING?" SIMON ASKED MARIA. Maria glanced down at him, surprised that he would ask. She had told him the night before that she was going to visit Sophie.

"To see your mother," Maria said.

"Who's going to take care of us?" Flo asked.

"I told you last night, Duncan and Jamey are coming over. Is that okay?"

"I like them. They're nice," Flo said. She made her way slowly to the front door, where she ran her fingertips across the fine-mesh screen and kept watch for the Murdochs.

Simon seemed to be gauging the level of Flo's interest in the screen and the imminent arrival of Duncan and Jamey. When he seemed satisfied that she was really absorbed, he handed an envelope to Maria. Maria read the address:

Mrs. Sophie D. Littlefield
Hatuquitit Jail
Hatuquitit, Connecticut

"You wrote your mother a letter?" Maria asked.

Simon nodded. He looked up but did not quite meet Maria's eye.

"What a good idea, Simon. What's wrong?"

"Do you think she'll read it?" he asked.

"Of course she will. Why would you think she wouldn't?"

"If she won't see *me,* what makes you think she'll read my letter?"

"I just know she will, that's all," Maria said, although she could see Simon's point.

Sophie entered the visitors' room smiling. "I'm glad to see you," she said.

"And I'm glad to see you," Maria said. "It's so nice and cool in here—it's scorching outside." She had some hard things to discuss with Sophie today; she floundered around with small talk.

"They keep the air conditioning turned up so high," Sophie said. "It dries up my throat. All I can think about is getting out of here." Her smile dissolved. "This'll be the first summer I haven't gone to Hatuquitit Beach."

To Maria, for whom it was the first summer in nine years that she had gone to Hatuquitit Beach, that statement put Sophie's situation in a real and bleak perspective.

"It'll be years before I get there again," Sophie said.

"You don't know that."

"Steve told me the prosecutor has suggested a plan. If I plead guilty to manslaughter, I'll be eligible for parole in six years."

"Six years?" Maria asked, calculating Simon's and Flo's ages. Flo's age would double and she would be twelve; Simon would be sixteen. "Why would you agree to that?"

"There's some question about the gun," Sophie said. "They're not convinced it was Gordon's in the first place. You know what I'm talking about, don't you?"

"Stamford?" Maria asked, and Sophie nodded. Maria held Sophie's hand. With her other hand, Maria felt in her pocket for Simon's letter. She laid it on the table.

"Oh dear," Sophie said. She smoothed the envelope, then lifted it to her face. She took a deep breath, as if the envelope contained Simon himself and she wanted to catch his scent.

Maria pushed her chair back from the table and faced the barred window, wanting to give Sophie some privacy. She stared across the treeline toward Hatuquitit Harbor. The railroad bridge had opened, and the *Deep Blue IV,* a party fishing boat, was steaming through. Now and then her eyes flicked back to Sophie; it made her feel like a voyeur. Although Sophie read without expression, her mouth slightly open, tears trickled down her cheeks. Maria had to look away.

Sophie snuffled a few times. Her eyes were red-rimmed and tired. "I've got to see them," she said.

"Is that why he wrote to you?" Maria asked. "To ask you if they could come?"

"No," Sophie said. "He just wanted to tell me he's having a nice summer fishing with Peter and Duncan and having cookouts with you. That's all he said. That, plus he hopes I'm not too worried about him and Flo." This released a new flood of tears. Sophie rested her forehead on the Formica tabletop and cried. "That's a good one," she said. "Not too worried about them."

"You want to see them?" Maria asked.

After a long stretch of snuffling, her head in her hands, Sophie looked up. "I've always wanted to *see* them, Maria."

"And now you *will*?" Maria pressed.

When Sophie didn't speak, Maria imagined what she was thinking. Perhaps she had been hoping for—counting on—an early release: in a few weeks or another month. She could force herself to wait that long without seeing her children. She could endure that if it meant sparing them having to see her in the jail. But now, with six very real years to contemplate, her need to see them might have risen to the surface.

"Six years," Sophie said again, shaking her head. But then her expression changed. "It's not that I don't deserve it."

"That's just one possibility," Maria said with what sounded— to her—like phony optimism.

"Hmmm," Sophie said.

Maria watched Sophie frowning, tapping her fingers. "Was that all Simon put in the letter?" she asked after a while.

"Just about. Why? Did something happen?" Sophie asked, her antennae up.

"We were telling ghost stories the other night," Maria said evenly. "Flo told one about a dead baby. Simon got very upset and said that she wasn't supposed to talk about it, that he was going to tell you she'd told."

The blood rushed out of Sophie's already pale face. "He didn't mention it in the letter."

"Do you know what Flo was talking about?" Maria asked, on pins and needles.

"She was talking about my baby," Sophie said.

Maria sat very still, watching her sister's face contort with something close to agony. Maria felt helpless, as if she were sitting beside a friend at the funeral of the one that person had loved most in the world. "I didn't know you had another baby," Maria said.

"No one knew I was pregnant," Sophie said. "Gordon wanted it that way. He said we should keep it secret, that it was a sacred thing for our family to share alone until the last minute. It was the same with Simon and Flo."

That was true: Maria remembered how hurt she'd been to get Sophie's letter telling her she was three months pregnant with what turned out to be Simon. Aldo had accused her of being a possessive older sister for dwelling on how Sophie could have kept such a momentous event secret from Maria for so long.

"How come no one in the family ever knew?"

"I'd been gaining weight," Sophie said. "They must have thought that's what it was . . ."

"When, Sophie?"

"It happened last fall," Sophie said. "One weekend when the leaves were brilliant, when we'd planned to take the kids on a foliage cruise. We'd made reservations at that place on the Mohawk Trail."

"That one by the river?" Maria asked. Hallie and Malcolm had once taken them through the Berkshires to look at fall leaves, and they had stayed in a beautiful white hotel with tall columns. It had overlooked a wide green river that reflected the red, yellow, and orange sugar maples. Maria hadn't thought of it in years. "You were there?"

"We never left home," Sophie said. "I was cross with the kids or something, and Gordon and I had a fight."

"The baby had been born?" Maria asked, not understanding how the entire family could have been fooled.

"I only made it to six months," Sophie said. "She would have been born around Christmas. Remember that time when you were deciding to rent the house at Squaw's Landing? And I told you I'd miscarried?"

"Oh, Sophie," Maria said, stricken. "It was true." That day, she had known Sophie couldn't lie about something like that; remembering how angry she'd been at Sophie after Gordon said that he didn't know what Maria was talking about, she felt full of shame.

"It was true," Sophie said.

"What happened?" Maria asked.

"Gordon pushed me into a wall and I started going into labor," Sophie said.

"At six months?" Maria asked, aware of an acrid taste that filled her mouth, nose, and lungs like ether, which Maria realized was horror. "What did Dr. Salter say?"

"Dr. Salter never knew," Sophie said. "Gordon delivered the baby himself."

"Sophie, no," Maria said. Watching her sister, she could see that Sophie was reliving it. Sophie's hands shook; Maria could believe she had left the jail, had traveled back ten months. Maria wondered about the pain, about what Gordon knew about delivering a baby, about how Sophie could just let it happen. But above all that, she remembered what Sophie had said months ago about the miscarriage, that it had been just like giving birth.

"It happened in our bedroom," Sophie said in a voice like a sleepwalker. "On our bed. I felt the baby coming, and I just wanted to die."

"Sophie, no . . ."

"Yes, I did, Maria."

"Why didn't you call someone?" Maria asked. "Peter? Or the police?"

Sophie seemed to come back. She gave Maria a long, direct stare. Then she faded away again. "It hurt so much, just as much as when I had Simon and Flo. I mean, I was giving birth. Going into labor and having a baby. But the worst part was knowing I would lose this one. I knew it the whole time." Sophie paused. "She was born alive."

"She was born alive?" Maria repeated.

Sophie nodded. "Gordon put her on my stomach and she lay there until she stopped breathing. It's unimaginable, how tiny she was. Hardly like a baby at all. Then he picked her up and wrapped her in Flo's christening gown. He cried . . ."

"He was sorry?"

"I don't know," Sophie said, her voice empty. "He just cried. The next day we told the kids I'd lost the baby, and we all walked down to Bell Stream. He let me choose the spot to bury her."

"Didn't the doctor make you put her in a cemetery?" Maria asked. "Isn't that the law?"

"The doctor never knew I was pregnant. I just healed myself. We never told him. We baptized her in Bell Stream, and dug a hole to put her in."

"She's there now?" Maria asked. She could see the whole thing: Gordon slamming Sophie into the wall, delivering their baby, leading the family in a funeral procession to the stream. "You buried her near the stream?"

"Under a little statue of an angel," Sophie said. "We put it there to mark her grave."

Maria felt as if she'd taken a step into the Littlefields' world. She felt covered with a film of cobwebs; she squirmed in her seat. "Why did you let it happen?" she asked, wanting to shake herself free. "Why did you let him do those things to you?"

But Sophie was lost to her. She rose without meeting Maria's gaze, and walked toward the door.

"Sophie? Will you see Simon and Flo?" Maria called. "Will you let them visit?"

"Can you really imagine that will help them?" Sophie asked, turning toward her. "Even Hallie's a good mother compared to me. And look how I feel about Hallie. I hate her, I swear I do. And if I hate her, how do you think my kids are going to feel about me?"

"Let them decide how they feel about you," Maria said harshly. "At least do that for them."

Sophie leaned against the door, seeming to consider Maria's idea. "Okay," she said. "Bring them." Then she left the room.

Maria sat at the table for a long time, until a matron tapped her on the shoulder and told her it was time to leave.

For the first time since the night of Gordon's murder, Maria returned to the Littlefields' house. Signs of the police investigation were evident: a notice stapled to the door, an orange plastic tape that had once blocked off the driveway but now lay on the pavement, an empty McDonald's bag. Maria could almost see the white outline of Gordon's body. Clumps of orange daylilies were in full bloom. Weeds had taken over Sophie's herb and perennial gardens. The lawn needed to be mown.

Maria sat in her car for several minutes taking in these and other details: two dishtowels hanging on the line, a living room window left open more than a crack, Simon's red Sting Ray bike leaning against the garage. Then she not so much climbed out as launched herself from the car. Without another glance at the house, she headed through the tall grass toward Bell Stream.

The day she had received the letter from Hallie telling her Sophie and Gordon had bought this property, Maria had felt jealous. She had been living in London without Aldo for the summer, giving a series of lectures at the British Museum. Of all the places she'd lived, London made her the least homesick, but she remembered the true, heart-piercing pang she had felt to think of Sophie settling down on Bell Stream.

When Aldo had come for the weekend from Edinburgh, where he was lecturing, Maria had told him about it. He had reacted with amusement. "She'll live within sight of your mother?" he had asked, incredulous. "Poor Gordon!"

"What's wrong with that?" Maria had asked. "Sophie loves Bell Stream."

"But so close to home!" Aldo had said.

It was the apogee of their struggle over where to live: Maria claimed that she didn't care where, as long as they made it permanent. She wanted her own house or apartment, a garden or terrace where she could grow flowers and vegetables, an address she could have engraved on stationery. Over the years she had thrown out pounds of stationery because the printed address had become obsolete.

"At least she'll own a place," Maria said. "She'll have her own land."

"I'm surprised at you, Maria," Aldo had said, sounding genuinely disappointed. "You of all people not realizing the futility of ownership. Okay, so you buy your little square of earth, and you occupy it for how long? Twenty years? Fifty? When you think of the hundreds of people who will occupy that earth before time is done . . . think of Rome."

"Oh, why don't you just say 'dust to dust'?" Maria had asked, feeling so misunderstood.

She had always thought he was just being cheap, applying his archaeological nihilism to real estate, but now, walking through the Littlefields' deserted property, she felt the pessimism he had preached. She could easily believe that no relative of hers would ever live here again. The place would be sold, the funds put in trust for Simon and Flo. Not right away but years later it would add value to the place, the fact that a murder had taken place there. That it was haunted.

Now Maria left what had been the lawn and walked into the field Sophie and Gordon had always left wild. Daisies, asters, thistles, black-eyed Susans, and hawkweed grew among the yellow grasses. She kept to the path: although it hadn't actually been cleared, it had been trod often enough to show her the way.

Maria thought she heard a voice and looked up. Wind brushing through pine needles sounded like a whisper. She had come to the edge of Bell Stream. Glancing north, she saw a thicket too dense to penetrate, and so she walked south, toward Hallie's. She wondered where the Littlefields' property ended and the neighbors' began. The ground turned muddy in the shade. Maria walked along, and suddenly she realized she was looking for the baby's grave.

She walked much farther than she had expected, and still she hadn't found it. Surely by now she had crossed the Littlefields' property line and one or two others. Hallie's land was just around the bend. Maria was about to turn around, retrace her steps, when she saw the stone angel.

She'd been damaged. One wing had broken off, and her nose was chipped. She was nestled at the foot of a small hill, nearly hidden by bayberry. In spite of the stone's relative newness, moss grew in its crevices. She had stone curls and a sad smile; Maria imagined there was no sweeter angel in any chapel anywhere. She was small, just twelve inches tall.

Disoriented, Maria glanced around. Sophie had said Gordon let her choose the burial site, but why here? This wasn't their yard; it might have been Hallie's, but just. Then Maria realized: Sophie's stone heart was just around the bend. She walked to it, uncovered it with the toe of her shoe, then returned to the angel.

Maria knelt in the mud before her, to say a prayer, and as she did so, she saw that someone had chiseled a name in the stone: HATHAWAY DARK LITTLEFIELD.

Maria remembered Hallie's pride, telling her that Sophie had been planning to name the miscarried baby Hathaway, after her. Holding branches back from the angel, she felt her eyes fill with tears. She thought of the secret Sophie had kept inside, letting it out bit by bit when its weight became too great. Telling a little to Hallie, a little to Nell, a little to Maria, then backtracking with lies.

She remembered when she and Sophie were little girls, playing by this stream every day. How could they have known that one day Sophie would bury her daughter on its banks? And then, at the thought of the little girl she would never know, who would never play with her own sister and brother, tears fell down her cheeks. Her hands held back the bayberry, and Maria wept for Sophie's daughter and for the fact that Sophie had named her Hathaway after the mother Sophie claimed to hate.

36

MARIA KNOWS THE WORST THING. IT FEELS strange, having someone else know. When I was telling her, I felt like an angel myself, hovering over our heads. I kept track of my voice, of Maria's reactions. I could see her thinking: *How could you have let it happen? Why didn't you make him take you to the hospital?* She just couldn't believe it. Who could?

Maria, does it help you to know I'm glad it happened? I can rest, thinking of that baby at peace. Buried deep in the ground on the bank of Bell Stream, just across the border of Mom's land. She died in her mother's arms, my daughter. She's the only one in our family who will ever know peace. Simon won't. Flo won't. And Gordon and I . . .

That morning when we were packed and set to go, I was feeling queasy and heavy; I had misgivings about taking such a long drive. I'd told Simon to stop dawdling—yelled at him, really. Gordon shoved me into the wall as hard as he'd ever done. I gaped at him—he'd never hurt me before when I was pregnant. But all he did was tell me to leave Simon alone.

A few minutes later we were climbing into the car, and I had a contraction. I told Gordon.

"Well, kids, your mother doesn't want to go," Gordon said. He told them I'd spoiled the trip before it even started, and without saying anything else, he headed the car toward Gwen's. Simon started fussing, defending me, asking Gordon to give me another chance. But Gordon just kept driving. I was thinking *Good, let's drop the kids off, let them get away from all this.* Because by then I was cramping pretty badly, and I didn't want them to see me in pain. I just wanted to crawl into bed.

When Gordon and I were on the way home, every bad thing he'd ever done to me flooded into my mind. The hurting, the cruelty, the threats. All of a sudden I felt a warm rush of liquid. I reached down, under my skirt, to make sure it wasn't blood, but it wasn't: my water had broken.

"Take me to the hospital," I said.

"I'm taking you home," Gordon said.

I started to cry because I knew then that I'd lose the baby. The oaks and maples along the shore were such bright colors I wondered why we'd ever decided to go north in the first place. I blamed myself for planning the trip, for convincing Gordon we should stay at that inn where I'd stayed as a child. He'd been out to sabotage the trip from the beginning.

Gordon drove with his teeth clenched. He kept glancing at me. At first I imagined he was feeling guilty because he realized I was losing the baby and that it was his fault. Or maybe I was just annoying him. At that point I stopped worrying about what Gordon thought. I began to realize that losing the baby would be a blessing. One less soul for Gordon and me to make miserable.

By the time we got home the contractions were strong and constant. I was crying too hard to breathe properly, and Gordon had to carry me into the house. He carried me upstairs and laid me on our bed. He lifted my skirt and took off my panties, and then he put his head down on my stomach, which had just begun to be big, and started to sob. "I'm so sorry," he said.

Other times when Gordon said "I'm sorry" it would feel like a revelation. *Things will start to get better,* I'd think. But by that day in October, I was past all that. I could believe that Gordon was sorry, but I had learned enough by then to realize it didn't mean that he was going to change.

Having that baby was just like having Simon and Flo. Maybe it took a little less time: the contractions seemed to come one after another right away. I lay on our bed doing my breathing, with

Gordon right there coaching me. He was wiping the sweat off my brow with a cool washcloth, telling me it wasn't time to push yet.

Between contractions I'd look around our room at the familiar things: our wedding picture, Simon and Flo's baby and school pictures, the picture of Hatuquitit in the twenties, our mahogany bureau, Gordon's rolltop desk, the open closet full of our clothes. To distract myself I'd pick out outfits and remember where I'd worn them. The white silk jacket with black piping I'd worn on our cruise to Bermuda, the faded peach sundress I'd worn all last summer because it was baggy enough to hide my pregnancy, the gray wool slacks I'd bought with Hallie on our last trip to New York.

Gordon gave me a pain pill and I took it. I didn't care about the effects of any drug on this baby. A haze settled over me, and I stopped caring about anything. I stopped crying. I felt very cold and analytical. At one point, watching Gordon sob, I said, "Why did you push me if you didn't want this to happen?"

He didn't answer; he only cried.

Finally, she was born. A tiny pink kitten opening and closing her mouth without making a sound. Gordon laid her on my stomach while he cut the cord. I held her in my arms, touching her little fingers, feeling her chest quiver with each breath. She was a perfect little baby, just like Flo only smaller. She might even have lived, if there'd been an incubator, if we'd been at the hospital. But of course we weren't.

Gordon asked me what we should name her. I said "Hathaway," after Mom. I didn't even have another choice. Mom may have bungled motherhood from the start, but it wasn't because she didn't love us. She loves us the way she loved her parents and Dad—with all she's got. She just didn't know how to turn it around, go from being a daughter to being a mother. She never knew what to do with us.

The next day we picked up Simon and Flo from Gwen's, and we told them that they'd had a sister but she died. They wanted to see her. Gordon took them to the nursery, where she lay wrapped in the christening gown, and showed her to them. And then I put on my black dress, and Gordon got a shovel, and we formed a funeral procession through the meadow.

Gordon was so good to me that day. I carried Hathaway's body, and he let me do it alone. Somehow he knew I didn't want to be touched. When we reached the stream, I turned left. "Sophie, our land stops here," he said.

"I know," I said, and I just kept walking.

He and the children followed me. No one said anything; they must have figured I was heading for Hallie's stretch of stream. I had it in mind that that land had belonged to the Dark family for generations and probably would continue to. Maybe I already knew what would happen between me and Gordon.

Also, I wanted to bury my daughter near the heart. I'll always remember walking down Hatuquitit Beach, Maria, with you and Nell, to gather stones, then carrying them home to Bell Stream and arranging them on the ground in the shape of a heart.

To me, it's one big story about love. The story of the boy and girl who wanted to marry so badly they'd stand on opposite sides of the stream in a storm. But also the story of you and me and Nell and Peter and Mom and Dad. When we were forming that heart, I was thinking about our family and how much I loved you all. That's why I wanted to bury Hathaway near the stone heart. Burying her, I felt dizzy with love for her and Simon and Flo, for all of you. And, in spite of everything, for Gordon.

37

SIMON AND FLO PUT ON THEIR BEST CLOTHES TO visit Sophie. Simon wore his chino pants, a red striped shirt, a Covey School tie, and a blue blazer. Flo wore her tutu.

"What about your yellow party dress?" Hallie suggested. "Or even your pink and white seersucker?"

"Let her wear the tutu," Maria said.

Hallie obviously didn't care much for the idea of the Dark family trooping into the prison auditorium looking anything like a show themselves. Maria imagined Hallie thinking of the Darks as diplomats of Hatuquitit, the reigning local family making an appearance—a dignified appearance—amid other prison families from Waterbury, Bainbridge, and Milford.

The whole family wanted to give their support to Sophie. Because of the large number of visitors expected for the show, the prison had scheduled specific visiting hours. Sophie's allotted period was one hour before curtain time, at two o'clock.

Everyone squeezed into Peter's station wagon. He and Nell sat in front; Simon, Hallie, and Maria sat in back, and Flo and Andy rode in the third seat. Hallie had judged it best that Julian not come; she had thought that by talking to Sophie he would take up time better left to Simon and Flo.

"What is 'wardrobe mistress'?" Simon asked. He wriggled with excitement.

"It means that your mother is in charge of all the costumes," Nell said. "She has to make sure everyone gets changed and buttoned up on time."

"Are we there now?" Flo asked for the second time.

"Almost. Another minute, sweetheart," Peter said.

Maria wished that Duncan were with her. Knowing how nervous Maria felt about the first meeting between Sophie and her children since her imprisonment, he had offered to come. But after much consideration, they'd decided that his presence would only add to the family's tension.

"I just have a feeling . . . ," Hallie said happily.

"What?" Peter and Nell asked at once.

"I don't know . . . it's probably just a fantasy, but I think Sophie is going to sing today."

"On the stage?" Simon asked.

"No," Maria said with a stern look at Hallie. "She is not. She's wardrobe mistress, and we should be very proud of her."

"Mommy's good at getting people dressed," Flo said.

"Yeah," Simon said. "Being wardrobe mistress is awesome."

"It's just a feeling," Hallie said, singsong.

But the family's jolly mood evaporated as Peter stopped at the prison gates and spoke to the guard. Maria squeezed Simon's hand, viewing the now-familiar scene as if for the first time, as the children must be seeing it. The red brick building, as imposing as any New England state capitol building except for the window bars; tall anchor fences topped with coils of barbed and razor wire; unsmiling uniformed guards everywhere.

"This is where she lives?" Simon asked doubtfully.

"You know that, sweetie," Nell said. "Haven't we driven past a hundred times?"

"Yes," Simon said.

"Can we get out of prison when we want to?" Flo asked.

"Yes, we absolutely can," Peter said.

"Your uncle comes here all the time," Nell said. "He's an officer of the court."

"Do you visit Mommy *every* time you come here?" Flo asked.

"Well, not every time," Peter said, chuckling.

"He has lots of clients here," Nell said. "Other ladies who need his help."

To Maria, Peter and Nell sounded like proud residents of a picturesque coastal town, showing it off to friends visiting New England from Arkansas for the first time.

"This had better be some show," Hallie said ominously, her left hand gripping her throat.

Based upon discussions among the family and with Dr. Middleton, Steve Grunwald, and the prison psychologists, it was decided that the entire family should meet Sophie in a conference room first, and not leave Simon and Flo alone with her until everyone felt comfortable. Maria had coached everyone to act as normally as possible, taking the focus off the children and Sophie, specifically not watching them for the moment of reunion.

The Darks and the Littlefield children walked silently down a long hallway. Maria felt relieved that it seemed no more threatening than the average elementary school corridor. Peter located Conference Room B, and he threw open the door.

Sophie sat in an easy chair, her legs crossed, reading a magazine. She wore her usual lavender-blue dress. She had brushed her hair until it shone, and she had gotten a yellow bow from somewhere. The matron, who had been standing by the door, exchanged glances with Peter, and then she left the family alone. Sophie looked up.

"Well, well," she said. "Hi, everyone." Although she spoke to the family at large, she had eyes only for Simon and Flo. They stared at her for the first few seconds, frozen in place. When everyone walked toward Sophie, to greet her, they hung back.

Sophie beamed, kissing Hallie, Peter, and Maria. She gave Nell an extra-long hug. "I haven't seen you in so long!" she said.

"I'm really sorry, I've turned into Annette Funicello," Nell said. "Andy won't let me leave the beach. We get there at ten, and we don't leave till naptime."

"Oooh, all that *sun*!" Hallie exclaimed disapprovingly.

"That's okay," Sophie said, her eyes seeking out Simon and

Flo. "I understand. There aren't enough beach days in a year, are there? Are there, Simon?"

"I don't like the beach anymore," he said.

"You don't?" Sophie asked. For three seconds her face threatened to fall, but then she grinned brilliantly. "Neither do I. Too much icky sand. And sand fleas. And jellyfish."

"And eels!" Flo called. She moved, hesitantly at first and then like a missile, toward Sophie. Sophie opened her arms and pulled Flo into a hug so tight Maria heard them both gasp. After a while Simon went forward. He paused for half a second, then tried to yank Flo out of Sophie's arms and wedge himself in.

"Hey, hey, *gentle*," Sophie admonished, kissing him.

"How come they made you wardrobe mistress?" Simon asked.

"Because I'm so stylish," Sophie said.

"You're skinny, Mommy," Flo said.

"I am? Do I look good?" she asked.

"You look great, Sofe," Peter said.

"You do," Simon said.

"Yes, dear, you do," Hallie said.

Maria and Sophie exchanged a smile—as long as Sophie *looked* good . . .

"Where's Julian, anyway?" Sophie asked, looking around.

Peter, Nell, and Maria started to laugh. "Mom wouldn't let him come. She didn't want to give him an unfair allotment of time with you," Peter said.

"Well, what's so bad about that?" Hallie asked, pretending to be indignant. "He can talk the ear off a brass monkey. He'd start talking about the Isle of Wight or somewhere, and the next thing you know, our time would be up. What time does the show start, anyway?"

"Three o'clock," Sophie said.

"Wardrobe mistress, eh, Sofe?" Peter asked, grinning. "You got lots of costume changes in this show?"

"Sixteen, to be exact," Sophie said, surprising Maria by how proud she sounded. Sophie didn't seem as pale as she had on

Maria's most recent visits. Her eyes sparkled, gazing at her children, who leaned against her.

"It's a shame to be dressing others when they should be dressing you," Hallie said.

"It's a shame?" Sophie asked, her voice cooling off.

"Yes, that's what I say," Hallie said, as if she was giving Sophie a challenge.

Sophie's eyes flashed, trying to stare Hallie down, but Hallie wouldn't back down.

"Well, it may be a shame, but it's the way it is," Sophie said.

"I think it's nice, the way you're in charge of everyone's clothes," Simon said eagerly. "What are they wearing?"

"Let's see. Bess is wearing a magician's cape and holding a magic wand. Peg and Tamara are dressing in a camel suit. Marla is disguised as Donny Osmond."

"What's that act?" Nell asked, giggling.

"She's lip-synching 'Puppy Love,' played at high speed," Sophie said.

"What are you singing?" Hallie asked.

"Mom . . . ," Maria said, trying out a warning glance that Hallie promptly ignored.

"I told you, I'm wardrobe . . . ," Sophie stammered, her face losing color.

"I know, Sophie," Hallie said, standing beside Sophie's chair and placing her hand on Sophie's head. She stroked her hair with obvious affection. "I know, I know. Maybe I'm being an old bore, but I still hear you singing that aria from Donizetti, you know the one . . ."

"I don't remember it," Sophie said. Her voice faltered slightly, and when she smiled it wasn't as brightly as before. Maria could see that she had patched herself together bravely, but seams were beginning to open.

"What do you say we—" Maria began, but Hallie interrupted.

"I wish you were singing in the show, that's all," Hallie said stubbornly. "I'm sure you'd be the best one up there by a mile, and I'd just about faint with pride to hear you. I see that dirty look, Maria. Is it such a crime for a mother to be proud of her daughter's voice?"

"Except for the fact that she's not singing, no," Maria said.

"Come on, everyone," Peter said heartily, clapping his hands. "Let's give these kids a little time alone with their mother."

"I'm coming, I'm coming," Hallie said, leaning down to kiss the top of Sophie's head. "Break a leg, will you, darling?"

"Thank you," Sophie said, staring stonily ahead.

But when Maria leaned down to kiss her cheek, Sophie's face came wildly alive. "Will you stay with us? Me and the kids?" Sophie asked.

"Sure," Maria said, waving Hallie, Peter, Nell, and Andy out the door.

"Why did Gram say that?" Simon asked, frowning. " 'Break a leg'?"

"Oh, it's an old saying in the theater," Maria said, because Sophie wasn't talking. "It means 'Good luck.' "

"It's stupid, telling someone to break their leg," Simon said in his sullen voice. As if a spell had been broken, the children had pulled away from Sophie and were drifting around the room.

"It is stupid, isn't it?" Sophie said.

"And *dumb!*" Flo said.

"Come here, my little Flopsy," Sophie said, patting her leg. Flo obeyed, settling onto Sophie's knee to suck her thumb while Sophie twirled her hair.

Simon had found some chalk and began to write his name on the blackboard. Pretending to concentrate, he was watching Sophie and Flo out of the corner of his eye.

"You two look pretty spiffy," Sophie said. "I can see your Aunt Maria is taking good care of you."

"She does," Flo said, not taking her thumb out of her mouth. Although Flo's words made Maria feel absurdly happy, she tried not to show it. Tension made the room buzz like an electrical storm. Sophie had been watching her with the kids, the kids were watching Sophie, and Maria just wanted everyone to get along and plan their next visit.

Suddenly Simon planted his feet at shoulder width, put his hands on his hips, and faced Sophie. "When are you coming home?" he asked.

"I'm not," Sophie said steadily.

"Yes, you are," Simon said. He walked to her, grabbed her hand, and tried to pull her out of the chair.

"Simon . . . ," Sophie said, not budging.

"Come on," he said, pulling. "Come on . . ."

"Simon," Maria said sharply. "Cut that out. You know your mother has to stay here—"

"Shut up, you bitch!" Simon said.

Sophie slapped him. It happened in one motion: she dropped Flo's hair, lifted her hand, brought it across Simon's mouth, and drew it back. Everyone, including Sophie, gasped. Simon's cheek turned white, and then the red imprint of a hand appeared.

"I want to go home," Simon said.

"Simon," Sophie said, her voice shaking. "I'm sorry I slapped you, but you cannot call your Aunt Maria 'bitch.'"

"Why not? Daddy called you one."

"Daddy was very, very wrong to do that," Sophie said. "And I was wrong to let him. We both set bad examples for you. But maybe even worse than that, we didn't have any respect for ourselves or each other."

"Not ever?" Simon asked.

"We used to," Sophie said slowly, as if she were paying close attention to the weight of every word. "We used to love each other. But first Daddy got sick, and then I did."

"Are you getting better?" Flo asked.

"I'm trying, very hard. But it takes a long time. You guys know the awful things that happened. You know how hard it is to feel good again, don't you?"

Simon nodded. Seeing that, Flo nodded too.

"Dr. Middleton is very smart," Sophie said. "She's going to

help you talk about all the things that happened. To stop keeping secrets. There's nothing you can't tell her."

"Even things you and Daddy said not to tell?" Simon asked.

"Even those."

"Even about...," Flo said, then whispered something in Sophie's ear.

"Even about the dead baby," Sophie said, looking straight at Maria.

"I told already," Flo said sadly. "I told Aunt Maria."

"You can tell Aunt Maria anything you want to," Sophie said. "She loves you. Don't you, Maria?"

"Very much," Maria said.

"Give me kisses," Sophie said. Simon moved close, and Sophie spent a long time kissing his and Flo's noses, their eyelids, their ears, their shoulders, their lips. "Now it's time to go." Her voice was warm, steadier than it had been at any time during the visit.

"I don't want to," Flo said, starting to cry.

"It's time to go," Sophie said. She gestured for Maria to take them away. They were both wailing, resisting her.

"I love you!" Sophie called above their cries. "Good-bye!"

As if on cue, or perhaps because he had been listening, Peter opened the door and took the children out. Maria turned to wave good-bye, but Sophie called her back. "Close the door," Sophie said.

"That went well," Maria said, not quite meaning it. "The circumstances were hard, but..."

Sophie just shook her head. "I'm not going to see them again," she said, sounding exhausted.

"I'm sure you'll feel differently when you've had a chance to think about it."

"I have thought about it."

Maria checked her watch. "We'd better get moving. The show's about to start. People must be waiting for the wardrobe mistress."

"I'm not going to do it," Sophie said. "I'm tired. I just want to go back to my cell and lie down."

"Oh, come on," Maria said. "Think of how disappointed the kids will be. And the performers! You'll mess up the entire show."

"Look at it this way: they're a bunch of grown women, and they know how to dress themselves. If I was singing a song and I didn't show, then there'd really be a hole in the program."

"Don't let Mom ruin it for you, Sophie—you know how she is . . . ," Maria said, worried by Sophie's tone of resignation.

"It's not her fault," Sophie said. "My heart was never in this show in the first place. The kids look good. You're doing a great job, and that makes me relieved."

"Thank you," Maria said, feeling really uneasy. "Sophie? What's going on?"

"Do you know why I killed Gordon?" Sophie asked. "Know why I shot him?"

"Because he caused the miscarriage," Maria said.

"No," Sophie said. "I bought the gun after he did that, but I didn't use it until he smashed the angel. He broke our daughter's gravestone."

"Why?" Maria asked, stunned.

Sophie's lips thinned, and she shook her head. "To upset me. That's the only reason. I thought he really loved her, Hathaway. I thought he grieved for her. But he didn't, not at all. It was just a trick to make me think he cared about her."

"What did he do?"

"That night, the night I killed him, I told him I wanted a divorce. I told him I wouldn't take it anymore. We had made love, and he ridiculed me. He told me I looked like a horror show. He made me look in a mirror, and he was right. Fat and bruised and . . . disgusting. I'd kept gaining weight even after the baby died and I didn't need to hide anything. I just ate and ate—I wanted to keep on till I burst. I told myself it was to fill up her place in my body, but that afternoon I realized: I wanted to take myself away from Gordon. By getting fat, I was depriving him of something. Of the thin woman he'd married, anyway."

"You did that," Maria said. "But you look wonderful, now. Even Simon said so."

"We were standing in front of the mirror," Sophie said, continuing as if Maria hadn't spoken. "When I asked for the divorce. He didn't say anything, he just left. I got dressed."

Sophie wore a faraway look, remembering that day. Maria, watching her sister's face, could imagine the relief Sophie must have felt, to have found the strength to ask Gordon for a divorce.

"It's strange," Sophie said. "But once I'd told him I wanted him to leave, I felt hopeful. I could imagine getting better. I thought it might be possible to forgive him someday."

If only she could have held on to it, Maria thought: *hope. If only that night had gone differently.*

"He wasn't gone long," Sophie said. "Hardly long enough for me to finish dressing. I heard him coming up the stairs—I made myself feel strong, so I could stand my ground no matter what he said. I knew he'd beg me to change my mind." Her eyes flickered. "But he didn't say a word. He had Hathaway's gravestone. The stone angel."

"He'd taken it off her grave?" Maria asked.

Sophie nodded. "He raised it over his head and just stared at me, like he was daring me."

"To do what?"

But Sophie continued without answering Maria's question. "All that strength I'd stored up just went away. I began to cry. I asked him to give me the angel, I told him he didn't know what he was doing. I was thinking of her grave, all bare and cold. I had a terrible thought, what if we couldn't find it again?"

Sophie shivered, remembering that thought.

"He listened to me. He lowered the angel, and I thought I'd gotten through to him. When I first saw him with it, I hated him. I thought that nothing we'd ever done together—getting married, having children—meant one thing to him. It was all a sick game. But when he lowered the angel, I had hope that it was going to be okay."

Sophie touched her throat, as if she was having trouble swallowing. "But it was a game after all. He just raised her up again and threw her against our bedroom wall. He stared at me, smiled at me, while he was doing it. I started to scream at him. I was screaming 'You broke her' over and over," Sophie said, "and then my head cleared and I got the gun."

"The kids heard you screaming."

"Yes. The kids ran into the room. Flo was hanging onto my knees, and I didn't care. I just shot and shot. I didn't even see his face."

Maria went to Sophie and held her. She felt Sophie breathing hard. "Afterward, all I could think of was putting the angel back on her grave. I couldn't stand thinking of it unmarked, and I left Simon and Flo alone to do it.

"I walked through our field, carrying that angel, and I remembered carrying the baby along the same path. It was so cold that night—much colder than when we buried the baby. I guess there was a moon out. I found the spot with no trouble. There was a little indentation from the angel's base, and in the mud I saw the footprints Gordon had made when he took her. And there was the stone heart, of course."

"I saw her grave," Maria said, her voice thick. "You buried her near the stone heart."

"So I put the angel back on Hathaway's grave," Sophie said. "And then I threw the gun in Bell Stream." She glanced up at Maria. "I made her as solid as I could, but the ground was wet and slippery. She's still there, right?"

"Right," Maria said.

"Could you make sure her base is deep enough? So she won't move?"

"I will," Maria said.

Sophie nodded, appearing to be satisfied. "Thank you," she said.

"You're welcome."

They sat there for a while, and then Maria knew it was time to go.

"I love you," Maria said, kissing Sophie good-bye. "I know how horrible things have been for you, but they're going to get better."

"I love you," Sophie said, hugging her hard. "Good-bye."

Maria turned for one last wave, and she left the room intending to perpetrate an illusion: she planned to shepherd Sophie's family into the show, allowing them to think all the costume changes were thanks to Sophie, to think that Sophie was backstage in charge. Maria did not realize that she was under an illusion herself. She did not realize that when Sophie had said good-bye, she had meant forever.

EPILOGUE

WITH ALL THE ARCHAEOLOGICAL TREATISES available on troweling, geophysical prospecting, fieldwalking, soil sampling, sample trenching, and gridding, Maria thought it noteworthy that no good guide existed for the filling in of an excavation. She shivered slightly. She held her hand over her eyes, visorlike, as if the day were too bright. Opaque white sunlight glanced off the bay. Crouched in the stern of Duncan's boat, which they had driven to Lookout instead of Maria's because its cabin was heated, she assembled her tools. It was the fourth Wednesday of November.

Lugging her knapsack and her spade through the shallow water, Maria was glad she'd worn boots. She left deep footprints in the sand. The children's voices came to her from somewhere down the beach: the next cove, perhaps. She felt sorry that Jamey hadn't come, and she knew Duncan was disappointed. This long weekend was Duncan's turn to have him, but Alicia's parents had come for a visit, and so Duncan and Alicia had traded.

Clearing the rise, Maria sighed. There was the Pequot squaw's grave, just as she had left it last July. Although Duncan had come out periodically to check it, to make sure the tarpaulin was securely tied down, this was the first time Maria had been able to force herself to come, and only now because snow had been forecast.

While farmland and marshy ground would already have frozen, the sandy soil on Lookout remained soft and easy to move. Maria tested it with her foot, burying her boot entirely, the way a child might bury her foot at the water's edge on a hot summer day. She glanced up, shielding her eyes again. High clouds filmed the sky, giving the sun a corona, or a "snow crown," as Hallie used to say.

Maria walked around the site, her gaze occasionally sliding to the plastic sheet. A loud splash made her turn around: an osprey was rising from the bay, on great slow wings, with a fighting fish in its talons. Maria watched it clear the water, then head for its nest in the Lovecraft Refuge. It surprised her to see an osprey so late in the year; she thought they would have migrated by now. She had a vague childhood memory of all the summer birds having left Hatuquitit by Thanksgiving. And Thanksgiving was tomorrow.

Finally she turned to the grave. She sighed, staring at it for a long time. She dug her spade into a heap of soil, then hesitated. Last night, Maria had been unable to sleep. She had always planned to fill in the grave before the first snowfall, and now it was coming.

The details of how she would rebury the Pequot squaw had kept her awake. She did not want to view her bones again. Then, suddenly, it had come to her: she could throw soil directly on the site as she had left it. She could consider the tarpaulin the woman's shroud. Although she had something she wanted to place in the grave, she could simply lift the sheet's corner and slip it inside. The revelation had allowed her to sleep. She had, in fact, when she finally dropped off, programmed herself to sleep right through the alarm, and if not for Duncan, she would have. Without any discussion, he had informed her that he was taking the day off from work to accompany her. Since the children's Thanksgiving vacation had begun, they too came along.

She tossed a couple of spadefuls of soil on the tarpaulin, then stopped. It didn't feel right. The tarpaulin was plastic. If it were canvas, or cotton, she might be able to leave it as a shroud. But she knew the sacrilege it would be to bury the Pequot woman in this chemical sheet. She dropped the spade. Her gloved fingers tingling with cold, she untied the ropes from their stakes. Gently she drew back the tarp.

The bones lay in their grave, just as Maria had found them months ago. Her eyes traveled from the squaw's feet to her pelvis to her skull. It was the skull with which Maria usually had the most trouble, since it reminded her that the skeleton had once been a person with hopes and fears and a family to love. Her heart flipped, once, at the sight of the squaw's skull, but that was all. She knew this skeleton intimately, the squaw who had loved Charles Slocum, and she loved her as bones—as she was now, not as she had been.

Maria patted the pockets of her down coat. Finding what she was looking for, she slipped off one glove and reached into her right pocket. When she pulled out her hand, she was holding the gold goddess. She had driven to Blackwood one day in September, and she had bought it with this purpose in mind.

"Sophie," she said out loud. In the days after they had cut Sophie down, Maria had not had the presence of mind to find the goddess. The children had wanted to send Sophie into the ground with gifts. They had sat in church, Flo clutching framed school photos of her and Simon, Simon holding the pearls Sophie had worn to her wedding. Maria and Hallie had sat side by side, not touching, staring dry-eyed at Peter, standing at the pulpit, reading some lines from Yeats:

> *Too long a sacrifice*
> *Can make a stone of the heart.*
> *O when may it suffice?*
> *That is Heaven's part, our part*
> *To murmur name upon name,*
> *As a mother names her child*
> *When sleep at last has come*
> *On limbs that had run wild.*
> *What is it but nightfall?*
> *No, no, not night but death;*
> *Was it needless death after all?*

Maria had felt too confused and angry at Sophie to be moved by the poem. She hadn't been thinking straight, and by the time the idea that she should have buried Sophie with the goddess occurred to her and became a passion, it was too late.

Now, standing in the cold sand, Maria gazed down at the woman's bones. Reverend Hawkes had been granted permission by the state archaeological commission to keep the grave goods Maria had found here for Historical Society exhibits. Maria knew an excavation promised no answers, and the science of archaeology guaranteed no definitive conclusion. She would never know for sure whether this woman had loved Charles Slocum. But someone had loved her enough to bury her with a gold ring, and to take its place, Maria had brought Sophie's goddess.

Maria pressed her lips to the statue and kissed her. As she did so, a strange thing happened: Maria felt that she was kissing Sophie herself. Although it wasn't Sophie's grave, it might as well have been. Then, pierced by a complete and overwhelming feeling of closeness, Maria fell to her knees, clutching the goddess, and wept.

After a while, tears continued to run down her cheeks, but she felt herself smiling.

"Good-bye," she said, and this time she knew what she meant. She laid the gold goddess among the squaw's bones. Then, rising to her feet, she took hold of the spade's handle and began filling the grave with dirt. She found a rhythm, throwing one spadeful after another into the grave, and by the time Duncan and the children came over the hill, Maria had buried the woman.

Worry clouded Duncan's eyes, but cleared when he saw Maria smiling. She knew that she hadn't been smiling much lately.

"Hello," she called.

"Did you do it?" Simon asked shyly.

Maria nodded and gestured toward the freshly turned soil.

"Good, it's *done*," Flo said, her voice full of relief.

"Were you worried about it, Flossie?" Duncan asked.

"Well, it was getting cold out," she said.

"Skeletons don't get cold, do they?" Simon asked.

"No," Maria said. "They don't."

"I know they can't feel anything anymore, but I'm glad Mommy and Daddy are together," Simon said. "That's all."

"I just feel so bad for that baby, all alone," Flo said, frowning.

Maria had considered having Hathaway moved to the cemetery, to bury her with Sophie and Gordon. But one of Sophie's last wishes had been for Maria to look after her grave, to make sure the stone angel was in place. And so Maria had left her buried on the banks of Bell Stream.

"She'll be fine, Flossie," Duncan said, giving her a hug. "You don't have to worry about her."

"At least *Thanksgiving* will be the same as ever," Simon said. "At Gram's."

"Yes," Maria said, smiling at Duncan. With his mother in Florida and Jamey spending the holiday with Alicia and his grandparents, Duncan would have been spending Thanksgiving alone if Hallie hadn't invited him to come with Maria, Simon, and Flo to her house.

"Every year Uncle Peter says we're having hot dogs, and every year we have turkey," Simon said, laughing.

"That's your Uncle Peter for you," Maria said.

"But it's sad . . . *you* know," Flo said.

"Because Mommy and Daddy won't be there," Simon said.

"Yes, that's sad," Maria said.

"What if we forget them?" Simon asked.

"You never will," Maria said. "You'll always remember your parents." She believed in her own words. Saying them, her mind filled with an image of herself, Sophie, and Nell, at ages eight and eleven, playing Pilgrim in the Darks' meadow. Frost had hardened the ground, and the November wind whistled like a gale in their ears. Maria had found a gully in the lee of a pine grove; the three girls had nestled there, imagining how tough the Pilgrims' first winter had been. Sophie had pulled a half-eaten candy bar from her pocket, and they'd passed it around.

"The Pilgrims didn't have *chocolate*," Nell had said, dismissing the candy as inauthentic.

"You take your comfort where you can get it," Sophie had replied, resolute.

Maria remembered it exactly, the words her sister had spoken as an eight-year-old, and, laughing, she told the story to Duncan, Simon, and Flo.

They all laughed, but then Simon asked, "What's so funny about that?"

"It's just a very old thing for a little girl to say," Maria said.

"I don't care if it's funny or not," Flo said. "I like that story."

"We should tell more stories about Mommy," Simon said.

"*And* Daddy," Flo said.

"We should tell them and tell them, and not ever stop," Simon said.

"Never stop," Maria agreed.

Then everyone noticed they all were shivering, and they decided to climb into Duncan's boat and turn on the heat. The sun was hidden in clouds now. A stray snowflake fell, then another. Maria hoisted herself over the gunwale; Simon clambered in, right behind her. Turning toward Duncan, who stood in the water, waves licking his rubber boots, Maria reached out for Flo. Duncan held Flo over his head, passing her through the air like an angel in a snowsuit, and Maria took her into her arms.

"Ready?" Duncan asked when he had climbed aboard.

"Ready," everyone said, snug in the cabin.

Then Duncan revved the engines, and the boat swung around, bow into the wind. It chugged out of the bay, away from the Haunted Isles, heading for home.

AUTHOR'S NOTE

"That's where bad girls go."

Who said those words? My mother or father? My grand-mother? I can't remember, but I can hear them so clearly, ringing in my ears, whenever I drive east along the Shore Road. Back in my childhood, the women's jail looked a lot like a genteel board-ing school: red brick, surrounded by graceful oaks and maples, with a pot of yellow marigolds at the end of the driveway. The peaceful, bucolic appearance made those words, *that's where bad girls go,* seem all the more ominous.

Whenever we drove that road between Old Lyme and Niantic, my gaze would drift to the red brick building. I'd wonder: How bad? What kind of bad? Who decided someone was bad enough to go there? I knew about right and wrong. I was a good girl, wasn't I? I obeyed my parents, and my teachers liked me. I'd never have anything to worry about. I would take the path prom-ised to all good girls: I would go to college, and start a wonderful career, and fall in love, and get married and live happily ever af-ter. I saw a picket fence in my future. Still, my attention was in-eluctably drawn to that lonely dormitory, that alternate campus, and I'd wonder . . .

One time when I was in high school, driving down that same road, my mother told me that the mother of one of her former students was a prisoner there. She told me that the woman had killed her husband. The man had abused her—and her daugh-ter—for a long time. My mother told me that she was haunted by this. I asked my mother why the woman hadn't just left—why she hadn't just taken her daughter away, called the police, gotten help.

My mother's response was so quiet, so strange. It sent a shiver down my spine and still does, as I write this.

"Because she couldn't," my mother said.

Those three words had such mysterious power. Even now I can hardly understand or explain that in that one instant I knew for a fact that I would never, never allow myself to be hit. That if any man ever laid a hand on me, I would leave instantly. I made myself that promise.

As I grew up, my vision of "bad girls" changed. Childhood's easy morality gave way to a more complicated sense of where people fit in the world, how they navigated their lives. I reassessed my thoughts on happily-ever-after and picket fences. They don't necessarily go together. What matters is what goes on behind the white fence and front door, behind the pretty curtains hanging at the windows, beyond the neighbors' gazes.

And so I wrote *Stone Heart*. It's about a family with secrets. It takes place in a town whose main road leads past the women's prison. And it takes one of the characters—a "good girl"—inside the brick walls. It was, and still is, the only women's jail in Connecticut. Now it is York Correctional Institution. The new buildings are stark, gray—what you'd expect a prison to look like. They're surrounded by walls and fences topped with glinting razor wire.

The landscape of the setting—the Connecticut shoreline— and that of the characters—three generations of a close family— is very familiar to me, close to my heart. I set out to imagine two sisters, and the dawning awareness of one that the other was in serious trouble. Maria Dark knows that something terrible is happening to her sister, Sophie Littlefield—but she doesn't know how to help. The elephant in this family's living room is called "domestic violence."

It starts with words . . . or even silences. Controlling behavior can at first be taken for love. "Where were you?" "Who did you talk to?" "Why are you wearing that? I don't want anyone else to see how beautiful you are. . . ." It can seem so much like concern, like love. But it goes on for a while, and other factors get added in—scathing silences, explosive anger, the realization that there's really only one way to do things—*his* way—and before too long she may find she's abdicated herself, lost track of her own deepest self, in favor of whatever will keep the peace, keep him happy.

Many women know about the pattern of domestic violence—we've read about it, seen it in movies, heard stories on talk shows. But sometimes it is so insidious, it's almost impossible to recognize when it's happening. Men never just move in and start hitting—when battering occurs, the groundwork has already been laid by subtler means. Some abusers never use their fists. Instead, he plays a power game of drawing the woman in, pushing her away, devaluing and diminishing her. He doesn't have to use physical violence if he can control her in other ways.

The worst part is, he denies it. It's crazy-making. Wanting to improve the relationship, seeking mutuality, the woman expresses her hurt and confusion. But instead of truly listening, her partner turns the tables, blames her for being oversensitive. He might say she's being accusatory, hormonal, too demanding. She doubts herself a little more each time.

Verbal and emotional abuse chips away at a person's heart. At her soul . . . Fists aren't necessary to beat a person down. Splitting her off from her family and friends—as one husband does to his wife in *Stone Heart*—is one way to keep her from talking, from having any perspective on what is happening to her. By the time she realizes what he's done to her, it's too late.

Secrets feed denial—they keep people from getting help. Sophie kept her terrible secret until it nearly destroyed her. Following is a list of telephone numbers and web sites people can contact for help—for themselves, or for people they suspect may be being abused. Because this novel takes place on the Connecticut shoreline, I have included some regional help lines:

National Domestic Violence Hotline—www.ndvh.org
1–800–799–SAFE (7233)
For the hearing impaired: 1–800–787–3224

Connecticut Coalition Against Domestic Violence
1–888–774–2900

National Coalition Against Domestic Violence—
www.ncadv.org
1-800-799-SAFE (7233)

Domestic Violence Valley Shore Services (DVVSS)
(a tiny shoreline affiliate where great women with huge hearts
provide enormous help)
1–860–399–4300

Susan Caruso, director of program services at DVVSS, says, "Physical violence leaves marks; when you see bruises, you know. . . . But when you feel disparaged, put down, belittled, or ignored, the pain is inside, impossible to see; a person is more likely to question whether or not it is real.

"Our mission is to help women and children who are victims of domestic abuse—not only those who are physically abused, but also those who are emotionally, verbally, and financially abused—to let you know that you have someplace to go for help. We are here to listen to you, and to validate that emotional abuse is in fact every bit as damaging and painful, sometimes even longer lasting, because the emotional scars don't heal as easily."

Reality is relative. What once seemed impossible can be worked out. What seemed hopeless can be surmounted. Other women have been there, have lived through it. Help is waiting— it really is.

ABOUT THE AUTHOR

LUANNE RICE is the author of eighteen novels, most recently *Silver Bells, Beach Girls, Dance With Me, The Perfect Summer,* and *The Secret Hour.* She lives in New York City and Old Lyme, Connecticut.

Visit the author's official website at www.luannerice.com.

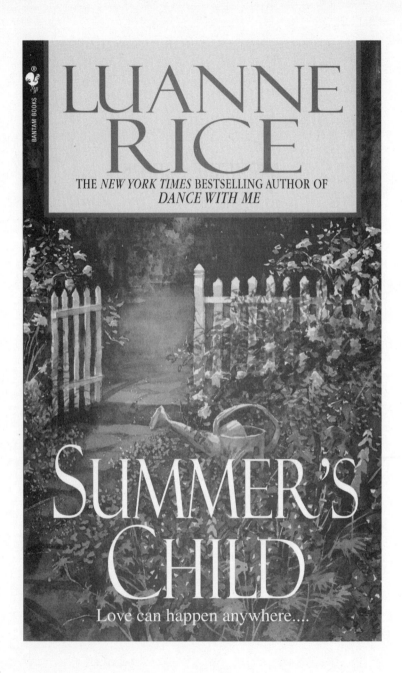

LUANNE RICE

THE *NEW YORK TIMES* BESTSELLING AUTHOR OF
DANCE WITH ME

SUMMER'S CHILD

Love can happen anywhere....

BANTAM BOOKS

COMING THIS SUMMER

Celebrate the Season with
Two Unforgettable New Novels from
New York Times Bestselling Author

Luanne Rice

Beginning with

SUMMER'S CHILD

On sale everywhere in paperback May 31st

At the time, it was the biggest story in the country. Every news-paper covered it on the front page. Her face was as well known as the president's—and beloved by all. She looked like every-one's favorite sister, best friend, and girl next door, all rolled into one. The fact that she was pregnant when she disappeared gave the story a terrible jolt of shock. . . . On the first night of summer, adorable five-foot nothing, pregnant-as-could-be Mara Jameson went out to water the garden. She was never seen again; no body was ever recovered . . .

Please turn the page for a Special Advance Preview
of *Summer's Child*

SUMMER'S CHILD
On Sale May 31, 2005

BEING RETIRED HAD ITS PLUSES. FOR ONE THING, it was good to be ruled by the tide tables instead of department shifts and schedules. Patrick Murphy kept the small *Hartford Courant* tide card tacked up by the chart table, but he barely needed it anymore. He swore his body was in synch with the ebb and flow of Silver Bay—he'd be pulled out of bed at the craziest hours, in the middle of the night, at slack tides, prime times to fish the reefs and shoals around the Stone Mill Power Plant.

Stripers up and down the Connecticut Shoreline didn't stand a chance. They hadn't for the two years, seven months, three weeks, and fourteen days since Patrick had retired at the age of forty-three. This was *really* the life, he told himself. He had lost the house, but he had the boat, the truck. This was what people worked their whole lives for: to retire to the beach and fish the days away.

He thought of Sandra, what she was missing. They had had a list of dreams they would share after he left the Connecticut State Police: walk the beaches, try every new restaurant in the area, go to the movies, hit the casinos, take the boat out to Block Island and Martha's Vineyard. They were still young—they could have a blast.

A blast, he thought. Now—instead of the fun he had thought they would have together—"blast" made him think of the divorce, with its many shocks and devastations, the terrible ways both lawyers had found to make a shambles of the couple they had once been.

Fishing helped. So did the Yankees—they had snapped their losing streak and just kept on winning. Many the night Patrick combined the two—casting and drifting, listening to John Sterling and Charlie Steiner call the game, cheering for the Yanks to win as he trolled for stripers, as his boat slipped east on the current.

Other things pulled him out of his bunk, too. Dreams with dark tentacles; bad men still on the run after Patrick's best waking efforts to catch them; a lost girl; shocks and attacks and bone-rattling fears that gave new meaning to Things That Go Bump in the Night. Patrick would wake up with a pounding heart, thinking of how terrified she must have been.

Whether she was murdered, dead and buried all these years, or whether something had happened to drive her from her house, her grandmother's rose garden, to someplace so far away she had never been seen again, her fear must have been terrible.

That's the thing he could never get out of his mind.

What fears had Mara Jameson felt? Even now, his imagination grabbed hold of that question and went wild. The case was nine years old, right at the top of his unsolved pile. The paperwork had been his albatross, his constant companion. The case was the rock to Patrick's Sisyphus, and he had never—not even after it promised to ruin his marriage, not even after it made good on that promise, not even now, after retirement—never stopped pushing it up the hill.

Mara's picture. It sat on his desk. He used to keep it right beside his bed—to remind him of what he had to do when he got up. Look for the sweet girl with the heartbreak smile and the laughing eyes. Now he didn't really need the picture. Her face was ingrained into his soul. He knew her expressions by heart—the way other men knew their wives, girlfriends, lovers . . .

She'd be with him forever, he thought, climbing out of bed at five-thirty a.m. He had only the vaguest idea of what his dream had been—something about the blood spatter on her kitchen floor, the spidery neon-blue patterns caught by the luminal, trickles and drops . . . spelling, in Patrick's dream, the killer's name. But it was in Latin, and Patrick couldn't understand, and beside, who could prove she'd been killed when her body had never been found?

He rubbed his eyes, started the coffee, then pulled on shorts and sweatshirt. The morning air felt chilly; a front had passed through last night, violent thunderstorms shaking the rafters, making Flora hide under the bed. The black lab rubbed up against him now, knowing a boat ride was in their future.

Heading up on deck, he breathed in the salt air. The morning star blazed in the western sky. The just-about-rising sun painted the dark eastern horizon with an orange glow. His thirty-two-foot fishing boat, the *Probable Cause,* rocked in the current. After the divorce, he'd moved on board. Sandra had kept the house on Mill Lane. It had all worked out fine, except now the boatyard was going to be turned into condos. Pretty soon all of New England would be one big townhouse village, complete with dockominiums . . . and Patrick would have to shove off and find a new port.

Hearing footsteps on the gravel, he peered into the boatyard. A shadow was coming across the sandy parking lot; Flora growled. Patrick petted her head, then went down below to get two mugs of coffee. By the time he was back on deck, he saw Flora wagging her tail, eyes on the man standing on the dock. Angelo Nazarena.

"Don't tell me," Patrick said. "You smelled the coffee."

"Nah," Angelo said. "I got up early and saw the paper; I figured you needed company so you wouldn't get drunk or do something really stupid. Longest day of the year's tomorrow, and the articles are starting already . . ." He held the *Hartford Courant* in one hand, but accepted the heavy blue mug in the other as he stepped aboard.

"I don't drink any more," Patrick said. He wanted to read the story but didn't—at the same time. "Besides, I'm not speaking to you. You're selling my dock."

"Making millions in the bargain," Angelo chuckled. "When my grandfather bought this land, it was considered crap. The wrong side of the railroad bridge, next to a swamp, stinking like clam flats. But he was smart enough to know waterfront is solid gold, and I'm cashing in. Good coffee."

Patrick didn't reply. He was staring at Mara's picture on the front page. It had been taken in her grandmother's rose garden—ten miles from here, at her pretty silver-shingled cottage at Hubbard's Point. The camera had caught the light in her eyes—the thrill, the joy, that secret she always seemed to be holding back. Patrick had the feeling he so often had—that if he leaned close enough, she'd whisper to him, tell him what he so desperately wanted to know . . .

"These papers really get a lot of mileage out of nothing," Angelo said, shaking his head. "The poor girl's been gone nine years now. She's fish food, we all know that."

"Your Sicilian lineage is showing."

"She's gone, Patrick. She's dead," Angelo said, sharply now. He and Patrick had gone to school together, been altar boys at St.

Agnes's together, been best man at each other's weddings. He and Patsy had introduced him to Sandra. Patrick's dream came back, the luminescent blood spelling out the killer's name . . .

"The husband did it—right?"

"I thought so, for a long time," Patrick said.

"What was his name, though . . . he had a different last name from Mara . . ."

"His name is Edward Hunter. Mara had her own career. She kept her own name when she married him."

And now Patrick saw Edward Hunter's handsome charm-boy face, his politician's desperate smile—as wide and bright as Mara's, but without one ounce of her heart, soul, depth, integrity, authenticity, spark. . . . As a state cop, Patrick had encountered smiles like Edward Hunter's thousands of times. The smiles of men pulled over for speeding on their way home from places they shouldn't have been, the smiles of men at the other end of a domestic violence call—smiling men trying to convince the world they were better than the circumstances made them seem and reminding Patrick that "smile" was really just "slime" spelled sideways.

"Everyone thought so—not just you. But the bastard didn't leave a body behind. So you can't try him, and it's time for you . . ."

"We could have tried to pull a Richard Crafts," Patrick said, naming Connecticut's infamous killer convicted of murdering his wife, whose body was never found, on the basis of a few fragments of hair and bone found in a rented wood chipper, "but we didn't even have enough for that. I couldn't even find enough evidence for that . . ."

"Like I was saying, it's time you moved on."

"Okay, thanks," Patrick said, his expression saying *why didn't I think of that?*, his Irish rising as he faced his friend Angelo—who had brought over the morning paper with Mara's face on the front page, who was about to sell his boat slip right out from under him.

"What I mean is . . ." Angelo said, trying to find the words to fill the hole he'd opened up.

"What you mean is, it's time I got a life, I know," Patrick said, giving his old friend an old-friends' glance, the look that tells them they know you better than anyone, that they were right all along, when what you really want is to just shut them up and get them off your case.

"Yeah. To be honest, that's what I mean," Angelo said, chuckling with relief even as Patrick was folding up the newspaper and tossing it through the hatch—purportedly for disposal but actually to save forever.

As he saved all of Mara's pictures.

Because, he thought as he started up the engine and Angelo cast off the lines, it was one of the ways he had found to keep her alive. That, and one other way . . .

The whole world assumed that Mara Jameson and her unborn baby had died all those nine years ago, and they still did. Patrick thought back to his Catholic childhood, that phrase in the Creed: *We believe . . . in all that is seen and unseen.* It was pretty much impossible to have faith in what you couldn't see. And the world hadn't seen Mara in over nine years.

Backing out of the slip, hitting the bow thrusters, he eased into the channel. The boat chuffed through the deepening water as gray herons watched silently from shadows along the green marshy shore. The rising sun shone through scrub oaks and white pines. Bursts of gold glittered on the water ahead.

The dead never stayed hidden. The earth gave them up, one way or another. Patrick knew they were relentless, in their need to be found. The Tibetan Book of the Dead described the hungry ghosts, tormented by unbearable heat, thirst, hunger, weariness, and fear. Their realm seemed familiar to Patrick; having spent his career investigating homicides, he believed that the dead had their own emotions, that they haunted the living until they were found.

And Mara had never been found.

Patrick believed he would know—deep inside his own body, if she were dead. He felt Mara Jameson in his mind, his skin, his heart. He carried her with him every day, and he knew he'd never be able to put her down until he knew for sure what had happened to her. Where she was . . .

The birds were working up ahead, marking a school of blues just before the red nun buoy. Angelo got the rods ready. Flora stood beside Patrick's side; her body pressed against his leg as he hit the throttle and sped toward the fish and tried in vain to escape the thoughts that haunted him wherever he went.

AND LOOK FOR

SUMMER OF ROSES

New York Times bestselling author Luanne Rice
continues the story begun in *Summer's Child*
in an unforgettable novel destined to take its place
as one of her most beloved works.